# Dragon Born

## The Rainbow Sands of Aljonnah

Rachel N Kaufman

Dragon Born and the Rainbow Sands of Aljonnah
Copyright © 2022 by Rachel N Kaufman
Publisher: Pylertchia Publishing
Bremen, AL 35033

First Edition

ISBN: 978-1-7362992-2-7 (Paperback)

Library of Congress Number -

*This is a work of fiction. The characters and events that appear in this book are products of the author's imagination. Any similarity to real persons, living or dead, is coincidental and not intended by the author.*

Editors: Chelsie Miller

THIS STORY IS FOR EVERYONE

One | The Ambush

Brantley was by my side, blocking the blow that would have cut me in half. With a spark, the slave's sword was flung back, and Brantley whipped me behind him.

The slave quickly regained their composure and threw back their hood.

The breath I had in my lungs escaped as my eyes fell on their face, with one whispered word riding on the wind.

"Darsey."

Our eyes met, but before another word was spoken, Brantley knocked Darsey down and stepped on his throat.

"Take off your gloves," he growled at me. "It's an ambush!"

I shoved him off Darsey with all the momentum I could muster. "Don't hurt him!" I screamed.

Gavyn's shrill cry rang through the trees and many men I recognized from the slave ship emerged from the forest, weapons and binds in hand.

*"Adalee,"* Uri cried out frantically.

Before I could take in their faces, Brantley was upon them, swinging his sword with perfect execution.

Darsey jumped to his feet and time stood still as our eyes met. In that moment, the tumult around us seemed inconsequential. He was alive. He was back. And I could see the same love in his eyes that had always been there. A look I thought was lost to the depths of the sea.

He reached his hand out to caress my face, and I angled my chin toward him, anxious for the touch I never thought I would feel again.

Gavyn's shrill cry once more pealed forth and a blast of light erupted between us, sending me flying to my back.

Uri jumped to my side, fear in his eyes. The awareness of the surrounding battle resonated in my mind, and I realized that the only thing standing between those men and us, was Brantley.

And Darsey.

My eyes sought him out as he snatched up his sword, his back to me.

Before I could go to him, one of the men was upon me, binding my gloved hands behind my back and ripping my dagger from my side. Instantly, the tingle I hadn't realized was vibrating through my body left, and I was dragged to my feet.

I didn't fear for myself. Darsey was nearby. Brantley could fight. But I couldn't stand the thought of Uri being bound and put in the dark again.

"Uri, run!" I screamed and, to my relief, he disappeared into the trees.

The clanging of swords echoed around me as the man who held my binds forced me into the woods.

I fought against the ropes and turned to see Brantley standing against five men twice his size. He looked winded, but none of their lumbering swings came close to touching him, and I knew he would get us out of this. My only fear was that he would mistake Darsey for one of them, though I couldn't find his face anywhere in the struggle.

The man shoving me along stopped abruptly and I turned to see Darsey standing before us, his sword dangling in his hand by his side.

"Stop," he said, his voice strained.

The man behind me sucked in a breath and said, "She goes to Surin."

I tried to meet Darsey's eyes, though they stared past me to my captor.

His grip tightened around the hilt of his sword.

A cry erupted behind us and I turned to see Brantley fall to the ground. One of the men easily kicked his sword from his hand and another picked it up.

I desperately looked back at Darsey. He pulled his hood up and I could no longer see his face. Then he turned away, sheathed his sword, and said, "Let's get her to Surin."

His words sent chills through my body and my mind reeled out of control.

"Darsey!" I cried out in disbelief, but the only reaction I received was a minute pause at my voice.

The rest of the men joined us, and we began walking. I looked back at Brantley, a still heap on the ground.

So much for being a warrior. It would be up to me . . . and Darsey.

I whipped back and whispered, "You're alive," to him, seeking a glimmer of hope that he had a plan.

He slowed down to match my pace and snapped, "No thanks to you."

My heart wrenched. How could he say that? What of the love in his eyes? Had I imagined it? Had I only seen what I wished to see?

How cruel would the dragons be to spare him, only to torture me with a now unrequited love?

There had to be an explanation, and I was determined to find it.

"I can't believe you're—"

The man holding my binds shoved me and said, "Keep quiet or I'll gag you."

I regained my footing and quieted. I looked at Darsey again but could only see the side of his hood. Then, as though he could feel my stare, he walked ahead of the group and all I could see was his back.

My heart hurt. He wasn't acting like my Darsey. My Darsey would have done anything to keep me from being taken back to Surin. I feared that what I was looking at might only be a shadow of the one I had loved.

*Of course he is. I told you he was weak.*

I audibly gasped at the sound of Madame in my head. It had been weeks since I had heard her voice, and I wasn't excited about harboring it again.

"Bag her," I heard Darsey yell. "I can't stand the feel of her eyes on my back."

The men laughed amongst themselves and a moment later, a bag was pushed over my face and cinched around my neck. I stumbled forward and felt my body lifted from the ground and thrown over one of the men's shoulders.

Not again. I couldn't go back to the ship. I was free.

I tried to struggle, but he only tightened his grip and panic immediately spread through me. Each bounding step that took me closer to a fate I feared stole more of my breath and soon my body began to shake.

Every wretched moment of my previous imprisonment played before my eyes, reeling through my memory like a tortuous dream with no escape. I began to sweat and fight against the tears. I couldn't go back. Surin would see to it that I never escaped again, even if it meant transfiguration.

The doctor!

I froze at the thought of seeing him again. His twisted methods and ability to skew time to fit his desires made me sick. A churning burned in my stomach and I felt as though I would retch into the bag. It took everything I had to hold it back. The doctor's evil grin played over in my head and memories of his voice barraged my being. I tried to shake them away, yet they persisted and slowly morphed into the sound of Madame's cackling.

*All for nothing,* she said to me through the face of the doctor.

A hopelessness fell over me like a cold, heavy blanket and my limbs felt weighed down with the pressure of my future. I could see nothing but confinement, shackles, and slavery.

Then we were on the ship, and I could barely stand as the man put me on my feet, cut my binds, and ripped my hood off. I stumbled to the ground on my sore legs and looked around at the most unwelcome sight. The men on deck stopped what they were doing and stared.

I turned and focused on the wood grain my hands were pressed against and tried to regain control of my breathing. My heart was pounding erratically, and I felt the remaining color drain from my face. My vision blurred and my head began to swim.

I couldn't believe what was happening. How had I come to be there again? My arms weakened and failed me. The deck crashed against the side of my face and my eyes drifted shut. My whole body trembled beyond measure, and I didn't know how to, or if I wanted to, regain control of it.

I felt a boot on my shoulder, followed by an aggressive and painful shove that rolled me to my other side. I didn't fight it. What would be the point?

A firm hand gripped my shoulder and distant shouts echoed around me as my mind tried to block everything out. I felt my body lift and fall, though the movement felt like a dream. Then peace, for only a moment.

A gentle touch grasped my shoulder and a familiar voice cut through the distance and whispered in my ear, "You need to get up."

I forced my eyes open and looked up at the blurry silhouette before me, though I didn't need to see him to know him.

"Get up," Darsey repeated, firm, yet gentle. Not lovingly as I desired, but not angrily like the others.

He tried to pull me up, and despite my desire to lean into him and trust his presence, I couldn't find the will to obey. Alone or not, I was staring the life of slavery in the face, and my mind refused to bear it.

I felt my head lay back on the wood and those angry voices were around me again.

"Give me a minute!" Darsey hissed at them, the only clear voice to ring out.

He leaned close and took my face in his hands. "Look at me," he ordered.

His touch spread through me and replaced the numbing cold with familiarity, comfort, and warmth. I opened my eyes and tried to focus, his presence only a blurred silhouette.

"Adalee, look at me," he repeated.

Hearing my name in his voice forced cognition to come barreling to the forefront of my mind, like a battering ram ready to burst forth into the comfort of a kingdom. My eyes cleared and took his face in. It was exactly as I remembered.

His deep brown eyes were nestled under thick, black brows, only now they held in them reservation and uncertainty rather than love and hope. His hair was loosely tied back, wavy strands danced beside his face in the wind. His naturally tanned complexion was colored even deeper by the sun since I had last laid eyes on him. His lips were still perfectly plump, though they spread across his face in a tight grimace and no longer looked soft and inviting.

But his skin . . . it was still as smooth and flawless as a serene pool of water, untouched by the world around it. I found in myself the strength to reach up and lay my hand on his face, catching him off guard. His jaw dropped and he sucked in a shallow breath.

Our eyes met for only a moment, then he pulled his face just out of reach and once again ordered me to stand.

The voices of the other men around us cleared and I could hear their frustration. Darsey was standing between me and them, risking himself to help me. I couldn't put him at their mercy by not honoring his request.

I nodded and kept my eyes firmly set upon his face while, with his help, I stood on shaky legs and brushed myself off. The panic tried to set in again, so I sucked in a deep breath and forced it out slowly. I had to be strong.

Darsey led me to Surin's cabin, though I remembered the way all too well. I kept my head down, avoiding the gawking faces of the crew. I focused on putting one foot in front of the other and recalled that soon my shoes would be taken. I felt the comfort of the clothing that rested against my body, and the security the cloak offered as it flowed freely around me. I anxiously rubbed my fingers together, feeling my new gloves that would soon be torn from me and repurposed. Not that it mattered. Without my dagger, I didn't need them.

We entered Surin's cabin, and the darkness gave me pause as my eyes adjusted and I concentrated on calming the pounding of my heart. The door closed behind me and I felt Darsey's hand on my back. The others stayed outside, and I took my opportunity and faced him in the dark.

"Darsey," I said, almost pleading.

"Keep moving," he said coldly, as he firmly turned me back around and pushed me toward the opening that would lead to Surin's banquet room.

I didn't resist the order and though I wanted to force my head up high, and show I was confident and powerful, I felt only small and weak. I rounded the corner and blinked against the bright morning light that shone through the massive windows in the banquet room.

I tried to stop and Darsey pushed me forward, rougher than before. I stumbled in and regained control just before I bumped into one of the cushioned, fabric-laden wooden chairs at the end of the imperial table that was fit more for a king than a slave-trading pirate.

Though the room now held an air of gloom, physically everything was the same. At least, at its most basic adornments.

The table no longer housed the elements of an ornate feast, and the curtains were now black, instead of crimson and gold. Each chair was dressed in black lace, matching a runner that stretched the full length of the table and draped off each end. Each seat housed a setting of empty platters and simple cups, save the vacant place where Therese once sat. Only at the end of the table was there an ornate place setting.

My eyes stopped wandering the room when they fell on Surin, sitting stoically in his seat. His expression indecipherable, though I could feel his eyes burning through mine, holding me in place.

Then, without releasing me, he coldly asked, "What say you?"

I remained motionless, no answer for him. I knew not what to say.

"Step forward," Darsey said behind me, his voice cold and indifferent.

He pushed me further, making no move to follow.

The motion broke Surin's hold on me and I tried to breathe deep, though only shallow breaths graced my lungs.

I dared to turn and cast my eyes at the boy I loved. He stared off, refusing to see me. Emotionless.

"Darsey," I whispered again.

*He certainly changed his tune since the last time you were together*, Madame mocked.

"Face me, slave," Surin snapped.

I jumped at his anger and spun back.

Before he could go on, Lapis crashed into the room, questioning in his squeaky voice, "Where is she?"

Surin silenced him with a stiff wave, but Lapis still seethed noisily as he stepped closer to me, his breath shooting out in hot erratic blasts upon my skin.

I tried to stand my ground while still attempting to put space between us without moving away.

Surin cleared his throat and I looked back at him. "If they survived the sea, which I imagine they did," Surin said methodically as he glanced at Darsey before returning his gaze to me, "then I would find it difficult to believe you do not know the whereabouts of Nadine and Veda."

My breathing quickened and nervous sweat beaded on my brow.

"Just as I thought," Surin said satisfactorily.

So, they didn't want *me*? I was just their way to Nadine and Veda? Yet had me, they did. I helped in the escape. I was privy to, and part of the plan.

Both Surin and Lapis stared at me like an enemy more than a slave. I couldn't tell them what I knew. I couldn't betray Nadine and Veda. Yet, I feared silence would only earn me a visit with the doctor. I had to say something.

"Why do you want them?" I asked in a small voice.

Surin took a deep, shaky breath and pointed to the chair Therese used to occupy.

I looked over and saw one of her dresses laid ceremoniously upon it, as though it was ready to be served in her stead. "Nadine took her from me."

"And she took Veda from *me*," Lapis added.

"You—," I tried to say, my voice barely audible. I cleared my throat and started again. "You took them from their homes," I said weakly. "You *made* Therese think she loved you."

He slammed his fists on the table, making the ornate goblet that sat before him tremble. "She *did* love me!" he roared.

I jumped but refused to let my fear encumber my movements any longer. I angled my face down at Lapis and boldly spilled forth, "And Veda does not love you. She left because she wanted to."

"Lies," he accused, pointing his finger at me.

Surin regained his composure and said, "So, am I correct in assuming you know where they are?"

I silently looked away.

"You will take us to them," he said as though it were fact, and not a request.

I took another shallow breath and shook my head in refusal.

"I'll take you to them," a familiar voice said behind me.

I turned to the doorway, as did everyone else, and was shocked to see Brantley casually leaning in the threshold, unharmed and armed with his sword and my dagger.

Relief flooded through me and I couldn't help the sigh that escaped my lips. He noticed and casually winked as he strode into the room.

"The ship now belongs to the Dragon Born," he announced triumphantly.

"Who are *you*?" Surin demanded.

He angled his sword at Darsey and said, "Disarm."

Darsey, with a look of disdain, stared Brantley in the face as he unsheathed his sword and tossed it down.

"Don't disarm!" Surin shouted. "Kill him," he ordered as though he were speaking about a fly on the wall, and not a seasoned soldier.

Darsey ignored Surin, held up his hands in surrender, and backed away. Surin pulled his sword and futilely called for more men to come. When no one answered, Lapis nervously went to his brother's side, but Surin shoved him away and said, "Get off me, you coward."

Brantley approached, and bowed down in royal fashion, presenting me my blade. "Demonstrate for them, Lady Dragon, what will happen if they resist."

With great relief, I ripped my gloves off and took the blade, quickly securing it back to my side. "Enjoy your revenge," he whispered with a smile.

I turned back and looked at Surin and Lapis standing at the opposite end of the table. I felt the power of the blade surge through me, and I was no longer afraid. I no longer felt small. It was my turn to make him feel small, and I relished the thought.

I reached down and turned the chair next to me to ash.

There was a mutual gasp in the room, and I let the power continue to pulse through me. How had I forgotten so quickly what I was capable of? The mere thought of being in Surin's clutches again had scared me beyond my senses, but I wasn't helpless anymore. He had no power over me.

I glanced over at Darsey and saw a smile play on his lips. He looked at me with an admiration and anticipation that made my heart flutter.

"If I recall correctly," Brantley said as I walked to the next chair and turned it to ash with a dainty caress. "You don't *believe* in the Dragon Born."

I picked up a plate from the table and let the ash from it fall through my fingers.

"You imprisoned this girl," he continued, and I grabbed a cup and savored the look in Surin's eyes as it too turned to ash. "You humiliated her."

Surin snatched up Therese's dress and backed away from the table.

I grabbed another chair and stared him right in the face as it became a gray pile of dust. "You did everything you could to break her."

I grabbed the chair nearest Surin and Lapis and turned it to ash. "Fools," Brantley said with a chuckle. "Don't you know? No one can stand against the Dragon Born."

I stepped up to Surin and he jumped back and swung his sword at me.

"Adalee!" Darsey screamed, terror in his voice.

The sword cut through my cloak and tunic but sizzled and burned to nothing the moment it touched my skin. Surin stumbled back, tripping over his chair and falling to the ground. Lapis darted towards the door, his frightened screams cut short when Brantley grabbed his collar and easily held him in place.

The shock of the blade striking against my skin was there. The sting of its blow resonated over me. And somehow, I was left whole. No blood was spilled.

I looked at my arm in awe, then met Brantley's eyes from across the room. His amazement turned to satisfied excitement and he smiled and nodded at me in approval.

Then I turned and laid my hands on the table and it easily dissolved, leaving nothing in the room but the five people, and piles of ash.

Lapis was cowering by the door. Surin slowly stood, sucked in a steady breath and quietly said, "I made a mistake when I enslaved you. My apologies."

"There are girls in the barracks," Darsey informed us.

Brantley approached Surin, dragging the terrified Lapis behind him, and said, "Call together every deckhand and slave so that we may speak to them."

Surin, still gripping Therese's dress protectively, stared at me, unmoving.

"Perhaps," he began quietly in a diplomatic voice, "I can allow you and your husband to go. I will not pursue you, or the others who escaped."

"We are not here to bargain," Brantley said smoothly.

I reached out and touched the hem of Therese's dress.

He sucked in a deep, pained breath as it turned to ash in his hands. Then he nodded and rigidly made his way to the door, followed closely by a whimpering Lapis. Brantley motioned for me to go first, and eyed Darsey.

I stood between them and said, "He's one of us."

"Then I wouldn't stand so close," Brantley grunted, slipping past me.

I realized how dangerous I was to Darsey and began to slip my gloves back on. Brantley turned back and laid a hand on my bare arm. "No," he whispered. "We are not yet done with your power."

I nodded and tucked the gloves into my belt. I would just have to keep my distance.

The three of us followed Surin and Lapis closely. Walking through his study we had to step over the men Brantley dispatched on his way to rescue me. The same men who had our weapons. Surin and Lapis paid them no mind, but Darsey whispered, "They weren't bad men."

"A pirate would befriend pirates," Brantley remarked.

I wanted to take Darsey in my arms and apologize for his loss. For everything he had been through. For the time that was stolen from us and for giving up on him. I couldn't imagine the torment he had gone through whilst on the ship, and I hoped when we were freely facing each other again, I could make amends.

As we made our way out onto the deck, Darsey muttered, "Do you really believe these men are here by choice?"

His words reminded me of Nadine's frustrations when she realized I had forced her hand. She had said something about having to kill the men now, too. She had been on the ship so long, perhaps she felt the same way Darsey did.

"Call the men together and let them know you are no longer their captain," Brantley ordered Surin.

"I'll call them together," Surin snarled, "but will relinquish no such right to you."

Brantley only smiled and caught my eye, nodding toward the largest mast of the ship, from where Surin liked to make his addresses.

Surin nodded at Lapis, and the mouse-like scoundrel obediently rang the large bell that would summon forth the crew.

I watched as more and more men approached, filling up the deck with an enormous presence we would not be able to stand against if not for the power I wielded. Darsey was near enough to me that I heard him suck in an uneasy breath when the doctor emerged, carrying a sly and unaffected smile on his face.

I must have reacted as well, because Brantley laid eyes on the doctor and asked who he was.

"The doctor," I whispered.

He nodded and whispered to Surin. He eyed Brantley with derision while motioning for the doctor to join them. The men moved aside, and the doctor easily made his way up, a smile still on his face.

Darsey whispered, "Come with me. We can get the slave girls."

I turned toward him, ready to obey, but Brantley grabbed me by the elbow and pulled me back. "How many are there?" he asked, as more men continued to show up on deck.

Darsey's eyes fell on Brantley's hand on my elbow, and his lips tightened. "Seven," he said through his teeth.

Brantley turned back and again whispered something to Surin, who then told one of the men to retrieve the slaves.

The men on deck were beginning to shuffle back and forth on their feet and whisper amongst themselves. No doubt they were wondering who Brantley was and why Surin was listening to him. Many of their eyes were on me, though I couldn't stop focusing on Darsey's eyes as he continued to glare at Brantley. I felt guilty for the look on his face and had so much I wanted to say.

The man returned quickly with the seven slave girls, and my heart lurched at how frightened and frail they looked. They were dirty and not as well kept as I expected, aside from their attire which was exactly as I recalled.

Rags. Short, revealing sacks of fabric barely passable as clothing. Humiliating.

"Get them something to wear," I pleaded.

Brantley nodded and announced, "You have been called here for good news. Each and every one of you is now free."

No one moved. Their silent stares were unsettling, giving the impression that any voice other than Surin's fell on deaf ears.

"Your captain, the crying one, and the one known as 'the doctor' are at *my* mercy. Anyone who chooses to fight for them, may do so now."

I looked at Brantley, my eyes wide. He could never take them all, and he knew how I felt about killing!

Still no one moved.

The doctor laughed and asked, "What is this, eh?"

"This is your end," Brantley said with a menacing confidence that sent chills up my spine. I was glad he was on my side. He smiled as the doctor's look of confused jest turned to reserved horror and motioned toward me. "Demonstrate for them, Lady Dragon Born, what they are now facing."

I looked up at the massive mast and gently laid my hand on it. It sizzled away beneath my touch, and spread aggressively to the tip, high in the sky. The wood and sail rained down in ash and the wind carried some of it away while the rest left everyone covered in gray.

There was a tumultuous uproar of shouts and fear. Some men turned to run, while others grabbed hold of the would-be deserters and shook them back to their senses. After fear had thoroughly spread throughout the crew, Brantley raised his arms and called for quiet.

"Now, men," Brantley said once he was sure he had their attention again. "I say to you, embrace your freedom, and leave this cursed place in the past. Surin and his kin are no longer a threat to the people of this world. They will meet their ends this very day. If you choose to die with them, so be it. If you choose to go out into the world and be destructive, then the Dragon Born will know, and she will end you as well. Now go."

As soon as the realization of his words set upon them, they quickly abandoned the ship, and the sound of their scrambling reminded me of thunder rolling through the sky in unending spells of havoc. Some rushed off the ship where it was docked, and some jumped overboard and swam to shore. Soon it was only Darsey, Brantley, me, the slaves, and the three men Brantley was ready to take the lives of.

The girls were staring at me; unmoving, trembling, and huddled together. "Get them some clothes," I snapped at Brantley, annoyed it had not yet been done.

He looked at Darsey and lightly said, "Your first test, lad. Prove to us you're with us, and get them something else to wear."

Darsey looked at me, his face unreadable, then disappeared below deck.

"So . . . you *are* special," the doctor said softly.

Brantley aimed his sword at the doctor and ordered, "Don't speak to her." Then, he smiled and said, "Actually, don't speak at all." He angled his head toward me and said, "Don't let them move. I'm going to give them the same graces they offered others."

I approached them and held my hands up. Lapis covered his head and cowered, the doctor forced a nervous smile, and Surin stood motionless, refusing to look me in the eye. It was nice to see them not in power anymore.

Brantley returned with binds the same time Darsey did with clothes. The girls quickly dressed while Brantley gagged each man and tied their hands behind their backs. He moved to do the same to Darsey, but I grabbed his arm.

"What are you doing?" I asked, appalled.

"Just to be safe," he said assuredly.

"No," I said firmly. "I told you, he's one of us."

"How can you be sure?" he asked, frustration in his voice.

"Because I *know* him," I asserted.

"Or you *knew* him," Brantley countered. "There's no telling what happened to him while you were apart. We can't let him be free unless we know for *sure*."

"It's fine," Darsey interrupted. "Bind me."

"No!" I shouted as Brantley shoved a gag in his mouth, a satisfied smile on his face.

I grabbed Brantley's arm again and scowled at him.

"What?" he asked, clearly enjoying the moment. "He said bind him." He spun Darsey around and tied his hands as he had the others.

I was seething but could do nothing to help. Because of the dagger if I touched Darsey I might turn him to ash. Without it, we wouldn't be impervious to retaliation. I crossed my arms and shook my head.

*"Adalee!"* Uri said as he came bounding up.

"Stop!" I said, holding my hands out.

He slid to a stop, and I could hear his loud purrs. *"I know. The dagger. I saw what you did! This is so neat! Where are we taking them?"*

I had no idea where we were taking them, so I looked at Brantley and asked, trying to relay the exasperation I felt toward him in my voice, "What now?"

He faced the slave girls and said, "If you know where you are, and wish to go home, you can. We are headed to a safe place, guarded by the blessings of a shaman. They have room for you and will gladly take you in. Don't get near, or touch the Dragon Born unless you want to end up like the mast."

I was displeased that he was using fear to keep the girls safe from my touch, rather than explanation. He faced me and smiled at my scowl. "Walk in the back, will you?" he asked. "If any of the men try to run, kill them."

I didn't like him ordering me about, but this was not the time for arguing. I nodded, and we left the ship and headed to the Shaman's Clearing.

## Two | The Shaman's Clearing

When we were close to the Shaman's Clearing, Brantley stopped the company and hooded the three men. My glare gave him pause when he reached Darsey.

He acquiesced my silent request and I added, "We should unbind him as well."

Brantley shrugged and said, "Go ahead."

I cut my eyes at him and whispered, "You know I can't." The risk was still too great.

"Then he stays bound."

"*I'll do it!*" Uri offered. Then he climbed up Darsey's pants to his arm and began gnawing and pawing at the binds around his wrists.

"I'll do it," one of the girls said.

Uri stopped and looked at me. I nodded and he hopped down.

The girl stepped up to Darsey and stared him in the eyes as she reached around and untied his gag. She gently pulled it away and I saw a small, grateful smile and something akin to affection in Darsey's eyes. She blushed and looked down with a smile, then walked around and untied his hands.

"Thank you," he said softly, and she nodded.

The exchange made me angry. Who was this girl to lovingly lay her hands upon Darsey? And what right did she have to deserve such a look from him?

She looked at me and said softly, "He was always kind to us."

I wanted to let her know that *my* Darsey was a kind man, and to not look too much into it, because he was *mine*. Instead, I didn't say anything; only nodded as she went back to the other girls.

"Okay," Brantley said. "We're about to come upon the dialons. I don't know what will happen when we try to take the four of them through."

"Three of them," I corrected. "Darsey will have no problem passing the wall."

Brantley smiled and said, "Let this be another test, then." He looked at Darsey and clarified, "No one with ill intent can enter the Shaman's Clearing."

"I know what dialons do," he snapped back. Then, without looking away from Brantley, he motioned to me and said, "I was raised in a shaman's village. I'm not a fool."

"We'll see," Brantley said. Then we slowly moved forward.

I wanted to focus on the task at hand, but I couldn't help peeking over at the girl who had so intimately unbound Darsey.

Who was she, and what had she experienced with him? *How* was he kind to her? I had never known him to have eyes for anyone else. Had he changed? The uncertainty made me sick.

*Just another reason why shamans should never marry,* Madame interjected. *It's a distraction. Look at you. Worrying about something so trivial at a time like this.*

As much as I hated it, she was right. Darsey was back. Whether his heart was still mine or not didn't matter. My heart belonged wholly to him, and as such, I only wanted him to be happy. Maybe.

We came upon the wall, and though I had passed through it earlier that very morning, I was still taken aback by the beauty of its magnitude. Darsey stopped and stared up, his eyes wide and mouth agape.

I whispered to him, "Madame wasn't what we thought. *This* is a shaman's Dialon Wall."

He didn't turn to me as I hoped he would, and instead closed his jaw and nodded. I wanted so badly to look in his eyes. To see the love I had held onto my entire childhood.

"Here we go," Brantley said. Then, as he stepped forward, the dialons parted, allowing a path. He walked in, leading the three hooded prisoners, who were tied to each other in a line by their necks.

Darsey followed, and the girls behind him.

I stopped at the edge and looked down at Uri.

*"Are you ready?"* he asked cheerfully. He couldn't sense the pain and uncertainty in me regarding Darsey. Probably for the better.

"Yes," I said, and we walked through the Dialon Wall.

The dialons quickly filled in the space behind me and once I was through, it was as though they had never parted. Our presence didn't go unnoticed, as the girls in the clearing began talking to one another and someone ran to Veda's tent.

Immediately, Nadine and Veda emerged. Nadine ran to Brantley, her sword drawn.

"What's wrong?" she asked, ready to battle. "What happened? Are you okay?"

He smiled at her fussing over him and said with a bow, "Actually, I have brought you a gift!"

I rolled my eyes. Of course, he would take full credit for bringing them here.

She looked past him at me, then her eyes fell on Darsey and went wide. Brantley leaned in and whispered something to her. Her face hardened and she nodded. Then she glanced at me, pity in her eyes, and I worried she was assuming the same thing I had refused to entertain. Darsey was not transfigured! I wouldn't let them hurt him.

She then saw the three hooded prisoners, and the look on her face was a mixture of relief and ferocity. "Bring them to the center," she told him and then she turned and whispered to Veda, who had been standing by quietly, taking in the sight before her.

Veda nodded and called some of their girls over. She approached the new girls and spoke gently to them, lending them comfort. They visibly calmed and joined the clan.

Brantley led the three prisoners to the center of the clearing and cut the bind joining their necks with a small knife he pulled from his boot. Then he forced them to their knees.

I joined Nadine, feeling as though I needed to be there. Darsey stood beside me, but Uri asked if he could go stand with the girls.

He loved scratches and since I was unable to touch him as often due to my weapon, he had taken to the girls for his cuddles. I nodded at him and he bounded off to them. The mute girl, Dimah, immediately picked him up and started rubbing his back.

"Vengeance is yours," Brantley said to Nadine. "Their crew has scattered, the slaves are free, and these three are at your mercy. Do with them as you will."

She placed a hand on his shoulder and smiled. "There really is more to you than meets the eye," she said, reverence in her voice.

"I told you there was," he said with a smug smile.

The feelings of relief I had felt when he showed up made me sick and ashamed. He let them take me to use me as bait. He made me think I was getting *my* revenge, when in fact he used my power to his own advantage to impress Nadine.

Scoundrel.

He walked through and ripped their hoods off. Surin quickly found Nadine, and a cold defiance mixed with rage set into his face. The doctor had the look of a wild animal trying to escape a snare in his eye. And Lapis . . . he found Veda almost immediately and a calm relief set into his shoulders. He tried futilely to speak through his gag.

I looked at Veda and saw her hanging her head, visibly shaken at his presence.

Brantley saw her reaction too, and strode over to Lapis, slipping his gag down.

"Veda," Lapis said in an exhausted and exasperated tone. "My love," his high voice squeaked out.

I noticed that the dozens of dialons that had been buzzing throughout the clearing were thickening into hundreds. They concentrated near Veda, and I realized they were reacting to her discomfort.

"She is your love?" Brantley said, acting as though he was shocked at the revelation. "My apologies, good sir," he mocked.

He went behind Lapis and unbound his hands. "Anyone who is favored by the lovely Veda is, of course, favored by the lot of us. Please, retrieve your love and be on your way."

Lapis' round body fell forward with the motion of his pudgy arms being freed. He looked up at Brantley, winded and said, "A trick! You will have that witch burn me the moment I move."

Brantley noticeably looked around as the dialons in the air thickened. "Oh," he said, "I don't think the Dragon Born is the one *you* need to worry about. By all means, retrieve your love and go. If she chooses you, your life will be spared. If you choose to abandon her, *I* will personally end you."

Lapis looked up at Veda and after a moment, his breathing slowed and calmed. A small, relieved smile played on his lips. "I found you," he said. Then he awkwardly stood and approached her, not offering even a backwards glance to his brothers. "Come," he said, as he held out his hand for her. "I will take you far from here and we can begin our life anew."

She instinctively stepped back from his hand, and the dialons gathered and began to swarm near her. Lapis looked at the little bugs, then back at Brantley, who smiled and tapped the hilt of his sword, reminding him what running would mean.

Lapis looked back at Veda and took a shallow, somewhat aggravated breath. "What have they told you about me?" he asked. "Haven't I always treated you with kindness and love? Never have I said a harsh word to you or raised my hand to you."

"I know," Veda admitted in her sweet, young voice. "But I hate you, nonetheless."

He looked visibly shocked at her admission. "Hate me?" he asked, hurt and anger in his voice. "They *poisoned* you against me!" His anger was rising, surely fueled by the panic that death was both behind and before him. "Come with me," he pleaded, jutting his hand out further.

"No," she muttered.

"Come with me!" he demanded, his voice cracking.

"No!" she shouted.

Brantley pulled his sword and Lapis rushed Veda and reached for her arm. Before he could touch her the dialons swarmed him, covering every inch of his body, and buzzed so loudly nothing else could be heard.

Seconds after swarming him, they dispersed, leaving nothing behind. Not even a pearl.

I had never seen the dialons in action before, and I now knew for sure why those with evil intent would fear them. They were unforgiving, unceasing, and unassailable.

Yet, they gently returned to Veda, with a change in demeanor that could only be described as affectionate. It reminded me greatly of my relationship with Uri. Though he was filled with more innocence and uncertainty.

Veda didn't seem afraid of the dialons as they returned to her. Instead, she breathed a sigh of relief, smiled, and slowly began to laugh. It wasn't a maniacal cackle at the destruction of Lapis. It was instead the joy of a girl who had been trapped in the dark for years, finally seeing light again. Her demeanor spoke of full freedom, and tears streaked her face.

Slowly her laughing ebbed to silence. No one spoke. Everyone stared. Brantley made everyone jump with a loud assertion of, "Okay, who's next?"

The doctor began struggling against his binds and crying out behind his gag.

"Thank you for volunteering," Nadine said with a grin.

Brantley whispered something to her, and she looked at him, slightly shaking her head. "Therese," she softly asserted.

He nodded and whispered something else. Her eyes fell on Surin and a coldness shot across them. After a moment she nodded.

Brantley smiled at her and extended the hilt of his sword to Darsey. "You! Kill the doctor."

I realized this was yet another test, and I was angry they wanted my precious Darsey to sully his hands with death. I didn't know what he had experienced since we had been separated, but if there was even a chance he had made it through without blood on his hands, I wanted to protect that with all my strength.

I shouted, "He doesn't have to prove anything—"

However, he was already upon the doctor with the sword in hand. Without hesitation he plunged the blade through the doctor's chest all the way to the hilt.

The doctor shook on the weapon and blood dripped from his mouth. I heard gasps from the girls, and many looked away from the savagery. I wanted to do the same, yet I couldn't stop staring at the look on Darsey's face. It was full of anger, sadness, and thirsted for revenge. It was a look of pure hatred I didn't know he was capable of. A darkness overcame his demeanor and for a moment, he truly wasn't the boy I once knew. He drew his face close to the doctor's and stared into his eyes. He growled, "Do you feel that? It's more than you deserve." The doctor sputtered blood up and it sprayed across Darsey's face, though he didn't react save a flinch to protect his eyes from the splatter.

"Okay," Brantley said. "Return my weapon."

"Not yet," Darsey growled, not breaking gaze with the doctor. "I want to see the life leave his eyes."

His words struck a blow to my core and I turned away, my stomach lurching. I faced the girls, and while many of them were looking away, many still were watching, a sense of the same satisfaction resting in their eyes. I found the one who had unbound Darsey, and not only was she watching, but she was also smiling with a silent gratitude that told me he wasn't only doing this for himself. It was for her as well. For all of them. For all of us.

I forced myself to turn back and watched as the doctor breathed his last and fell to his side. Darsey knelt over him, staring down at his lifeless face for a few moments longer. Then he stood, pushed his boot into the doctor's shoulder, and yanked the sword from his chest. He was breathing heavily, no doubt from the weight of what he had just done. He tossed Brantley's sword to the ground at his feet and turned, quickly walking away, running his hands through his hair and rubbing his face. I watched as he brought his hands back and stared at the blood that dripped from them.

"Finally," I heard Nadine say. Darsey turned back, tears balancing on the brims of his eyes. His breathing looked erratic despite his long, forced gasps, and I wanted so badly to go to him, if not for the blade that stood between us.

"I told you the day you brought me on the ship that you would die at my hand," Nadine said, savoring every word. "Do you remember that?"

"Yes," Surin said boldly.

I turned toward them and saw a slice on his check where I assumed Nadine lowered his gag with the tip of her sword. She was standing before him, poised and ready to strike. "It looks like that day has come," she said satisfactorily.

"You killed my bride," he said evenly. "You can't hurt me any more than you already have."

My eyes widened and I looked at her face. Her lips were tight, and her eyes were raging. "*You* killed her," she growled. "By turning her against me—"

"All I did was help her understand her true feelings. I didn't force her to love me. I didn't force her to hate you. It was how she truly felt."

Nadine screamed and lifted her blade above her head.

Surin smiled up at her and said, "She was always mine."

In one swift motion, she brought her sword down upon his head, slicing him in two to his chest. He fell back, taking her blade with him.

She spun and screamed, clenching her fists. I wished her scream was one of satisfaction. Instead it was filled with rage and dismay.

Brantley was by her side instantly, laying his hand on her back and talking softly to her. I looked back at Darsey and saw him stumbling away. The girl who unbound him broke from the group and followed.

I quickly unlatched my blade and went to Veda. "Please, take this," I begged.

She understood and nodded. I laid it at her feet and rushed off to Darsey, Uri on my heels.

*"Can I come?"* he asked.

I patted my shoulder without slowing and he leaped up and climbed my flowing cloak.

"Darsey!" I shouted when I caught up to him and the girl.

He spun around and finally took me in his arms. "Adalee," he breathed into my hair, relief in his voice.

I cared not that he was covered in blood. I held onto him tightly and relished the feeling of his arms around me.

The girl stood by awkwardly, then returned to the group without a word.

"I thought you were dead!" I cried, glad to finally have the freedom to speak with him.

"I know, I know," he repeated as he caressed my hair and held me close. "I'm sorry. I'm sorry."

"No, I'm sorry," I cried. "I left you out there. I let you sink. I should have—"

"No," he said firmly. "All I wanted was for you to be free, and you escaped."

"But you—"

"It doesn't matter," he said, stepping back and looking at me. Instead of the clear love I had expected to see, I only saw a looming storm settled within his gaze.

"I feel like I need to explain myself," I admitted. The guilt of giving up on him and trying to move on was overwhelming.

"All I want to know," he said, "is *what* that was?" A smile played on his lips, and I knew instantly he was speaking about my power. There was so much for him to learn. So much to say.

"Adalee," Brantley called from the tree line. Irritation swarmed me at his interruption, and I turned.

"What?" I asked, not trying to hide my annoyance.

He held out my blade and motioned for me to follow. "We need you."

I turned back to Darsey and said sadly, "I'll explain later. Just know that when I take that blade in my hand, you can't touch me."

He nodded and stepped away. Uri jumped down and ran up to Darsey, rubbing against his legs. Darsey leaned down and picked him up, holding him as Papa Theo used to, and rubbed his belly.

I turned and took the blade, annoyed that Veda had handed it off so easily. He led me back to the bodies of the doctor and Surin.

"Turn them to ash," Nadine ordered, the presence of a cold soldier resonating through her.

It didn't occur to me to argue or resist the order. They were already dead and had wreaked so much havoc throughout the land. If anything, I hoped turning them to ash would give closure to everyone they had harmed.

I nodded and stepped up. I looked down at the doctor and remembered the pain I had felt in his presence. The fear he instilled in everyone. The joy he experienced from other's pain. Everything he had done to hurt so many. We were all his victims at some point. I reached out and laid my hand on his shoulder and he turned to ash instantly and blew away with the wind. Just like that, his reign of terror was at an end.

I looked at Surin and did the same. As his body turned to ash and began to blow away, I knew so many women were now safe from him. He would never entrap and control anyone again. He, too, was gone.

Brantley approached with their pearls and set them before me. "You know what's next," he said.

I flashed back to the days after the battle in the other clearing, when so many had died. Brantley and Nadine had brought me everyone's pearls and insisted I turned them to ash. I resisted, as I felt everyone deserved to have their story known. But . . . those pearls were of men who were just as evil and deranged as Madame. And with that knowledge, I reluctantly acquiesced.

This time, I felt no such reserve. The dialons had chosen to destroy Lapis and his pearl, and I trusted their enacted justice as chosen ambassadors of Pylertchia. They were world given judges, and they had ruled in our favor.

I took the pearls from Brantley without hesitation and watched as they both turned to ash in my hands and fell through my fingers.

Now those monsters would live on only in the memories of their victims. It was up to us to decide what to do with those memories.

"Well done," Brantley said as though I cared about his approval.

I shoved my knife at him and said, "Just hold this so I can go speak with Darsey."

"You trust me with it?" he asked, surprised.

"Not at all," I admitted, "Though it doesn't seem to matter since anyone else I give it to will hand it over at your behest."

He smiled and shrugged. "That is true. Don't take long, we still need to get on the road."

I huffed and went back to Darsey, who wasn't where I left him.

"Darsey?" I called.

*"We're by the grave,"* Uri sounded in my head.

I ran to where I had chosen as Darsey's final resting place, and found him standing there, staring at the flower laden memorial. He had done his best to wipe the blood away, though it still caked his hair and smeared his skin.

"Who is this?" he asked softly.

Suddenly I was fully aware of how blessed I was by the dragons, and I whispered in a broken voice, "You."

He turned to me, and the tears he had been holding back finally slid down his cheeks.

"I'm sorry," I said. "I didn't know what else to do."

"No," he said quickly, waving my words away. "It's beautiful."

"Now you're here," I said as I stepped up to him.

He faced me, closed his eyes, and pressed his forehead against mine. The tears I hadn't realized I'd been holding back sprang forth and slid down my cheeks. I sucked in a shaky breath and closed my eyes, relishing the closeness to him.

"I hate to break up the beauty of this moment," Brantley interrupted as he approached.

I let out a frustrated sigh and faced him, not stepping away from Darsey.

"He really needs to explain *how* he's alive," Brantley finished.

"There is plenty of time for that," I snapped.

"I'd like to know too," Nadine said as she approached.

"He doesn't have to—"

"Merpeople," Darsey interrupted as he stepped up beside me. "As soon as I lost hold of Adalee's hands, I was grabbed from beneath by merpeople. They took me back to the ship. I was barely conscious, or I would have resisted. They thought they were helping." He looked at me. "I guess, in a way . . . they did."

"What happened after that?" Brantley asked.

"How is that any of your concern?" Darsey challenged.

"We need to know," Nadine pressed.

I realized they still believed he had been transfigured and was filled with indignant rage. "He is still *him*!" I shouted, stepping up. "He doesn't have to explain or prove anything to anyone!"

Nadine looked at me with pity in her eyes and asked, "Can I speak with you? Please?"

I looked at Darsey, and Brantley said, "Don't worry, I'll watch him."

I sucked in a deep breath and stepped up to Brantley, but Uri offered, *"I will stay with them."*

His precious innocence immediately calmed me. I loved that he found himself to be an extension of me, and thus capable of standing on guard for Darsey. I nodded at him and said to Brantley, "Ask him nothing. Uri is watching you."

He snickered and said, "He has proven to be quite useless in a tight situation."

I continued to stare at him, and he shrugged.

"I'll humor you this one time. Not a word." He smiled in his cocky fashion and I ground my teeth and looked at Darsey.

He nodded and said, "I'm okay. Do what you need to do."

I followed Nadine some paces away and she turned. "I know you want to believe he is still himself."

"Because he *is*," I insisted.

Nadine paused for a moment, then said, "I'm not so sure."

"I can see it in his eyes," I persisted.

"Brantley said he tried to kill you in the woods."

"No," I said firmly. "He didn't know it was *me*."

"He also said Darsey spoke harshly to you and did nothing to free you from your captors. That he, himself, took you to Surin. How do you explain that?"

"I . . . I don't know," I admitted. "He probably had a plan. I trust him."

"I don't," she said. "When did he start seeming like himself again?"

"Well, he's been through a lot—"

"So have you!" she said.

"It isn't the same."

"I just want you to be careful. Therese remembered me. She remembered everything. If she wanted to pretend to be on my side, she could have."

"He isn't pretending."

Nadine laid her hands gently on my shoulders and said, "For your sake, I hope you're right."

"I trust him," I reiterated.

"I know," she said as she removed her hands. "Can you do something for me?"

I crossed my arms, preparing for whatever request she might present.

"Can you trust Brantley, too? He *is* on our side."

I scoffed, and she shook her head.

"I know you don't get on well with him. I know he annoys you, and to be fair, you aren't his favorite either, but it is in both of your interests that he helps you get to the next dragon. Can you at least trust *that*?"

I nodded and said, "I can trust that."

"Okay," she said, somewhat satisfied.

We walked back to them together and they were facing off.

*"They didn't say anything, and I don't think they like each other,"* Uri said with a panicked voice.

"Okay," I said as I stepped between them. "Do you want to stay here and recover before we go?"

Darsey looked at me and said, "Just long enough to clean up. Then I would like to put as much distance between us and this place as we can."

"Great!" Brantley agreed. "I was ready to go this morning."

Nadine laid her hand on his back and Darsey scoffed. "Your services are no longer needed," he said to Brantley.

"Well, she certainly isn't going anywhere without *me*," he said smugly.

"We'll see about that," Darsey said, stepping up to him. "Give me back my blade and let us settle this."

"Lad, if you have to ask for your blade back, I assure you, you won't win."

"Darsey, please," I pleaded as I stood before him and placed my hands on his chest. The Darsey I knew wasn't aggressive like that.

He looked in my eyes and asked, "You wish for him to stay?"

"He . . . knows the way," I lied. I couldn't bring myself to tell him about the bind. Seeing how he reacted at the simple thought that Brantley might choose to stay with us made me worried about how he would react to the story behind his presence.

"How does he know the way?" he asked, confused. "I've never seen him in my life," he bit as he glared past me at him.

I then realized that Darsey thought we were going home.

"No," I said softly. "He isn't taking us home."

"I will go nowhere he leads," Darsey growled. "I learned *my* lesson."

"Even better," Brantley said. "You can stay here while Adalee and I go on our way."

"You will be taking her nowhere!" Darsey shouted, stepping in front of me.

I looked at Nadine and she was giving me a look that I hated. She was taking his reaction as proof that he might not be himself. That he wanted to get me alone to hurt me. I knew they were wrong, and I had to prove it.

I knew Darsey's reservations stemmed from the mistake of trusting Garroway, which was understandable. I touched his arm tenderly and said, "I have to free the Dragon Lords."

His eyes widened and he looked at me. "I don't understand," he said softly.

Brantley laughed and said, "Honestly, lad, where do you think she gained the power to turn things to *ash*."

Darsey shot a glare at Brantley, but it softened as I turned his face back to me. "I freed the Red Dragon Lord. He bestowed upon me the power of Dragon's Fire. It comes from the stone in the blade I carry."

"And where does *he* come in?" Darsey asked, blowing past the revelation I had just laid on him.

"I have been chosen by the Dragon's Fire to accompany her to the next Dragon Lord," he said, baiting Darsey with his tone.

Darsey huffed at him and faced me again. "Is that true?"

In a sense it was. I nodded. "Only until the next Dragon Lord," I reiterated.

Darsey sighed heavily and begrudgingly nodded. He looked at Brantley and asked, "Can I have my weapon back?"

Brantley gave out a short laugh and tossed it on the ground before him. "If you knew how to use it, I would have said no."

Darsey clenched his fists and he slowly squatted to retrieve his blade.

Brantley held my blade out to me, and I paused.

"Don't forget the task at hand," he warned when he saw my hesitation.

I nodded and took out my gloves. After I slipped them on, I took the blade and secured it to my side.

Nadine and Brantley returned to the clearing. I pulled my hood up and Uri bounded beside me as Darsey and I followed.

"How do you *know* he has been chosen?" he asked, eyeing Brantley suspiciously.

I was somewhat grateful Brantley had caught on to my hesitation and concocted the lie. I hated being untruthful to Darsey, but it was for his own protection. If he chose to challenge Brantley, I didn't trust the man to spare him.

"The fire doesn't harm him," I said honestly.

Darsey didn't push any further and we entered the clearing.

Veda had the girls dispersed in groups. They were getting to know each other and learning about their new home. Brantley and Nadine were speaking near the Dialon Wall where we had left that morning.

The young girl who unbound Darsey earlier broke from her group and stopped to stare at him, a hopeful expectancy in her eyes. He paid her no mind as he went to the well and drew water to wash the blood off.

I waited for him, then we walked toward Brantley and Nadine. While my steps were feeling lighter and more carefree with the knowledge I had him back, his steps were more of a saunter, and I hoped he was as grateful to be back with me as I was with him.

When we reached them, Brantley said, "We'll retrieve the supplies we left by the tree and be on our way."

Before I could move, Darsey stepped past us and through the Dialon Wall. I looked at Brantley and followed, ignoring the shake of his head that told me I was crazy for trusting Darsey.

They would see.

## Three | On the Edge

I tried to mask my labored breathing from the weight of the supplies while we trekked the woods, as it was much more than I was used to carrying.

Darsey and Brantley didn't seem to be phased by the weight on their backs, though they took the heaviest of the supplies. I hid my struggle and pushed on, Brantley ahead, leading the way, Darsey on one side of me, and Uri on the other. I couldn't believe Brantley had expected Darsey to carry all the supplies himself when he purchased him.

The thought of anyone using Darsey in such a manner made me fume. I glanced over at his quiet, still face. He showed no emotion. No incline toward me. He just followed along, stoic and contemplative.

I wanted to know what was going on in his mind. With the slave ship behind us, I hoped he would open up and start showing me the old Darsey again. But the longer we walked with no conversation, the more Nadine's warnings creeped at the edges of my mind. It wasn't long before Madame spoke up.

*Better safe than sorry.*

I shook my head slightly, willing her voice away. I didn't want to give her a say.

*He's not himself. Any fool can see that.*

I took a steady breath and tried to ignore her.

*Don't pretend you trust him! You lied about why Brantley is here. Think about that.*

I ground my teeth and glanced at Darsey again. It wasn't like that. I was afraid for him with Brantley the same way I was afraid for him with Madame. Two different monsters. Two different captors. Same Darsey.

I nodded to myself. Yes. I trusted him. If I thought he'd been transfigured I would have told him about the bind. The Darsey I grew up with would react with unrivaled indignation and challenged Brantley to a duel of some sort. A fight he would lose.

*Because he is weak.*

No! Not weak. Brash. Caring. Inexperienced. Never weak.

I had to be mindful to never let Madame affect my thinking again. I felt her voice played a part in mine being bound to Brantley, and I needed to do all I could to resist her.

The day continued in uneventful fashion. At least, by outward standards. Inward, my mind was reeling in a never-ending battle with my demon. She was determined to undermine my confidence in him, and I could not let her win.

The scenery hadn't changed much as night approached. We were still in the forest, though Brantley assured us we were on the right path.

We stopped by a group of trees that shared the soil with large boulders, their partially exposed roots slithered along the ground, creating sectioned places to recline and rest. The heat stuck to us like the soft green moss that clung to everything on the ground.

I happily dropped all I had been carrying when Brantley said we were stopping for the night. With a heavy breath I disguised as a sigh, I fell into the rounded crevice of a low root and leaned back on it, stretching out the ache in the middle of my back. My arms were exhausted, and I didn't relish the thought of how sore I would be in the morning.

Darsey chose a space close to me, yet far enough that we wouldn't accidentally touch in the night. A precaution I assumed he was taking because of my warnings about the blade. Brantley chose a completely different tree and root system across the way to rest in. He quickly cleared a spot and started a small fire. I watched tiredly as he surrounded the blaze with stones, forcing it to keep its shape. I didn't want the warmth of it to reach me, as the heat of the day hung around like an unfriendly illness.

Brantley pulled his canteen up and drank sparingly from it. I followed suit and heard Darsey do the same. I decided a sparing drink was not enough and proceeded to drain more into my mouth.

"Don't drink it all," Brantley said, much closer to me than I thought he was.

I jumped and some of the water spilled down my chin. I sat forward and wiped it with the back of my gloved hand. "I'm not," I said, coughing and sputtering slightly.

He grunted and grabbed one of the bags I had been carrying. I jumped up and followed him to the fire. "We can get more water from the stream," I defended.

He nodded and squatted, focused on retrieving bread and cheese from the bag. He quietly held out a piece of each and I took them, turning to offer them to Darsey.

Uri was standing on a root near Darsey's face, leaning close and sniffing his hair.

*"I think he's asleep,"* he said.

"Okay," I whispered, and turned back to Brantley.

*"Can I sleep on him?"* Uri asked.

I turned back and smiled. "Of course, you can."

Uri excitedly stepped to Darsey's shoulder and moved down to his lap. I could hear him purring and sat down by the fire, despite not wanting to be near the heat.

Brantley was already eating, and I lifted the bread and took a bite.

"So, your tippoo isn't as in control as you led me to believe," He accused softly, not looking at me.

"What do you mean?" I asked defensively.

He laughed quietly and said, "When those men attacked us, he ran off."

"So?" I asked. "I told him to."

"All I'm saying," he said as he readjusted his seat, "is that if he *can* leap at will, then he isn't very loyal."

"He's obedient," I tried to counter.

"He was okay with letting you be taken," he accused. "Now, I don't know *much* about tippoos, but before, when you were threatening me, he seemed pretty loyal. Now, tell me, he can't leap at will, can he?"

I didn't take another bite, having lost my appetite, and I crossed my arms, avoiding his eyes.

He laughed and said, "Okay," as though he had it all figured out. "You *lied*."

"You lie about *everything*," I hissed. "I don't trust a word that comes out of your mouth."

"I don't hear you denying it," he said smugly.

I huffed and shook my head. He knew. There was no point in hiding it now. And Nadine had begged me to trust him. Though I didn't, I did trust her. I sighed defeatedly and said, "He's a baby. I'm all he can remember. He didn't even know he could leap until the first time it happened. He doesn't know how to control it yet."

"So, what you're telling me is—" he began, but I cut him off quickly.

"As you've seen, he *does* leap when it really matters."

"You mean, when *I* need to be held in check?"

I looked up at him and nodded with taut lips.

"Okay," he said. "That would have been useful to know before. It changes things."

My heart began to race, and I shook my head. "Don't think you'll turn me from my path," I warned.

"What?" he asked, looking at me shocked. "No, it doesn't change *that*. All I mean is that now I know *I* am the only line of defense. He's useless in a fight."

"Excuse me," I said, pointing to my blade. "I am way more powerful than your sword."

"When you have the dagger at hand," he added. "It isn't hard to disarm you. We should probably fix that."

"How?"

"I can teach you how to defend yourself."

"What about him?" I asked, nodding towards Darsey as he slept soundly.

He shrugged and said, "Maybe . . . if I feel I can trust him."

"He wasn't transfigured," I whispered harshly.

"Maybe not," Brantley agreed.

I took in his demeanor and asked, "Why do you say so?" I was eager to hear anything that would give me hope I was right.

"He reminds me of a soldier recovering from being over enemy lines," he admitted. "I didn't know him before, so I can't be sure. Was he always so quiet?"

"No," I said, shaking my head. "He was always vibrant and full of life. He could make anyone love him."

"And with you?" he asked. "Nadine said he is your husband. What is he normally like with you?"

I looked down and shrugged. The danger had passed. There was no reason to hide that we weren't actually married anymore.

I looked back up and said, "We aren't married. That is just something we said because his father told us I would be safer on our travels if we were."

He nodded as though he understood completely, which surprised me.

When he didn't speak, I continued. "Normally he is completely devoted to me. He would do anything for me. Whatever it took to keep me safe was always his aim."

"Was?" Brantley asked, raising an eyebrow.

"Is," I quickly corrected. "*Is* his aim."

"Is that why you lied about this?" Brantley asked, holding up his wrist.

I absently rubbed the mark beneath my glove and nodded. "It's best he doesn't know the truth."

"Or it would be a good test. If he reacts how you think he should, then we'll know if he was transfigured."

I quickly shook my head. Now that I had lied, I couldn't let Darsey know! I glanced back at him. Our relationship already seemed strained, and I couldn't stand the thought of him knowing my deceit. "He has enough to worry about," I defended. "And he *would* react the way I think he would. And it wouldn't be good."

"He can't hurt me," Brantley said with a small laugh.

"I know," I said in low voice through my clenched jaw.

*Go ahead,* Madame goaded. *Tell him about how you had to protect him from me,* she said with a sneer I could almost see.

I ignored her and glanced back again to make sure Darsey was still asleep, and satisfied that he was, I scooted closer and whispered, "As much as I hate to admit it, he is no match to you."

Brantley arched his brows and nodded as though he were trying to act humble at my words but couldn't deny them, and it infuriated me.

"He is nothing like you," I said, a little louder. "He's a poet. An artist. He can see beauty where no one else can. And trust me when I say it is better for everyone if he doesn't know about the bind."

"For everyone, or just you?"

"Him too," I said. Then, taking in his judging face, I scoffed and spilled, "Okay, maybe it wouldn't matter to you if he knew. Everyone hates you already, so what is another reason, right?"

He nodded with a smile and shrugged.

"Well, this isn't about *you*. It's about *us*. And once the Blue Dragon Lord is free, we will be unbound, and you will be able to go wherever you wish. Then it *will* be just the three of us, again."

He scrunched his brow in confusion, then smiled and nodded when I saw his eyes fall to Uri. "Yes," he said. "The *three* of you."

"How it was meant to be," I added.

"Just do me a favor until then," he said as he began to arrange the packs to lay on for the night.

"What?" I asked warily.

"Don't do anything stupid, like entrust your dagger to him."

"Why?" I asked suspiciously. "Because you would rather I entrust it to *you*?"

"I would *rather* you be able to control it and keep it on *you* at all times."

"I'm the only one who can wield it, so what does it matter to you if I entrust it to Darsey? I trust him way more than you."

He sat back up, clearly agitated and said, "Because if you are wrong about him, and he *isn't* himself anymore, then he could easily get rid of it and you would be powerless. We may need your power to release the next Dragon Lord. Did you ever think about that? You need to treat that weapon as more than just an accessory. It is your *life*line."

"What do you care?" I snapped. "Why do you care what happens to me?"

He looked surprised at my question and shook his head. "I don't," he said matter-of-factly. "Right now, your decisions affect me too. After I'm gone, do what you want. Good luck saving the world," he said sardonically as he stood and doused the fire with dirt, kicking some of the ground onto me as well.

I stood and angrily felt my way back to my tree roots. Once I heard him settle down for the night, I whispered harshly, "I never said I was going to entrust it to anyone. *You* said that."

He didn't respond.

I fumed at his words. I worried about Darsey. I could hear Uri purring on him nearby, and I wished the kitten could be cuddled up to me, though I was grateful Darsey didn't have to sleep alone.

One thing Brantley was right about was that I needed to gain better control over the dagger. Even though I hated admitting he was right about anything.

It was dark. It was cold. There was great pressure all around me. The frigid air pushed in on me though it didn't move.

I didn't have to be cold. I had fire.

No!

I couldn't control it. I might hurt Darsey. He was near. I needed to find my way without the fire.

I held out my hands and could see the gloves. They protected others. They protected me. I tried to peer into the unrelenting darkness.

"Hello?" I tried to ask but could make no sound.

The darkness ebbed, and around me was a piercing blue.

Water. I was swimming.

I began to kick my legs and move my arms, but I didn't know which way was up. I would need air soon. Had I been holding my breath? I couldn't remember.

I sat up and breathed deep.

Dawn was breaking through the trees and Brantley was moving about. He stopped and looked at me.

"Bad dream?" he asked, though he sounded very uninterested.

I rubbed my eyes and said drowsily, "I think it was a calling dream."

He nodded and said, "Get the lad up. We need to eat and be on our way."

I nodded and turned toward Darsey on the other side of the roots. He looked so peaceful. His face was still and serene. Relaxed. I hadn't realized that the day before he had had a scowl on his face and his brow had been furrowed. Now, he looked like the Darsey I knew.

*"It got hot last night,"* Uri complained, as he stretched from a low tree branch.

"Fall should be upon us soon," I said, but I agreed with Uri. I desperately wanted to remove my cloak and gloves and cool off, despite the danger.

I reached out to gently nudge Darsey with my gloved hand, then paused. I wanted so badly to touch him. I glanced over at Brantley, and satisfied he wasn't paying me any mind, I discreetly removed the blade and set it down beside me near the trunk of the tree. The pulsing disappeared as soon as I let it go. I felt normal again.

I pushed back my hood and pulled off a glove. I reached for him, and just as I laid my hand on his shoulder, he grabbed my arm and shoved me back, pulling his sword and aiming it down at me with a ferocious rage in his eyes.

"Hey!" Brantley yelled as he knocked Darsey away from me.

I scrambled up, slipped my glove back on, and grabbed my dagger before anyone noticed.

Brantley faced me just as I wrapped my cloak around the secured dagger and asked, "Are you hurt?"

I shook my head and Darsey said, "Adalee . . . I'm sorry. I'm so sorry."

I looked past Brantley and saw the pained look in Darsey's eyes. "It's okay," I assured him.

"It's not," he argued, tossing his sword down and putting his head in his hands.

His pain made my heart wrench and I wanted to comfort him, but even with the gloves I couldn't risk it. He meant too much to me.

Uri jumped down beside me and said, *"It's a good thing you took the dagger off. He would have been ash if you hadn't!"*

I didn't look at him, as I couldn't tear my eyes from Darsey. "Really," I said. "I'm okay."

"Good," Brantley said, eyeing me. "We need to move."

"What about breakfast?" I asked.

"You've wasted too much time. You can eat on the road."

Darsey avoided my eyes as he took his sword back up and began gathering his things.

I took up my packs and ignored the soreness in my arms. We quickly set back out; Brantley ahead, and me between Darsey and Uri.

I was expecting the same quiet as the day before, so I was surprised when Darsey softly said, "I'm really sorry. On the ship I was woken by loud noises and calls. Any time a hand was laid on me when I slept, the doctor was where I went."

I cringed and asked, "Did you endure him often?"

"More often than I'd like to remember," he admitted.

After a pause I asked, "Why? What reason did Surin have to send you to him so often?"

"You," he said gently. "He told me I would be with him forever, and that I would never see life off the ship again. He said he wouldn't transfigure me, because he wanted me to remember *whose* fault it was I was there." He looked at me with sad eyes. "He wanted me to hate you. He sent me to the doctor every couple of days." He looked away and shook his head. "Never for more than a few hours, because he didn't want to waste time on recovery," he said bitterly.

"I'm sorry," I said breathlessly.

"No," he said firmly as he looked back at me. "It *isn't* your fault."

I looked away and nodded. I wanted to hold his gaze longer, but the guilt of what he went through made me feel as though I didn't deserve it.

"It doesn't matter," Darsey said, his voice edging on a colder tone.

I looked at him and he was looking forward, his eyes hard and face firm.

"It does matter," I said.

"No, what I want to know now is about that dagger and how you turn things to ash." His voice was distant and hard. As though he were a stranger questioning me, and not my beloved inquiring of me.

However, I didn't want to wait for a more appealing tone of voice. I desperately wanted to share with him all I had been through.

I quickly recounted what had happened in the days after we were separated. I told him about meeting Serefina and what she had told me about my destiny. I told him about meditation and how I had tried to find my way home first and was met with an angry Dragon Lord. I told him about the journey up the mountain, though I skipped over my embarrassing lack of survival skills and how I couldn't start a fire. He showed a bit more interest when I mentioned the jeweled wall that turned out to be fire in disguise.

He breathed out at that part and said, "I wish I had been there to see it."

"Me too," I said with a smile. I told him about how I freed the Dragon Lord and how he had returned to the Shaman's Clearing with me and Uri on his back. I told him how Serefina was his rider, and what he said to me before he left. Then I told him about the blade, and what I knew so far about my abilities with it.

"That is amazing," he said.

I nodded and added, "It really is. I had no idea it was all true."

"And what about Uri?" he asked, motioning to the kitten as he bounded along.

"What do you remember of the night we escaped?" I asked.

"I thought I was crazy but hearing all that, I am thinking I might not have been wrong. Was he . . . big?"

"Yes," I said with a smile. "He is a tippoo. I don't know a lot about it. He is *attached* to me, I think. I don't really know what that means, though. He said something about being sick until he met me. I think he was dying when you brought him to me. And when he saw me, he attached and that healed him. Or something like that."

"Wait, he *said* something to you? He can talk?"

*"And you finally stay awake to listen!"* Uri added excitedly.

"Yes," I said, remembering what it was like before we could speak. "The swooning!" I added excitedly. "The swooning was Uri speaking to me. For some reason I couldn't hear him, and it made me swoon."

Darsey looked at Uri again then back at me. "So you can hear him now? Is it a Dragon Born thing?"

*"Nope! It's a Gavyn thing!"* Uri happily answered, though his nonchalance didn't carry over to me. I warily glanced up at the trees and looked for the Falcone, knowing he wasn't far.

"What's wrong?" Darsey asked, grabbing the hilt of his blade and looking around.

"Nothing," I assured him. "I was just looking for the Falcone that has been following us. I don't know what he wants, but Uri and I were only able to speak after he showed up. Uri says it's Gavyn that makes it so I don't 'sleep' when he talks."

"Sleep," Darsey mumbled, mulling over the word. He nodded and took his hand from the hilt of his sword.

"And his size?" he asked.

I nodded and said, "It's called leaping. The ship was the first time he had done it. And he's only been able to do it once since then, though he tries every day to learn."

*"Tell him about how I looked tough and made Brantley go with us,"* Uri urged, wanting to be seen as a hero in Darsey's eyes.

His blatant confession immediately sent me into defense mode and I shook my head and said, "It's great, anyway. Having him." I cleared my throat and wanted to make sure Darsey didn't suspect anything like what Uri exclaimed could be true, though I was the only one who could hear him. "And Brantley, he's great. Very useful. I'm . . . glad he was *chosen* by the Dragon Lords to help. You know . . . until the next dragon."

Darsey nodded slowly and looked down. "I missed it all," he chastised himself.

"No," I said, not wanting him to feel guilty for his imprisonment.

"If I had been here, maybe the Dragon Lord's would have chosen *me*—"

His reasoning pained me to hear because it was without merit. I touched his arm and said, "You *survived*. And you're here now."

He looked down at my hand and I realized the danger and pulled it back to my chest. "Sorry," I whispered.

"Should I have burned?" he asked, hopefully.

I shook my head and said, "Only if my skin touches you. My clothes help block it."

He looked me up and down and asked, "Is that why you look like it's the dead of winter?"

"Yes," I exclaimed. "And I'm dying in this heat!"

He turned toward me and said, "Let me take your packs. You shouldn't have to carry the burden of the blade *and* supplies."

I shook my head again and said, "I'm okay." I couldn't bear the thought of making him carry my supplies as well as his.

"You could take some layers off and cool down if you didn't have to carry supplies," he added.

"Not in the forest," I pointed out.

He looked around and nodded. "Right. I didn't think about that."

"It's okay," I assured him. "I'm okay."

"Could I carry the dagger *for* you?" he offered. "Or would it burn me?"

"I am the only one who can wield it. To anyone else, it is nothing but a charred blade."

"Then that would fix our problem," he said. "You could lighten your load and not die from the heat."

"She said she's fine," Brantley bit as he turned around. "Getting your hands on that dagger will do nothing for you."

His blatant accusation knocked the wind out of me as Darsey drew his blade and walked up on Brantley quickly. "The only one here who should be met with mistrust is *you*," he growled.

Brantley drew his own weapon and stopped Darsey at blade's length. "You might want to reconsider your actions, lad. As we discovered yesterday, and as your own Adalee attested to me last night, I *will* best you in a match."

His disregard for what I had said in confidence sent me reeling and I shouted, "Brantley! Put your sword away!"

Darsey let his blade fall and looked at me with hurt in his eyes. "Did the Dragon's choose him, because *you* chose him?" he asked, pain in his voice.

"No," I said vehemently. I realized then that he thought Brantley and I meant more to one another than the unhappy circumstances that were forcing us together. "He means *nothing* to me," I promised.

"Happily so," Brantley agreed, sheathing his sword. "I am only here until the next Dragon Lord. Upon my release, I will be all too happy to leave you two to the task. Though, I personally don't think trusting a pirate is in the lass's best interest."

Darsey gripped his blade tightly again and faced Brantley. "Me? A pirate? *You* are the one who *purchased* me."

"And you tried to kill your beloved and set a trap upon us," Brantley said coolly.

"I didn't have a *choice*," Darsey yelled, getting angry again.

*"Adalee,"* Uri said, but I couldn't focus on him.

"Please, stop," I begged.

"You always have a choice, lad," Brantley chastised.

"Don't patronize me," Darsey yelled. "You had a choice too, and you chose to *buy* a human. Don't pretend like you're any different than me."

"So, you admit it, then? If I am so evil and we are just alike, what have you to say about *yourself*?"

"I think this trek would be a lot better without *you*," Darsey growled, raising his sword.

"Stop!" I screamed.

Brantley drew his sword again and easily blocked the blow. "You won't get your hands on that blade," he teased darkly.

Darsey roared and swung his sword again. Sparks flew as the blow was once again blocked.

"Brantley, stop! Don't hurt him!" I cried.

I felt like every emotion in me was running rampant and out of control. Every inch of my body was on fire and I was terrified I was about to lose Darsey again. My vision began to blur and turn red. "Stop," I cried out again.

The clanging of blades continued to crash, and I covered my ears, willing the men to think reasonably, though my ability to do so was long gone at the moment.

Then a loud scream erupted, and a blue flash streaked through the air, breaking through the red before my eyes. The two men were blasted away from one another, Brantley landing inches from me.

He scrambled up and quickly snatched the blade from my side.

Instantly, the red cleared, and I found myself staring at his bewildered face, my body calm though my heart racing.

"Get control of yourself," he hissed, motioning around us.

I realized the ground was singed and the trees were hot to the touch. I remembered what had happened when Brantley and I became bound, and I looked at his face. "You too," I said through my teeth, trying not to let him see how worried I was about how out of control I had just been.

Darsey limped over, holding his arm and aimed his sword at Brantley. "Give her the dagger back," he ordered.

Brantley sighed and laughed. "Fine," he said, handing it back to me. He sheathed his fallen sword and remarked as he passed Darsey, "*I'm* not the one who will get burned." Then he continued on his way as though nothing had happened.

"Are you okay?" I asked, rushing to Darsey.

"I'm fine," he said coldly. He sheathed his sword and began walking.

I quickly tied my dagger to my belt and looked around for Uri.

"Uri?" I called out when I didn't see him. I heard rustling in the woods as he approached and was relieved when he jumped from the trees.

*"Gavyn told me to run,"* he said.

"I'm glad he did," I admitted, looking around for the Falcone that had disappeared yet again.

I wondered what his purpose really was, but at the moment I was more concerned with how Darsey was feeling. He now knew I didn't have full confidence in him, and I feared he was hurt.

Much to my dismay, I was also concerned that he did try to get me to hand the dagger over. What if Brantley *was* right? I shook my head.

No. Darsey was still Darsey. He had to be.

## Four | A Little Thief

I caught up to him and called his name as I approached. "Darsey," I pleaded.

"Stop," he snapped.

"I'm sorry," I said as I matched his stride.

"Don't be," he growled.

"No, you need to know that I don't doubt you—"

"Well, you should!" he yelled.

I jumped back at the roar in his voice and tried to take in his face, though he turned away as we continued walking. Had he been transfigured and was fighting it? Was he wanting to hurt me and couldn't because of his previous devotion? Nadine said Therese remembered everything about their life together, and only met it with indifference. Maybe he wasn't with them long enough for a transfiguration to really take over.

"Why?" I asked when he didn't go on. "Why would you say that?" I needed to know what was going on inside his head.

"Never mind," he deflected. "Where are we going, anyway?"

I sighed at his change of subject and said, "To get starrunners."

"What is that?" he asked, frustration still on his voice.

"They are celestial steeds. I've seen one before and Brantley knows the way."

"Of course he does," Darsey said flippantly. "Where is he even from? His accent is foreign."

"Forget that," I said. "Forget him. Tell me what you meant. Why would you say I should doubt you?"

After a pause he sighed and grunted. "Because I've done nothing but cause you problems," he whispered, glancing up at Brantley who was a good six paces ahead.

"What are you talking about?" I whispered back. "You've been back with me for less than a day."

He shook his head and said with a trembling voice, "You never told me about how the shaman treated you, because you didn't trust my reaction—"

"That's not fair," I said quickly.

"No, let me finish," he said, waving his hand.

I quieted and he continued.

"Then, when we got on the road, I trusted Garroway and got us taken. Then, on the ship I could do nothing to save you. *You* ended up saving *me*."

"And what a terrible job I did," I pointed out.

He shook his head. "Regardless, you are still the one who ended up coming back and saving me again. I had this ridiculous plan to bide my time and find the perfect opportunity to get us out of there, and then *he* showed up, gave you that weapon, and in a matter of minutes you took down one of the most successful slavers in the region. Maybe the world. And I did nothing to help."

"What could you have done?" I asked, trying to show him it wasn't his fault.

"Exactly!" he agreed. "Nothing! I could do nothing. And now, I see that without me, you *thrived*. You rescued a Dragon Lord, *on your own*, and can now wield dragon's fire. Where do I fit in? The Dragon Lords even chose someone else to accompany you. You may not have known I was alive, but *they* did. And the Dragon Lords chose *him*."

I hated that he was beating himself up for nothing! I hated that my lie was doing this to him. Worse than that, I now knew that I could never tell him the truth. He would never forgive me if he knew I lied and let him feel so much pain. I was too far in and had to keep it hidden.

"It isn't like that," I assured him. "He was just in the right place at the right time."

"*I'm* here now," Darsey said. "Couldn't they change it so *I* am the one who isn't harmed by your fire?"

I shook my head. "I know he is irritating, and frustrating, and cocky, and—"

"And remarkably handsome," Brantley added from up ahead.

We both looked at him and Darsey made a disgusted face while I shook my head and scoffed. "If I'm being honest, the three-day trek it took me to rescue the Fire Dragon Lord should have only taken one. I almost died because I couldn't start a fire in the rain or find shelter. I couldn't find food, and a landslide almost took me with it. Then, I almost burned to death passing the fire. I didn't *thrive* without you. I barely *made* it without you.

And the whole time, all I could think of was how much better things would be if you were with me."

He didn't say anything, and I continued, "I didn't make that grave for you until after the Dragon Lord told me my work wasn't done. I knew if I couldn't have you with me, I wouldn't make it unless I was able to say goodbye. And even then, I would have traded it all to be with you again."

He looked at me and nodded, understanding in his eyes. I smiled and he smiled back, though it was small.

We continued walking and he quietly said, "I still don't like that you talked about me to *him*."

"It won't happen again," I assured him, glaring at Brantley's back.

We walked in silence for the rest of the day, and I just enjoyed the peace that had settled between us. The day was hot, and I often thought of taking Darsey up on his offer to hold the dagger for me, but I didn't want there to be another fight, so I just endured it.

Birds created a melody of chirps in the trees around us that blended with the sounds of critters scurrying about on the ground. And although Uri's scampering seeming abrupt and out of place, I loved watching him jump from bush to bush and run up trees, only to dive from them and land in his tiny form. He didn't have to say anything for me to know he was trying to leap.

Madame stayed quiet as we walked, and I was grateful she wasn't barraging my mind with her unwelcome advice and comments. As the day progressed, we slowly got closer to Brantley, until he was only one pace ahead. I noticed Darsey often glaring at his back or at his feet. I could tell he was imagining how he wished the fight had gone, and though I wanted to turn his thoughts away, I didn't want to disrupt the flow we had going. We were moving well, and I felt that even a tiny interruption might put them at each other's throats. I also had no idea how I would be able to endure an alliance with Brantley if he hurt Darsey.

The day continued, and the heat never let up. As we approached evening, just before bright daylight gave way to an evening glimmer, Darsey lunged at Brantley, catching him off guard and sent him flying forward in a tumble.

"Darsey!" I screamed at his sudden aggression.

Brantley scrambled up and pulled his sword, "Arm yourself, Adalee!" he shouted as both our eyes fell on Darsey's non-aggressive composure.

He was laying on his stomach, staring at a circle of small stones with wildflowers at their center.

"Explain yourself!" Brantley boomed, shaking his hair from his face.

"It's a fairy ring," Darsey said breathlessly.

Brantley scoffed and sheathed his sword. "That's why you attacked me?"

I jumped down beside him and looked more closely. Uri edged in alongside us and sniffed the stones.

"You were about to step in it," Darsey said.

*"I can smell* something*, but I don't know what,"* Uri admitted.

"And so, what if I did?" Brantley asked, obviously annoyed.

"Don't you know anything?" Darsey asked as he looked up at him, matching his annoyance. "Fairy rings mean that they are nearby. My father taught me that when a fairy is lost or on a mission or quest away from its Frollick, they will create the rings just before nightfall, and if you come upon one, you should leave an offering. Something useful for them."

"Like what?" I asked, intrigued by his knowledge.

He smiled at me. "Something sweet, or useful like a piece of cloth or sewing thread."

"Why would we do that?" Brantley asked.

"Because if you know what you should do, and choose not to do it, you will be counted an enemy to the fairy realm," Darsey said seriously as he stood and faced Brantley.

"You want to stop the Dragon Born on *her* quest to indulge in something from a children's tale?"

Darsey clenched his fists and I stood quickly and said, "*I* want to do it. Papa Theo traveled more than anyone in the village. If he says it is true, then, if for nothing else," I looked at Darsey then back at Brantley, "it would help us feel close to him while we're out here on our own."

Brantley sighed again and shrugged. "Fine. Make camp."

As Darsey and I smiled and began to unload our supplies I could hear Brantley mumbling that this is what he gets for traveling with children. I ignored him because for a moment, when Darsey was looking at the fairy ring, he had the same boyish wonder in his face that I knew so well. That I wished for him to return to.

We were settled in with full bellies by the time night was upon us. We had replenished our canteens from a nearby stream and drank our fill. Uri and I were nestled into the base of a tree, though he minded the space between us.

Darsey had placed offerings in the fairy ring and was sitting back, watching for any sign of the magical creatures.

Brantley kept his distance, still irritated that we stopped before he wanted to. I was surprised he didn't make a bigger deal of it. I smiled as I watched Darsey try not to doze as he watched the ring. The light of the fire danced gracefully on his face, lighting up his features and showing the boyish charm I had missed. Seeing him struggle to keep awake for something so innocent took me back to our time in the village together. When, I now realized, things didn't matter as much as I thought they did. And now, just having him back seemed to diminish the severity of Madame's hold on me. Her voice was merely a memory.

I stayed awake until he lost his battle to the day and drifted off. He seemed more relaxed than the night before, which set me at ease. I looked over at Brantley and saw him staring across the fire at Darsey as well. My irritation flared up and I couldn't help the scowl that crossed my face.

Like he felt the glare, he glanced at me, then smiled smugly and doused the fire. I wanted to smack him for sharing what I said with Darsey. I began to fear that he might tell Darsey about the bind. I hoped I was wrong and tried to reason myself out of my concerns. Surely, *he* enjoyed pretending to be *chosen* by the Dragon Lords to accompany me. It would suit him. He disgusted me.

I turned a cold shoulder to him and aimed my gaze back at where I believed Darsey to be. I couldn't make out his silhouette in the night and found him by the hum of his steady breathing.

Uri purred deeply from a low branch above me.

"Not sleeping on his lap again?" I inquired softly.

*"It's too hot,"* he explained. Then, when his purring slowed down and eventually stopped in his slumber, I let myself drift to sleep.

The cold pressed in around me. I knew where I was this time. The Dragon Lord was calling me to her. I was feeling what she felt.

"I'm coming," I tried to assure her, but I had no voice.

The darkness was expelled violently from around us, revealing clear, beautiful blue water.

It went on forever, and though I tried to find her, I realized I was alone and couldn't move.

*No one can come to me.*

*"I'm coming,"* I tried to force my thoughts into hers. There seemed to be no place in the dream for me. It was all about her, just as I experienced with the Red Dragon Lord. I focused in, letting her share her experience with me. Maybe she would share something to help me know where she was.

*The people will die. Don't you care?*

What was she talking about? What people?

*You're stealing their home!*

Who was she arguing with?

*I will not be held by the waters* she decreed boldly.

Then the water around me began to rush and spin. I futilely tried to break out of the powerful current. It continued to wrap around me until it no longer touched me, and I felt myself land on a silty floor. My limbs tightened and froze. I tried to call out to my breath, but it was trapped away from me.

*No one can come to me.*

I awoke to the sound of a crash and feared the water had come down upon me.

I quickly checked my chest and limbs, and found them intact and dry, save the sweat that constantly beaded and dripped from my skin.

She was trapped in water, I marveled to myself. Why then, when I meditated, did she lead me to the desert?

"Wake up!" Brantley shouted from across the dark.

I shouted back, "What's wrong?"

I heard Darsey shuffle and draw his sword.

A moment later there was a spark and a small fire started beside Brantley. He was gripping the arm of a young, scantily clad, girl.

"Here she is," Brantley mocked Darsey. "Your *fairy*. Take a good look! She was sneaking in to steal supplies."

I jumped up and rushed to them, being careful not to get too close as I could feel the power of the blade pulsing through me with the sudden alertness.

"Let her go," I said to Brantley as he laughed and bound her hands behind her back before he shoved her down. "Don't take pity on thieves," he warned.

"You're a savage," Darsey growled as he ran up and took off his cloak, wrapping it around her. "Are you okay? From whom did you escape? We won't make you go back we just want to know how to help you."

"You can help me by untying me, giving me food, and letting me go," she said in an even younger sounding voice than her face portrayed.

I realized Darsey thought she was an escaped slave, but Brantley looked at her with a furrowed brow after hearing her speak.

"How old are you?" he asked, with a calmer tone.

"Older than *you*," she shot back with a mischievous grin.

I marveled at the fact that she showed no fear. Her face was dirty and wore a sheen of sweat, though her skin looked cold and carried a purple undertone to it. She had very little hair atop her head, and it looked cropped and spiky, and also carried a strong purple tone to it.

"Darsey," I said softly, as my healing tendencies kicked in, "touch her skin and tell me what you feel."

66

He held out his hand to her gently and waited for her to give him a little nod before he laid the back of his hand on her cheek.

"She feels normal," he said as he pulled his hand back and looked at me. "Sweaty," he added.

"What's your name?" I asked her sweetly.

"What's yours?" she countered.

"I'm Adalee. This is Darsey, and *that* is Brantley."

"And the tippoo?" she asked, looking past me to Uri, who was facing us from the base of the tree.

Darsey and I looked at each other, curious that she knew what he was so easily. "His name is Uri," I said, looking back at her.

She cocked her head said, "Alright, I'll let you live. Since he's so cute and all."

Brantley laughed and said, "You are the one at our mercy, child. Not the other way around."

"Are you sure about that?" she said with a snicker as she darted up and disappeared into the dark, leaving Darsey's cloak behind. In place of her binds were flowers.

"Goldenrods!" Darsey said excitedly as he picked them up. "Maybe she is of the Asteraceae kingdom."

Brantley scoffed and rubbed his face. "She's not a fairy," he said as though he were exhausted. "She is just a little thief."

"No," Darsey said firmly as he stood, still showing excitement. "Didn't you see her skin and hair? They were unnatural. Not like a human."

He shrugged and said, "Regardless of that, why would you assume she was a *fairy*?"

"The ring!" he said, pointing to it.

"A trick!" Brantley said as though he was revealing some great mystery. "If you think she is something other than human, why not an imp? *That* would be more believable."

"Now that is just rude," the girl's young voice sounded from behind us. We all spun just as she ducked out of sight. Brantley hurried past everyone and looked behind the tree she disappeared by just as her voice rang out from the other side of the fire.

"Imps are mischievous and mean-spirited," she said, but was gone by the time we spun back.

"Seems about right to me!" Brantley shouted, humor edging on irritation.

From above in the trees we heard her say, "I'm just playful. You should learn the difference."

"We know you're not a fairy!" Brantley shouted into the trees. "Come down so we can talk."

"No! We don't know that! I believe you!" Darsey called after.

I grabbed Brantley's arm so he would look at me. "She already doesn't like you," I pointed out. "Maybe let Darsey handle this?"

He shook me off and said, "I got you to come to me easily enough. And *you're* the Dragon Born. I think I can handle this child."

"I *knew* she looked different!" the young girl called down from above.

"Yes," Darsey called up. "She is the Dragon Born. So, can you see that we are accepting of magical creatures? Please come down and join us."

Brantley shook his head and looked at me, with humor in his eyes. He motioned to me and mouthed 'creature' with a small laugh.

I cut my eyes at him and looked back at Darsey.

"If what you say is true," Brantley whispered, "which I still doubt, how can we trust her?"

She hopped down and landed in the middle of the camp and said, "Now you're just being mean," in a light-hearted tone, hinting on laughter.

"How so?" he asked, moving to take a step closer, only to pause when Darsey stilled him with a motion from behind the girl.

She crossed her arms and said, "I said I would let you live. I wouldn't have said it if I didn't mean it. I have honor, unlike *imps* which you so rudely compared me to."

"Please," Darsey pleaded and she turned to face him. "Please, grace us with your presence and let us give you whatever you need."

"Well," she said smugly, glancing back at Brantley briefly, "at least someone here is a gentleman."

"If you want to stay, you must prove to us that you are a fairy," Brantley challenged.

Darsey shook his head and said, "You needn't prove anything. My father taught me about the signs of a fairy, and I believe you."

"No, it's okay," she said as she faced Brantley. "It's proof you need?" she asked with a twinkle in her eye.

"Aye, it is," he said with a nod.

"Draw your blade from your boot and throw it at me," she said calmly.

Darsey quickly sidestepped so he wasn't directly behind her and made his way to me.

*"He shouldn't do that,"* Uri said. *"There are two others with her. I can see them."*

"Uri says she isn't alone," I whispered, looking around.

"Yes," she agreed. "Those are my sisters he sees."

Brantley eyed her and asked, "Why would I do that? I never said I wanted to *hurt* you."

"You won't," she laughed.

I noticed him glance at us before he straightened up and asked, "And what will happen if I do?"

She laughed again and said, "You *won't*."

He shook his head. "You may be a fairy, you may not. Either way, I'm not throwing my knife at an unarmed child."

"I told you, I'm older than you."

"You look about ten," I offered.

She smiled and said, "I'm one hundred and twelve, thank you very much."

Brantley shook his head again and said, "I'm not throwing my blade at a child."

"Okay," she said, seeming offended. Then she looked at Darsey and said, "You do it."

"You want *me* to?" he asked, taken aback.

"Well, someone needs to," she said.

"What if we just say we believe you now?" I offered, growing nervous about her persistence.

She shook her head and said, "*He* doesn't. Besides, now I *want* to show you."

Darsey slowly nodded and held out his hand for Brantley's blade. Brantley sized him up, then reached down and pulled the knife from his boot, handing it over, hilt first.

"You're about to see what kind of man he really is," Brantley whispered to me so low I barely heard him.

Despite Darsey's nervous look, he took a more balanced stance, held the knife by the tip of the blade, and threw it towards her with a great, sharp motion.

I jumped when the knife released from his hand, and all our jaws dropped when it split in two just before it reached her, falling in twin piles of pink flowers on either side.

She smugly looked from side to side, then picked up three of the flowers. She skipped up to Darsey and held one out.

"Dahlia?" she asked sweetly.

His eyes were wide with shock and excitement as he took it from her hand.

Then she skipped to me and held one out. "Dahlia?" she repeated in the same tone.

I took it, a smile on my face. She really was a fairy.

She skipped to Brantley and held out the flower. "Dahlia?" she asked.

He took it, no humor on his face. "Where is my blade?" he asked.

She looked surprised then tapped his hand. "You're holding it. Well . . . part of it."

He looked down at the flower and furrowed his brow. "Can you change it back?" he asked, obviously annoyed, though I couldn't tell if his irritation stemmed from being wrong about her, or having his knife turned into a pile of flowers.

"Fairy magic doesn't work that way," she said with a look that playfully suggested he should have already known that.

She skipped toward the trunk of one of the trees and Darsey faced Brantley and held up the bloom. He mouthed, "It doesn't work that way," with a smile on his face.

Brantley rolled his eyes and tossed the flower down while I tried to stifle a giggle. *This* was the Darsey I knew.

The girl spun around and hopped up on one of the massive, exposed roots of the tree. "Now that I have your attention," she said in her sweet voice, "I am in need of clothing, shelter, and food."

Darsey quickly retrieved his cloak from the ground where she left it and handed it to her. "Will this do for now?" he asked.

She smiled and wrapped it around herself. "For now," she agreed.

"You can share our food and shelter," I offered as I dug into one of the bags and handed her some bread and cheese.

"I thought fairies didn't need to eat?" Darsey asked, genuinely curious.

She took a ravenous bite of the bread and pointed to my canteen, which I grabbed and handed to her. Before she had swallowed the bread, she took a long drink.

"Not usually," she said with a full mouth. "But, as you can see," she paused to swallow, then took a bite of cheese, "I'm not exactly in fairy form."

I looked down at Uri and whispered, "What do you see?"

*"There is a pink one and a yellow one. They are very fast."*

"One what?" I asked.

"I told you," the girl interrupted. "Those are my sisters. He's seeing fairies."

"And we can't see them because they don't want to be seen," Darsey filled in, with a smile.

She nodded at him, her cheeks full of food.

"What do you mean, you're not in fairy form?" Brantley asked as he knelt down and fed the fire.

She didn't answer his question until she finished gorging on the food and drinking all the water in the canteen. When she was done, she burped and shook her head. "I hate this body," she mumbled, then laughed as she looked around at each of us. "Humans are *disgusting*."

"Then why are you in 'human form'?" Brantley challenged.

"She doesn't have a choice," Darsey said as though he had just discovered the greatest revelation of the trek.

She smiled at him and said, "I like you. You're clever."

He looked down and smiled. I noticed a blush in his cheeks and was thrilled to see him looking so happy.

"It seems to me you have a story to tell," Brantley said, motioning for her to sit by the fire.

"We all do," she said as she looked at each of us, as though she were sizing us up. "I think I will require *your* story," she settled on Darsey.

"Me?" he asked, seeming shocked.

"Mm," she confirmed with a nod.

"Why should we help you if we don't know from whence you came or where you're going?" Brantley challenged.

"Brantley," I scolded.

"She could be our enemy," he whispered.

"Still don't believe me?" she asked, eyeing him. "Shall I turn your sword into goldenrod?" she suggested with a giggle.

He protectively grabbed the hilt of his blade and said, "No, that's okay. I believe you can do *that*."

"You just don't trust me?" she asked curiously.

"Why should I?" he asked. "I caught you trying to steal from us."

"No," she defended. "You caught me going *through* your things. You didn't see me steal *anything*."

"What were you looking for?" he asked.

"That's *my* business," she said as she leaned back and pulled her knees up to her chest, balancing perfectly on the root she was perched on.

"You said you needed shelter," I reminded her. "We can share what we have—"

"We have none to share," Brantley interrupted.

She shrugged lightly and said, "I don't mind!" Then she hopped down and skipped over to me, grabbing my arm and leaning on me as though we were close friends. "We don't mind sharing, right Dragon Lady?" she asked, as she looked up at me.

"Wait . . ." Brantley said as he stood. "Are you planning on staying *with* us?"

She looked surprised at his question. "Of course," she said as though he should have already known that.

"Really?" Darsey asked excitedly.

Her arm around me was very strong and I became more aware of the pulsing by my side, so I pulled away from her. She looked surprised and I said, "It isn't you. I just . . . um . . ."

"She doesn't want to turn you to ash," Brantley finished smugly. "You see, you say you aren't going to hurt *us*, but you are in presence of the Dragon Born. The Child of Essence. Her Dragon Fire can destroy you quicker than you could turn her to flowers."

She looked me up and down and said, "I knew I felt something. I had no idea it was *dragon's* fire. Be careful with that," she warned me. "Some magic is too powerful for humans to wield."

I nodded and crossed my arms. "I'm learning," I admitted. "I'm getting better."

"Why are you staying with us?" Darsey asked, moving on from talking about the dagger.

"I want a star-runner," she said matter-of-factly. "*He*," she added as she motioned to Brantley, "knows where to get one."

Brantley nodded and said, "You're a thief and a spy."

"I already told you I'm not a thief," she countered.

Darsey came to her defense and said, "Stop insulting her."

"She's been following us!" he shouted. "I just can't believe I didn't notice."

"I'm a fairy," she reminded him. "I may be in a human form, but that doesn't mean I lose everything. If I don't want to be seen, I'm not."

"One condition," Brantley said as he stood. "There is one condition to you staying with us."

"If a fairy offers to travel with you, you don't place conditions on her," Darsey argued.

"She's not offering to travel *with* us," Brantley countered. "She needs something from us. So yes, I will make a condition."

I noticed their faces growing tense, and I said, "Maybe we should calm down."

"No, it's okay," the girl said to Darsey. "I don't mind, so long as I get my star-runner."

Darsey crossed his arms and shook his head.

"Great," Brantley said with a smile. "The condition is that your party can be seen at all times. I don't want fairies flitting about the camp, out of sight, doing whatever they wish. If you can see us, we can see you. All of you."

She cocked her head and thought for a moment. "Let me ask them," she said before she raced up the side of one of the large trees and disappeared into the darkness above.

*"I don't know how I feel,"* Uri said.

"Why is that?" I asked.

*"They smell different. Weird. And they are so fast."*

"Then if they agree, that will be good. We will all be able to see what you see," I comforted him.

He nodded and said, *"Okay. That sounds okay."*

She hopped back down in the middle of camp and said, "They agreed."

Then a small pink sparkle flashed beside her, and when the sparkling ebbed, a tiny figure was flittering in the air. We all drew closer, and I was amazed to see a small woman, with pink tones to her skin and long pink hair that cascaded from her head down to her toes. Only her face and arms were seen, with her wings working fiercely and yet easily to keep her afloat.

Next to her a similar sparkle erupted, and when it calmed, she looked exactly the same, only yellow.

"This is Mathilda of the Dahlia region. This is Doria of the Goldenrod region. And I am Plume of the Thistle region."

"Is that why your hair is short and spiky?" Brantley asked.

"No," she said flatly. "My hair is short because the imps are trying to kill me."

# FIVE | Mean Magic

"What?" Brantley asked, drawing his sword and looking around. "What trouble did you bring on us?"

"It's only trouble if the pimeys find me," she said nonchalantly. "I've evaded them well enough."

"What are pimeys?" Darsey asked, fully intrigued with no sense of fear.

"Death for those not of the fairy form," she said as she looked at her sisters.

"What do they look like?" I asked, pulling my hood up and making sure no part of me was exposed. The way she had said the word sent my dagger reeling and it was resonating powerfully through me.

"If I'm going to talk about the pimeys, I would like for you to grow the fire," she said to Brantley.

He let his sword rest and eyed her. "You act like a child telling a night story. Will the fire protect you?" he added with some mocking condescension.

"Yes," she met his tone with equal sass.

Darsey grabbed some dry underbrush and quickly tossed it into the fire. It burst forth with new life, but quickly died back down to its former self.

"What about you?" Plume asked me. "Can you do something with your Dragon's Fire?"

I shook my head and said, "It doesn't work like that. It burns too hot and turns things to ash right away."

She sighed and rolled her eyes. "Humans and magic," she muttered.

Darsey tore some dried limbs from the nearby trees and broke them into smaller pieces before he returned and used them to make the fire blaze brighter.

"How's that?" he asked, eager to make her happy so he could learn more about what she had to share.

She smiled at him and said, "Better. Thank you." As she walked past him to the blaze, I heard her whisper, "I like you more than the others."

He smiled, and his eyes instantly met mine. It didn't surprise me. Everyone liked Darsey the most. It was one of the things that made him Darsey.

I moved toward the fire when Uri's frightened cry rang in my head.

He was spinning around, and the fairies were grabbing his fur and making him jump and shake.

"Hey, stop that!" I yelled at them.

They quickly flitted back to Plume and she was staring at me, her brow furrowed. "They were only playing. Tippoos are fun to mess with. When you get them worked up, they leap," she said with a giggle.

*"I don't like it,"* he whined.

"Leave him alone," I warned.

She shrugged and turned away, sitting by the fire. I sat on the other side and Uri got as close to me as he dared. Darsey sat between Plume and I, and Brantley sat across from him.

"What are pimeys?" Darsey eagerly asked again.

"They are darkness," she said, looking around at the shadows dancing on the trees in the firelight.

I found myself glancing around as well, and Uri's fur was on end.

"You're afraid of the dark?" Brantley asked lightly.

"Not the dark," she corrected. "The darkness. Pimeys. They are different than the dark. They are void of all light and if they capture you, they pull the light from you."

"What does that even mean?" Brantley asked.

"Fairies are not flowers," she said simply. "Though we do share many of their characteristics. Like, we need sunlight to thrive. Put us in darkness for too long and we become immobile. It's the worst fate for a fairy. We don't die, but we can't move. Frozen in time, yet aware of all that goes on around us."

"So, they aren't trying to kill you," Brantley pointed out. "They're trying to paralyze you."

"I'm a human now," she reminded him. "If they pull me in like this, then I *will* die."

"How will we know if they are upon us?" Brantley asked, becoming more serious.

She relaxed slightly and said, "I'll tell you."

"And if they pull one of us in?" he asked.

I looked at her face and could see Darsey staring at her intently.

She looked around at each of us and hesitated. "If they pull you in . . ." she said slowly, "then you will die."

"Great," Brantley mumbled, as he sat back.

"How do we stay safe?" Darsey asked, leaning in closer. "There has to be a way. There is always a way with magical creatures. What are the pimeys' weakness?"

She smiled at him and said, "I'm glad you asked. Unlike *some* of you who lack total confidence in me," she eyed Brantley.

"Why would I have any confidence in you?" Brantley asked. "My confidence is in myself. My loyalty is to myself."

I shot him a glare, silently reminding him of the belief that the Dragon Lords chose him to accompany me.

"And her," he added flippantly, motioning to me.

I shook my head and rolled my eyes with a huff. Way to make it believable, I thought. Yet, Darsey was still solely focused on Plume.

"The pimeys can't enter light. Firelight, sunlight, even moonlight keep them at bay."

"Then why are you in the forest at night?" Brantley challenged.

"I didn't have a choice," she said as though she thought he was stupid.

He thought for a moment then his eyes opened wide. "The new moon," he said softly.

She nodded and added, "There is nowhere safe for me right now. I don't know how to make fire . . . or clothes, or shoes, or how to find food. All I keep finding is Brownie fruit, and I'm not foolish enough to touch that."

"You came into the forest hoping to find food," Darsey said.

"And water," I whispered.

"And people," Brantley finished firmly. "People to keep *you* safe."

Darsey glared at him and stated boldly, "I think she's worth protecting."

She looked at him, appreciation in her eyes. Her sisters settled on each shoulder and caressed her face.

"At the risk of Adalee's life?" Brantley challenged.

His blatant use of me as a reason to turn someone away from our company was frustrating. "My life is not in danger," I argued. "I have Dragon's Fire. You are only worried about yourself," I accused.

He jumped up and said, "I didn't make it this far by helping every hapless wanderer I came across. We don't have time for this."

Plume jumped up and her sisters flitted off her shoulders and hovered near her. "Don't have time for what?" she asked. "All I'm asking is for you to let me stay with you until you reach the star-runners. Once I have one, I'll be *gone*."

"If you want to stay, you tell us *why* they are after you," Brantley warned.

"Fine," she acquiesced. "But once I do, I don't want to hear another word from you," she said firmly. She eyed Darsey and smiled brightly, almost changing the whole mood of the conversation. "Now from *you*, I want to know *everything*."

He leaned back, seeming surprised and looked at me. "Why me?" he asked.

"Like I said before, you look like you have a story to tell, and I greatly wish to hear it."

Darsey looked somewhat relieved and nodded bashfully.

"Great!" she said as she lightly plopped back down in her seat. "Then I will share mine. I am of the fairy people, as you already know. Our kingdom is the largest in Pylertchia. We are the Asteraceae."

"I knew it," Darsey whispered.

She smiled at him and continued. "While there are many kingdoms of fairy blooms, ours is the most powerful. As such, when dark times present themselves, the other kingdoms come to us for protection and guidance. My mother . . ." she paused and looked at her fairy sisters, then amended, "*our* mother, was the queen of the Asteraceae. We didn't know the imps were moving through the meadows, taking down the lords and ladies of every province. Before we realized what had happened, the three of us were the only leaders left in the Asteraceae. We went to the queen to tell her of what was happening and just as we arrived, an imp-witch cut off her hair, leaving her to die on the steps of her throne.

"We rushed to her, using all the magic we had to ward off the witch, but she wasn't alone. We were set upon quickly by her army of imps. I was the first one they captured, and just before they sliced through my long, purple hair, my queen mother expelled her last bit of energy, and covered me in a powerful magic that would keep me alive."

"It turned you human," Darsey said breathlessly.

She nodded solemnly and continued, "They cut my hair just after the magic settled in, then I grew. I became this clunky, clumsy, weak bodied human." She looked around at us and continued, "I suppose it isn't all terrible. My growth initially frightened the imps and they scattered. I scooped up my mother just in time to find her pearl resting on her chest. Mathilda and Doria are now the keepers of her pearl, as it is too delicate for human hands to touch."

"Do fairy pearls work the same as human pearls?" I asked, surprised that other creatures had them.

She nodded and said, "They can be gazed into once, then they perish. It is very difficult for a fairy to resist the call of a pearl," she admitted. "With the lives of every fairy in Pylertchia depending on it, we know we must succeed."

"We're not helping her on her quest," Brantley said to me in a low voice.

I looked at him, surprised and annoyed that he knew where my mind had been.

"I don't need help on my quest," she shot at him.

"What is your quest?" Darsey asked. "Why are you resisting the pearl?"

"We must hasten it to the council of blooms. They must see for themselves what the imps are doing. Without proof, they will do nothing."

"And the pimeys? Where do they come in?"

"They are in league with the imps, though I don't know their purposes. All I know is that if I am taken by one, I will die. If my sisters are taken, they will be hastened back to the imp witch and she will cut their hair and take their pearls, along with our mother's."

"What can we do to help?" Darsey asked.

"Nothing," Brantley scolded, jumping up.

Then he gasped and gripped his chest. He stumbled sideways and fell to the ground with a dull thud.

Darsey jumped up and asked, "What's happening?"

I immediately recognized it as the mysterious wound he refused to tell me about. Before I could say anything, Plume was squatting beside him. She tore open his tunic and sucked in a surprised breath.

"Wow," she whispered. Then her tone turned light and playful and she said, "That is *mean* magic. Who did you cross?"

"Get away," he tried to grunt, but she swatted his hand back like a gnat.

"Okay," she said with a smile. "I'll help you," she added as though he had begged for her assistance.

Suddenly, the two fairy sisters flew to him and settled upon the fierce, pulsing scar. A great light emerged from them and I shielded my eyes.

When it ebbed, Brantley's breathing returned to normal and he slowly sat up, rubbing where the scar had been. He looked down, then back at Plume.

"It's . . . gone," he said, bewildered.

"No," she said, holding up a finger. "Not gone. There's only one way to heal a wound like that, and I think you know what it is."

"Aye," he said darkly. "So, what *did* you do?"

"It's hidden," she said lightly. "Suppressed. And so long as you help me, it will stay that way."

"How?" he asked.

"All you need to know, is that my sister's will have no more 'light' magic until the sun rises. So . . . you owe me."

He sighed and leaned forward. "What do you want, fairy?"

"Just get me to the star-runners," she said with a smile.

"We are weeks away from the star-runners," Brantley informed her.

She shrugged and said, "Then I guess you'll be pain-free for weeks. Now, if you want to live, I suggest we keep the fire burning all night."

"I'll take first watch," Darsey offered, smiling at Plume.

"I was hoping you would," she smiled back. "I want to hear what you have to say."

"I might have a few questions of my own," he said, breathlessly.

Brantley breathed deep and laid on his back. "Okay," he said softly. "Wake me in a few hours, and I'll take the next."

I eyed Brantley, wondering what Plume meant by calling his scar 'mean magic'. What was he hiding?

*"I can help you keep watch,"* Uri offered excitedly.

I smiled down at him and asked, "When do you want us to watch?"

"You don't watch," Brantley said firmly. "You sleep. You need to stay in control."

I couldn't deny his reasoning, but his delivery was infuriating. I decided it best to just lay down with my back to the fire. Uri laid near my head, accepting the command. The firelight glowed gently against his fur.

*"Do you think the pimeys are going to get us?"* he asked nervously.

"I won't let anything get you," I promised him.

I heard Darsey's whispers as he began telling Plume of his parents and our life in the village before everything had happened. I wanted to stay awake and hear the telling for myself. He had a way of making stories come to life and I wanted so badly to feel like I was back in those carefree days again. However, the heaviness of my eyelids won, and I drifted to sleep with the soft caress of his voice mingling with the crackling of the fire in my ears.

The fairies settled in quickly. We were able to fashion clothing and shoes for Plume, though she spent much of her time pulling at them and complaining of discomfort in the heat.

Darsey was very protective of her and they spent much of their time together. At first, I didn't mind because their exchanges were friendly and curious. However, her presence had driven a wedge between Darsey and I, simply by the fact that she left no time for me to spend with him.

Madame's voice constantly tried to draw my attention to his dismissive behavior towards me. And it was true. No matter how often I tried to speak to him, or pull his attention back to me, he stayed focused on her. I was as unimportant as crickets in the night.

Nonetheless, I fought against Madame. Nothing good ever came from her evil words. I was forced to focus on the positives of Plume's presence, though my jealously increased daily.

One of the good things I clung to, was that Darsey was getting back to his old self. Whether it was by magic, or simply having someone he felt he could talk to, he was getting better.

So, after a few days, I let them be, and turned to suppressing Madame.

I wished I could say that my ability to let him focus on himself and find comfort in the presence of another was because I was confident in his love for me and knew we would be together forever, no matter what. Alas, it was more because those dastardly little fairies wouldn't stop tormenting my precious Uri, and I found most of my time was spent shooing them away or focusing on harnessing the power of the blade so he could seek refuge in the safety of my hood.

Much of Brantley's time was focused on keeping an eye out for dangers, and fashioning a new blade for his boot, since his was turned to flowers. However, his irritation at the fairies ebbed, and pretty soon he was back to being his annoying, carefree self.

With Darsey distracted, I had found myself more willing to speak with Brantley as we trekked each day. However, every moment spent in his presence only fueled my distaste for him.

He was sarcastic, smug, arrogant, and controlling. Every question I asked about the star-runners, he met with cocky condescension. Every time I suggested somewhere to stop or something to eat, he would tell me to leave the decision-making up to him.

Madame loved using those moments to slip in and try to convince me to regain control of the quest, always trying to poison my mind against his leadership.

He *did* know the way to the star-runners, however, and he was skilled in survival. Although I wanted to take him down a few notches, I still needed him.

So, I found it best for Uri and I to maintain our distance from everyone, and just try to make it to the star-runners without incident.

Then, Plume and the fairies would be gone, Darsey's attention would be back on me, and I would take the reins of the quest from Brantley.

One night, roughly a fortnight from when they joined us, the full moon was rising and we were settled into camp in a very bright part of the forest that butted up next to a looming rock-wall with a wide-mouthed cave.

The moon was shining through the scattered trees, and the ground was a mixture of compacted dirt and rock. Though heat still hung firmly in the air, a small breeze occasionally found its way through the camp, which was an unexpected relief.

I was trying to find a comfortable place to lay for the night, as the trees were tall and slim, and didn't offer the same root systems as they did in denser parts of the forest, and the cave would be too dangerous to enter at night. Darsey was already laid back on Plume's lap, as they often did, and she was playing with his hair as he spoke softly to her. While I was trying to settle in, I couldn't help the jealousy creep up that there was such intimacy between the two of them.

I wasn't worried about his affections, as she only looked like a child, and fairies and humans were not even the same species. My jealousy was rooted in the fact that he spoke so freely and openly with a level of comfort that even surpassed what we had. I had *never* played with his hair while he rested his head in my lap and spoke to me of his desires for the world. It was always him, offering me comfort. I found myself lamenting all the times I could have shown him that kind of affection, and now those opportunities were gone.

My focus was suddenly drawn away by Mathilda and Doria tugging at Uri's ears.

*"Ow!"* he complained, and I spun around and hissed, swatting at them, so they scattered and rushed back to Plume.

*"Why are they so mean?"* Uri complained.

"I don't know," I admitted. "But if they don't stop," I shot a glare at Plume and the other fairies, "the blooms will be missing two more leaders."

She met my eyes briefly, before returning her attention to Darsey. He didn't notice and continued talking.

Although I had done well rejecting Madame's whispers about doing away with Plume, I had to admit that the thought seemed less heinous by the day.

I huffed and laid down, rolling over. Brantley was already sleeping on the other side of the fire. He was growing exhausted from staying up half the night to watch for the pimeys. I could see it in his face, though he hid it well behind his humor.

Darsey was full of an unnatural energy, despite getting the same amount of rest as Brantley.

As I stared, Brantley's shirt fell open and I saw where his scar used to be. I still wanted to know about it, but he was close-mouthed every time he noticed me looking or when I tried to bring it up.

I guess it didn't really matter. He would be gone after the next Dragon Lord, and his issues would be his own. I glanced over at Plume and Darsey again, and Madame made her way into my thoughts.

*She sure does enjoy his company* she said, nonchalantly. *Suppose she enjoys it so much she decides not to leave?*

The suggestion took me aback and I tried to shake it away. "She has her own quest," I whispered. "She's only here until she gets a star-runner."

I had found it easier to be bold against Madame when I spoke out loud, though I was always careful to keep it discreet. No one knew about my battle with her. Not even Uri.

*You're right,* she said as though I made a good point.

I smiled.

Then she added, *I suppose she'll just take him with her, then.*

I was horrified at the thought, and immediately recoiled against it. He couldn't go. I wouldn't let him. I glanced at them again and thought about breaking them up. Telling her to back off. Asking him where his allegiance lied. If he wanted me or *her*.

*"Ouch!"* Uri whined.

I whipped around and saw him swat at the little fairies as they pulled his tail.

"Stop!" I snapped, swinging at them to break them up.

They flitted back to Plume and I jumped up and faced them. "Keep them away from Uri," I demanded, yet again.

Darsey sat up and looked at me, bewildered. "Are they still bothering him?" he asked.

"Yes," I said, exasperated.

"Why don't you let him sleep under your hood?" Plume asked, shooting me a mischievous smile.

I glared at her. I was not enjoying the company of these fairies. "You know I can't," I snapped.

"Okay, it's okay," Darsey said, trying to calm the situation. "Why doesn't Uri sleep with me?" he offered. "I promise I won't let them bother him."

Plume looked annoyed, so I quickly nodded and asked Uri if he wanted to.

He was already bounding to Darsey and climbing up his cloaked arm. He quickly settled in and Darsey turned to the fire, not laying back on Plume's lap.

Somewhat satisfied with the outcome, I laid down and rolled away with my back to the fire and closed my eyes. Once she was gone, Darsey and I could start rebuilding our relationship.

The water rushed around me. Same as before. Same as every night. It was powerful and encompassing. Yet, it wasn't designed to trap me. It was designed to keep others out.

*No one can get to me.*

She needs me.

"Wake up!"

My eyes shot open to the sounds of blades clanging together. They were fighting again!

I jumped up and spun, but it wasn't Darsey that Brantley swung his blade toward. "Watch out!" Brantley shouted at me.

More blades clanged beside me and I turned to see Darsey blocking the blow of another bandit.

"Knock them into the cave!" Plume screamed in a terrified voice. "The pimeys have come!"

I faced the darkness, more terrified of what was in the cave than in our camp.

The man Brantley was fighting stumbled back, too close to the shadows of the cave, and was sucked in, flying off his feet, his scream quickly stifled.

Brantley and I both froze, our eyes wide and jaws dropped.

Plume jumped in and helped Darsey shove the man he was fighting into the shadow and drawing too near she was quickly sucked in as well. Her scream resonated across the stone walls.

"Plume!" he cried, preparing to dart into the darkness after her.

"No!" I shouted, running past him. He was foolish enough to go. He was foolish enough to die. He had no protection. I had Dragon's Fire.

I darted into the shadows.

*"Adalee, come back!"* Uri cried, but I couldn't stop. I couldn't let Darsey sacrifice himself for her. I couldn't lose him.

The sounds of the camp and their shouting disappeared behind me, and even Uri's voice faded.

I heard Plume's scream and found her gripping the side of a stone, head and arms still in the light of the moon; the pimeys slowly pulling her in.

She wasn't exaggerating when she described them as the darkness. It was so dark it hurt my eyes to look at, and nothing existed inside it. Her legs were hidden from inside the pimeys and I quickly wrapped my arms around the rock she was gripping and grabbed her shoulders.

"I've got you!" I grunted.

"Don't let it take me!" she screamed, sounding more like a petrified child than a lady of the bloom.

"I won't!" I promised, as I pulled her harder. The blade was firing at my side, and the stone began to weaken beneath my feet.

"No," I said defeatedly.

The blade was too powerful. I was burning through the rock!

Plume reached out with a pained grimace on her face and grabbed a hold of my cloak. I braced myself, and she screamed, "Pull me out!"

With a great effort, I pushed myself off the rock and her feet slowly came back into view. Then, as though a powerful strap broke, she came flying to me and we scattered on the ground beside one another.

"Adalee!" Darsey's scream echoed from nearby.

"Get out of here!" I yelled at him.

"Run!" Brantley ordered.

Plume jumped up and pulled me to my feet with surprising strength. "It won't stop!" she cried.

"Darsey, run!" I screamed past her toward his petrified face.

"Use your power," she begged, then she shoved me violently toward the pimeys.

In an instant, I went from hearing the frightened and shocked cries of my group, to a deafening silence. The silhouettes of the rocks disappeared and only darkness surrounded me. The cold was unbearable, and the air offered no respite for my lungs.

Immediately I felt myself crumble, though there was nothing for me to land on or touch. Only an unencumbered void mixed with the discomfort my body was feeling as the life was being sucked out of it.

Worse than when I was beneath the sea with Darsey, my lungs cried out for air. I gripped and grasped at myself. The cold was freezing my limbs. The emptiness around me sent terror reeling through me. I spun out of control, trying to fight off the invisible enemy that was taking hold of my senses. I had no choice but to see and hear nothing, as the cold deepened its grip on me. It seeped past my cloak and tunic. It relentlessly bore into my skin. Like a fall there was no escape from. I was falling into death, and nothing I did was going to change it.

Suddenly, a spark of warmth shot through me. It rolled throughout my body, and ended at my fingertips, then rolled back. Then it rolled larger and faster. The blade was fighting. I could feel it forcing its energy through me.

I curled up, trying to help it move faster. I wasn't alone. The dragons were with me!

The rolling became a steady rumble as it shot through me so quickly, I could find no beginning or end. Then it began to spill forth, amplifying itself into the emptiness around me. I braced myself for what was to come, letting my fear and anger at Plume's betrayal fuel the fire.

I opened my eyes and no longer saw black. Now I saw red. And I knew the time had come. The blade exploded beside me, reacting to the desperation I felt, and I could see fire shooting out around me. The pimeys disappeared immediately, dropping me roughly on the cold stone.

I sucked in a much-needed breath and looked up just as Darsey came running to me, torch in hand.

Brantley grabbed a hold of his collar and shoved him aside. "Don't touch her!" he yelled.

I rolled to my hands and knees and could see the red still emanating on the edges of my sight. The ground around me was becoming dusty, and a swirl of ash began to circle its way out, turning everything it touched.

"Brantley," I cried desperately when I realized I wasn't going to be able to reel the blade back in.

Suddenly the red was gone. The ring stopped spreading. The tremble of the blade coursing through me gave way to the trembling of my limbs. I sucked in a relieved breath and let go of my weakened arms and legs. I fell to the ground in the ash but was quickly lifted by Darsey's warm touch.

He laid my head on his lap and I stared up at him through exhausted eyes.

"You *killed* it," Plume said excitedly.

"You shoved her in," Darsey snapped at her.

"She's fine," Plume said dismissively.

I heard Brantley draw his blade and say, "The same can't be said about you."

"Kill her," Darsey growled.

Then my eyes drifted shut, and I let the darkness of sleep take me.

Six | The Dangers of the Honeycomb

When my eyes opened again, they were met with daylight beaming through scattered treetops.

I was exhausted. I felt so heavy it took effort to suck in enough air to make my chest rise.

"Are you okay?" Darsey asked me tenderly. I heard him rush over before his face entered my vision.

"I think so," I whispered.

"She's awake!" he called over his shoulder.

I heard Brantley respond, "Good, get her up. We need to move."

"Give her a minute!" Darsey snapped.

"We can't waste the day," Brantley warned. "When night falls, the pimeys will come and next time the fairy might sacrifice one of *us* instead."

"It wasn't a sacrifice," Plume argued lightly. "I was testing a theory, and I was right."

Frustration spread through me. Why was she still with us? I thought they would have killed her, or at least sent her away for what she did.

"Just relax," Darsey whispered when I tried to sit up. "I'll handle this." Then he was gone from my side.

Uri ran up to me and bumped his head against mine. *"That was scary, but I'm feeling better now."*

"What happened?" I asked him.

*"I don't know. She pushed you into the cave, and then I went to sleep. I woke up a little bit ago."*

"You went to sleep?" I asked.

He nodded and rubbed his head against mine again.

I sat up and steadied myself. Other than feeling weak, I was okay.

Plume jumped down next to me and smiled. "That was pretty impressive, what you did. You *killed* one. I don't know if that has ever been done!"

Her voice annoyed me beyond comprehension, and I looked at her. "Why are you still here?"

Darsey came running over and snapped, "I told you to stay away from her! Don't get near her again!"

She jumped back and held her hands up in unconcerned defense. "I just thought she should know how amazing that was," she said dismissively as she skipped away.

"If you don't want to get moving just yet, we can wait. I don't care if I have to take all the pimeys on at the same time. You just let me know."

Brantley forced a chuckle that turned into a growl as he neared us. "We need to either get away from the mouth of this cave or get through it. I don't want the pimeys to take any of us, but if you are going to insist on being a fool, I won't be able to protect *anyone*."

"We don't have to be afraid of the cave anymore," Plume called from a small distance.

"Why would we trust you?" Darsey argued.

"*He* does . . . or I wouldn't still be here," she said, motioning toward Brantley.

He held his head up and smiled tightly. "No, not trust. Tolerate." He looked at her and called, "I tolerate you. If your theory doesn't work, then you *will* be in danger from more than just the pimeys."

"It will work," she said as she came closer with some black goo in her hand.

"What is that?" I asked as Darsey allowed her near me, with a scowl on his face.

"It makes fires burn longer," Brantley explained. "If you cover your wood, it can make the fire burn all night."

I realized they were thinking we light our way through the cave using the goo as fuel. "I don't want to go back in there," I argued. "I want to find another way."

"Okay," Brantley acquiesced quickly, much to my surprise. "Just remember we are on a time limit. We need to get to the other side. The fairies told Plume it was an empty vastness of flat, rocky terrain. It should be easy to trek, which is good because we still have far to go if we are going to get to the starrunners by the next new moon."

I scrunched my brow and thought for a moment. I looked up and knew we would not be able to climb over. It was too steep. The rock face also disappeared on each side of us into the forest. We could go around . . . if we knew how far we had to go.

"Maybe I could meditate on it?"

"You think that would work?" Brantley asked.

"What is that?" Darsey inquired, confused.

"Sometimes if I need help and meditate, the dragons will show me the way," I explained, without realizing how amazing it really sounded.

Darsey looked dumbstruck, and Plume and her fairy sisters came close to me. "Do you really speak with dragons?" she asked, excited.

Darsey swiped at her and she jumped away, holding her hands up. "Okay, I'm sorry," she said with the attitude of a child not getting their way. "I forgot."

"Don't forget again," Darsey warned.

"What do you need?" Brantley asked.

I was surprised he remembered that meditating wasn't easy, and even more surprised he didn't give me a hard time for it.

I eyed him and said, "Just quiet and patience."

He nodded and stepped away, whispering to Darsey, "Let's give her some room."

Darsey looked at me eagerly, concern and frustration on his brow. I nodded and his face softened. He stepped away and I turned my back to them and sat in the position I was taught.

I played Serefina's instructions over in my head and began to push everything from my mind. This time I felt my heart warm at the realization that Darsey was not one of the things I needed to push away. He was really with me. I hadn't meditated since I had him back.

But a new darkness loomed on the horizon. The pimeys were a primal threat that sent shivers throughout my being. They were there, waiting in the recesses of the cave, and for a moment, I feared closing my eyes and them finding me in the darkness behind my eyelids.

The fear of the pimeys brought everything rushing back. The discomfort of traveling with the fairies, the distrust I now had of them, the frustration that they liked to torment Uri, and the most unwelcome and overbearing presence of Madame.

*You can't open your mind without bringing me back* she goaded.

I moaned in frustration and rubbed my face.

"What's wrong?" Brantley asked, his voice edging on irritation.

"Nothing," I answered quickly, refusing to look back. They were watching me. They were waiting for me. They were counting on me. If I couldn't find a way around this wall, we would have to go through it, and I couldn't stand the idea of letting everyone down.

I sucked in a deep breath and forced my eyes closed upon exhale. Nothing happened. The pimeys didn't come for me. I took another breath and focused on the spots of sunlight that shone through the trees and illuminated my skin. It was warm. It was bright. It was safe.

*Don't think I'm going anywhere* Madame growled.

She was too prevalent to push away. I sighed curtly and focused on the others in my way. Plume was easy get rid of, the fairies tormenting Uri were next, Brantley's sense of ownership over my quest disappeared, and even my fear of the pimeys were pushed aside with the warmth of the sun on my skin. Madame lingered still, like the phantom she was.

*Go ahead. Bring forth the Dragon Lord so I may show her my glory* she challenged.

I clenched my jaw. What if she was right? If I couldn't push her away, would the Dragon Lord think her more powerful than me?

I tried again to force her away, but she clung to me and seemed to seep in deeper, entangling herself with my thoughts and reaching through my mind into my body. She was determined to take me over.

"What's taking so long?" Brantley asked.

"Just give me a minute!" I snapped, not meaning to sound so aggressive. Now I had to start over, as everything came flooding back. It was harder to keep my problems at bay without Serefina walking me through it with her steady, confident voice.

I closed my eyes again and refocused. I tried to play Serefina's voice in my head. Then it morphed into Madame's.

*Go ahead. Get rid of everything* she said. I could hear the smile in her voice. She was determined to speak to the Dragon Lord.

I shook my head and she laughed.

*You can't get rid of me that way* she goaded.

"Get out!" I roared, opening my eyes. Both Brantley and Darsey's swords slid from their sheaths and I turned around. "Put your swords away," I snapped. Darsey looked confused and Brantley eyed me with steady observation.

I turned back and closed my eyes. This time I couldn't feel Madame's presence. She had left . . . for now. I focused on clearing my mind, which was easier with her gone.

Soon, the sound of the wind in the trees stilled. The chirping of birds faded. The ground began to soften, and I opened my eyes to my vision.

Water swirled all around me and the great blue Dragon Lord stood before me. She was beautiful and serpentine. Massive and long. Instead of wings, she had wispy tendrils that cascaded from her body from the edges of her mouth all the way to the tip of her tail. She lowered her head and the water quickly deepened until we were submerged. I swam to the top of her head and held on. She began to swim along the wall. I forced the first few breaths in and out, remembering that I could breathe in my meditations, no matter the circumstances. We continued along, at incredible speed, for far too long. We would never be able to walk it and get there in time. Then the wall tapered down to the ground and ended, leaving a mixture of forest and rock. It looked much like where she had taken me the first time I meditated. By following Brantley, we were too far off track and now we had to go through the cave to reach the star-runners.

She continued over the threshold and moved across the vast, rocky terrain Plume had described. It truly was massive and stretched far beyond the horizon. Though I knew only moments were passing where I sat, it felt as though many days were passing on the back of the Dragon Lord, and she swam with great speed. Once again, we stopped at the edge of the desert. She froze and hovered. Then burst into a mass of bubbles that lowered me gently to the ground. All the water sank into the sand before me.

I consciously opened my eyes, and was back in the forest, sitting undisturbed. I stood and brushed myself off.

"You have taken us far off the path," I accused Brantley.

"What do you mean?" he asked. "This is where the stars led me. We're on the exact right path."

"No," I argued. "The Dragon Lord showed me we would need to travel for days by foot *that* way," I said as I pointed along the wall, "to reach where we could cross.

"If we don't follow the path the stars lay out, we won't find the star-runners, even if we were to stumble across exactly where they descend."

"Surely, we could spare a few days," Darsey suggested. "The moon was just full. We have at least a fortnight before the new moon. And if we miss it, what is so terrible about taking our time and waiting until the next moon cycle?"

Brantley rubbed his brow and said, "That's a great idea, if you don't plan on getting any star-runners." He stared at Darsey like he was an idiot.

I crossed my arms and said, "What does that mean?"

"They won't be there *next* moon cycle," he argued. "This is our only chance, and I hope I don't have to explain to you the great favor the stars are bestowing upon us by descending the star-runners so close. They could have been *anywhere* in Pylertchia, and they chose to funnel down within a moon cycle's trek from us. If we miss it, we may never have the chance again."

I looked at Darsey and he met my eyes. "So . . ." he asked, "we need to go *through* the cave?"

"It looks that way," Brantley responded.

I sighed.

"Great!" Plume said excitedly. "Are you ready for my plan?"

"I suppose," Brantley mumbled as he faced her.

We stood at the mouth of the cave, ready to traverse the darkness. Our supplies were already on the other side of the wall, waiting for us. With the help of the fairies and some rope, we were able to heave everything over.

I was trembling at the thought of willingly entering the lair of the pimeys, but this time Plume was risking herself as well, which gave me a small sense of hope. Except her plan placed her and Darsey together, and a part of me feared she would throw him to the pimeys if it came to it.

However, Brantley seemed confident enough, which strangely set me at ease. Though I couldn't stand him, he knew how to survive. And he seemed determined to bring us through with him, for whatever reason. For that, I had to give him credit.

He and I had completely covered our cloaks in the black goo. After testing it, it burned Dragon's Fire for many minutes. Minutes only. Plume said her sisters claimed it would be enough time to get through the cave if we ran.

Brantley was to go first, followed by Darsey and Plume. Uri would stay tucked in Darsey's hood and I was to follow behind. Darsey and Plume both had torches dipped in the black goo, ready to be lit. The light from mine and Brantley's cloak would hopefully burn brightly enough to protect them, along with the torches they had in hand.

"Are you ready?" Brantley asked as he pulled my knife from his belt. I was slightly surprised it didn't bother me much that he had yet to return it since pulling it from me after killing the pimeys.

I sucked in a deep breath and nodded. He handed me the blade, hilt first, and I took it from his hand, immediately feeling the blaze course through my arm. It was still wild from the battle, but I was in better control this time. He held out his sleeve, and Darsey and Plume held out their torches. I quickly swiped my bare hand over each item, including my own, and everything covered in black goo erupted in Dragon's Fire.

Brantley pulled up his hood and dashed into the cave. The rest of us followed quickly and closely.

It felt counterintuitive to lift my head and open my eyes whilst on fire, though the fire didn't feel like anything. No heat. No sound. No pain.

I forced my eyes open and lifted my head. I could see the fire on the edges of the hood around me. It was surreal, yet familiar. Like when I lost control when I was inside the pimeys and with Brantley when he was still called Finnian.

This was different because it was outside of myself. I wasn't angry or overwhelmed or frightened, and yet the fire burned around me. Dragon's Fire.

Maybe this was how I could control it. If we found more of the black goo, we could use it to harness the power of Dragon's Fire, and everyone in the group could wield it.

I looked ahead, minding my distance from Darsey and Uri . . . and Plume. Brantley was rushing through the darkness, lighting the way, convinced he was the only one who could lead us safely through the cave.

Darsey was rushing behind him, keeping just enough distance to not be in harm's way, while staying in the safety of the glow. His back was still illuminated by the light from the mouth of the cave behind us, and not my fire.

I feared getting too close to him, but if we went too far into the cave and the daylight disappeared, his back would be exposed to darkness and the pimeys might take him.

I quickened my pace until I could see the fire's glow on his back. I stayed just close enough to illuminate him, and desperately hoped it wasn't so close it would harm him.

Suddenly, the ground quaked beneath me, knocking me off my feet. I saw Darsey stumble and regain his footing. Uri's back end came flying from his hood, his claws holding tight to the cloak.

The daylight behind us began to disappear and I saw Brantley turn. His eyes went wide and he yelled, "Go! They're trying to trap us!"

I scrambled up as he turned and ran. I looked back to see the mouth of the cave swamped in darkness as boulders fell from all around, blocking the entrance, and all the light.

Quickly, I spun and followed, both trying to keep the perfect distance from Darsey and hoping Brantley knew where we were going. How long would the fire last? How long until the goo burned up and we were in the dark?

Darsey and Plume's cloaks bounced and waved as they ran ahead, and the only indication of Brantley was the glow before them.

Then the ground quaked again and split between my running legs. I jumped to one side and Darsey and Plume jumped to the other as the ground opened and steam sprayed forth, blocking my view.

"Darsey!" I screamed, petrified of losing sight of him.

Brantley was at my side in an instant, gripping my arm. "Keep moving!" he barked as he dragged me along. I frantically obeyed while still staring past the chasm through the water that shot up in heated defiance, standing against our plight, one with the will of the pimeys.

"Darsey!" I called across the chasm as we ran.

"I'm here!" he yelled back. "Keep going!"

Relief swarmed me and I screamed to Brantley, "We have to jump across!" We couldn't leave Darsey so unprotected.

"That's what they want!" he argued, nearly as breathless as I was.

I looked again and realized he thought the water would put out the Dragon's Fire. I knew it wouldn't. I had seen the fire dry up water in an instant. Nothing could stand against it. I opened my mouth to protest just as the ground shook again and crumbled beneath us, stealing my footing as I felt myself falling freely through warm, wet air.

I could only hear myself screaming, and then my mouth was filled with water as my entire body became submerged in a winding torrent of confusion and aggression.

The only thing keeping me grounded was Brantley's tight grip on my wrist that never let go. While I was trying to figure out which way was up, he was dragging me through the water and onto land.

He sputtered once, sucked in a deep breath, and said in a coarse voice, "Come on!"

I was still coughing up water as he continued to drag me along the rocky floor.

"Let me go!" I screamed when I finally could, trying to tear my wrist from his grasp. "Darsey!" I screamed into the dark.

Then he drove his shoulder into my stomach and lifted me from the ground. Everything spun as he ran with me tossed over his back. The bouncing was nauseating, and I could do nothing to stop him as disorientation and fear overcame me.

Moments later we emerged from the darkness and he threw me to the hard, rock-slabbed ground. I jumped up and screamed into the empty mouth of the cave for Darsey.

I spun on Brantley and threw myself into him, beating at his chest with my fists. "Why did you leave him?" I demanded angrily, tears in my eyes. "He needs us!" I screamed.

He grabbed me by the wrists and threw me down. "Because I'm not willing to die for him!" he roared.

The ferocity in his voice made me pause, though my vision still quaked with tears and my body was shaking breathlessly.

"And I'm not willing to die for you!" he continued. The indignation and anger in his face would have been frightening had my mind been able to fully comprehend it. I was too overcome with grief and despair. "You are going to get us both killed if you don't stop acting like a child! Pay attention! Look around you! Our fire is *out*. They would have taken us!"

I looked at my hands supporting me on the ground and realized he was right, and it only aggravated my fear. "If our fire is out, then so is his!" I cried.

"Then he's gone!" Brantley shouted. His face and voice softened slightly as he added, "And I'm sorry. I'm sorry he's gone again."

I jumped up and felt my side for the blade. "I can save him," I said definitively.

He grabbed my shoulders and held me in place despite my struggle. "You're still not listening!" he screamed again. "What are you going to do? Fly in there and blast the pimeys with fire? Then you would kill him if he *was* still alive. You would kill him *and* Uri."

"I can't stand here and do nothing!" I shouted, trying again to pull away from him.

His grip tightened and he growled, "If you don't learn when to stand by and do nothing, then you will not make it to the end of your quest. He is useless to you like this. Uri is useless to you like this. So long as you wield Dragon's Fire, you are better off alone."

"Let me go!" I screamed.

"It is better he dies at the hand of an enemy than by your carelessness," he argued heatedly.

"Release her!" Darsey shouted behind us, and the relief that flooded me was overwhelming. Brantley released my arms and I turned.

Darsey stood there, on the edge of an overhanging rock that jutted from a smaller opening in the wall, sword in hand, looking winded and ragged. His clothing was torn and soaked, his torch was nowhere to be seen, and he had minor scrapes all over his body and face.

Plume broke from his side and quickly climbed down, rushing to her fairy brethren, whom I had not noticed were hovering nearby.

Uri clung to his shoulder, looking mangy and pathetic, yet so perfect. He jumped down and quickly plodded toward me. Darsey sheathed his sword and climbed down as I broke from Brantley to run to him. He pulled me back harshly by the shoulder and ripped my blade from my side, giving me a disgusted look before he shoved me away.

I ignored his attempt to prove his point about my carelessness and ran to Darsey, throwing myself into his arms. He wrapped them tightly around me and I buried my face into his neck and pulled him into the embrace I had wanted since the moment I saw him in the forest. Since the moment I knew he hadn't died at sea. This was that moment.

Uri climbed up my cloak to my shoulder and rubbed into the back of my neck, and I was grateful he was okay.

Our embrace deepened with each passing moment, and I felt myself melt into him with ease. The happiest moments of our childhood flashed across my memory as I breathed in his scent. Our running across the bank to the willow tree, weeding his family's garden, feeding the dialons . . . it was all still there. Right there in my arms. I didn't have to say goodbye. I didn't have to try to imagine a future without him.

"You're alive," I whispered.

"So are you," he said, his voice soft with relief.

I couldn't help the ironic laugh that shook my chest. We both pulled back just enough to see each other's face.

"What's funny?" he asked, a soft smile in his eyes.

I wiped my eyes with the back of my hand before returning it to his shoulder. "Of course *I'm* alive. I can kill them. But you . . ."

He laughed softly and said, "I'm tougher than you think. You don't have to worry about me."

"What did you do when your fire went out?" I asked, genuinely curious.

He shrugged and looked away for a moment. "I drew my sword. They stayed away."

*"Gavyn saved us,"* Uri chimed in.

"The Falcone might have helped a little," Darsey admitted just after Uri's private confession.

"Gavyn saved you?" I confirmed.

He looked down and smiled bashfully as his hair swept into his face. He nodded and said, "Yeah, he really did. His light kept them at bay, and he led us from the cave."

*"He might not be so bad,"* Uri suggested.

I looked up at the rock wall behind Darsey, as it loomed greatly, emanating a darkness I was sure could be attributed to the pimeys inside. It expanded as far as the eye could see on either side, only this side was riddled with holes like a honeycomb, some black as night, others with roots and leafed limbs reaching from them. Above the wall, the forest stretched out over it, like a mischievous child desiring to climb into the neighbor's garden and explore.

I spotted Gavyn perched on one of the outstretched limbs and tried to study him. He looked as though he didn't notice or care about my focusing on him. If anything, he seemed slightly put off that his assistance was needed. To my surprise, I was both grateful for his help, and annoyed that we needed it. We needed to do better. Be better. I didn't want to owe the Falcone anything, and I didn't trust his intentions.

"Let's get away from this cave," Brantley ordered. "We need to find a place to camp for the day."

I turned away from Darsey. He continued to cradle my elbow in his hand, and I leaned into him. "Camp for the *day*?" I asked.

Brantley didn't look at me, nodded and said, "Now that we are in the open, I can follow the star path at night."

"Won't that leave us vulnerable?" Darsey asked.

He didn't respond as he took up his portion of the supplies. Darsey and I did the same while Plume stayed with her sisters, paying us no mind.

I looked out over the rocky terrain. "It looks so barren," I commented. The wind picked up and blew past us, whipping my hair to the side. My waterlogged cloak pressed against me uncomfortably.

"We'll dry out quickly," Brantley said, ignoring my concern. He started to walk and Darsey grabbed my hand.

I looked at his face, our noses inches apart, and smiled. He smiled back and laced his fingers with mine. "Want me to get your blade back?" he asked softly.

I tightened my grip on his hand and whispered, "He can hold it for a while."

Brantley had not gained my trust. If anything, I was more wary of him than before. But I knew he could not wield it. And since he liked to use me as a weapon, I knew he would give it back. I didn't need the blade on me. We would see danger coming for miles.

We stepped from the shade of the looming wall and into the sunlight. Uri put his paw on my head and lengthened himself toward the sun. I imagined his sweet face, eyes closed, basking in the glow and warmth.

I enjoyed feeling the sun on my skin. The forest had been stifling at times, and I had never seen such openness on land before. During my time on the ship, I had seen the open water, yet here there was nowhere I couldn't tread. It was a freedom I hadn't realized I had been missing. The forest offered shade and sometimes protection, along with many dangers that loomed in the shadows. Out here, there were no shadows. Nowhere to hide. Nothing to hide from.

Just miles and miles of empty, flat faced stony slate. It swelled and dipped in some places. It was broken and jagged in others. There were hundreds of forms around us of the stone. Pieces both large and small. Some areas compacted and strong. Others, broken and dusty. And yet, all the same. The stark change from the ground to the sky was the only thing that gave the scene depth, as strange as that felt. Vastness of stone so difficult to comprehend that the blue sky was needed to make it seem real.

Panic and relief fought for control within me. I tightened my grip on Darsey's hand once again, and reminded myself that with him by my side, it didn't matter how expanding the terrain was. We were doing it together.

SEVEN | The Rocky Plains

The rocky plains were windy.

That was an understatement. Their gusts were violent. If not for Brantley's survival skills, our tents would have been lost the first day, and though the sound of the shelters whipping in the wind was ferocious, they stayed firmly tethered in place.

Nighttime gave us no relief from the unending wind. We had all grown accustomed to hiding inside our cloaks, shielding our faces from the assault and Brantley kept reminding us to get used to it, because the desert would be much worse.

After a few days and nights of letting Brantley carry the blade for me, he insisted I take it back. To my surprise, I was dismayed at the idea of bearing it again. I had enjoyed my time being close to Darsey, unhindered by the fear I might turn him to ash with a touch. And I enjoyed having Uri sleep on my neck again. I had missed his furry body purring against my skin. But Brantley was right. It was my gift from the Dragon Lord, and I did him a disservice to be ungrateful.

Over the course of the following days, I noticed a change in the party. Plume was no longer trying to steal all of Darsey's attention, though she looked forlorn about it. He refused to have anything to do with her, which made me happy. His focus was solely on me, and the task ahead.

And though I was unsure if it had anything to do with what happened between Darsey and Plume, the fairies had stopped tormenting Uri. In fact, the opposite happened. They spent the nights playing a game that seemed much like tag. They would see how close they could get to him before he noticed and he would pounce, sometimes grabbing them, sometimes missing. Everyone unharmed. I was grateful for the change, and I was thankful Uri had someone to interact with since I had to stay focused.

Especially with the blade back at my side. My gloves were lost in the cave, and Brantley's warning continued to resonate within me. I would never forgive myself if *I* was the reason something happened to Darsey, *or* Uri.

So, I resigned myself to staying at a distance from everyone. It really was unfair that Brantley was the only one I could be close to, when I despised him so. Where I kept my distance from others for their safety, I stayed distant from Brantley for my sanity. In light of his confession after the pimeys, I felt more distant than ever before. Nadine was wrong about him.

I had no doubt that if we had not been tethered together, he would have left me to die in that cave. Of course, without the tether he wouldn't be on the trek at all, which was his own fault.

For mere days shy of a fortnight we followed his lead, trusting his ability to read the stars. Darsey stayed as close to me as I would allow, and our conversations had slowly returned to the ease we had before.

However, the secret I held of Brantley's presence loomed over me, always darkening our moments together. I feared he would sense the darkness and ask about it, though he seemed oblivious to my dishonesty.

Plume was slowly becoming more agitated as the night of the new moon neared. She often looked about, as though something was lurking nearby, ready to strike.

"What's your problem?" Darsey asked her one night.

"The moonlight was the only thing keeping the pimeys at bay," she admitted. "As soon as the new moon rises, they will come for me. For us."

"They are far behind us," Darsey said. "We have a head start."

"You think time is their weakness?" she scoffed. "Time doesn't bind them. Light is their only restraint. And tomorrow night they will be upon us as soon as the sun sets. We need to be prepared."

I felt nauseated at the thought of fighting off the pimeys again. What would we do? The wind wouldn't allow fire to survive. We had nothing to burn. I could only protect myself and Brantley. Gavyn was soaring high above us, keeping an eye on the trek, but I couldn't count on him to help out a second time. He didn't save Darsey in the sea, why would he do it again out here? The cave was probably a fluke.

"We'll have starlight protecting us," Brantley called back.

"It isn't enough!" Plume shouted, looking up at the barely visible moon. "We're lucky there hasn't been any clouds in the sky since we began."

"I promise you, it *will* be enough," Brantley argued nonchalantly.

"No," Plume insisted. "You don't understand."

"*You* don't understand," he reiterated. "The star-runner trails are almost *blinding*. If the pimeys come for us, they will be destroyed instantly."

There was a pause before Plume muttered, "*If* we get to them before the pimeys find us."

"We're there," he answered, as he pointed through the darkness. Barely visible in the distance was a large pillar of stone, backed by a mountain side. The first deviation from the emptiness we had seen for almost two weeks.

"What is that?" Darsey asked.

"That is where the star-runners will descend. We will camp here for the rest of the night and continue in the morning. We'll need light and rest to make it to the top."

"Top of *what*?" I asked.

"The pillar," he said simply.

Without any more discussion, we made camp and settled into our tents. Plume shared Brantley's tent, as he didn't trust her and wanted to keep an eye on her. Uri and Darsey stayed in another, and I had my own. I settled down in the darkness, wishing I could have Uri on my neck. I had to learn how to control the blade better. I was the Dragon Born. Controlling Dragon's Fire should be at the forefront of my mind. And I would try. I needed to be better.

I stood at the bank of black waters. They were still. There was nothing around me, and in the center of the black pool, stood the great Blue Dragon Lord. She was beautiful and serene. The pool reached out with tentacle-like features and wrapped around her, pulling her beneath the water. Her expression didn't change. Didn't look away from me. Then she disappeared below.

*Pimeys* a voice echoed around me.

I turned and saw only darkness.

*Pimeys* the voice screamed.

I forced my eyes open and stared at the darkness of my tent.

"Pimeys!" Plume screamed.

I jumped up and felt the blade blazing at my side. I dove from my tent, determined to save Darsey and Uri, if no one else.

There was a loud screeching all around us and I saw Plume and the fairies disappear into the darkness without a trace.

I ran to Darsey's tent and with all my strength resonated the power of the blade throughout my body, willing it to extend beyond my skin to the air around me, only with control. I could do this. I could control it.

The fire burned into existence on my skin and rested there, as though it belonged. I smiled and as Darsey came out of his tent I ordered that he stand behind me.

"It's too dark!" he screamed.

I sucked in a deep breath and closed my eyes. I was the Dragon Born. I was in control.

The fire reacted to my calm. I told it where to go, and it seeped from me in a blazing line. It slowly and methodically surrounded Darsey, soaking him in light from every angle.

"Stay away from the flames," I said in a voice not my own. It was deeper. Primal. Dragonesque. I was doing it. I was the Dragon Born.

"Stay back!" Brantley's voice warned.

He didn't care to protect us, and I didn't have time to protect him. I needed to focus on Darsey and Uri. He was on his own.

"Adalee!" Brantley shouted at me.

I couldn't respond. I couldn't move. Controlling the fire took all my concentration and if I faltered, Darsey's life would be forfeit.

Then the pimeys had me. They gripped my wrists. They stole my blade.

"No!" I roared. How could this be? They had no power in the light. They couldn't take my protection!

They wrapped their violent limbs around me and began to shake.

I felt myself slinging from side to side. I knew soon they would be finished with me, and when they were, Darsey and Uri would be next.

"Get off her!" Darsey screamed, and I felt the pimeys release me.

"Run," I tried to scream, my voice refusing to do anything but whisper.

I felt his hand reach through the dark and touch my face. "Open your eyes," he said.

"The pimeys," I tried to warn in an unwanted whisper.

"We're safe," he said. "It's okay. Just open your eyes."

I sucked in a deep breath and forced my eyes open, shocked at the light that assaulted them. I instinctively shielded them from the sun and tried to look around. It was easily midday. Darsey stood before me, concern on his brow.

"You were sleep-walking," he explained slowly.

"The pimeys were upon us!" I exclaimed. "I used my fire to protect us!"

Brantley scoffed and said, "All your fire did was destroy your tent."

"Hush," Darsey hissed at him.

I looked around and realized I was standing in a pile of ash that was once my tent. The wind quickly finished carrying it away and I felt greatly disappointed in myself. "There were no pimeys?" I asked.

Darsey shook his head and said, "No."

"Do you think you can handle this?" Brantley asked, annoyed, holding my blade toward me.

I felt my face flush in shame and embarrassment as I realized what had happened. Similar to what happened at the Shaman's Clearing the night the Blue Dragon Lord first called me. Only this time I had done some damage. My tent was gone. I could have hurt Darsey.

"I can handle it," I said softly as I stepped away from my love and took the blade.

"It's okay," Darsey assured me. "You can share my tent."

I kept my head down and pulled up my hood, then fastened the blade back to my side. I needed to do something with the blade during the night. I couldn't risk anyone again, or Brantley's warning might come to pass.

Plume skipped ahead, indifferent to what had just happened. Darsey and Brantley quickly broke down their tents and packed them up then we were on our way to the pillar ahead.

During the day we could see it much better and I wondered how he expected us to climb it. It was a sheer rock wall.

The walk to the pillar took longer than I expected. No matter how long we walked, it didn't seem to draw any nearer.

"How long until we get there?" I finally asked.

"We should get there a few hours before dusk," Brantley called back.

"It looked closer than that," Darsey said to me.

*"Can I play with the fairies?"* Uri asked from Darsey's shoulder.

I nodded and he climbed down and ran off to wrestle with Mathilda and Doria.

"I mean it when I say you can share the tent with me," he said softly. "I'm not afraid."

The image of me accidentally turning him to ash flashed across my mind and I cringed and shook my head. "You should be. I'm dangerous now."

"You're not dangerous," he argued lightly. "At least not to me. You just need practice. I know you can control it. You're the Dragon Born." His last statement was made with such perfect confidence that I wanted to earn it.

I tried to smile and said, "I know I can. It's just a lot to handle."

He nodded.

"It is nice feeling so safe though, from enemies," I added.

"What you did to the ship was amazing," he agreed. "And seeing you standing there in a pile of ash this morning . . . I know you think I should have been scared, but I wasn't. You're incredible."

I couldn't help the smile that played on my lips.

"I mean, everything you're doing," he continued. "You speak with the Dragon Lords, and they come to you in your dreams, and you destroyed one of the most notorious slave traders in the world, and you are wielding Dragon's Fire. Of *course*, it is going to be difficult. It's *Dragon's Fire*. It isn't meant for humans, and the only reason you can do it is because of the Essence."

My smile widened and I glanced at him. "I guess you're right."

"I am," he assured me. "And honestly," he said in a lower voice, "I don't know what they were thinking when they paired *him* with you."

I cringed and hid my face. Brantley's behavior was making it more and more difficult to keep the lie believable. How much had Darsey heard outside the cave?

"Maybe after this Dragon Lord is freed, he will be released and I can take his place," he suggested.

I sighed. I wished it were true. Brantley would be gone, but it wasn't a Dragon Lord who bound him to me. I stayed silent, unsure of what to say.

"Unless . . . you don't think I can help," Darsey whispered.

I looked at him and realized he thought my silence meant I doubted his ability. "No," I assured him. "I will definitely ask if you can be bound to me instead of him." As I said it, I realized what a wonderful idea it was. Maybe they *could* make him immune to the Dragon's Fire. I could at least ask. For Uri too! She was a Dragon Lord, after all.

"So . . ." Darsey continued. "You dreamed you were protecting me from the pimeys?" he asked with a smile.

I blushed and nodded.

His smile widened and he asked, "Tell me?"

"Okay," I acquiesced. I had missed sharing my dreams with him. We spent the afternoon talking about my dream, and I told him about all my Calling dreams and the one I had had in the clearing when Brantley pulled me out of it.

"So, he is always there to save the day," he said sardonically.

"Or make it worse," I accidentally mumbled.

Darsey laughed softly and said, "At least I'm not the only one who dislikes him."

"No, you're definitely not alone," I agreed.

"You ready?" Brantley interrupted.

We both looked at him and realized we were standing steps away from the pillar.

The closer we had gotten to the massive rock face, the less aggressive the wind had become. Now, it was naught but a breeze, and a happy change. My wind-chapped cheeks were ready for relief.

"How are we going to climb it?" I asked, staring up. It was even taller than I imagined.

"With everything we have," he said as he began to unbundle his supplies.

Darsey silently did the same and I watched as they lengthened out their ropes and tents.

"Why doesn't the Dragon Born just burn footholds into it?" Plume asked, looking toward where the sun would set in a couple of hours.

Brantley looked at her with surprising frustration in his eyes. "Because if the stars feel they have chosen an unsafe place, they won't descend. They chose the pillar because they know how difficult it will be for the star-runners to be found.

"Wait, they don't *want* to be found?" Darsey asked, confused.

Brantley began tying the tents and ropes together to climb. "The star-runners *do* want to be found. It's the stars who don't like releasing them to Pylertchia."

"So, you've done this before?" I asked, thinking of his old star-runner who was destroyed in the fiery blast. "I mean, you know how to get up the pillar, right?"

He sighed and looked at me, shaking his head. "They are never in the same place twice. That's why we *followed the stars*," he reminded me with attitude.

"Don't talk to her like that just because *you* don't know if you can get us any further than this," Darsey snapped.

Brantley spun on him, eyes wide. "Me?" he asked. He dropped the items in his hands and threw them out wide. "Have I not brought you far enough? Did I not come to your rescue on the ship? Or help you bring those slavers to their rightful end? Did I not keep us well fed and hydrated as we traversed the forest and rocky plains, all whilst getting less sleep than *everyone* because I had to watch the stars *constantly* to follow them? I have kept us sheltered and safe. I have more fighting, survival, *and* common-sense skills than anyone here! I got her out of the cave and away from the pimeys' reach. I have played along with your little games and put up with your harping after each other." His passion continued to grow into irritation as he got louder. "Night after night, day after day. When will it end? And you expect *more* of me? Maybe when we get to the star-runners you can get yours and go home. We don't need you. You are a distraction and, in all honesty, a liability."

Darsey's frustration was growing as well, evidenced by his passionate shouts of, "As soon as this next Dragon Lord is freed, and *you* are gone, *I* will be the one commissioned to be with her. She wants *me* here. She doesn't even like you."

Brantley laughed ironically and said, "Is that what matters? How much I am *liked?* Well, let me ask *you* something. She may like you, but how confident are you that she trusts you?"

Darsey scoffed and shook his head, crossing his arms. "She trusts me more than *you*," he argued.

My heart quickened and I stared Brantley down, imploring him not to tell Darsey the truth of the bind. To my horror, he refused to look at or acknowledge me.

"Really?" Brantley asked, mocking the idea that Darsey knew something he didn't. "Because from what I've seen, she doesn't even trust you enough to hold the blade for her and give her respite. *I've* held the blade," he pointed out.

Temporary relief swam over me, hoping that *that* was the only point he planned on making.

Darsey shook his head and said, "I'm glad she's being cautious. She should be."

"Even if *I'm* the one who warned her to be?" he asked with a smile.

Darsey looked down and smirked. I could tell he was trying to pull in his emotions. "You can't take credit for that," he said softly.

"Oh, but I can," he said smugly. "See, I specifically asked her not to entrust the blade to you. And now I see she listened. So, tell me again who she trusts more?"

"Stop it!" I snapped. "I *don't* trust you," I added, glaring at Brantley. "I've only tried giving you the benefit of the doubt because Nadine begged me to. I trust *him* way more than you."

I looked at Darsey, hoping to see his spirits raised, only to find a small smile that didn't say much. I spun back on Brantley and yelled, "And just to clarify, I have *never* entrusted the blade to *you*. You *take* it when you deem it necessary. *Darsey* has always demanded you give it back. So, if you are trying to make it seem as though you are somehow higher than him in my eyes, you are wrong."

His eyes turned stony and cold. His mouth flattened and his gaze darted toward Darsey. He glanced back at me and a smirk played at the edge of his lips, not reaching his eyes.

Somehow, I could see what he was about to say. That he was about to give up our charade. I feared Darsey would leave once he had a star-runner. I feared he wouldn't love me anymore. Worse still, I feared he would challenge Brantley and not stop until he paid with his life. I had to fix it.

"But," I said quickly, "you *do* know how to survive. The Dragon Lord *did* choose you to help me."

He looked at me, and the stoniness in his eyes softened. Instead, they filled with a hint of pity.

"And for that alone," I continued, "I should trust you more." I looked at Darsey and tried to smile. "This is hard for me," I said with tears in my eyes. "We need to get along so we can get through this."

He tried to look away, so I moved into his line of sight. "I'm not asking you to trust him, or even like him. *I* don't like him. That's okay. But he isn't wrong. And he *has* done well keeping us alive. Before we were bound . . . by the Dragon Lord's will," I covered for my almost mistake, "I was in constant peril. I almost died so many times. I barely made it. So, trust me when I say, this has been so much better, even if he is difficult to be around."

Darsey huffed and nodded.

I leaned in and said, "And just so you know, I do plan on sharing your tent and letting you keep the blade at night so I can sleep without hurting anyone." I owed him at least that.

"Can we get moving?" Plume asked, irritated. "You know, *before* the pimeys devour us?"

Darsey and I didn't look away from each other, and Brantley said, "Yes. We need to hurry. It will take some time getting up there."

"That won't reach," Plume argued.

"Then we will use our cloaks as well. Our satchels. Our clothing. Whatever we need to make it up there."

Plume scoffed and said, "It still won't be long enough."

"Do you have an idea, then?" he turned on her.

She whispered something to her sisters, and they flew to the top of the pillar, disappearing for a moment.

We stood silently while awaiting their return and she said smugly, "I am older than you, after all."

The fairies came back and whispered in her ear. She smiled wide and nodded. "Great," she said to them. "Adalee, give Darsey your blade."

I took off the blade and laid it on the ground for him to take. He picked it up and attached it to his own belt.

"You may want to regather your supplies," she said to Brantley with a smile. "We won't be needing them."

He sighed deeply and undid everything he had done with harsh motions. Then he put his own away and tossed Darsey his.

The fairies flew back to the top of the pillar, and Plume stood close to the base. She instructed everyone to follow. Uri climbed up to my shoulder and we stood near Darsey. Plume stood between me and Brantley.

"Whatever you have planned, it better not scare off the stars," Brantley warned.

"It won't," she assured him.

There was a rumble in the ground beneath us and the rocks split open, revealing a dahlia bloom that sprang up and quickly began to grow in width.

"Jump on!" Plume ordered and we all obeyed. It continued to grow until we were each settled in our own petal. Then the flower began to rise.

"This won't work!" Brantley shouted as it began to fall away from the pillar with our weight.

Then a powerful stream of goldenrods grew up beside it, grasping the stem and pulling it back to the pillar. We all tried not to spill out of the flower with the movement and held tightly as its growing slowed greatly.

*"Did you know they could do this?"* Uri asked me.

I shook my head. I knew they had magic, but *nothing* like this.

The bloom stretched up over the top of the pillar and began to bend over the edge. We were not met with a flat top as I expected. Instead, the flower continued to grow and lower *into* the pillar.

"It's not a pillar!" Darsey exclaimed.

"It's hollow!" Brantley followed.

Then the flower fell forward and we all cried out as we gripped tightly to our petals. My legs dangled from the bloom as it slowly lowered us to the ground. After what seemed to take forever, I felt my feet touch the stony earth.

We all let go together and it lifted away from our grasp with the freedom from our weight.

"Wow!" Darsey heaved, as he bent over, breathing heavily.

I turned and marveled at the stony walls around us. They were massive and the center of the pillar rested in what I was sure was perpetual shadow. Most importantly, there was no wind, and I was immensely grateful for it.

Brantley looked up at the enormous dahlia and shook his head. "It's too much. The stars won't come with it here, I'm sure of it."

"That's where *she* comes in," Plume said, and I turned.

"Ah," Brantley said with understanding.

The flower continued to grow, even after it settled on the ground with the weight of the bloom.

Darsey loosened the dagger and laid it before me. I waited for Uri to understand and jump from my shoulder.

I lifted the blade and felt the power surge through me. I approached the flower and when the tingle was dripping from my fingers, I touched the bloom. The beautiful pink hue quickly turned dull as it faded away in an ashy dust that spread up and over the lip of our hideaway.

Once we are alone in the center of the pillar, Plume said, "You better be right about this being where the star-runners are descending. Because if you aren't, we won't make it out of here."

"Because of the pimeys," Darsey clarified.

She nodded solemnly and whispered, "The sun is setting."

Brantley drew back to the wall of the pillar and motioned for us to follow.

"Don't let them take me," Plume begged breathlessly as she slipped in beside us.

"The star-runners will come," Brantley whispered.

Then all sound ceased. A quietness so overpowering, it left ringing in my ears. They began to throb, and I looked at Plume as terror struck her face.

The pimeys had come.

EIGHT | The Coming of the Pimeys

I slowly turned and looked at the fear-stricken faces of Darsey and Plume. The power of the blade surged at my side and determination settled into my being with the heavy pound of each heartbeat.

"Darsey," I whispered. "Hold Uri close and stay behind me." I stepped out and unlatched my cloak, letting it fall from my shoulders, revealing the skin of my arms. If they were to come for us, I would destroy them all.

"No!" Brantley yelled, and I felt his weight bend me in half as I slammed into the ground and he grabbed the blade from my side and tossed it away. The last thing I heard was the clanging of metal against stone, echoed by Darsey and Plume's distant screams of terror.

Then silence. Emptiness. Pain.

Brantley's grasp loosened from my body and disappeared. The cold was even more painful than I had remembered, and it touched my core.

My body twisted and convulsed violently. I tried to suck in air where there was none to be had.

Before I could try again, the expanding darkness dissipated. I landed, not on stony ground, but on the softest earth I had ever felt. I welcomed air into my lungs and dared not move what felt like a broken body.

The ringing was overcome by the powerful roar of water. Where had they taken me? Why had they released me?

A light twinkled delicately above me, and I forced my eyes to focus.

Gavyn?

As the vision cleared, I realized it was not the aura of the Falcone hovering above me. Rather it was a dazzling column of sparkling light that danced between many colors, the collective brilliance a blinding prism. It was breathtaking.

It poured down from the heavens and landed not a stone's throw away from where I lay.

I forced myself up, surprised at how much strength I still had after the pimeys attack, and turned to see the light billowing out from where it landed, spreading across the ground, layer after layer.

I looked down and realized I was laying upon it. I lifted my hand and watched it cascade from between my fingers like dry sand, moving seamlessly like a stream of water.

"They came," Brantley's voice sounded from behind me.

I turned and saw him sitting up, staring at the column, its light reflecting in his wide eyes.

I quickly spun, the light around me reacting in waves, and searched for Darsey and Uri.

Darsey was leaning against the stone wall, staring up at the column, and Uri was perched on his knee, staring down at the light flowing on the ground.

I stumbled on weak legs as I tried to run to them. I crawled the rest of the way and he met me when he saw me coming.

"Are you okay?" he asked as he wrapped me in his arms.

I nodded. "Are you two okay?"

*"What is this stuff?"* Uri asked as he climbed up my tunic from the beneath the light.

"Yes," he said gruffly. "They got us, and then let go."

"Me too," I cried, remembering the fear I had experienced moments before.

"They let go because the stardust killed them," Brantley called as he approached us. "Like I said it would."

"We could have died," Darsey growled.

"If she had used the blade, the stars wouldn't have descended and we *would* have died. So . . . you're welcome."

"No, no, no," Plume cried out.

We all turned and saw her on her hands and knees, digging through the stardust that was now up to our ankles.

"What's wrong?" Darsey asked.

She sat up, shaken and panicked. "My sisters. They took my sisters."

"The stars didn't—" Brantley began.

"Not the stars! The pimeys!" she cut him off as she jumped up.

Brantley shook his head and said, "The pimeys are dead!"

"Not all of them," she growled as she fell back and put her face in her hands. "They've been taken to the imps," she sobbed.

Despite the trouble she had caused amongst us, I felt bad for her. I opened my mouth to reassure her that we would help her get her sisters back, but Brantley spoke first.

"You're on your own," he declared. "We have brought you to the star-runners. What you do with that is up to you."

"Brantley," I snapped.

"You don't speak for us," Darsey added.

*"I liked them,"* Uri cried.

"We have our own mission," Brantley said coolly, as though his words were final.

"I don't *need* your help," Plume bit as she stood. "You'll just slow me down."

A blast of light exploded from the top of the column and drew all our eyes.

The fullness of the column ebbed and thinned, until only a stream of stardust was pouring down. Then another blast resonated and from it a ribbon of light streamed down and around the pole, creating a spiral ramp from the heavens to the ground.

"Watch this," Brantley breathed, anticipation in his voice.

A ball of stardust landed on the top of the ribbon and slowly bounded down. Another one followed not too far behind, and another after that. More continued to appear as others descended. Once the first one reached the bottom, it landed on the dusty ground and exploded with light and a small, white horse ran out of the ball of dust, letting it spill to the ground and mix into the flow.

Before I could take in the beauty of the beast, Plume was upon it, and the stardust rumbled around us and shot to the creature as it gained speed, becoming nothing more to the eye than a streak of light. The dust spread up the walls of the pillar and the creature easily ran around the base and up the sides until it disappeared over the lip, and the dust settled back at the bottom.

Just like that, she was gone.

"Should we go after her?" Darsey asked.

"No," Brantley said quickly.

Then he grabbed his chest and cried out in pain as he fell to the ground.

I instinctively rushed to him, fearing the pimeys had harmed him before the stars vanquished them.

I tore open his tunic and instead of a fresh wound, my eyes fell upon his old scar re-emerging, burning a fierce red that pulsed across his skin.

His arm fell away from the mark as he arched his back and cried out in primitive grunts and growls of torment, akin to the sounds that came from the doctor's lair.

Every muscle in his body tensed up and his face turned red with unbridled agony.

The air was knocked out of me by his cries, and I spun away, covering my ears.

Then I saw Darsey, a disconnected look of great discomfort on his face as he also tried to block out the sound.

The doctor's face flashed before my eyes, as I was sure he was doing to Darsey. His slimy, yellow smile spilled forth cockney questions and confessions, offering no mercy from his deranged devices. It surrounded me, and Brantley's screams intermingled with my own. It had been so long! How did the doctor still have such a hold on me?

I didn't notice when the screaming stopped, as I was so focused on trying to see *anything* except the doctor's face.

It wasn't until I felt a hand on my shoulder that I looked around and saw Brantley standing there, tunic closed, covered in a sheen of sweat.

"The fairy magic wore off," he grunted.

I stood, fighting my nausea, and nodded.

We both looked at Darsey who was curled into a ball in the light that still spilled across the ground.

"Honestly, I didn't know you two cared so much," he said, still winded.

"You . . . sounded like the doctor had you," I admitted softly.

His face changed from minor amusement to one of concern. "Oh." I moved to comfort Darsey, but Brantley stopped me and said, "Let me, lass."

He approached Darsey and knelt down, speaking to him.

I moved closer to hear them and Brantley was saying, "It's okay, lad. He's gone. It was just my own tormentor returning with a vengeance."

Slowly, Darsey sat up, then Brantley gripped his arms and helped him stand.

"Let's get ready. It will be time to choose our star-runners soon."

We turned toward the staircase and the intensity of my fears melted away as soon as my eyes landed on the star-runners. They continued to bounce off the end of the ramp and turn into horses as they darted about the star-laden quarry. They ran in circles around the staircase. They jumped and pranced and danced about happily, completely care-free. It was beautiful to watch.

The star dust was thrown up behind them like splashes, only to quickly descend and rejoin the swell of the sea of light. They moved within inches of us with barely a breeze as they rushed by.

Much to my amazement, Darsey was spinning around with each passing star-runner, a smile wide on his face. The joy of the steeds spread to me, and I was overcome with contentment and delight.

Brantley leaned over and said with a light-hearted tone, "There is nothing like being amongst them when they descend."

And from what I could tell, he was right. Everything else was gone for that moment. No angst. No worries. No quest. Just us, taking in the beauty of the stars.

"Astraeus!" Brantley shouted and Darsey and I both turned to see a large star-runner trot over, its head bobbing happily. Brantley wrapped his arms around its neck and said, "I've missed you, my friend."

"He knows him?" Darsey asked, confused.

Brantley laughed and said, "He was with me until Adalee sent him back to the stars."

Darsey looked at me and arched his brow playfully.

"Accidentally," I added. "I hadn't gotten the hang of the blade yet." Then I remembered Brantley throwing my blade just before the pimeys attacked.

"Where is it?" I panicked, looking around.

"You lost it?" Brantley asked as he faced me, his hand still on Astraeus' cheek.

"You *threw* it!" I corrected as I began searching around the walls where I heard it clang.

Uri jumped from my shoulder, disappearing beneath the light, and said, *"I'll help!"*

Darsey and Brantley also began searching, Astraeus staying near Brantley's side.

"Found it!" Darsey exclaimed, as he held up the blade.

"Keep it, for now," Brantley shouted from the other side of the staircase.

Darsey looked at me and I nodded.

*"Good!"* Uri said excitedly as he emerged and climbed up my tunic, making my back arch with his little claws.

"Where's my cloak?" I asked, smirking at him.

A star-runner came trotting up to me with my cloak in its mouth. It stopped suddenly before me and I slowly took the cloak, jaw dropped. "It . . . brought me my cloak?" I asked, bewildered.

"They understand all language," Brantley explained as he approached. "And they want to be chosen. She is taking initiative. I would give her a name if I were you."

"A name?" I asked, still staring in awe at the beautiful face before me. She was as delicately white as Astraeus, yet softer, with wide, round eyes that bore into mine, beseeching something of me.

"When you name them, they are chosen. The stars allow them to stay for as long as you tend to them."

"Let's name them all!" Darsey laughed, as multiple star-runners were surrounding him, licking at his face and neck, pulling lightly at his hair, and nudging him with their noses, as he tried to pet and pay attention to all of them.

"Only one per rider," Brantley said. "By order of the stars."

I nodded and said, "Okay. Then I will call you Starla."

She nudged me with her nose, and I pulled her face in and nuzzled back.

"Whoa! Stop! How do I get them off me?" Darsey cried, his laughter turning to concern as one of the star-runners grabbed him by the hood of his cloak and dragged him from the group, dropping him on his back and standing over him, neighing loudly.

"Name one!" Brantley called.

The other star-runners began to rush over to Darsey again and he quickly grabbed the one by the face that had dragged him away and shouted, "Cosmo!"

The other star-runners stopped immediately and trotted off, continuing their earlier play.

Cosmo began licking Darsey's face like a dog and Darsey laughed as he struggled to get up. "I hope I didn't hurt the other's feelings."

Brantley laughed and said, "They're happy to be on the ground playing. They have until the end of time to find chances to stay."

"They're ageless?" I asked.

"Timeless, ageless, immortal. They have a long and complicated story. One that I do not know all the details to."

"I think I chose a good one," Darsey laughed as Cosmo nuzzled him.

"They're all good ones," Brantley corrected. "You just need the *right* one."

The last star-runner bounded off the ramp and released its dust as it took off running.

I stroked Starla from her head, down the length of her back, which came to my chest, all the way to her tail. She was beautiful. She was magnificent. Her coat was like the softest fur. It almost felt like nothing beneath my hand, yet it filled me with joy. The aura around her was strong and made her appear truly celestial. I couldn't believe that I now had a star-runner of my own.

"We should go soon, while the night is young," Brantley said, breaking me from my awe. He took one of his extra canteens and began filling it with star dust. "Fill your extra canteen," he instructed, and Darsey and I did so. It flowed in easily, coating the outside and my hands.

"This stuff gets stuck to everything," Darsey mentioned.

Brantley shrugged and said, "It'll disappear at dawn. You must never let light touch the stardust."

Neither of us questioned him, and we continued filling our canteens.

When we were done, we all stood and my attention was grabbed once again by the star-runners, leaping around us in a joyous celebration, while our own stood by expectantly, patiently waiting.

"Which way?" Brantley asked me as though I had a map.

His abrupt switch from leader to follower was astounding, and I found myself not wishing to undermine his confidence. I looked around without any idea where we were in relation to the Blue Dragon Lord. Brantley had led us astray, good reason or not, and I was lost. Not to mention, we were still in the pillar so all I saw was a festival of star-runners and tall, stony walls.

I decided we should get going and I would figure out the way once I gained my bearings.

"That way," I said, trying to sound confident as I pointed in the direction I believed to be generally right.

Everyone's gaze followed my finger, and Brantley turned back and asked, "Are you sure?"

I put my hand down and nodded. "Yes," I said when he didn't accept my nod as an answer.

"Maybe you should meditate?" he asked, a smirk playing at his lips.

Of course. I had forgotten that I *was* the map. The Dragon Lord would lead the way. However, I could do without his smug expressions.

I sat down in the stardust and crossed my legs. I took a deep, calming breath and closed my eyes. The excitement of everything we had experienced was coursing through me, and I was having a hard time calming down.

The sound of the star-runners suddenly ceased, and I imagined them all standing still, watching me. I couldn't disappoint.

I pushed all the distractions from my mind, one by one, and let myself go. It was easier than ever before, and I felt the comfort of the stardust had something to do with it.

I simply pictured the Dragon Lord, and suddenly she was before me. Only, the stardust was replaced with frothing waters that she raised out of, despite their shallow appearance.

I stood and she dove under, then raised up beneath me, lifting me into the air. I held on to two tendrils that floated from her head and had to remind myself this was only meditation and I needn't hold my breath as she dived back down. She swam in circles along the stony wall, and the water rose with each lap until we were at the top and it spilled out into a vast sea, which flowed over the stony earth that surrounded us.

She spilled out with it and we set off across the terrain. We moved quickly, and I held on tight. Our direction never changed, and we traveled for many hours in a straight line until we again reached the edge of the desert. She stopped and, just like before, the water descended and she burst into bubbles, which slowly lowered me to the ground.

That was it. A straight shot.

I opened my eyes and saw Darsey kneeled before me, looking amazed and enthralled. Uri had a similar look on his face even though he had seen me do it more often. I searched for Brantley and saw him oblivious to me, talking softly to Astraeus, which irritated me slightly.

"I know the way," I declared as I stood.

"What's it like?" Darsey asked in wonder.

I smiled at him sheepishly and opened my mouth to speak, but Brantley cut me off.

"She can tell you later. We need to go," as the star dust around his feet mounded up beneath him and made it easy for him to mount Astraeus.

I smiled at Darsey reassuringly, then faced Starla and the dust did the same for me, though my balance was thrown off by the sudden movement. I fell forward across her back and as the mound began to shrink away, I quickly threw my leg over her and almost fell off the other side. She stayed completely still, showing immense strength. I gripped her mane, and immediately felt bad for it, afraid I hurt her. I clumsily adjusted until I was sitting atop her back, and I was surprised that dragons seemed easier to ride than horses.

I looked over and saw Darsey was having as much difficulty as I was.

Uri climbed from my shoulder to my satchel. *"Can I ride in there?"* he asked nervously.

I smiled and held open the flap for him and he quickly disappeared inside. I let the flap fall and looked at Darsey again. He was finally atop Cosmo, looking nervous. He smiled at me goofily, then seemed as though he were about to lose his balance despite not moving.

"Okay. . ." Brantley said, and I saw him staring, his expression seeming embarrassed for us. "So, you've never ridden, I take?"

I shook my head, and quickly added, "Only dragons."

"And it is for that reason I won't fault you for this. You will be pleased to know that star-runners are much easier to ride than regular horses. It's nearly impossible to fall from them or be thrown unless they want you to be, or if they go to sleep with you atop them.

"You grab them by the mane, don't worry, it doesn't hurt, and you lean forward near their neck." He demonstrated, then continued. "You hold with your thighs and knees, though it isn't really necessary on nights of the new moon." He looked up at the sky and back at us. "When you have had your star-runner for many moons, you will learn how to connect with them. The stars will begin to trust you. You will be able to be one in mind with them. For now, however, you need to tell them the direction you wish to go." He sat up and looked at Darsey. "We are following her. We will be moving very fast, so make sure Cosmo knows to only follow Starla."

He looked back at me and said, "Say their names often. Introduce them to everyone. Their names are the only reason the stars are allowing them to stay, and if they forget their names, the stars will take them back."

I nodded and rubbed the side of her neck. "Okay, Starla," I said. "Are you ready to go?"

She whinnied, making me jump, and bobbed her head excitedly.

I gripped her mane and leaned in close to her neck. I tightened my grip with my knees and thighs and said, "Um . . . can you take us out of here?"

She whinnied again and lurched forward. To my surprise, it felt as natural as if I had decided to run myself. She began galloping around the bottom of the cistern near the wall, a barrier of light protectively cloaked around us. I felt nothing except her movement beneath me. No wind, no pressure, not even an imbalance from her movements. Uri poked his head from the satchel and said, *"This isn't bad at all!"*

He was so comfortable, he came out of the satchel and climbed back up to my neck. Starla steadily picked up speed, and I twisted around and saw Darsey and Brantley very near our flank. They, too, looked relaxed and Darsey smiled and waved at me from Cosmo.

I waved back and then was surprised that Starla broke from the wall and seamlessly began running back up the spiral ramp. Once we reached the top of the cistern, she leaped from the edge and giant wings of star dust erupted into existence at her sides. We glided down on the outside of the cistern, gentle and slow, then landed lightly and the wings melted away.

She stopped after a few more steps and I turned to see Brantley and Darsey landing in the same way. I watched as their wings melted away and Darsey and I both cheered and laughed when they stopped.

"They're showing off," Brantley said, unable to hide his smile.

"Let's see what else they can do!" Darsey shouted.

"If they do anything along the way, you will," Brantley said. "Adalee, go. We've wasted enough of the new moon already."

I nodded and smiled at Darsey one more time before I turned and lowered myself to Starla's neck. "Starla," I whispered. "It's a straight line that way," I said as I pointed.

She took off and I was amazed and relieved at our speed. The shield that wrapped around us both, making me one with her, was incredible. The rocks moved past us at the same speed as they did in my meditation. I was unsure what Brantley's lesson on riding was for. I could let go and stretch my arms above my head, which I did many times during the night, and not budge from my place.

Starla was smooth and graceful. If not for the passing land outside of the glowing shield, it would have felt like we weren't moving at all. I looked around often and saw Darsey and Brantley close behind.

Brantley was always rubbing Astraeus's neck and speaking to him, though I couldn't hear his words. Darsey was always playing around with the shield. Pushing his hands against it, stretching his legs out, trying to see what would happen if he leaned back. He seemed to be having a wonderful time, and I decided throughout the night that I should talk to Starla.

I told her what a good job she was doing, and how smoothly she ran. I used her name often and rubbed her neck like Brantley did for Astraeus. I talked to her about how I hoped she liked the name I chose for her.

I didn't hear much from Uri, so I assumed he had fallen asleep, or Gavyn couldn't keep up for us to keep our connection open, which made me feel a mixture of relief and angst. It would be okay if Gavyn disappeared and didn't come back, as I didn't trust him, however I really loved being able to communicate with Uri and didn't want to go back to silence and swooning.

The night passed quickly, and I never ran out of things to talk about with Starla. I told her about who I was and what we needed her help with. I told her about how I freed the first Dragon Lord and all that he said to me. I told her about how I had accidentally sent Astraeus back to the stars, but that I would be careful not to do the same to her.

She began to slow down and eventually stopped, not even winded, at the edge of the desert. Exactly where the Blue Dragon Lord continually led me in my meditations.

"That's it for tonight," Brantley said as he pulled up beside me and dismounted.

I slid from Starla's back easier than I had mounted, and Brantley grabbed my elbow to steady me as I landed.

Darsey pulled up suddenly and dismounted easily, though not as gracefully as Brantley.

I pulled my elbow away and laid my hand on Starla's back. I didn't question why we were done for the night, because

I honestly didn't know where to go, or what to do next. This was where the Blue Dragon Lord had always brought me.

"Why are we done?" Darsey asked, full of life. "Let's keep going! This is amazing! Cosmo is incredible!"

"The sky is edging on dawn," Brantley explained.

I looked up at the night sky that was not as deep blue as it had been moments before, and the stars were beginning to fade. With them, the glow around Starla faded as well.

"What's happening?" I asked, panic streaking through me. "What's happening to her?"

"Cosmo?" Darsey asked, catching my panic. "Are you okay, buddy?"

Brantley reached up and stroked Astraeus's muzzle and said, "Relax. They're just going to sleep for the day."

I calmed and nodded. "Okay, good," I said, relieved. "You go to sleep then," I whispered to Starla. "I'll be here when you wake."

"You'll be the one to wake her," Brantley said as he turned and said his goodnights to Astraeus.

Darsey was also saying goodnight when I turned back to Starla. The sky was a pale blue, and the horizon beyond the sand glowed a warm orange. We were standing at the precipice where stony ground gave full way to sand. I looked behind us and realized that as the wind blew the sand across the ground, it fell between the rocks and disappeared. I wondered briefly where it went and marveled at the stark difference between the grey slate and golden sand.

With my hand still on Starla's neck, I looked out over the new terrain before us. Meditation had brought me no further than where we were.

What now?

How could the Blue Dragon Lord be trapped in water when this was nowhere near water?

The sun broke over the horizon and Starla disappeared beneath my hand into a pile of star dust that quickly blew away.

It happened too fast! I spun and faced where the dust had blown and cried out her name in terror.

"Adalee," Brantley snapped, and I looked at him, tears of shock welling up in my eyes. "She's fine," he said quickly, pointing to the ground.

I looked where he motioned and saw a perfectly clear little orb resting atop the sand. I let out a relieved sigh and Darsey said, "Wow! Is that what they look like when they sleep?"

"It is," Brantley answered. "Catch."

I looked up just as he tossed me some vines. They landed lightly against my chest and I grabbed them before they fell. "What is this for?" I asked.

"We're going to make some jewelry," he said with a smile.

"The mossy vines will protect the orbs!" Darsey said excitedly as he sat and began going through his materials.

"Until we can get something more suitable, yes," Brantley confirmed as he went to work with his vines.

I looked at my vines in confusion and asked, "Where did you get these?"

He cocked his brow and said, "Some of us plan ahead."

"We've been out of the forest for weeks," I wondered aloud.

"And while you two lazed about every night, I stayed awake and made preparations."

Darsey turned, light-heartedness still in his voice, and said, "You and I *both* stood guard in the night."

"With your attention so divided by the blasted fairy, I could hardly relax on your watch."

Darsey rolled his eyes and turned back to his work.

I gently picked up Starla's orb and examined it. It was perfectly clear, yet solid. Like a bubble that resisted the elements. It was about the size of a plum, and similar in weight. It was hard, like a piece of ice over a pool of water in winter, only not cold.

"You can stare at it all day, but I recommend you make something quickly so we can get some sleep," Brantley pulled me from my thoughts.

I looked up at him, bewildered. I had forgotten they were even there while staring into Starla's orb.

"I'm finished, I can do yours if you like," Darsey suggested with a smile.

I smiled back and nodded, handing him my vines. I watched him work and protectively cradled Starla's orb against my body. Cosmo's orb was attached around Darsey's wrist and I watched as he quickly twisted and braided the vines finely, as though he was bred to do it. He held out his hand for Starla's orb and I gently handed it over. He slipped her into the center of the cradle and wrapped the vines up around the top, fastening her in securely.

"She'll sleep well in that," he said with a smile as he handed her back.

I tried to tie the loose vines around my neck, and soon found they weren't long enough. I copied Darsey and secured her around my wrist.

Brantley stood and began setting up his tent. "Get some rest. We have a few days yet."

I didn't understand his meaning, but I wasn't worried about it either. He had no idea where we were going so what business did he have deciding how long it would take to get there? *I* was the map, after all.

I helped Darsey set up his tent and we tied up the flaps so air could travel through. Brantley warned us that the days in the desert would be sweltering, and we needed to try and keep cool while we slept. After it was set up and we ate and drank enough to satisfy our needs, we laid on the ground. Laying on a mat on the sand was much more comfortable than laying on rock and I was excited about the rest I was going to get.

Darsey fell asleep quickly and I settled in, Uri purring on my neck.

*"I really like her,"* he said.

I was surprised to hear his voice since he had been so quiet the whole night. That meant Gavyn *was* nearby. How fast could a Falcone fly?

"I'm glad you do," I whispered.

*"I think she likes us too,"* he added.

His observation made me swell with glee. "Really?" I asked. Then I remembered that they could understand all languages, and I wondered if Uri could speak to her. "Did she say that?" I asked, hopeful.

*"No,"* he said as he yawned and stretched. *"Well, she might have,"* he amended. *"She talks funny."*

I looked at him and asked, "Talks funny? What do you mean?"

*"Her words are like . . . sounds. Her voice is really pretty, and her words sound like wind. And water. And rain. But, I think she likes us."*

I smiled and rubbed his neck. "I bet you're right," I said, trying to imagine what her voice sounded like.

Then I yawned and stretched my arms above my head, letting them rest where they laid, and closed my eyes. I was exhausted.

I walked through the darkness toward something familiar. The only thing reaching my senses. No sounds, nothing beneath my feet, no movement in the air, and only one vision in my sight.

That tree.

I missed them. Too many days of staring at rocks. Now only sand waiting before me.

And yet, there it was. A tree.

But not one I was used to. I reached it and looked upon the bark. Instead of lines etched gently throughout the trunk, like dry, cracked ground, it was rippled and thick. Large pieces stacked upon large pieces. Some fanned out, some held close.

I stared up at the tree, gently laying my hand on the bark, and saw the trunk standing tall and thin. No branches. Just singular strength. A large, knotted pod settled atop it, and a couple dozen leaves spread out from the pod, sprouting firmly and boldly. Between the leaves were more pods that flowed out from the center and sank beneath their weight.

A trickling sound began dancing all around me, and I slowly turned, as though I was moving through water. The darkness opened up to reveal many pools of different colors. They seemed to be fed only from themselves, as each pool had its own cascading stones that continually poured forth the color that engulfed and illuminated the water. Like magic.

I stepped away from the tree and moved toward an orange pool. I peered into it and saw Madame's face.

I gasped and stepped back, stumbling into shallow green waters. The green pool sucked me in and for a moment, I felt as though I were once again riding upon the Red Dragon Lord.

I was quickly thrown from the pool and landed roughly on the sand. I stood and spun around, trying to wipe the water from my already dry hair and skin. Everything returned to black, except for a new vision in the distance. A dragon.

I calmed. It was a Calling dream. Of course.

I approached the Dragon Lord slowly, prepared to greet her and discover where she wanted to lead me. As I neared, her vibrant blue tint turned to an ashy grey. I slowed my gait as she continued to morph until she looked completely different than in my meditations.

I stopped a little way off and stared. The dragon shook her head and when she slowed, even her feminine features were replaced with bony, masculine details that spread out from the sides of *his* face. Who was this? It wasn't the Blue Dragon Lord.

Beyond him, the blackness began to shimmer and move, like a puddle catching light. He was guarding another pool. A dark one.

I continued my approach. Was I being Called by another Dragon Lord before rescuing the Blue Dragon Lord? How desperate were they becoming? Did our trek to get star-runners put the quest in peril? I needed to move faster.

I stopped a few feet from the new Dragon Lord and looked beyond him. The pool was serene and still. So dark I couldn't make out the color. I took a step toward it, and the Dragon Lord stepped in front of me. I looked up at him, and he stared down, a snarl forming around his mouth, showing rows of dangerous and threatening teeth.

I backed up, and he closed his mouth.

I mustered up my courage and asked, "Where is the Blue Dragon Lord? Who are you?"

My eyes shot open, and I didn't know why. Did the Dragon Lord wake me because he didn't like my question? The tent was bright orange with the power of the sun beating down on it from the highest point in the sky. There were many hours left before nightfall.

"Hey," Darsey said softly beside me.

I rolled toward him and realized I was drenched in sweat. "Wow," I breathed out softly as I took in the heat that was pushing in around me.

"Yeah," he agreed in as exasperated a voice.

I sat up and looked around for Uri. He was sprawled out near the edge of the tent, taking in as much of the breeze as he could, though only hot air was blowing through.

"Sorry to wake you," Darsey whispered. "I just . . . I couldn't sleep and I really wanted to get a chance to talk to you. You know, *without* Brantley listening in."

I wiped the sweat from my brow and shook my cloak off. "Yeah, me too," I agreed.

"A lot has happened," he said, looking down.

I nodded. "It has."

"What you did back there . . . just before the pimeys came . . . it was amazing."

I shook my head and said, "I didn't do anything. They got us. They took the fairies."

"No," he said firmly. "You *did* do something. You showed a part of yourself I always knew was there. You *protected*."

"I tried," I said with an ironic laugh.

Darsey's face darkened and he whispered, "What was his problem? He almost got us killed."

The memory of Brantley knocking the blade from my hand played over in my head and I tried to brush it off. "He was afraid a fight would scare the stars away. He thought the star-runners might not descend."

Darsey shook his head and looked at the orb around his wrist. "I suppose it worked out, either way. Just know if he does something like that again, he'll taste the bite of my blade."

I wanted to get his attention off Brantley. I didn't want him obsessing over him and doing something foolish.

Before I could think of anything to say, he looked at me and asked, "Do you think Plume is okay?"

His question surprised me and I cocked my head. "Are you worried about her?"

"I don't want to be," he defended. "I hate her for what she did to you. How she just threw you to the pimeys."

He looked down and began fidgeting with his fingers as though he was worried about what he was about to say. "Every time I sleep, I *see* her."

Pity and concern stabbed at me and I reached out to comfort him but stopped and pulled my hand back. I could feel tears wanting to well up and I fought against them.

He really did care about Plume. And I was beginning to feel like, had she not taken off so quickly, he *might* have gone with her.

"I see her throwing you to the pimeys, and I strike her down," he growled.

Then I realized his feelings were more vengeful than remorseful.

"Then I wake up," he continued. "And I feel *guilty*," he said as though the emotion confused him.

Then he shook his head and put his face in his hands. "That's why I feel so bad about caring what happens to her. I feel like, if I don't hate her, then I'm against you. But, hating her *hurts*."

I scooted closer and put my hand on his shoulder. "You don't have to hate her," I said softly. "You don't have to choose. She made her choice and left without us. She was never going past this point with us. She had her quest, and we have ours. We helped each other. We got her a star-runner and she made me see how strong I can be."

He looked up at me with tears in his eyes and nodded.

I took a deep breath and continued, "Being with her made you different. It made you more like . . ." I hesitated to say what I was thinking, because I didn't want to hurt him.

"More like how I was before Surin," he finished my thought.

I looked away.

He shook his head and said, "I was able to talk to her. And it isn't anything about you," he defended. "It's just . . . it was a release to be able to talk to someone who didn't know me. Who wasn't trying to fix me."

I cringed.

"Who just let me talk. I was able to tell her *everything*. For some reason I felt I could really open up to her. And now I don't even get to repay her for it. Instead, I wanted to kill her for what she did. Then I ignored her and treated her poorly. And, just like that, she's gone. I don't have a chance to apologize to her. To thank her for helping me feel like I can be me again. I did her such a disservice."

What all had he told her? If she cared about him so much, why did she treat Uri and I so terribly. How could I help him see how not okay that was?

"What did you say about us?" I asked.

He looked at me, eyes wide. "Everything," he said softly. "More than everything. I told her things I never thought I'd say. . .."

"Good things?" I whispered.

He looked up at me, shocked. "I only have good things to say about us."

I sighed in relief and nodded. "So, she knew how you felt about me, and she still threw me to the pimeys."

I let the statement sink in and he tightened his lips, furrowed his brow, and nodded. "You're right," he said. Then he smiled at me and added, "I feel better."

"You don't still wish you could tell her all those things?"

He shook his head. "No. What she did was wrong, and she did it knowing how it would hurt me. I think everything is as it should be."

I smiled and nodded. "Me too."

He took a deep breath and lifted his head, resting it in his hands. "I think I can sleep now."

I leaned over him and touched my forehead to his, closing my eyes. It was bold, but I wanted him to know I was there for him. That I would always be there.

He moved and I sat up a little as he lightly stroked my chin.

I smiled and said, "Goodnight . . . or . . . good day?"

He laughed and said, "Good day," then he rolled away from me toward the open flap, facing the desert.

I laid down and scooted over until my back was against his. Just close enough to feel comfort. It didn't take long to fall back to sleep, which was good because I needed to find out who the new Dragon Lord was.

# Nine | Only a Legend

"How far do we have?" Brantley asked as we packed up our tents.

Dusk was coming quickly, and we were preparing to wake our star-runners.

"I'm not sure," I admitted. "I did have a new dream last night, so that might give us some answers."

Uri, who was perched on my shoulder, purred and butted my head lovingly. I smiled and scratched him behind the ears.

"Okay, I don't care about all that. Just tell me how far we need to go."

"What's your problem?" Darsey asked, stepping up to him.

"It's fine," I said, loudly. I was surprised at how quickly everyone's happy moods had dissipated since the night before, and I hoped with the waking of the star-runners, they would return. "He doesn't have to care. Let me meditate so I can have some answers."

"You don't answer to him," Darsey reminded me. "*He* is helping *us,* remember?"

"I'm keeping you two alive, *remember*?" Brantley challenged, sounding more irritated than I felt he should.

"Just do your job and follow the Dragon Born," Darsey said condescendingly.

"The only thing I'm doing here, is making sure we make it. And by 'we', I mean Adalee and myself. *You* are not an important part of this trek, and I beg you to not forget it."

Darsey's fists balled up and I quickly stepped in. "Fighting won't get us anywhere," I pointed out.

"Aye lass, you're right on that point," Brantley agreed. "Call the lad down, and we'll get on with it."

"Darsey," I said softly.

Without looking away from Brantley he said, "*I* respect her authority, so I will do as she asks."

"That's well and fine, lad, just do it from a distance. Away from me."

Darsey took a moment to step away, while Brantley never showed any signs of unease at the challenge, which made me nervous.

Once I felt nothing more was going to happen, I sat down and closed my eyes, taking a deep breath. Uri hopped down and stepped away.

I was full, hydrated, rested, and ready for answers. Upon exhale, I let my concerns come to the forefront of my mind so I could push each one aside.

Darsey and Brantley's constant bickering was the most obvious one to me. It would be easier for me if they got along, but for the moment, I pushed it away.

More concerning was that the next Dragon Lord was already emerging and beginning to Call. The Blue Dragon Lord had yet to be rescued, and my dreams offered no answers. I hoped I would figure something out in the meditations.

The last worry I focused on pushing away was Brantley's disregard for my leadership, only to realize it was no longer a problem. He *was* following me. He wasn't trying to take over like when we were seeking the star-runners.

*You're a fool if you think he isn't in control of this quest,* Madame sneered.

I stiffened, trying desperately to maintain the calm I had created as she continued.

*What about your lie? Hm? Do you honestly believe he is playing into it because he is loyal to you?*

A touch of angst shot through me, and I battled against it, not wanting her to be right. I took another deep breath and slowly released it, determined to get rid of her without a verbal shout like the last time.

*He wants something. He expects something. Just wait. The moment you do something he doesn't like he'll use it to force you into submission. You are his slave now,* she laughed.

Sweat beaded down the back of my neck despite the cool air that now rushed over the sand.

She was right. He *would* use it to control me. How could I combat that? I couldn't tell Darsey the truth. Not now. I finally had him back.

I shook my head and decided those worries could wait. Then, with another deep breath, I pushed down all my concerns with Brantley, and focused on the meditation.

I pictured myself where I sat. The darkening sky, vast sand, and cool breeze that Brantley said would turn freezing once night fully fell.

Slowly, everything else disappeared. Then, the sand turned into bubbles that frothed up on gentle waves. The Blue Dragon Lord appeared and swirled around me. She lifted me up and I grabbed on to the back of her head as we swam through the desert.

It felt like I was entering a new world beyond all that I knew. She had shown me the way to the edge of the desert many times, and finally we had entered it. I was both excited and anxious to see how much farther we had to go and hoped I would get answers about the other Dragon Lord in my dreams.

We continued over the sand with nothing to see that differentiated one place from the next. It was just miles upon miles of dunes and sand with an occasional shift in direction. Then, once we rose to the top of one of the dunes, before us was miles and miles of colorful sands.

I leaned forward, shocked at the sight. We continued down the dune and into the rainbow sands until, after not too long, we came upon a tropical oasis that rested at the bottom of an unanticipated, colorful mountain. The mountain was not as tall as the ones where I lived, though it was quite broad. She continued into the oasis and stopped at the center of six pools.

Colored pools. Just like my dream.

She burst into bubbles that gently lowered me to the ground. Before I could take any more in, I felt myself being thrown to the ground.

"I warned you!" Brantley shouted at Darsey.

I jumped up, having been yanked from my meditation, and shouted at them. "What happened?"

*"They got mad again!"* Uri shouted, rushing over to me.

"*He* wants to fight," Brantley said, irritated.

I looked at Darsey and he was breathing heavily. The side of his face was covered in sand and I realized he had crashed into me. "Why?" I asked, pleading.

He took a deep breath and retrieved his sword from the ground. "I'm sorry," he said. "He just doesn't respect you, and I can't stand it."

"He doesn't respect *anyone*," I said. "Don't get upset. I don't respect him either and it's fine. We just need to endure it for a little longer."

"Some choice the Dragon Lords made," Darsey mumbled, and I quickly spun on him.

"Don't speak ill of the Dragon Lords," I warned. I didn't know how much they could see or witness from me. I had no idea what kind of connection the Essence created, and I didn't want Darsey being blasphemous because of my lie.

"I'm sorry," he sincerely apologized. "I'll . . . try to let things be."

"Enough," Brantley snapped, raking his fingers through his disheveled hair. "What did you see?"

I held eye contact with Darsey until he visibly calmed. I turned to Brantley and said, "We will travel through the desert for many miles. Then we will come upon more miles of sands of many colors. Once we enter that part of the desert, we will find an oasis—"

"With colored pools of water?" Brantley asked, a surprising anger in his voice.

I was taken aback, and it took me a moment to regain my composure. "You've been there," I whispered.

"No, I haven't," he said firmly. "*No one* has."

"Then how do you know of it?" Darsey challenged.

"You've never heard of the Rainbow Sands of Aljonnah?" Brantley asked skeptically.

"Should we have heard of it?" I asked.

"I suppose not," he said, calming slightly. "It's desert lore. I heard of it in my travels when I neared the desert the first time." He looked at me and clarified, "To come find you."

My heart skipped anxiously, and I glanced at Darsey who looked confused.

Brantley continued, "The people who dwell near the desert warn travelers not to cross. Not because of the dangers of the desert, which are perilous enough, but because they may happen upon the Rainbow Sands, and be lost forever."

"It's a good thing Adalee is a human map then," Darsey declared, laying his hand on my shoulder.

"Not lost like that," Brantley continued. "They say there are a people there. People who will kill any who happen upon Aljonnah."

"That is where the Dragon Lord is leading us," I argued. "We can't ignore her."

"We won't," he shouted, then rubbed his face. "I'm not saying we shouldn't go. I'm just saying we need to be ready. The people who warned me were . . . dark. A little darker than you," he said, motioning toward Darsey. "Even they say the people of Aljonnah are as dark as night. That you can't see them coming. Some don't believe they are people at all, but wraiths of shadow."

"Like pimeys?" Darsey asked, intrigued.

"Maybe," he agreed.

"I can fight off pimeys," I said, though I didn't feel very confident in the statement. How would I protect everyone if they *were* pimeys?

"Not if we don't get there. How long will it take?" Brantley asked.

"We should be there by morning," I said confidently. The Dragon Lord seemed to carry me at a pace the star-runners could match.

"Good," Brantley said, relieved. He looked up at the darkened sky and said, "Enough stars are out. We can wake the star-runners."

"Yes!" Darsey exclaimed, pulling the orb from his wrist and holding it close. "Wake up, buddy," he said.

I remembered the first time I had seen Astraeus, and I leaned close to Darsey and whispered, "I don't think it works like that."

Brantley laid Astraeus's orb on the ground and opened the canteen he had filled with stardust. He touched the tip of his finger to the glowing dust and tapped the top of the orb.

He quickly stepped back as the dust multiplied upon itself, springing up from the orb with newfound freedom. It piled higher and higher, then spread across the sand, taking the shape of a horse. Once the shape was fully sculpted, Astraeus stood up and shook off the extra dust, revealing his milky white coat.

Darsey was already doing what he had seen Brantley do, and I set Starla down to do the same. I carefully opened my canteen and marveled at the treasure inside. As he had done, I dipped my finger into it.

I expected it to feel warm. Instead my finger was met with a chilled, soft, sand-like texture. It was pleasant to touch, as the rest of me was covered in a sheen of sweat from the day. I gently caressed Starla's orb and quickly put the canteen away as she awoke, exactly as Astraeus had.

Uri stayed as near her as he could, jumping away just before any of the stardust could touch him.

When she stood, I watched as the stardust disappeared before it hit the ground, and immediately touched her soft mane.

I rubbed my hand over her back and spoke gently to her. "Good morning, Starla. How did you sleep?"

She whinnied and Uri climbed to my shoulder. *"I'm ready to get going!"* he said excitedly.

I loved touching her coat. I imagined it felt similar to a cloud.

Darsey's laughter caught my ear and I turned to see Cosmo nosing around his chest and arms, grunting. He knocked him over and began smelling all over him, and I let a little laugh slip out.

"Hurry up," Brantley shouted. "We need to get moving."

Madame was right. Brantley was trying to take control of this part of the trek as well, even though *I* was the only one who knew where we were going. I had let him lead us to the star-runners because he was the only one who knew the way. Now it was *my* time to lead. *I* was the Dragon Born.

I was torn from my thoughts as a mound of stardust formed at my feet and lifted me to Starla's back. I held on and positioned myself easier than before and sat up tall, proud of my grace.

"Lead the way, Dragon Born," Darsey shouted once he was atop Cosmo.

I smiled wide at his declaration of my leadership and laughed at his theatrical performance. Then I leaned forward near Starla's head and pointed where the Blue Dragon Lord had taken me. "That way, Starla."

She neighed and darted forward, though I felt none of the movement, just like the night before. I was also relieved that the blatant chill in the air disappeared once we were moving and I was surrounded by her shield. The other two fell in line behind me and I paid close attention to the path ahead, though I was unsure of exactly where the Dragon Lord had curved and turned.

I felt as lost as I was when Uri and I had headed up the mountain alone after the Red Dragon Lord had shown me the way. How could I memorize the path when everything looked the same?

Dunes and ridges surrounded us, endlessly sprawling across the golden sands that presented black in the night. How was I to know where we were going when there were no landmarks to guide us?

Yet, I carried on through the night. I couldn't let Brantley know I was unsure, lest he take the quest from me by force. He was already overcome with a sense of superiority proven by his blatant mention of coming to find me.

I had told Darsey he was chosen because he was in the right place at the right time, and now he had given me something I had to explain away.

*An accident,* Madame sneered.

I ignored her snide remark and focused on my task. Everyone was depending on me. I knew Starla and I could find the rainbow sands. At least, I thought we could. Then the stars began to fade.

Brantley pulled up before me and Starla slid to a stop, bobbing her head.

He dismounted and dragged me off Starla by the arm. While I shouted at him to release me Darsey ran up on him and Cosmo neighed in his face. He let go and stumbled back, bumping into Astraeus, who was there to catch him.

I fell to the ground, quickly recovering as Darsey dismounted and drew his sword. "You don't touch her!" he shouted, fury in his voice.

Brantley drew his sword and swung it at Darsey. The blades struck and sent sparks through the air. They froze with their blades crossed, glaring at one another.

I jumped in the middle and pushed Darsey back. "Stop it," I demanded. Then I spun on Brantley and asked, "What is your problem? You've been angry ever since we got the star-runners. You keep trying to be in charge and take over even though you have no idea where we're going! Only *I* do!"

He growled and sheathed his sword. "Do you?" he spat. "Because you said we would be there by now and we're not!"

"Who cares?" Darsey shouted. "What matter is it to you how long it takes?"

He grabbed the water canteen from his side and held it up. "This! This is what matters! We are deep in the desert and what we have in these canteens is *all* we have left!"

The realization that we were low on supplies dawned on me for the first time. I hadn't even thought of water since I got Starla. The star-runners didn't need food or drink, and neither did Uri, so I had been happily indulging in my supplies, too distracted to notice how low they were.

"She'll get us there!" Darsey shouted back. "And if we need to, she can take us *out* of the desert so we can get more water, then bring us back in. We have *star-runners*. Time belongs to us!"

I felt relieved at Darsey's comment. It wasn't over. He was right. Time was on our side so long as we had the star-runners.

"You don't know anything," Brantley snapped, tying his canteen back to his side and brushing his hair from his face. "This is the last night of the new moon. The star-runners will slowly begin losing their power until they are like normal horses."

"What?" I asked, stepping up and grabbing Starla's muzzle. "They only have their powers for a few nights?"

"During each new moon, when the stars are the brightest," he confirmed.

"Will they be okay?" Darsey asked, sheathing his sword and stroking Cosmo's forehead.

"You're not focusing on what's important!" he shouted. "*They* will be fine. *We* might not be. If we don't get to the oasis tomorrow, we may not make it through another day."

*"Are we going to die?"* Uri asked innocently.

"No," I said, firmly. I was only speaking to Uri, but all eyes fell on me. They were looking to me as their leader, and I needed to lead, even if I didn't know how. We would have been there had the desert not been so hard to navigate. However, as I met their expectant eyes, I knew I had to say something. Give them something to hold onto.

I shook my head and said, "We *will* make it tomorrow. I just misjudged how far we had to go. We're on the right path and tomorrow you will see."

"I hope you're right," Brantley said as he walked past me and began setting up his tent.

"Of course, she's right!" Darsey said with a smile, laying his hand on my shoulder. "I know you'll get us there," he assured me. Then he turned and began erecting our tent.

Truly, I had no idea if I was right or not. I didn't know where we were, how far we had gone into the desert, or how much farther we needed to go. And now my nearly empty canteen battered against my side like an omen.

*He will try to take control* Madame said. *You know he will.*

I knew she was right. If I didn't get us there, he *would* try to take over. And, though it shouldn't matter how we got there, so long as we did, I feared for what the Blue Dragon Lord might say if one other than myself was the reason she was freed.

Would she take the Essence from me and pass it to him?

*You're starting to see what I tried to tell you all along,* Madame goaded.

I shook my head, silently disagreeing with her.

*Yes,* she continued. *That you are unworthy of the Essence. Even a common soldier from a foreign land is more worthy than you.*

I quickly walked away from the group about ten paces and stared off over the horizon. I couldn't let her get to me, and I didn't want them to see my struggle.

"Adalee?" Darsey called. I held my hand up toward him without turning, begging him to let me be.

"I am worthy," I whispered.

She scoffed.

"I *am,*" I pressed.

She needn't say anything for me to picture her condescending smirk. And I loathed it. She was wrong. I wouldn't let him take over because I *was* worthy. The Dragon Lords chose me. For whatever reason, they chose *me.*

The first rays of light shined into my eyes from over the horizon and I turned away quickly, shielding my face. The star-runners erupted into dust, leaving behind their little orbs. Brantley and Darsey were retrieving their orbs while Uri tried to catch stardust before it completely disappeared.

I quietly picked up Starla and secured her to my wrist. They returned to making camp and I helped Darsey set up our tent. I saw my blade securely fastened beside his sword, and I suddenly wished I could carry it like a normal weapon, without the threat of turning anyone to ash with my touch.

*How can you call yourself worthy when you lament the gifts bestowed upon you by the Dragons?* Madame scoffed.

I shook my head, trying to push her out, while Darsey shared his idea of how we could change the directions of the flaps to maybe keep the sand from coating us while we slept as it had the day before. I silently nodded and helped him bring the vision to life. It would offer shade and hopefully more shelter while we slept.

I laid my cloak out to sleep on, as it was too hot to wear, and Uri pranced into the tent happily, settling himself upon the cloak and attempting to groom the sand from his fur.

Afraid that my silence would be an invitation for more of Madame's pestering's, I asked Uri, "Did you enjoy last night?"

"It was great!" Darsey exclaimed as he laid his cloak out. "Cosmo is incredible. He has such a personality!"

I must have had a look on my face, because when Darsey looked at me, smiling wide, I noticed him blush and look away. "You weren't talking to me, were you?" he asked, sheepishly.

I smiled and said, "That's okay. Keep going."

He shook his head and laughed softly. "I don't know how long it will take me to get used to you and Uri talking."

I nodded. "I know. I was surprised at how easily I fell into the habit of just speaking with him. Like it was second nature. Often, I forget there was ever a time we couldn't talk. And even though I don't trust Gavyn, I suppose his presence is good for something."

"Gavyn?" Darsey asked, confused.

"The Falcone," I reminded him.

"Right," he said with understanding. "I keep forgetting it has a name."

I closed up my canteen and began to put it away.

"You didn't drink enough," Darsey said in a low voice.

"I'm fine," I said.

"No," he said as he shook his head. "Don't let Brantley scare you. I trust you. Drink what you need so you can focus. If you run out, you can have mine."

"You need water too. Don't worry. I'm fine," I lied. My throat was a little dry, and I could have easily finished the canteen in a few thirsty gulps, and despite what I had said, I wasn't positive we would make it the next night. I had no idea where we were.

Darsey, stubborn as always, laid his canteen beside me and said, "I'm not thirsty. It's there if you need it." Then he rolled over and prepared to sleep. "And just so you know, Brantley isn't as great as you, or the Dragon Lords, think he is."

"I don't think he's great," I said firmly. "I don't like him any more than you do."

"You seem to trust him, though."

"I trust his skills," I specified. "That isn't the same as trusting him."

"His skills are lacking, though. He didn't prepare for a few days in the desert? We should have more water than this if he was worried."

"I don't fault him," I said, feeling guilty about taking so long to get us to the oasis.

Darsey sat up and turned toward me, looking hurt. "Why not? Why do you constantly defend him?" he asked.

I shook my head. "I'm not trying to defend him. He doesn't want to be here anymore than we want him here."

"Then why doesn't he leave? Let's be honest. Does he really seem like the type to obey the commands of a Dragon Lord? There's another reason he's here, and I don't trust it. He's no better than the shaman."

His reference to Madame and Brantley's similarities struck me and I recalled that the only reason he chose to trap me was because he thought I *was* Madame. Darsey wasn't far off the mark, but I didn't want him worrying about it more than he needed to.

He continued, "And what did he mean when he said, 'came to find you'? What am I missing?"

There it was. I quickly spilled the excuse I had come up with while riding through the night.

"I didn't know he was coming to find me. I thought it was coincidence he was there when the Dragon Lord bound him to me." I hated lying to him even more, especially since I knew Brantley had *something* to do with Madame, though I didn't know the details.

"You see?" Darsey asked. "He's a liar, and he's hiding something."

"What are you afraid he's going to do?" I asked, bewildered by his aggressive accusations.

"I don't know," he admitted. "I just feel like he doesn't have your best interest at heart like I do. I want to know what he's after. What he's *really* after."

"He won't hurt me," I said confidently.

Darsey looked at me as though I were speaking of a venomous snake. "You can't know that," he warned.

"I can," I said. "When he became immune to my fire, he also became incapable of harming *me*. We can't physically hurt each other."

Darsey sucked in a deep breath and nodded as he let it out. "That does make me feel better," he admitted.

"But," I added, hesitant to say more. "He *can* hurt *you*. So please, please, stop challenging him. Let me handle him."

"He thinks he's better than you," Darsey said, frustrated.

"And do you think rushing to defend my honor is going to change that?" I asked, gently. "*I* need to earn his respect on my own," I added. "You can't force him to respect me."

"You don't *need* his respect," Darsey rushed to say.

"Exactly!" I said. "So, who cares? Let him say what he wants. He can't hurt me. Let's free the Blue Dragon Lord so we can be done with him."

Darsey nodded slowly. "Okay. I'll back off. I still don't trust him or like him."

"I'm okay with that," I said.

He sighed and laid back down. It wasn't long before he was snoring softly.

Uri stretched, having finished his bath. *"I like her,"* he said, answering my earlier question. *"Why didn't you talk a lot last night?"*

"I was concentrating," I said softly. "I'm just trying to get us there."

*"You will. Darsey is right. You can do it."*

I smiled at him as he curled against my leg and closed his eyes. I was exhausted too, and wished I had the freedom to lay down and sleep.

Instead, I knew I needed to spend my time in meditation. If what Brantley said was true, and I believed it to be, then this was our last chance to get there.

Lest we die.

I was exhausted, and riding upon Starla seemed more taxing than the nights before. Either the shield wasn't as strong, or I grew weaker as I rode. Every gait and leap felt rougher and bumpier, though only barely, which was why I wasn't sure if it was because a sliver of the moon was peering through the darkness, or because I was only able to steal a couple of hours of sleep before nightfall.

The Blue Dragon Lord and I had spent the day in meditation. She had shown me, at least one-hundred times, the way to the oasis. I focused on every dune, curve, rise and fall on our way to the rainbow sands. I meditated until I was so exhausted, I couldn't see straight.

When I did sleep, I dreamed again of the colorful pools and the mystery Dragon Lord. He didn't speak to me. He only made sure I didn't approach his pool. I planned on seeking Darsey's insight once I knew we would live through the next day.

Though my rest was minimal, reaching the oasis would make it worth it. Everyone's life depended on where I lead them tonight.

I stayed hunched over Starla, focusing fiercely on the desert markings around us. A few times I realized we were off course, and quickly adjusted. I was unsure how many miles those times cost us, but Starla did very well listening to me. As the night wore on, my mind grew more and more muddled.

A few times my eyes drifted shut and I had to force them back open, only to realize we were off course again. It was still difficult to know exactly where to go, and as dawn drew closer, my confidence and optimism shriveled. The rainbow sands were nowhere in sight.

*And you thought you could do this,* Madame's voice whispered in my mind.

I tried to push her away.

*You got lucky with the Red Dragon Lord,* she persisted.

"It wasn't luck," I whispered back.

*You have allowed yourself to be distracted. Just like the fool you've always been.*

"You're the only one distracting me," I growled softly.

*Your failure only proves one thing,* she accused. *You believe Brantley to be worth following,* she said in disgust.

"He's following *me*," I pointed out.

*You followed him through the forest. You followed him to the star-runners. Perhaps the Dragon Lord is leading you to your doom so the Essence can pass on to someone who is capable of leading.*

I shook my head. I could see Brantley pulling up beside me on Astraeus.

"Don't let them stop us, Starla," I ordered, and she shot forward, jerking me back a little with the extra speed.

It took a moment longer for Brantley to catch back up and when I looked over, he was yelling something I couldn't hear beyond his barrier. I could see the anger in his eyes, and I didn't care to hear it. This was *my* mission, and *I* was in charge of when we stopped.

He tried to pull in front of me again, so Starla jumped sideways and continued running up a dune.

On my other side, Darsey and Cosmo appeared. I looked over and saw Darsey trying to talk to me though, just like Brantley, I couldn't hear him.

*They are fighting for control over you*, Madame laughed. *And you will let them. One way or another, you need someone to tell you what to do. Without me, one of them will win.*

"Keep going," I growled at Starla, and she didn't slow.

*"It's almost morning,"* Uri said.

*Even the beasts have reign over you*, Madame mocked.

"*I* decide when we stop!" I growled at Uri.

He didn't respond, and we fiercely pressed on. I would show them I could handle this quest.

Suddenly, Starla disappeared from beneath me and I slammed into the sand, painfully rolling and bouncing.

When I finally stopped, I laid still, my face to the sky. It was a soft blue. The sun was rising. I had been thrown. My mouth tasted of sandy blood, and I licked my lips, finding the culprit.

Slowly, I sat up on the side of the dune I had crashed upon. I was sure nothing was broken though I was sore, and every part of my body resonated with burns.

I looked around and saw Uri not too far away. Fear at the sight of his limp little body shot through me and I jumped up and stumbled to him.

"Uri!" I exclaimed as I fell to my knees and scooped him up. "Are you okay?"

He opened his eyes and looked up at me as I cradled him against my chest. *"Are* you *okay?"* he asked, sweetly.

I pulled him up to my face and kissed his whiskers. "I'm sorry," I whispered. "I should have listened."

*"Where's Starla?"* he asked, becoming alert and looking around, his ears perked forward.

I put him on my shoulder and stood, almost falling down the side of the hill. "Look for her orb."

"Why are you so stubborn!?" I heard Brantley shout from behind. I turned quickly and saw him stomping up the dune toward me. The side of his face was scraped and bleeding, and he was gripping one of his arms.

"What happened to you?" I asked.

The look of indignation on his face made me take a step back. *"You* happened to me!" he roared. "Astraeus threw me because you wouldn't stop! We're lucky to be alive! Do you have any idea how fast we were going?"

"No," I said meekly, as I realized he had continued with me, knowing he would be thrown.

"Neither do I," he shouted. "You could have killed us. Nay, you *have* killed us. Look around you! Do you see the rainbow sands or an oasis? Because I don't! Daylight is upon us, and we don't have enough water to make it anywhere from here. We have no steeds—"

"We just need to find them!" I countered.

"Even if we do, what good will they be for us during the day?"

His point settled upon me and I realized I had doomed us. They followed me, and I had led us to our deaths.

"Adalee!" I heard Darsey shout and both Brantley and I looked for where his voice resonated from. "Adalee!" he shouted again, closer this time.

I looked up toward the top of the dune and saw him standing there, waving down at me. "Adalee! Up here!"

Between my concern for Uri and Starla, and my argument with Brantley, I hadn't even realized Darsey had been missing. "Was he thrown, too?" I asked Brantley as I began running up the dune with the little strength I had left.

"We all were," he bit back, not far behind me.

I reached the top of the dune and threw my arms around Darsey's neck. "Are you okay? Are you hurt?" I asked.

He grabbed me by the chin and turned my face, looking out over the desert. "I knew you could do it," he whispered.

The sun beamed over the horizon, blinding me and causing me to shield my eyes. Once they adjusted, they widened in disbelief. Before us were the rainbow sands.

## Ten | Into the Rainbow Sands

Darsey leaped in the air, letting out a whooping cheer that made me jump, then join in.

"I knew you could do it!" he shouted, lifting me up. We fell upon one another to the sand and he grabbed his arm. "Ow, ow, ow," he complained through the smile that never left his face.

I stood and helped him up.

"You're bleeding," he pointed out and I wiped the blood from my chin.

"I'll be okay," I said. Then I turned to Brantley and asked, "Well? What do you have to say now?"

He closed his mouth and nodded. "Okay, you got us to rainbow sands." He paused before adding, "I didn't think you would."

"You should apologize to her," Darsey said with a smirk.

He acted as though he didn't hear Darsey and said, "We need to find our star-runners and head for the oasis. You said it wasn't far once we reached the rainbow sands, right?"

I nodded, though I wasn't sure how far it would be on foot.

"Good. We have to get there if we want to live."

"I thought you said the people of the rainbow sands will kill us?" Darsey asked in a goading tone.

Brantley took a deep breath and said, "So will the heat. I told you what I was told, and if the people *don't* kill us, they'll have water."

We searched the sands and, with Uri's help, found each of our star-runners, though we couldn't be sure whose was whose once we gathered them. We each chose one at random and attached them to our bracelets and began the descent across the rainbow sands.

My excitement was quickly replaced by exhaustion once we began walking. The sand gave way and slid beneath my feet, making each step more arduous than the last. The cool of the morning burned off within the first hour of our trek, and soon the sun beat down upon us like an unforgiving rain, though instead of drenching us in water, it saturated us with fire.

Uri was nestled within my hood for only a few moments after we began. Then he realized it was cooler to cling to my cloak, attempting to hide in shadows as we walked. Darsey and Brantley trailed behind me, trusting my guidance, and no one spoke. No doubt the long night had taken its toll on everyone, and as the day wore on, the severity of our situation settled in.

*Reaching the rainbow sands does nothing for you if you die in them,* Madame said lightly.

I didn't have the energy to argue back.

She continued with her occasional comments, which I forced myself to ignore.

By the time the sun rose overhead, leaving no room for shadow, my water was gone. And though the blood on my mouth and chin from the stumble had dried, new blood joined it as my parched lips cracked and split. I hadn't realized how quickly the desert could deplete your water supply, even after you had taken it into your body.

Though I craved a fresh breeze and longed to remove my cloak, Brantley had insisted the cloaks protected us from the sun. I feared he was right and felt I had no choice but to trust him. Even Darsey stayed cloaked.

The sun seemed suspended once it reached the highest point. Too long it hung there, mocking us. Watching our efforts. Awaiting our imminent failure.

What would come of our bodies if we died out there? I saw no animals to drag our carcasses away. There was no wind to blow the sands upon our bodies and bury us deep within the desert. We were in a cursed land that none dared to trek. The only witness to our demise was the unforgiving sun, punishing us for entering his domain. A place where he reigned, unrivaled. A place without shade. Without shadow.

I focused on my feet. Determined to put one foot in front of the other. They were slower now than when we had begun. Less sure.

The colors of the sand danced before my eyes in swirls and twirls of glee. Did it, too, await our death?

I tried to focus on the colors that shot across our path, stretching endlessly to either side. Colors that ran beside one another, barely mixing.

Red, black, yellow, green, purple, and orange. Strong and vibrant. The opposite of how I was feeling while trekking their paths.

I looked ahead, to see if the oasis was anywhere in sight. All I saw was Brantley, stumbling ahead of me. When had he taken my place as leader? I hadn't noticed.

My vision blurred and doubled. I shook my head slowly and looked back down, focusing on my feet. If the sand hadn't been so hot, I would have removed my sandals.

I looked up again and saw Brantley slowly grab his chest, then fall to his knees. My eyes had to be mistaken. I closed them tight and looked again, but my vision was so blurred all I could see was a dark spot on the sand ahead.

Slowly, I looked behind me and saw Darsey's last moments on his feet. He stumbled sideways, reaching out to futilely grasp something that wasn't there. Then he fell.

It couldn't be true. I hadn't doomed us. The wretched sun was tricking me, and I would not be duped by its ruse. I looked back down and tried to take another step as the sand gave way and everything swirled around me, leaving me nothing to stand on or grip. I landed on my back and shut my eyes against my enemy. He burned down upon me, punishing me for my foolishness. If only night would come.

Aches. Burns. Whispers.

My head throbbed. My side hurt. My shoulders pulled. My wrists stung. My legs burned. I couldn't feel my feet.

When I found the strength to open my eyes, I was laying upon the colorful sand. It was muted and dark. Did the sun leave us alive? Had the night come to our rescue?

Weakly, I tried to lift my head. The side of my neck retaliated with intense waves of pain that spread through my muscles and into my shoulders.

I dropped it back down, which did nothing to alleviate the agony, and an unruly moan escaped my dry throat and pushed past my cracked lips.

"Adalee?" I heard an unrecognizable, equally weak, voice beside me.

I wanted to twist and see who it was, though I dared not move again.

There was a shuffling on the sand, and a momentary breeze wafted to my dirty, matted hair. Then it was dark, and I wondered if in my exhaustion, I had closed my eyes.

Despite my urging, they refused to open again.

Then another breeze briefly settled upon me, and the light returned, gently illuminating the sand I laid on.

"Who are you?" a gruff voice I didn't recognize sounded from my other side.

I was too tired to respond. Too thirsty. Too nauseous.

Then the most welcoming voice I had ever heard graced my ears with, "So, you speak the mountain language?" And I knew, despite the pain it would cause, I had to see her to believe it.

I forced my head up, bracing against the pain and stared into the torch lit face of a scowling Serefina. She had come back. She and the Red Dragon Lord had come back to rescue us.

"Se-se—" I tried to say her name. I sucked in a deep breath and forced out, "Serefina." Once the word was out, my energy was spent, and my head landed on the sand with a thud.

I heard her suck in a breath and then speak quickly in a language I didn't recognize. A man's voice responded and after a moment, she grabbed me by the hair and forced my face up.

"How do you know that name?" she hissed.

The agony of having my head ripped up rendered me immobile, and I didn't understand what she was asking, even if I could have found my voice.

"You're hurting her!" an angry, raspy voice shouted from my left.

"Tell me," she repeated, her face close to mine.

When I couldn't respond, she let go and quickly left, taking the light with her.

I wanted to understand. I wanted to know why I was in so much pain. I wanted to know where I was, what had happened to everyone, and why Serefina was so angry.

A moment later, the light returned and my head was yanked up again. This time, she leaned over me, the torchlight reflecting off her eyes, and poured something down my throat.

It was cold and bitter, and I would have heaved it from my body if she hadn't wrapped her arms around me and held my mouth closed until I swallowed it.

When she finally released me, I started coughing and sputtering, though nothing came up, and my mind cleared. With my body still aching, I finally had the sense to take in my surroundings.

I was laying on my side with my arms bound behind my back and after a moment, I realized my wrists were strapped to my feet. Slowly, breathing became easier, and I found my voice.

"Serefina," I said. "Why am I bound?"

The torchlight moved and her face was before me again. "I am not Serefina," she said angrily. "And I will not be taken by your lies, Dragon Born."

Although my mind was clearer, I still didn't understand what was happening.

"What happened to you?" I asked, my voice still gruff. "Where is the Red Dragon Lord?"

She looked up at a man standing nearby, then back at me. "You will be silent, evil mistress of the Dragons," she hissed.

"You will show the Dragon Born respect!" an angry voice sounded from my left. I forced my head up and saw a very exhausted and burned Darsey. His face was blistered, covered in dried blood, and swollen, with a fire blazing in his eyes as he glared at her.

"You mark your fate by dishonoring the Child of Essence," another, equally gruff voice came from the other side. I looked over and saw Brantley. He was in just as bad a condition as Darsey and I.

How close we had come to death out on the sands?

Then I realized I couldn't see Uri. Or hear him.

"Dragon Born," Serefina spat. "Child of Essence," she added spitefully. "She is nothing more than a mistress to the ones claiming to be Lords of the land."

"How dare you?" Darsey sputtered.

Deceivers.

"I can see you are *not* Serefina," I screamed, though my voice was weak. My rage was building from her blasphemous accusations. She looked exactly like Serefina, so I knew not who she was or why they bore such a striking resemblance, but I not only disliked this woman, my anger burned against her. "Now where is my cat?"

The man spoke to us for the first time and darkly said, "Out on the sands, no food goes to waste. You can thank Wanjala for your loss."

His words resonated over me like an overwhelming bell that shook me to my deepest self. "Food?" I said, barely above a whisper. "You *ate* him?!" I screamed, my voice cracking as angry tears sprang up and I futilely struggled against the binds, despite the pain that shot through my body.

I needed my blade. I needed my fire. I would burn these people and all they had to the ground!

Suddenly, the two ran from the tent, taking the torch with them.

"Adalee, what are you doing?" Brantley asked in a low, gruff voice.

I was lamenting. I was crying out. I was asking the Dragon Lord's to bring Uri back. To undo what these sacrilegious desert-dwellers had done.

They came rushing back in and the woman bent down to me and said, "How are you doing this? Please, stop!"

I was shaking my head and crying out still, unable to comprehend her words.

"Release us, and it will stop!" Brantley said.

Within moments my binds were cut, and I curled up, still wailing too loudly to hear anything other than shouts.

Hands were upon me, pulling me over. I didn't need to open my eyes to recognize Darsey's scent, though it was marred by desert stench. He held me close, his arms around my shoulders, and I cried into his dirty, sweat-stained, tunic.

Uri was gone. I would never hear his voice again. I would never sleep with his furry, purring body on my neck again. I would never get to watch him jump around and play again. Just like that, he was gone.

And suddenly I wished we had all died out there on the sand. What was the point of being rescued if all it meant was living the rest of my life without Uri? I didn't have it in me. I lost Darsey once, and now Uri was gone. Only this time, he wouldn't come back. He couldn't. I knew what had happened to him, and there was no miscommunication or confusion that would change the outcome of what the man had said.

No food goes to waste.

*"Adalee?"*

I could still hear his sweet voice in my head.

"Please, please, stop this!" the woman begged.

I pushed myself from Darsey's chest and glared at her through my tears. "You killed my Uri," I growled.

"And all of you will die if our demands aren't met," Brantley roared as best he could from his parched mouth.

"Please, spare us!" the man shouted.

I then realized that the tent we were housed in was shaking violently, much like the tents did on the rocky plains.

*"Adalee?!"*

I sat up quickly. His voice was really in my mind. "Uri?" I asked softly.

*"Adalee, are you here?"* he called out.

My weak legs buckled beneath me when I tried to jump up. The man and woman stepped aside as I crawled to the flap and flung it open. Sand immediately slammed into my face and I felt myself being dragged back in. I rolled over and saw Brantley and Darsey kneeling nearby, looking winded.

"You can't go out there," Brantley said with a cough.

I had to. Uri was out there. I *heard* him.

*"Adalee! Please! Are you here!? I'm scared!"* he called again.

I sucked in a deep breath and screamed as loud as my voice could carry, "Uri!"

There was a pause, and then he said, *"I hear you! Call again!"*

I didn't feel like I had any more in me when I sucked in another deep breath and screamed out, "Uri!" This time, Darsey's voice joined in.

I waited another moment, then he said, *"Keep calling! I'll find you!"*

"Again," I said gruffly.

Brantley looked at the man and woman and said, "You better call too if you want to live."

Then I took another deep breath and screamed out as loud as I could, "Uri!" This time, everyone in the tent joined in, though the man and woman seemed less enthusiastic than us.

To my great relief, Uri came flying through the flap and landed on my lap. I quickly pulled him to my neck and rubbed my head against his. "You're alive," I whimpered.

Then the sandstorm subsided as quickly as it arose. Uri was unscathed from the storm aside from some windblown fur, and I felt like I would never let him go again.

"You're alive," I repeated. "You're okay," I breathed in great relief.

*"I woke up in a basket. I tried to climb out, and someone grabbed me and tried to kill me. Then sand began to fly everywhere, and the man dropped me. Gavyn told me to run and I started looking for you."*

His words made me freeze. *Gavyn* saved him? Then I remembered it wasn't the first time Gavyn had warned Uri of danger to help him. Why?

"You are lucky the Dragon Born's tippoo is alive," Darsey said from behind me.

Still cradling him close, I looked up at them and, holding eye contact with the woman, I told Darsey and Brantley what Uri told me.

"The wind obeys you, and animals speak to you," the man said, awe in his voice.

"If you do not wish to be buried in the next storm," Brantley began, "then I suggest you—".

Before he could finish, the woman pulled a blade and dove at me.

Darsey threw himself upon me protectively and Brantley tackled the woman. The man pulled a blade and came at us.

Uri jumped from my arms and let out a furious growl as he lunged forward, swiping with a paw that quickly exploded in size.

The man stumbled back and Uri stood before him, his massive body heaving and shaking with anger. His growls were guttural and savage.

The woman scrambled away from Brantley and rushed to the man's side, holding her hand out.

"No," she cried. "Please, spare us! Please, Dragon Born. Forgive your servants." Then she prostrated herself on the ground before Uri and cried out, "We humble ourselves to you. You are truly one of awesome power."

The man silently did the same.

Darsey sat up and quickly grabbed the blades they had dropped in the scuffle. I sat up, sore all over, and many of my blisters had burst. My lips had cracked again and poured fresh blood down my chin. I looked at Darsey, sitting beside me, and Brantley, wavering on his feet, holding the torch they had thrown down to attack us. They both looked in as terrible condition as I, and I greatly lamented bringing them out there.

It *was* dangerous. We had almost died.

I looked back at the man and woman, still bowing to Uri, and realized we *still* might die. They had both tried to kill me just then, and if Uri hadn't found the will to leap, I might be dead.

*"I did it,"* Uri said, pleased with himself, his growls still emanating threateningly.

Darsey was the first to speak to them. "You will be spared if you bring us water, food, and medicine for our burns and blisters."

"Of course," the woman said. "Anything for the Dragon Born and her company."

They both scrambled up and turned to exit.

"Stop!" Brantley shouted, and they froze. They turned back hesitantly and he said, "You will have someone bring it. I do not trust you out of our sight."

They looked at one another and the man nodded. The woman knelt back down and the man lifted the flap and called someone over.

A thin young man equally dark as the woman came over, and the man spoke to him in another language.

"Speak in a language we understand," Brantley ordered harshly, and Uri let out a more threatening growl.

The woman looked frightened by Uri and bowed down again. "They do not know the mountain language. Joah and I are the only ones who speak it!"

Joah and the young man were looking at us, and I looked up at Brantley, who nodded with pursed, unhappy lips.

A moment later, the boy ran off and Joah sat down beside the woman. For the first time, I had a chance to take in his features, and it struck me as odd that he was pale in complexion, unlike the woman and the boy. They were both as dark as Serefina. Dark as night.

These were the people Brantley had heard of. The people of Aljonnah.

Except Joah. His hair was curly and blonde, and his eyes were wide and blue as the sea. He looked as though he were chiseled out of stone, with high cheekbones and a prominent chin. His eyes were deep set beneath thick, blonde brows, and his hair was short with tight, soft looking curls, ending just at the top of his ears.

I looked over at the woman and slowly began to see vague differences between her and Serefina. Her hair was much longer than Serefina's, and it was thick and strong, standing almost a hands-breath out from her head. She had a gold nose ring shining from one nostril and a wide, thick, gold earring clasped to the top of her opposite ear. Serefina adorned herself with no jewelry that I could remember, and her hair was barely long enough to cover her head.

Still, I found it hard to believe that this *wasn't* Serefina, as everything else, even her facial expressions, were exactly as I recalled.

"What's your name?" I asked in a squeaky voice when she noticed I was staring at her.

Her face was cold and still, and she said firmly, "Anahita."

Her accent was much thicker than Serefina's, which I felt I should have noticed earlier.

"And that is Joah?" I asked, motioning to the man without looking away from her.

She silently nodded.

"Is this Aljonnah?" Darsey asked, and they looked at him.

"No," Anahita said simply.

"If you try anything," Brantley warned, "the Dragon Born will end you and your people."

Had they not tried to kill both us and Uri, I would have detested such a threat.

But why? Why did they rescue us from the desert, only to try to kill us once we were awake? They should have seen I was the Dragon Born while we were out on the sands. Since they appeared to hate it so much, why wait to try and kill me?

"Why did you rescue us, only to try and kill us?" I asked.

"Good question," Darsey agreed.

They didn't answer.

Brantley waved the torch and said, "You will answer when the Dragon Born addresses you."

Joah took a deep, steady breath and said, "We wanted to question you."

"Shh," Anahita hissed.

He looked at her and whispered something in their language and Brantley said, "No! Speak so we can understand you."

They both looked back at us and Anahita said, "You will kill us either way, so why should we answer?"

Her words didn't sit right with me and I quickly shook my head. "We're not going to kill you. *You* tried to kill *us*."

"Because we know why you have come," Anahita spat venomously.

"All we wanted was justice for our son," Joah said woefully.

Anahita turned away and wiped her face.

Brantley scoffed. "What does that have to do with us?"

Darsey scooted forward and asked, "What happened to your son?"

The flap flew open and three young men stepped in. One held a skin of water. One held a bowl of grain. The last held a small bowl of salve.

"That's close enough," Brantley warned, holding the torch toward them. Joah spoke to them in their language and they each laid what was in their arms on the ground and bowed their way out.

Uri had yet to move from his tense position and I loved how intimidating he looked. I felt like we had the upper hand because of it, and I wished he could leap anytime he wished. I imagined how helpful it would be.

Brantley pointed the torch toward Anahita and said, "You, drink first."

"We did nothing to—" Joah began.

"Then you should have no problem," Brantley interrupted.

Anahita wiped the tears from her face and retrieved the water skin. She drank from it, and then held it out for us.

"No," Brantley said. "He's next."

Joah stood and walked over, taking it from her gently, then pouring some into his mouth.

I recalled how Veda had done the same thing on the ship with the wine she offered me, yet it was still drugged.

Brantley made them do the same with the food, eating a small handful each before allowing them to sit back down.

"So, can we drink now?" Darsey asked him.

He shook his head and said, "Not yet. Now we wait and see what happens to them."

Darsey sighed and I looked over at the salve, ready for something to soothe my burns and blisters, though I couldn't dismiss Brantley's concern. I had made the mistake before of accepting something from someone I didn't know, and it didn't bode well for me. Even accepting something from someone I *did* know almost cost me my life, as I thought back to Madame's deadly tea.

*So, you survived after all,* she said shrewdly.

It wasn't hard to mask my irritated sigh behind Uri's loud growls. I was frustrated that by merely thinking of her, I had brought her back to the forefront of my mind.

"I believe," Darsey said as loudly as he could, "that we may have had a misunderstanding."

*What would you have done, had they not found you in the desert?*

I looked down and closed my eyes for a moment, willing her away. I wanted to hear what Darsey was saying. I wanted to hear what Anahita and Joah had to say.

I couldn't focus. I needed her to leave.

*Shut the beast up, and maybe you'll be able to hear,* she mocked.

I looked up and realized Uri's growls *were* making it difficult to hear.

Gently, I reached out and laid my hand on his hip nearest me.

He didn't react, save a small flinch, and asked, *"What do you want me to do?"*

"You can relax," I said. "But don't let them leave."

He stopped growling and sat back on his haunches, wiping a little bit of drool from his chin.

The absence of his growl created more silence in the tent that I expected. Even Madame quieted.

I breathed a deep sigh of relief and looked at Darsey, offering him a small smile.

Brantley finally came off his feet and kneeled down as Darsey began again.

"You said some terrible things about the Dragon Born," Darsey said in a non-combative way. "But we are not your enemy."

"Unless you are an enemy of the Dragon Lords," Brantley added.

His declaration annoyed me. He didn't care about the Dragon Lords *or* me. He was just enjoying the feeling of being on the other end of Uri's threats.

"You have come to crush the rebellion and give Wanjala back his power," Anahita said. "So you *are* our enemy."

"What rebellion?" Brantley asked. "Who is Wanjala?"

"And what happened to your son?" Darsey asked, coming back to the earlier confession.

I held up my hand and said, "Before all that," and everyone quieted and looked at me. I stared at Anahita, desiring answers. "Who are you, really? You know Serefina, don't you?"

Joah glanced at Anahita, though she didn't take her eyes from mine.

"She is my sister," she said after a moment. "We shared our mother's womb and were born only moments apart. We look alike in every way, save one." She showed me a mark on her leg, and I recalled Serefina speaking of her curator who left.

"You were her curator," I whispered.

"So, now you know the truth. Our parents hid us from Wanjala as long as they could, and when we were of age and no longer willing to share an identity, we left together. Our skills protected us from those we came across. They needed us.

"After about a year of travel, we settled in the mountains. There we stayed for a few years, helping the surrounding peoples who had no shaman to heal them." She reached over and grasped Joah's hand tenderly. "Then I met Joah, and we married. We had a child, whom we called Zaire. As he aged, my heart grew troubled. I wanted my parents to know him. So, with Serefina's blessing, I returned to Aljonnah with my family."

Darsey leaned in, intrigued by the story, and asked, "And Wanjala didn't accept you back?"

She looked at him and said, "No, he did. Joah and Zaire completed the tribal initiation ritual and we found our place amongst the people."

"Why did you leave?" Brantley asked. "Why did your parents hide that there were two of you?"

They looked up at him and Joah said, "Aljonnah is not large enough to sustain the people if they grow too quickly. Each family is allowed one child. If that child dies, they have no other chances. If they accidentally conceive more than one, then one is chosen to live, and the rest are thrown into the pit."

"What's the pit?" Darsey asked.

Anahita looked at him and said, "A hole where all of the venomous creatures of the rainbow sands are collected. A single sting or bite will not harm you. However, covered from head to toe by them, you stand little chance of survival."

"And the rare ones who do survive," Joah added, "are usually marred for life. Incapable of speech. Unable to walk. Some are even unable to think. They only have emptiness behind their eyes."

"Tell us more," Brantley ordered.

"We have already thrown ourselves on your mercy. What more do you need to condemn us?" Joah asked.

Darsey sat back and held his hands up. "We're not here to condemn anyone."

"What have you said that would condemn you?" I wondered aloud.

"It's not what they've said," Brantley interjected. "It's what they've done. They attacked us, and they know it's wrong."

"They *saved* us first," Darsey pointed out. Then he turned back to them. "It doesn't make sense. You said you wanted to question us. You said you wanted justice for your son. Then you tried to kill us."

"You should replenish your strength," Joah said, motioning to the food and water.

"And heal your wounds," Anahita added.

Darsey nodded and said, "We will." Then he scooted closer and said, "We all have stories to tell, and the one we're most interested in is yours."

His words almost matched exactly those Plume had said to him when she first came upon us, and I glanced over, realizing he was trying to use the same charm she did to get information from them.

Brantley stood and retrieved the bowls and skin, one at a time. The three of us sat near one another and shared in the provisions. I was grateful to have water to drink, but between the three of us, it was gone quickly. I didn't have much of an appetite, but made good use of the salve, spreading it on my face and lips.

"If you have not come to condemn us," Joah said hesitantly, "then why *have* you come?"

"She is being called by the Blue Dragon Lord," Darsey said. "She is out here, somewhere, waiting to be freed."

"Darsey," I scolded, looking back at Joah and Anahita. I feared how the Deceivers would react if they knew I was coming to free a Dragon Lord.

Anahita and Joah looked at one another, confusion in their faces. Then they faced us and Anahita said, "Our Dragon Lord is grey, not blue. And he is male."

Brantley leaned forward now and asked, "You know where the Dragon Lord is?"

Joah nodded and said, "The Grey Dragon Lord reigns over Aljonnah."

The three of us looked at one another then back at them.

The Dragon Lord in my dream was grey. Was that why I was dreaming of them both? Were there two Dragon Lords in Aljonnah?

Brantley shook his head and said, "That doesn't make sense. You have mentioned a tyrannical ruler. Wanjala. Why does the Grey Dragon Lord not remove him from power? If he reigns over Aljonnah, why is he making the people fight for themselves?"

Anahita and Joah looked at each other then back at us. Then Anahita said, "Wanjala *is* the Grey Dragon Lord."

## Eleven | The Grey Dragon Lord

We stared at them silently, waiting for more.

"You seem surprised," Joah said.

I shook my head and said, "All the Dragon Lords are still trapped."

Joah shrugged and said, "No one in Aljonnah recalls a time when Wanjala was not ruler. He does not age. He does not weaken. How then, could he be anything other than a Dragon Lord?"

What he said made sense. Wanjala *did* sound like a Dragon Lord. And from what I saw in my dreams, I believed he was. But how was he free? Had another Dragon Born rescued him before the Calling? Had he escaped the Great Deceiver before all the Dragon Lords were turned to stone?

"I think we need to hear everything," Darsey said solemnly.

Joah and Anahita looked at one another, and when he nodded at her, she faced us and began, "When I returned with Joah and Zaire, Wanjala was unhappy. That is, until he laid eyes upon our son. He then decided we could stay, so long as Zaire placed himself in the running for tribal leader when the time came."

Joah interrupted and said, "I didn't understand what it meant at the time, or else I would have refused and we would have returned to the mountains."

Anahita hung her head and Joah placed his hand on her shoulder. "It's okay," he said.

She nodded and continued. "For ten years we lived in Aljonnah, and many moons ago Wanjala began the search for a new king to rule beside him."

I thought of Serefina, riding atop the Red Dragon Lord, speaking as one with him. I nodded and said, "He needs a rider."

Anahita nodded and said, "The king is old and close to death. Zaire was ordered to take his place amongst the candidates."

"Only, we had no right to promise him to Wanjala, and he refused," Joah said.

"He refused to be Wanjala's rider?" I asked, perplexed.

"No," Anahita said. "He refused to compete in the games. He felt it was unnecessary and barbaric. And he was right. He and his brother, Faraji, pulled together and convinced many of the candidates to step down and refuse Wanjala."

Brantley leaned forward and said, "You said only one child was allowed per household. And now there is a *brother*?"

Joah quickly explained, "Faraji was not born of Anahita. His parents died of sickness less than a year after our arrival, and he was Zaire's first friend. We took him in and raised them as brothers, with Wanjala's blessing."

"What happened?" Darsey asked. "What happened after they convinced other candidates to step down?"

Joah shook his head and said, "Stepping down from the games is a disgrace that comes with a price. Though it is allowed, your line ends with you. Wanjala does not believe there is room in Aljonnah for cowardice bloodlines."

"Zaire was not a coward," Anahita clarified fervently. "He was *smart*. He paid attention. He didn't let others do his thinking for him. And he didn't believe a Dragon Lord should treat the people as Wanjala does."

"Was?" Darsey asked softly. "Does that mean . . ."

"Wanjala threw him into the black pool," Joah said stoically.

There was a silence in the tent that rested over each of us. Without needing explanation, I think we all knew that the black pool was death. I thought of my dream, where the grey dragon was guarding the black pool, not allowing me near it. Was he protecting me from it?

"I thought stepping down was allowed?" Brantley asked, and I was surprised at how interested he had become in their tale.

"That wasn't the problem," Joah added as Anahita turned away to wipe her tears. "Zaire created a movement. He made the people see that they should not be made to compete for a position they didn't want."

"Wanjala killed Zaire, but it didn't have the effect he was expecting," Anahita said, facing us again. "In his despair, Faraji riled the people up against the king, and now the Dragon Lord is doing whatever he can to crush the rebellion. We fled into the desert because Wanjala was going to kill Faraji next, even though the people have spoken. They wish for Faraji to be their king. They trust him."

"All except the few who are continuing in the candidacy," Joah said darkly.

"And those who are ruled by fear," Anahita added.

"Wait," Brantley said. "So, let me make sure I'm understanding this. Wanjala is the leader of Aljonnah, and a Dragon Lord, and the people are against him. So, he is trying to kill the leaders of this rebellion to take back control?"

They both nodded and Brantley scoffed and asked, "What does that have to do with us? Why did you try to kill the Dragon Born? If anything, shouldn't you believe she can fix this?"

"Or at least get Wanjala to leave?" Darsey added.

I looked at them, taken aback by their confidence in me. How could I smooth over the discontent of a nation? How could I tell a Dragon Lord he had to leave his home?

"Wanjala has been threatening to summon the Dragon Born for generations," Joah said.

Anahita added, "This is not the first time there has been unrest amongst the people." Then she looked at me and said, "As I'm sure you know."

I shook my head and said honestly, "I didn't even know your people existed before a few days ago."

They looked at one another and then Anahita faced me and said, "How can I believe that? You knew my sister's name."

I quickly shook my head and said, "Your sister helped me. She is my friend. My mentor, even."

Brantley cleared his throat and eyed me angrily.

I ignored him and continued. "I knew nothing of where she came from. I knew she looked unlike anyone I had ever seen. She told me she had a curator who left, but nothing else."

Anahita nodded. "Because she didn't trust you," she said with finality.

"No," I said adamantly. "She showed me who I was. What my purpose was. When I met her, I was still just trying to get home. She showed me how to meditate and speak to the Dragon Lords that call me in my dreams. She told me I was blessed, and that she was highly favored for being in my presence. Does that sound like someone who doesn't trust me?"

My passion was growing and I was getting louder. "Does that sound like someone who doesn't trust the Dragon Lords? Does that sound like someone who would be okay with you leading a rebellion against one of them?"

I was standing on shaky legs now, and Uri moved over beside me, subtly letting me lean against him. "She would have never attacked me. In fact, she disenchanted me when—" I motioned to Brantley but caught myself, and stammered, "when— *someone* used magic on me to make me not myself. *And*," I said, "when I freed the Red Dragon Lord, he went back to her immediately. He rewarded her loyalty to the Dragon Lords by choosing her to be his rider."

Anahita's eyes went wide and I continued.

"No games. No candidates. He just went to her, she mounted him, they spoke to me in one voice, and then they flew away to await the arrival of the rest of the Dragon Lords. And *that* is why I have come," I said with finality. "Because I am being called by the Blue Dragon Lord. She is somewhere in Aljonnah. She takes me to pools of color. She wants me to free her so she can join the Red Dragon Lord and prepare for the battle that is yet to come."

"And what of Wanjala?" Joah asked. "Why has he summoned you here?"

"He didn't," I admitted. "He didn't appear in my visions until a few days ago. Around the same time the Blue Dragon Lord led me to the oasis was when I started seeing Wanjala. I believe he has been waiting for me and I'm sure he will leave with the Blue Dragon Lord."

"So, you have not come to establish his throne forever?" Anahita asked hesitantly.

"Forgive me," Brantley interrupted as he faced them. "What could Aljonnah possibly offer a Dragon Lord that is better than being back with his brothers and sisters?"

They looked at each other again and then Joah said, "Very well. Stay here. We need to speak to the others and decide what to do."

"Cross us," Brantley warned, "and you won't be able to withstand the horrors the Dragon Born will bring upon this camp."

They stared at him, eyes wide, then they nodded and left the tent.

My knees buckled and I grabbed Uri to slow my fall. He helped me sit and said, *"I don't know how long I'm going to stay big this time. How am I going to ride Starla when we leave?"*

I hadn't thought of that. Part of me wanted to get to Aljonnah so I could feel safe in the presence of the Dragon Lord, and the other part felt too worn to travel. What if we arrived in this condition? Would he deem me too weak to continue the quest? Would he give the Essence to another?

*Maybe he'll give it to me.* Madame sneered.

I didn't have time for her. I didn't have time to worry about any of that.

Darsey leaned in and whispered, "What do you think?"

I looked at him and asked, "About what?"

"Everything," he said. "Wanjala, these people, the story they told. Does it seem real?"

Brantley answered, "I don't trust them at all. We need to leave as soon as we get our weapons back."

*"What about me?"* Uri asked.

I shook my head and said, "We can't go anywhere until Uri shrinks. Starla can't carry him like this."

Brantley's eyes widened and he asked, "He can't control shrinking either?"

I shrugged helplessly and he rubbed his face.

"Fine." Then he looked at Darsey and said, "If they question us, you and I are her servants. She needs to be seen as powerful enough to not need us."

Darsey nodded and said, "I can do that."

Then he faced me and said, "And you don't need to be telling stories that make you look weak. Everything you said about her sister makes you look like an unsure child."

"I *am* an unsure child," I bit, immediately regretting the words.

He sat back and his face hardened. "Aye, you're right about that," he agreed. "Just don't let them see it."

"Adalee," Darsey said, drawing my attention. "You are more capable than you realize."

I shook my head and he went on.

"No, really. Think about the storm you summoned when you thought Uri was gone. How did you do it? You must have felt *something*."

Before I could respond, Brantley let out a short laugh and said, "She didn't."

I stayed quiet, because he was right, and Darsey whispered, "Uri?"

Brantley scoffed and Darsey turned toward him, taking a deep breath to say something.

"It was probably the Falcone," Brantley explained before he could speak.

*"It was,"* Uri agreed.

"It's still around?" Darsey asked.

I nodded and said, "So long as Uri and I can speak, Gavyn is near."

Darsey nodded and said, "That's right. Uri was causing your swooning."

"We need to figure out how we're going to escape," Brantley whispered.

"These people are scared," Darsey defended. "They might not be our enemies."

"They did save us from the desert," I pointed out.

"Only to bind us, threaten us, and try to kill us," Brantley said coolly.

"It was a misunderstanding," Darsey explained. "They know the truth now, and I'm sure they will *want* to work with us now that we can get Wanjala to leave them be."

"Maybe," I said, his words filling me with angst and doubt. "But what if he doesn't want to leave?"

They both looked at me and Brantley asked, "What do you know?"

"Nothing," I admitted quickly. "It's just that . . . he has only been in my dreams; not my meditations. I can see him, which is different than the other Callings. In the other Callings, I am one with the Dragon Lord. When he is in my dreams, we are ourselves, separate from one another."

Darsey shrugged and said, "Probably just because he isn't trapped. Maybe the Dragon Lord's can only show you what they see and feel."

I nodded. "Maybe."

Darsey laid his hand on my shoulder and said, "It'll be okay. He'll be as happy to see you as all the other Dragon Lords, trapped or not."

The flap flew back and Joah and Anahita entered. They were carrying the belongings they had stripped us of before we awoke. Our star-runners, canteens, satchels, and weapons. After laying them before us, they sat and I noticed Anahita holding golden pieces in her hands.

"It has been decided," Joah said as we quickly sorted and took our things back. I was careful when I touched the dagger, not wishing to destroy Starla's orb with my stress. "You will take as much time as you need to recover here, then go to Aljonnah and rid the people of Wanjala and the Blue Dragon Lord."

"Dragon Lords are a blessing," I reminded them softly. "Please don't forget that."

Anahita looked down at the jewelry in her hands and said, "The people will not take kindly to you. There are many who are too fearful to cross Wanjala, yet many more who secretly align themselves with the rebellion."

"And they will be terrified of Adalee for the same reasons you were," Brantley reasoned.

She nodded, then held up a wide, gold bracelet. "That is why you must adorn yourselves with these bracelets. When placed on the correct wrist, it shows a loyalty to the rebellion. Those who still follow Wanjala do not know of it."

"So, neither side will attack us," Brantley clarified.

Joah nodded and said, "So long as they see it."

Anahita held the bracelets out and Darsey took them and handed one to each of us. We waited for Anahita to indicate which wrist to put them on, and we did so.

Joah then proceeded to tell us how to navigate the sands to Aljonnah, and I was surprised at how simple it seemed. We had been travelling across the lines of color while the colored sands *came* from Aljonnah. They described the colored pools I had seen in my meditations and told us how each pool produced the colored sands that had spread out into the desert over time.

"You are free to leave tonight," Anahita finally said.

I shook my head and said, "We will not leave until I am comfortable with it."

I saw a smirk on Brantley's face from my peripheral vision, and I assumed it was because I was taking his advice, and trying not to appear weak, though we could go nowhere while Uri was still so large.

"Of course," Anahita said hesitantly. "Is there anything else we can offer you?"

"Just more water and salve," I said confidently.

"And clothes," Brantley said while clearing his throat.

I nodded quickly and added, "And clothes."

"Of course," Joah said, and they both exited once again.

"I like your spirit," Brantley began, "but he needs to try, because we need to leave as soon as possible."

"It's out of our control," Darsey smirked with an achy stretch.

"It wouldn't be if we would stop worrying so much about keeping the cat alive," Brantley snapped.

"He came through earlier," Darsey reminded him as he straightened back up. "It's clear they've never seen a tippoo before and that might have saved our lives."

"He's not reliable!" Brantley said as he shook his head. "Until he can leap at will—"

He grunted and grabbed his chest, squeezing his eyes shut and leaning forward.

Darsey looked at me, his eyes wide, and I shook my head gently, letting him know it would be okay. He stayed tense and silent as he turned toward Brantley.

After a moment, Brantley sucked in a deep breath and jumped up angrily. He let out a frustrated sigh and stormed toward the flap.

"Where are you going?" Darsey asked.

Brantley stopped at the flap with his back to us and turned his head just enough to be heard. "I'm going to wake Astraeus, so the stars don't take him back. You should do the same."

Then he stormed out, letting the flap close behind him.

We were halfway through the next day before Uri finally shrank back to his tiny size. I had been up most of the night trying to process everything Anahita and Joah had said. I failed at my many attempts to meditate, still too worn from almost dying on the sands. However, our blisters and burns were lessening by the hour with the potent salve the people had given us.

"You need to either sleep or meditate," Brantley interrupted my thoughts.

I looked at him in the shadows of the tent. The desert tents were much more capable of keeping out of the heat of the day than our thin tents from the hills.

Darsey took advantage of the shade by snoring away happily. Uri slept nearby, enjoying the cool as well. Brantley however, refused to sleep, and I was unable to.

"I can't do either," I admitted.

"We're not staying another night," he stated. "So, you better get some answers because when the sun goes down, we are leaving on the star-runners."

"I'm nervous about what we'll find in Aljonnah," I admitted.

"I think we have a pretty fair idea of what's waiting for us."

I nodded thoughtfully, then said, "Even so, I don't know why the Grey Dragon Lord would stay in Aljonnah if he was free. The Red Dragon Lord left right away. Almost as though they have a meeting place. Why would the Grey Dragon Lord not go there and wait too?"

Brantley shrugged and said, "That's a very long time to be alone, lass. Whether he was freed many years ago, or never turned to stone like you suggested, there is no reason anyone should have to be alone that long."

The idea of being alone for thousands of years was heartbreaking. How aware were the trapped Dragon Lords? Were they lonely?

"Either way," Brantley said, "when we get to Aljonnah, no matter the case, let's stay focused on the task at hand. We need to free the Blue Dragon Lord so she can undo this dastardly bind and I can be on my way."

I liked the idea of Brantley going his own way. We had learned enough from him in the last weeks to be able to make our own shelters and build fires despite the weather.

"Oh," I said as a new thought entered my mind.

"What?" he asked.

"What if Wanjala can undo the bind?" I suggested with soft excitement.

"Now that, lass, is the best idea you've ever had."

I scrunched my brow and said, "I wouldn't say it's the *best*."

"Aye, it is," he asserted as he laid down with his hands behind his head. "The best," he said again before he let his eyes drift shut.

When night finally fell, I was ready and eager to be on our way. Darsey, Brantley, and Uri had all slept through the day. I was the only one who couldn't find rest behind my eyelids.

We awoke our star-runners and mounted them as the small band of outcasts gathered around us. They were silent and stoic as they watched, making me nervous.

I took a deep breath and reined in my uneasy feeling. I had possession of the blade now and I needed to stay in control so I didn't accidentally send Starla back to the stars.

Uri was saddled with Darsey, just to be safe, and Brantley was the first to shoot off into the colorful desert, though not as quickly or with the aura glow of the nights before. I followed after him and Darsey was near my flank.

Holding on to Starla was significantly more difficult than our first ride, and I clung to her tightly, fearing I would slip off at any moment. Holding in the tingle of the dagger didn't help my nerves, so it took all I had to hold it together.

It was within the hour we climbed to the top of a dune and looked down below at a beautiful oasis, filled with warm light and many rainbow pools reflecting into the air, laying a blanket of color in the skies above.

It was full of a lush forest that looked to harbor people and animals alike. The dancing of the colored pools reflecting on everything gave the oasis a life of its own. There was only a handful of people gathered at the front of the oasis, and the back butted up to a colorful mountain.

"Here we go," Brantley said. Then he leaned forward and Astraeus took off down the dune, toward the oasis. Darsey and I looked at one another, then sped after him, with no idea how we would be greeted.

Twelve | A Warm Welcome

I focused on staying atop Starla and keeping the power harnessed. As we drew nearer, my heart began to race, and I could feel the blade trying to pulse out of control. I held on tight, closed my eyes, and pulled it back in.

I opened my eyes when shouts reached my ears.

Brantley pulled up amongst the armed men and held up his wrist with the bracelet, shouting, "Wanjala!"

I looked around at the men and was shocked to see fear in their eyes. I quickly pulled the sleeve of my desert tunic up and showed my bracelet as well. I looked over and saw Darsey do the same.

Then I realized they hardly saw us. Instead, their eyes were wide set on the star-runners.

The men calmed after a moment and one of them shouted at us in their language.

"What are they saying?" Darsey asked.

"You expect *me* to know?" Brantley hissed back.

The warriors looked back and forth at one another, then the man repeated his shout, though this time he seemed less confident.

"Wanjala!" Brantley called out again.

I was scanning the warriors for a bracelet like ours, surprised the only adornments I saw were earrings and nose rings.

My confidence began to waver until I realized they needed to see my hair. These were still followers of Wanjala and they would believe he had summoned me. I reached up to remove my turban when they raised their bows and tautly drew their arrows.

"Adalee, watch out!" Darsey screamed.

I threw my hands up defensively as one of the men loosed his arrow at me. It slammed into my palm and turned to ash, covering the sand around us.

With a gasp, each warrior froze, eyes on me.

I could feel the power surging, and I feared for Starla. I quickly slid from her back, sprawling onto the sand, making sure no part of my skin touched her.

Then the leader cried out and I jumped up as all of them loosed their arrows at me. Each and every arrow turned to ash, whether it landed directly on my skin or tore through my clothing first.

Thanks to the power of the blade, their weapons couldn't harm me, though I feared for everyone else.

I spun around at their stark white faces and yelled, "Take Starla and run!"

In response, Starla turned and took off into the desert, Uri entangled in her mane.

"I won't leave you!" Darsey shouted stubbornly, drawing his sword.

Brantley wrapped his arm around Darsey's neck and dragged him from Cosmo, throwing him awkwardly across Astraeus and they escaped into the desert.

I spun back just as they had filled their bows again and loosed more arrows. Knowing they couldn't harm me I made a spectacle, turning each one to ash. The arrows didn't pierce my skin but stung when they struck. I threw my arm out at one that came toward my face, and my bracelet slipped from wrist and landed silently in the sand.

They drew closer to me and pulled out whips, slinging them toward my arms and neck. Those too, were turned to ash as soon as they struck me.

One of the men ran toward me and I jumped back, screaming at him to stay away. He paid no mind to my warning and grabbed my tunic. His hand brushed against my skin where arrows had torn through and he immediately stumbled back, screaming as his thumb crumbled to ash.

I turned from him, searching wildly for my bracelet. Though it meant nothing to these few, I would need it when faced by others. I saw a shimmer in the sand and dove for it. As soon as I touched it, it turned to ash and blew away.

"No!" I screamed.

Then I heard a grunt behind me and spun just as one of the warriors lifted a large stone above his head and brought it down upon mine.

My head throbbed. My neck ached. My body felt stiff.

My eyes fluttered open and I saw the dancing flame of a torch in a stand. My body stung and I felt suspended in a forward fall.

My feet were surrounded by large sticks and as I came to my senses, I could feel wood against my back.

"Adalee!" Darsey's voice shouted in relief.

I winced with the pain but forced my head up and looked over. Darsey was tied to a pyre beside me.

"They caught you," I moaned in despair. How had they been able to catch the star-runners?

"No, we came back," Brantley scoffed, his voice laced with anger and irritation.

I turned and saw him in a similar state on my other side.

"Of course we came back!" Darsey said as though it were ridiculous to question the decision.

Fear struck me and I frantically asked, "Where's Uri?"

"Safe with the star-runners," Darsey assured me.

"Yes, he's *safe*," Brantley said as though the word meant nothing. "Until we die," he said matter-of-factly. "Then the stars will take back the star-runners and he'll be *alone*."

The realization frightened me, and I looked around for a way out. No one was present, guarding us.

"Where is everyone?" I asked.

"They brought us here and left," Brantley said, still in the same tone. "Probably to complete some ritual before they burn us."

"Stop acting like you knew this would happen the whole time!" Darsey snapped at him.

"I *did*," he barked back. "I knew you two would get me killed."

"Did you see anyone with bracelets?" I asked desperately. "I lost mine. It turned to ash!"

"The bracelets did nothing!" Brantley shouted. "It was a trick! A lie to make us feel safe. They couldn't kill us in the desert so they sent us here where their tribespeople could finish us off!"

"Adalee," Darsey said in a soft voice, drawing my attention. "Can you singe the binds?"

I sighed heavily and shook my head, tears springing to my eyes. "I don't feel the power," I admitted.

"They took our weapons," Brantley pointed out, as though we were foolish to believe otherwise.

"Just try," he said. "You can do it. I believe in you. You're the Dragon Born. Use the Essence and summon Dragon's fire."

"It doesn't work like that!" Brantley snapped at him.

I felt like a failure. Even with the blade at my side, I couldn't protect anyone. I couldn't do anything.

I felt a tug at my back and realized something was pulling at my binds. Then his whiskers tickled my wrists and I knew. "Uri," I said, relieved. Then my relief was quickly replaced by concern. "Uri, get out of here. It isn't safe."

*"I'm not afraid,"* he said as he continued gnawing at the ropes. *"If I could leap,* they *would be the ones running scared."*

"I know," I said. "Right now, you need to go. Go find someone. Someone that will take care of you. Please. I don't want you to be alone."

He didn't respond but gave up on chewing the ropes as they were sealed with something his teeth couldn't tear through.

"Uri, now," I ordered gently. "Go."

He climbed up to my shoulder and sat down. *"No,"* he said firmly. *"I'm not leaving."*

Before I could respond, a flutter caught my eye, and I turned to see Gavyn descending from out of nowhere. He turned into his warrior form just in time for his feet to touch the ground.

Once again, I was astounded by his presence. So many things resonated from him, and it created many contradicting emotions.

He emanated power and danger. An unrelenting constant I didn't understand. He was an enigma, and though I couldn't deny the help he offered in tight places, something told me his intentions were not for the Dragon Lords. The Red Dragon Lord detested his presence in the skies, and I couldn't bring myself to deviate from their desires, even if I wanted to. I was committed to fulfilling my purpose and bringing peace to the land. An enemy of the Dragon Lords was an enemy of peace.

He didn't look at me with his intimidating gaze and instead glided across the ground toward a golden basin of oil that was perched upon an intricately ornate stand. Without breathing deep, he leaned over it and blew out an unnaturally long breath, causing the oil to tremble and shake.

When it calmed, he turned away from us and with a flash of light, flew away in his bird form.

"What . . . was that?" Darsey asked breathlessly.

"The Falcone," Brantley said in equal awe.

"Gavyn," I whispered, not trying to understand what he had accomplished by blowing on the oil.

Just then, the voices of men came from the trees. Five men and one woman exited the oasis forest and strode toward us, adorned in body jewelry that rivaled the extravagance of the stand the oil rested upon.

I checked each of them and realized they didn't have golden bracelets like Anahita had given us.

"Be strong," Brantley ordered.

"They can't do this!" Darsey shouted.

Then I remembered that often times Gavyn would talk to Uri, and hope welled up in me. "Uri, what did Gavyn say to you?" I asked.

*"Nothing,"* he said, sounding as disappointed as I felt.

Three of the people stopped and grasped the torches that rested before each of our pyres. The woman stood before me, no emotion in her face.

One man stood tall behind them and the others went to the basin of oil and carefully lifted it from the stand. They carried it over and poured a third of it around Darsey's pyre. Then they did the same to mine and emptied the rest onto Brantley's. This was really happening.

They replaced the basin and went to stand on each side of the man who stood watching. He raised his hands to the sky and began a ritualistic recitation that I needn't understand their language to comprehend. The three before us held their torches high to sky and repeated some of the words in unison.

What would burning alive feel like?

"Adalee, I love you," Darsey cried out.

His panic spread to me, though I was trying to be strong like Brantley. My heart began to race, and nervous sweat beaded on the back of my neck. "I love you too," I told him, trying to hold back tears.

*"I'm not scared,"* Uri told me, though it seemed he was only trying to convince himself.

"You can run," I whispered. "I *want* you to run," I implored.

*"If you die, then so will I,"* he said bravely.

They shouted one last unified cry then abruptly brought the torches down and shoved them into the bottom of our pyres.

I sucked in a deep breath and clamped my eyes shut.

Nothing happened.

No heat burned the bottoms of my feet, and the air didn't thicken with smoke.

I opened my eyes and saw the three before us looking back and forth at each other. The ritual leader stormed up and yanked the torch from my pyre. The wood I was perched upon wasn't even smoking. He held the torch up, proclaimed the last word of the ritual again, and shoved it into the pyre. When nothing happened, he turned to the men who had poured the oil and began shouting at them.

They shook their heads and held up their hands defensively.

"Wanjala!" Brantley shouted.

I looked at him, and he nodded at me.

"Wanjala," we shouted together, looking into the eyes of those who would burn us.

We shouted it again, and I heard Darsey join in. We repeated the Dragon Lord's name until they ran from the pyres, back into the forest, leaving the torches stuck in the wood, though it refused to burn.

"What now?" Darsey asked.

"Hopefully they will bring Wanjala, and Adalee will fix this," Brantley said with no hint of irony.

I looked at him and saw no humor in his face. He was truly trusting me to handle it.

"Uri, at least hide until we know for sure what is going to happen," I pleaded.

*"I am strong,"* he assured me.

"He'll listen to you, right?" Darsey asked, and I looked at him.

"No," I said. "Uri isn't listening."

He shook his head, sweat pouring down his face. "Wanjala," he clarified. "He'll listen?"

"Of course he will," Brantley answered. "He needs her."

It was the first time Brantley had placed me above himself in any way, and I felt undeserving of the confidence, though he wasn't wrong. At least, according to the legend.

"What about us?" Darsey asked, a tremble in his voice. "He doesn't need us."

"Adalee will keep you safe," Brantley assured him.

I nodded at Darsey and he tried to force a smile. The nervousness in his face was undeniable.

"I'll probably die, though," Brantley added.

I glanced over and caught a smirk on his face.

He angled his head toward me and said, "After all, no one loves *me*."

His ill-timed humor was staggering. "Seriously?" I asked. "Are you serious right now?"

He shrugged as best he could with his arms tied to the stake; the smirk never left his face. I wasn't sure if I should be concerned by his madman assertion or read his demeanor as a sign that he felt we were no longer in danger.

There was a great tremble in the forest and the ground began to shake. A roar sounded in the distance and Darsey's breathing became panicked and excessive.

"Calm down," Brantley shouted at him as though he were reacting to a spider on the mat.

The trees parted and a great grey dragon emerged, appearing furious and ready to strike. I recognized him immediately as the same Dragon Lord from my dreams.

Many warriors came rushing from the oasis and stood beside the Dragon Lord, weapons ready.

*"Whoa,"* Uri said in awe.

The Dragon Lord's focus turned from us to Uri. His eyes opened wide as they stared at one another.

After a moment, the Dragon Lord's gaze bore into mine. He reached out with a long, curved talon and hooked the edge of my turban, pulling it from my head. My hair cascaded freely down my back and side.

The warriors gasped and began whispering amongst themselves.

There was movement upon his back, and an old man leaning on a walking stick, his eyes white with age, appeared at the crest of the Dragon Lord's head, donning a glorious gold crown.

He spoke in a weak voice the people quieted to hear.

To my surprise, Uri began to translate his words effortlessly. *"He says the Dragon Born and her companions will be released and treated as gods."*

I turned to ask how he knew, but quieted when our would-be executioners cut our binds. Other warriors caught us as we stumbled off the pyres and helped us find our balance.

"You're welcome," Brantley whispered, clearly proud of himself for getting us to shout the Dragon Lord's name.

The Dragon Lord turned and slowly began walking back into the trees.

*"We need to follow,"* Uri said. I started walking behind the Dragon Lord and Darsey and Brantley stayed close.

"How do you know?" I whispered. "How did you know what he was saying?"

*"That dragon,"* Uri said, still in awe. *"He's just like me."*

I was stunned. I was confused. I felt dizzy and nauseous.

"What do you mean he's like you?" I whispered.

*"He talked to me. He called me brother. He can see in my mind. He knows you're the Dragon Born."*

That explained why he took my turban off. He was seeing for himself. "So, he's not a Dragon Lord?" I asked softly.

*"No,"* Uri confirmed. *"He's a tippoo."*

Anger and fear battled for control. An imposter was living among these people like a deity. Letting them worship him. Forcing them to obey him. He was the epitome of evil. A false god. And he could see into Uri's mind. We could hide nothing from him.

Why did he spare us? If he knew I was the Dragon Born, then he had to assume I knew the truth. Or, at the very least, that Uri would tell me.

He could have killed us and not revealed me as the Dragon Born. The people would have never known. Instead he was risking being exposed. Losing his position and glory. Why?

What did he want from us?

My mind continued to race with possible explanations as we wound through the colorful oasis, passing by the glorious pools of colored waters I had seen in my dreams. Had I not been so distracted by the possible dangers that lurked ahead, I might have taken in their beauty as I was sure Darsey and Brantley were.

They stayed silent, for which I was grateful so I could think.

We came upon a massive, colored temple, built from blocks of the rainbow sands. It was perfectly camouflaged, only revealing itself when we were right upon it. It towered mightily above the head of the dragon, and we followed him into a great round hall, made from smooth stone.

I was momentarily distracted by the detail work of the columns and pillars, carved to perfection and intricately designed with images of their people.

The dragon stooped before a throne and let the old king hobble to his seat. Once he was settled, the dragon laid behind the throne, his back towering over it like a dog protecting his bone. He stared silently at us.

Uri began to tremble and said, *"He wants me to step forward and translate."*

"Don't trust him," I whispered as softly as I could in Uri's ear. "Don't tell him about the rebellion." I now saw Anahita and the others in a new light. If what she had told me was true, then he was despicable and had no right to rule them.

He gulped and nodded. I gently lifted him from my shoulder and sat him gingerly on the ground. He approached the massive beast, looking tinier than ever before.

The throne room was perfectly still. The king looked like a statue.

*"He says his name is Wanjala and we are most welcome,"* Uri shared.

"Ask him why the people tried to kill us."

There was a pause and then, *"They aren't used to intruders, but we need not fear. They will not harm us and will treat us with the respect we deserve."*

I felt out of place asking for respect from the people. A respect that came from the order of a false god seemed repugnant.

"What's he saying?" Brantley asked.

"We are welcome, and no one will harm us," I said.

"Tell him we want our weapons back," he ordered.

I made eye contact with Uri and nodded.

After a moment, Uri said, *"Before that, he wants you to demonstrate the power you used to burn the arrows that struck you."*

His request made me nervous and I whispered to Brantley, "He wants to see my power."

Brantley looked at me, shocked. "Does he not know?" he asked, and I realized he still believed Wanjala to be a Dragon Lord. A Dragon Lord would understand how the Essence worked and how I was powerless to harness it without a jewel.

I slightly shook my head and he looked down for a moment, then fed back quickly, "Tell him the Dragon Born does not perform tricks to entertain a court."

His words were bolder than I expected, but I couldn't let the imposter know I was helpless without my weapon.

I nodded at Uri.

Uri nervously said, *"He wants to know why the warrior is speaking for you."*

"Stop talking," I hissed at Brantley.

He nodded and whispered quickly, "Get our weapons back and make him see you as the leader." Then he bowed deeply to me and backed away, settling down on one knee. I noticed him shoot a glance at Darsey, who was still marveling at the beauty of the throne room. When he caught Darsey's eye, he too sank to one knee.

I turned back to Uri and after a moment of thought, I said, "Tell him I am tired and in need of rest. We would like our weapons back and the freedom to retrieve our steeds."

Uri turned toward the dragon and after a much longer pause, the dragon nodded. The king motioned with his hand and a servant emerged from between two of the pillars and bowed before the throne. The king spoke softly, and the servant quickly stood and disappeared from an opening hidden in the shadows of the pillars.

Another servant entered with hurried purpose and prostrated himself before the king. Once the king extended his scepter, the servant spoke and was dismissed.

*"He says the star-runners returned when they saw us released. They are waiting for us, and we will soon join them."*

Then three servants entered with our weapons laid delicately upon plush pillows. They approached and bowed down, extending them to us.

Brantley and Darsey both stood and retrieved their weapons quickly, sheathing them before returning to their respectful positions.

I stared at the dagger on the pillow, unsure of how to handle it. The fear of everything that was happening made my self-control too unpredictable. What if I grabbed the knife and turned the pillow to ash? Or even turned the servant to ash? The dragon would see me as a threat. And if he realized my power was solely granted to me by the jewel in the blade, it could shift the balance of control.

Brantley stood and grasped the blade, presenting it to me in the same fashion the servant had tried to. I gratefully took it from him, thankful he had read the situation and stepped in. Annoying he might be, but occasionally smart and useful.

Then he returned to his place behind me.

After I secured the blade to my side, Uri said, *"He says the servants will lead us to our huts."*

The three handed the pillows off to another servant and hung their heads, exiting the temple. Uri trotted up beside me and asked, *"Should I ride on Darsey?"*

"Walk beside me," I said softly.

He silently obeyed, and we followed the servants.

Just outside, the servants veered off the large path, to a smaller foot path that wrapped around the back of the giant temple. I was reluctant to follow. Only by Brantley and Darsey's confidence did I find the courage to continue. I wondered how their feelings would change once I told them the truth about Wanjala.

The path led out of the trees, and up the side of the enormous mountain the oasis butted up against. It widened the further up we went, and once we were even with the highest steeple of the temple, the ground leveled out and flattened wide, offering a large place for three huts overlooking the oasis to nestle safely against the mountain.

Our star-runners stood beside the huts. We all rushed to our own, and I stopped before Starla, making sure my blade was harnessed, before I stroked her neck. "Thank you for coming back," I cooed at her. She whinnied and bobbed her head.

One of the servants approached me and stood by the door leading into the mud hut set aside for me. I looked over and saw Darsey's hut beside mine, and Brantley's nearest the path we came from. They each had a servant standing at their door and both looked in my direction.

I looked down at Uri, then pushed the cloth aside and entered the hut. Once inside, I took a blazing torch from its mount beside the doorway and explored the tiny abode.

It was made from a mixture of mud and sand and was just as colorful as everything else in Aljonnah. It consisted of two rooms. The main room was plain and long, with empty shelves carved into the walls. There was nowhere to start a fire. Nowhere to cook food. Nothing with which to draw water.

To the side was a wall of loosely woven sticks, held together with globs of dried pitch. On the other side of the wall that only reached half the length of the hut was a low bed, covered in a luxurious lambskin.

Uri was quietly exploring the home when a knock sounded, making us both jump.

I spun and saw cloth hanging on the back wall of the main room. Another knock erupted from the cloth and I cautiously approached it, ready to let the dagger blaze fiercely if needed.

With the blade barely harnessed and an unsure hand, I moved the cloth aside and saw a wooden door. It was solid and thick. Very well built.

It shook with the next knock and I looked up, seeing a large metal latch protecting me from whatever was on the other side. I was unsure if I was willing to face another foe alone, and greatly wished Darsey and Brantley were beside me, brandishing their swords. However, with the servants outside our doors, they may as well have been miles away.

*"Open it!"* Uri said excitedly.

I looked down at him, surprised by his enthusiasm and furrowed my brow. I looked back up and heard Darsey shout, "Adalee, are you okay?"

Relieved, I quickly unlatched it and the door swung out. Darsey stumbled back and Brantley stood there, looking annoyed as always.

"About time," he whispered. "Get in here."

Uri ran past me and Darsey picked him up. I handed Brantley my torch and ducked under the jamb, minding my head. I quietly pushed the door closed and took my torch back, looking around.

We were in a small cavern behind the huts in the mountain. It was exceptionally cool, and I wondered if the huts were originally going to extend farther into the mountain, or if they had yet to finish building them.

"What did Wanjala say?" Darsey asked excitedly.

His voice echoed all over, and I shushed him quickly, looking around for listening ears. I didn't know who we could trust or if the tippoo had spies among the people. For all we knew, the servants stationed outside our huts were waiting to find out our intentions.

"Follow me," Brantley whispered, moving his flame toward a low opening near the back of the cavern.

We quietly followed and ducked into a small tunnel that opened up to a much larger cavern on the other side. The walls stretched up high, meeting a rounded dome top. Unlike the rest of the mountain, this cavern was dull and grey. Almost black.

It felt oppressive and I found it hard to catch my breath.

Darsey whispered my name and I looked at him as he moved slowly toward the wall and shined his torch upon it. The light of the flame revealed the face of a skull imbedded in the stone.

I audibly gasped and stepped back, tripping over a rock and landing on my side. When I retrieved my torch and went to stand, I realized it was a pile of bones I had stumbled into and screamed.

Darsey ran to me and reached for my arm. "We have to get out of here!" he hissed.

Terrified, I reached for his hand. Brantley quickly knocked him aside and grabbed my hand so I could touch nothing. "Don't move," he warned. "You're not in control, don't move."

"I'm in perfect control," I shouted at him hysterically.

He leaned in close and whispered, "Calm yourself. You're not in control."

My breathing was erratic, and everything started to spin and blur.

"Hey," Brantley said, grabbing my chin and making me look at him. "Breathe with me. Calm down and breathe with me." In that moment, he was no longer the annoying soldier who did everything he could to undermine me. He was more like Papa Theo, trying to help me regain myself.

He took a deep breath, raised his shoulders, and held it until I followed his example. Then he nodded and let it out slowly. I did the same, and he repeated the motion. I stayed with him until I was calm, and my heart was no longer racing.

"Okay," he said gently once he could sense my calm. "Look around you."

I looked down and saw that I was seated in a pile of ash, not bones, and the torch I had once held was gone.

I realized I had almost grabbed onto Darsey in my terror and sought him out. He was still laying on his back where Brantley had shoved him, staring wide-eyed at me.

*"Are you okay?"* Uri asked, approaching as Brantley stood and went to Darsey.

I nodded and said, "I am. I'm sorry."

I saw Brantley help Darsey to his feet and slap him on the side of the arm, like an encouraging older brother. Darsey nodded and Brantley came back to me.

"Now that we're calm," he said as though he were talking to children, "let's find out what's going on." He reached down and I grabbed his hand. He pulled me to my feet, and I steadied myself.

I looked back where we had come and said, "We should go back to the huts and talk."

Brantley shook his head and said, "We won't get more privacy than this."

Darsey looked around and said, "Unless the dead have ears."

"Have you never been in a tomb before?" Brantley asked, and I stared at him, trying to see if he was telling another joke. After a moment he said, "Okay, just me then."

"What did the Dragon Lord say?" Darsey asked again, trying to regain his composure from our earlier fright.

I took a deep breath and admitted, "He isn't a Dragon Lord. He's a tippoo."

"I knew something seemed off," Brantley whispered.

"Like what?" Darsey challenged.

He shrugged and said, "When we first laid eyes on him, I couldn't help but feel underwhelmed. He didn't seem lordly to me."

"Lordly?" I asked, arching my brow.

He nodded and added, "And when he didn't know how you harness your power, it really tipped me off."

"I didn't catch any of that," Darsey admitted, in frustration.

Brantley shook his head and said, "Let's just say I know a fraud when I see one."

I quickly relayed the details of what I knew and what was said in the temple.

Brantley nodded when I was done and said, "It was smart of you to let me retrieve your blade. Wanjala thinks you're our leader and we need to keep it that way."

"She *is* the leader," Darsey interjected.

"Okay," Brantley said with a chuckle.

Darsey opened his mouth to argue.

I cut him off, not wanting the situation to escalate. "What now? Now that we know Wanjala is an imposter, what do we do?"

Brantley thought for a moment, then said, "Is this where the Blue Dragon Lord Called you?"

I nodded.

"Okay," he said as though that settled it. "Then we stay. We play the part. We treat him like we are fools who believe he is a Dragon Lord."

"To what end?" Darsey asked. "Why should we treat him like a Lord when Adalee could end his reign with a single touch?"

"*I'm* more concerned with buying time so Adalee can free the real Dragon Lord."

"Why not free the people of Aljonnah while we're at it?" Darsey asked, throwing his hands out. "We have the power and it wouldn't be hard."

"No," I said, getting nervous by what Darsey was suggesting. "I don't want to kill *anyone*. The best thing we can do is free the Blue Dragon Lord. She can fix this."

"We should let *her* expose Wanjala," Brantley agreed.

"We need to get word to Anahita and Joah," Darsey suggested. "They need to know they are being hunted by a tippoo and not a Dragon Lord."

"And how do you expect us to do that?" Brantley asked, irritated. "We don't speak the language. Even if we knew someone we could trust, we would have no way of relaying the message."

Darsey got excited as though he had a great idea. "I could write a letter. I could send Cosmo to find them and deliver it."

"And let Wanjala see you sending out your star-runner, alone on the eve of our arrival?"

"Then I'll go myself," he volunteered.

"No," I interjected fervently.

"You're a fool," Brantley said as though he were annoyed with the conversation.

"Why?" Darsey asked honestly.

"They could follow you," he explained. "You would lead Wanjala right to them. If you really want to help them, we need to help Adalee free the Dragon Lord. *She* is the only one who can help them."

Darsey sighed heavily and nodded in defeat.

I let my anxiety ebb. I didn't want Darsey out of my sight again. Every time we separated bad things happened.

"We should get back to our huts," Brantley said.

Darsey nodded, his lips taut in frustration.

I didn't want to be alone. Uri climbed down from Darsey's shoulder and stood beside me.

"I don't have light," I said softly.

*"I can see. I'll help you,"* Uri offered sweetly.

Brantley handed me his torch and said, "Take mine."

I thanked him and we each headed back through the tunnel and into our own huts.

THIRTEEN | Settling In

Once the door was closed, I turned and saw Uri sniffing the air.

*"I smell something I think you'll like!"* he said as he trotted to the front curtain.

I followed him and pushed the cloth aside. Just outside the door was a bowl of food, and a large skin of water.

I brought the water in first, taking a long draw from it, not realizing how thirsty I was. Then I returned and brought in the bowl of food. I sat on the floor and took the blade off, laying it carefully beside me. My mouth watered as I looked at the tasty array in my lap. Steam rose enticingly as the smell of roasted meat and spices filled my hut. The first bite I took was of a round, flat cake. My mouth watered with a taste I had never experienced before. I then took a small bite of a reddish slice of citrus fruit that was surprisingly sweeter and more spice-like than I expected.

The back door opened and Darsey stepped in, a blanket tossed over his shoulder, a skin of water attached to his belt, and a bowl of food in his hand.

"Started the feast without us, I see," he said as he sat down beside me, his spirits higher than when we had left the cavern.

Brantley entered, laden similarly and carrying the extra torch. He attached it to wall near the back door and joined us.

"Have you two ever had lamb before?" he asked as he took a bite.

"Of course we have," Darsey said. "We're not *that* sheltered."

I hung my head sheepishly and lifted my hand in the air. "*I* have actually never had it," I admitted.

They both looked at me, shocked.

"She never fed you lamb?" Darsey asked in disbelief.

"What *did* you eat?" Brantley asked, taking another bite.

I cleared my throat and said, "Porridge, of sorts."

There was a moment of silence, and then Brantley said, "Wait, is that *all*?"

I nodded and Darsey snorted in irritation. "She was so evil," he remarked darkly.

"Porridge isn't *bad*," Brantley defended. "As soldiers we often eat something similar."

"It wasn't exactly a porridge," I clarified. "It was more of a gruel. I think. It was very oily and had no flavor."

There was silence again and I looked up at them. Darsey was pushing his food around, and Brantley was staring at me with a pitied look on his face.

"What?" I asked defensively.

He snapped out of it and shook his head. "Dig in. You should enjoy every opportunity you get to eat good food."

I took a bite of the lamb, and my mouth exploded with flavor. Juices dripped down my chin and throat and I froze for a moment, letting the warmth of it encompass me. Mama Iris's stew was divine, but this was other-worldly.

Darsey held up a wrinkled, brown, egg shaped item and said, "I think this went bad."

"It's a date," Brantley said as though he was surprised by our ignorance. He then picked one out of his own bowl and pulled it apart, prying out a seed. He tossed the rest in his mouth and said, "It's a sweet fruit," as he chewed. "I've only had them once before, just before I crossed into the desert on my way to the mountains."

Darsey pulled his apart and plucked out the seed, then tossed the remaining pieces in his mouth. He looked at me and arched his brow, nodding.

I pulled one out and did the same and was surprised at how sweet the brown fruit actually was. I had never tasted anything so sweet, and it almost hurt my face. Then I picked up the flat cake and took another bite, nodding. "The cake was sweetened with dates," I said while I chewed, a tiny piece of food flying from my mouth and landing on Brantley's knee.

He flicked it away and said, "You eat like a ravenous wolf."

I ignored him, and Darsey held up another unfamiliar food.

Brantley then went through his bowl and told us what each piece was called.

I picked my citrus fruit up again and saw Darsey examining a fig. Brantley took up a handful of olives and began tossing them into his mouth, while I tore into the spiced fruit.

We each finished our meals and drained our canteens before we spoke again.

"So, what are we going to do?" Darsey asked.

"Adalee needs to meditate," Brantley said. "Once she gets some answers, then we'll know what to do."

I agreed and immediately regretted it, as I was overtaken with exhaustion. "Actually," I backtracked. "I think I need some rest first."

"We don't want to lose the night," Brantley insisted.

"I know her," Darsey defended. "She will go until she kills herself. If she says she needs sleep, then we need to let her sleep."

Brantley sighed and, to my surprise, nodded. "Okay. We probably all need sleep."

"What about the star-runners?" I asked.

"The first one awake can go gather the orbs," Brantley said. "I think they'll be fine."

*"I'll keep watch,"* Uri offered, puffing out his chest heroically.

I relayed his pledge, smiling at the fact that he slept heavier and more often than anyone.

Brantley smirked, and laid out his lambskin.

"Good boy, Uri," Darsey applauded, scratching him between the shoulders. Uri began purring and pushing up into the scratches.

He nearly fell over when Darsey pulled his hand away. Once he recovered, he laid by the door, and peered out under a hole in the bottom corner. I was impressed that he really planned to keep watch.

I went to my bed as Darsey laid out his lambskin on the other side of the wall and asked Uri, "Are you sure you will be able to stay awake?"

*"Starla is my friend, and I don't want Wanjala to hurt her."*

His concern sent chills up my spine and I looked at Darsey and Brantley, forgetting that they couldn't hear him as I could. Brantley was on his back, sword in hand, eyes closed. Darsey was facing me on his side, his sword laying beside him, unsheathed and ready for action. I retrieved my dagger and laid it on the bedding beside me.

I sat on the bed and was surprised at how deeply I sank into it. It was softer than anything I had ever slept on and I eagerly laid down, letting the comfort surround me. I wanted to lift my head and check on Uri one more time. Instead, my eyes drifted shut, and I slept.

I stood in the midst of the oasis jungle. Daylight shined through the trees, casting bold beams upon the ground. A glistening caught my eye and I looked to see the beautiful yellow pool, its waters dancing happily with the gentle wind that moved the trees and made the beams of light shake and shift.

A small child ran past me, drawing my attention. He was naked, save a cloth diaper that was fastened around him. I watched him run up to three older children, and they all began to laugh and rush through the jungle.

Curious, I followed them, easily keeping up as their movements were slow, like they were moving through the weight of water. I followed them past the red, orange, and purple pools, before they stepped up to the green one. The oldest looking child picked up a stone and skipped it across the water.

A man in warrior garb rushed at them, with the same slow movements, and chased them away, though they appeared amused rather than frightened as they scattered into the jungle.

I watched the man return to standing sentry at the green water, and slowly walked past him. I saw no recognition of my presence in his eyes.

A date fell at my feet, and as I stared at it, another fell. I looked up and saw two monkeys swinging and jumping back and forth from branches. One had a handful of dates he was trying to escape with and were falling from his hands and scattering below.

Movement on the ground caught my attention and I turned and saw a snake darting across my path. Instinctively, I stepped back and heard the monkeys above howl in what sounded like a mix of laughter and frustration. As I looked up, my eyes were drawn to a curious looking lizard that was slowly moving along the bark of a tree. I almost missed it, as its colors blended in well.

I continued forward, taking in the vibrancy of the jungle and enjoying the life it had to offer. It was no wonder the people thrived here and didn't want to risk intruders upsetting the balance of nature they had learned to utilize.

I focused on the path ahead and stopped suddenly, as I was standing before the black pool of my dreams. The carefree sounds of the jungle immediately ceased, and the pool and I were left alone. The silence slowly grew into ringing as I stared into it, feeling confused and entranced.

I felt a wind brush against the back of my head and turned, only to find an empty desert, with muted grey colors. There were no pools. No jungle. No people or animals. No life.

A wind picked up in the distance and I watched in horror as it washed over the sand, mixing the grey hues into one. It grew large and drew closer, threatening to slam into me, when suddenly a great orange sandstorm blew in behind me. I didn't feel the pain of the sand whipping across my skin. The wind seemed to move around me, leaving me untouched as the orange sand grew larger than the grey, and it flew forward and consumed the grey sandstorm.

Then it was gone, and I was facing the black pool again, only this time I wasn't alone.

Wanjala was staring at me from across the pool, eyeing me as though he had caught me doing something wrong.

He bared his teeth and the dark pool slowly shrank between us. As he neared me, I noticed something jutting from his mouth and only once he was upon me, did I realize it was bones.

His snarl turned to a sinister smile as he stared down at me and the bones began to fall from between his teeth. I ducked and covered my head as they piled on top of me until I was buried in the dark.

I jumped up, prepared to run, and found myself in the tomb. The bones were glowing in an eerie muted grey, and they quickly drew in upon me.

I spun and sought the tunnel that would lead me to my hut. I found it and ran, diving for the hole as I could feel the bones piling up at my feet.

I crawled through though it became smaller and tighter around me. Once on the other side, I saw my door; a happy lit torch resting beside it.

I jumped up and stumbled forward, crashing into it.

Locked.

I slammed my fists into it, screaming for Darsey or Brantley to wake up and let me in.

I could hear the bones clattering against one another as they piled up behind me. I dared not turn to see what evil form they were taking to pull me back into the tomb and make me one with them.

I wasn't dead! I wasn't one of them!

I screamed and threw myself into the door, making it bounce back and fly open. I blindly stumbled into the hut and tripped over my bed, which was sitting right in front of the door.

I landed with my back to the open door, and I could still feel the frigid air blasting in from the cavern. I shut my eyes and prayed to the Dragon Lords that they not let the bones have me.

My eyes opened to daylight; my back drenched in warm sweat. I was on my side, facing the rainbow wall nearest my bed. I could hear movement and whispers behind me.

Uri was laying against my back and I glanced up, seeing that the dagger was gone. I sat up quickly, and Uri rolled down the bed into my hip.

*"What happened?"* he asked tiredly, as he sat up.

"Where's the dagger?" I demanded.

"Right there!" Darsey said, coming around and grabbing it off the ground by my bed. He put it near my pillow and said, "When I woke up this morning and saw you sleeping so near it, I felt it was unsafe so I moved it."

Uri yawned and jumped off the bed, elongating into a deep stretch.

I picked up the blade and attached it to my side. "I can't be without it," I explained. "Please, I need to keep it on me at all times."

"I'm sorry, I was just trying to help," Darsey said.

"I know. It's okay. I'm just nervous about . . . him."

"Wanjala," Darsey clarified.

"Shh," Brantley hissed. "Don't say his name."

I looked over at the door that lead to the tomb. A chill ran up my sweaty spine and buried itself deep in my bones.

"Even if the people don't understand our language," Brantley was saying, "they know his name. We don't want to draw any unwanted attention."

A pulse started low in my ears and resonated around me. The fear from the dream began to spread through me, still feeling so real.

"And what exactly is 'unwanted' attention?" Darsey asked.

Cold sweat beaded on my forehead and in my palms. I felt sick.

*"Adalee, look,"* Uri drew my attention.

I glanced at him, then followed his wide gaze to the bed, which was starting to singe beneath my touch.

*"Any* attention," Brantley said seriously.

I discreetly loosed the blade from my side and subtly pushed it away. The tingling left and I breathed deeply, trying to calm my fear, grateful no one else had noticed.

Darsey stepped back to the other side of the wall and brought me a bowl of porridge. "This is what they had for breakfast this morning," he said in a tone that seemed very bright compared to what I was feeling. "I know it doesn't look very good, but it tastes amazing."

I took the bowl and wooden spoon from him and wasn't worried about what I saw. It was a warm yellow color, speckled with dark bits, with pieces of fruit sticking out of the sides. There was something orange and smooth swirled throughout, and I found myself desiring a taste.

When I brought the spoon to my mouth, a mixture of sweet citrus and warm comfort spread through my face, erasing the dread that still hung on me from my nightmare. It was nothing like what Madame used to force on me. If gruel had tasted anything like this, I might have never found issue with my life, despite all the other shortcomings.

I snickered at the ludicrous thought but eagerly took another bite.

"Can you meditate?" Brantley interrupted.

"Give her a minute to wake up and eat breakfast," Darsey scolded.

"I forgot," he said sarcastically. "She needs everything to be *perfect* to do her *job*."

"Can I speak to you outside for a minute?" Darsey asked him seriously.

Brantley didn't say anything as he shoved the flap aside and stepped out. Darsey handed me Starla's orb and said, "I'll be right back." He also handed me a small bowl of water, then followed Brantley out.

I paid little mind to their whispers as I wrapped Starla up and attached her to my wrist. Though the dread had faded, I glanced over at the wooden door again, peering through the stick wall that split the hut into two.

What would my meditation reveal? If my dreams meant anything, as they often did, Wanjala had something to do with the tomb. Was he secretly killing people and hiding their bones? Was that where he would put all the rebels when he found them?

Then a grisly thought entered my mind. What if he trapped people in there whilst they still lived? What if it was the pit Anahita spoke of? And what if the only reason the venomous creatures it was said to house didn't come forward, was because of the Dragon's Fire I wielded?

Brantley and Darsey came back and I decided I should tell them about the dream. When I was finished laying it all out along with my concerns, Darsey sighed deeply. "That's really dark."

I nodded and said, "Trust me, I didn't like it at all."

"If that *is* the pit," Darsey asked, "then why would he put *us* in houses so near it?"

"He's threatening us," Brantley answered confidently. "Adalee knows the truth, and he's doing what he can to keep her quiet."

Darsey and I looked at each other and he shook his head. "That's insane. He thinks he can *threaten* the Dragon Born and get away with it?" he asked angrily.

Brantley held his hands up and clarified, "*Maybe.*"

"You didn't say 'maybe'," Darsey accused.

"Well, I'm saying it now!" he shouted.

"Let me meditate!" I interjected.

They both looked at me. "Is everything finally perfect for you?" Brantley asked sardonically.

"You have no right to say that," Darsey defended. "You have no idea what it's like."

"I need some privacy, please," I said. "Let me try to meditate and get some answers."

Brantley and Darsey stared at each other, each sucking in a deep breath.

"Of course," Brantley said, storming out the front.

"Call me if you need me," Darsey said softly as he followed Brantley.

Uri hopped up on the bed and stared. *"Do I need to go too?"* he asked.

I shook my head and offered a smile. "Never."

He happily settled in and I moved the dagger near him.

He looked at it, then back at me.

"Just to be safe," I whispered.

He laid on the hilt protectively, and I sat my empty bowl down and crossed my legs, ready to figure out what was going on.

I closed my eyes and let Serefina's instructions play over in my head. After not too long, the hut around me vanished and the Blue Dragon Lord appeared. Like always, she was floating in a world of water. I grabbed onto one of the tendrils snaking off her head and pulled myself up, ready for answers.

Though it had exhausted me, the day in the desert I had spent in meditation had really helped me hone the skill more than ever before.

She turned and leaped gracefully from the cliff edge, floating over the large temple, and slowly sank to the jungle floor. Then she swam forward, through the jungle and stopped at the black pool. The water slowly disappeared around us and she gently set me on the ground instead of bursting into bubbles. Then she jumped up high and dove into the center of the black pool. Her serpentine body eventually disappeared beneath the water, leaving the surface perfectly still.

That was where she was trapped. As soon as I stepped forward, Wanjala appeared and stood in my way.

In a fright, I pulled myself from the mediation, trying to let the new layer of cold sweat that had just covered my body disappear.

*"What's wrong?"* Uri asked innocently.

I shook my head and called for Darsey and Brantley.

They rushed back in and stood around my bed.

Brantley crossed his arms and studied my face.

Darsey eagerly asked, "Did it work?"

I nodded and said, "I know where she is."

Brantley sighed in relief, then asked, "She is *here*, right? We came to the right place?"

I nodded again and said, "She's trapped in the black pool."

Darsey furrowed his brow and asked, "Why don't you seem happy about that? We know where she is, so we can free her, right?"

I sighed and mouthed the name, "Wanjala."

"What about him?" Brantley asked through tight lips.

"He won't let us do it easily. He has been in my dreams, somehow. And just now he was in my meditation. At first, I thought he was the next Dragon Lord to free, until Uri revealed the truth to me."

"How is he in your dreams at all?" Darsey asked. "What kind of power makes him able to do that?"

I shrugged and said, "He might not be aware. He doesn't speak to me or do anything other than threaten me in the dreams, *and* meditation. It's almost like . . . like the Blue Dragon Lord is *warning* me of him."

"*She's* showing you a vision of him, rather than him invading and threatening the Calling," Brantley clarified for himself.

I shrugged again and said, "Maybe?"

"So, what do we do?" Darsey asked.

There were voices outside that drew all our attention. Brantley held out his hands for us to stay silent and went to the flap. He peeked, then stepped out quickly, letting it shut behind him.

The talking quieted, and a moment later he returned with a large stack of cloth in his arms.

"They brought us clothes," he said as he laid them down on the bed.

I stood and we each found what would fit best. They stepped into the cavern to change, and I quickly took off my singed desert clothes and put on the new ones they offered.

They were similar to what Anahita and Joah had given us except the headpiece was smaller and didn't cover my face and neck.

The guys came back, dressed similarly, though mine looked brighter and newer than theirs, then Brantley whispered, "They were trying to tell me something. I have no idea what." He looked at me and said, "Maybe Uri can help us out?"

"He doesn't know their *language*," I pointed out.

*"Wanjala,"* Uri said.

I looked at him and scrunched my brow. I didn't want to bother or seek Wanjala if we didn't need to, then the servants who brought us our clothes frantically began whispering his name.

Uri hopped off the bed and trotted to the flap. I made sure my emotions were in check, then grabbed the dagger and secured it before following him.

Darsey stayed beside me while Brantley went ahead and held the flap open. Coming up the path was Wanjala, the king seated on a throne secured to the base of his neck.

It took him only moments to reach our huts. All the servants bowed low while the three of us stood tall. I knew who he was, and I couldn't bring myself to bow.

He stopped and stared at us with an indecipherable expression. His long snout pulled into a sneer, and I couldn't tell if he was angry, or trying to smile.

*"He wants to give us a tour of the oasis and let us meet the people,"* Uri said. I hadn't even realized they were speaking already.

I nodded and said, "Very well." I needed to know where the black pool was. I shot a glance at Brantley and said, "Wanjala is going to show us his land."

Brantley and I made eye contact and he nodded. I hoped he understood that most of the information of the layout would be on his shoulders.

Darsey whispered, "Even the black pool?"

My eyes went wide, and I scolded him as best I could with only a look. Brantley didn't flinch. I didn't want Wanjala knowing we knew about the black pool, and who laid beneath it.

He hung his head and I was both grateful he read my face and regretful I made him feel bad.

Yet those concerns would have to wait. We needed to be ready for anything.

Fourteen | The Truth About Wanjala

Wanjala turned and began walking slowly back down the hill, his movements causing the ground to tremble. Uri looked up at me and asked, *"Can I walk near him?"*

"Stay beside *me*," I whispered. Without knowing Wanjala's intentions, I couldn't let anyone be alone with him. He was too large and dangerous. Too unpredictable.

We walked quietly down the hill, while the servants stayed face down until we passed. Wanjala turned along a wide path that lead into what looked to be the heart of the oasis.

He stopped once beneath the tall trees and Uri said, *"He wants to know if you will walk beside him and talk."*

I looked at Brantley first, who never took his hand from the hilt of his sword. He stared at me intensely and I whispered, "I am going to talk to him."

He nodded.

I looked at Darsey, who was aloof and gazing about in awe. I didn't think he would notice, and I knew Brantley would enlighten him if he asked, so I nodded at Uri and approached Wanjala.

*"He asks if you slept well."*

"Tell him the bed was very comfortable." Though I didn't sleep well, Wanjala had no business knowing my dreams, or nightmares.

*"He wants to know if the food was to your liking."*

"Tell him it was." I wanted to say it was unlike anything I had ever tasted. That it was the most delicious food I had ever placed on my tongue. That I couldn't wait until I could have another bowl, and I hoped that after we left, I could try it again one day.

*"He says he is happy you have come. Your presence is a great gift to the people of Aljonnah and he wants to make sure all of your company is treated in the highest regard."*

Wanjala stayed stoic and forward facing as he walked and spoke to Uri. His movements were smooth and regal, like a real Dragon Lord. The old king swayed back and forth with each step, seeming not to notice, no doubt from years of practice.

*"He doesn't want you to have the wrong idea about him."* Uri continued. *"He says he knows you must have figured out he is merely a tippoo being treated as a Dragon Lord, and he would like permission to share his story, so that you know you can trust him and his presence among the people."*

My heart began to race as his words made me anxious. I hadn't tried to give him any indication I was against him. That I would be an adversary to him, though I couldn't deny the legitimacy of the assumption. Anyone who falsely claimed to be a Dragon Lord in order to control others couldn't be anything other than evil.

However, I wanted to hear everything he had to say and tell Darsey and Brantley later.

I nodded and said, "I am interested in hearing how he came to be here."

After a moment, Uri said, *"He is very pleased you are willing to hear him out. He is going to talk slow so I can tell you word by word."*

I nodded and waited for him to begin.

*"I am over one thousand years old. Him, not me,"* Uri clarified.

I nodded and said, "I understand," though my mind was reeling. A *thousand* years old? How old was Uri? Were tippoos immortal?

Uri let out a little laugh and continued. *"The people of Aljonnah were once a barbaric, and war-ridden people. I was attached to a human many years ago, and we had become lost in the desert. He wasn't my first human, but I loved him dearly."*

I remembered that Uri had told me I was the first of his memories. The only human he knew. Did that make him a baby tippoo? How many people would he have after me? The thought of him loving another more than me hurt. I quickly pushed the feeling aside as he continued.

*"We stumbled across the oasis and were attacked when we tried to enter it for water and shelter. Frightened for my human, I leaped into my largest form. The form you see now. The people were so taken by the sight of me, they immediately fell down and began to worship."*

I looked around as we walked through the trees. I saw no statues of dragons as I expected to see. Of course, they had what they believed to be a real Dragon Lord, so why would they need a statue? Just like my village had no shrine because they had me.

*"My human didn't know their language, yet they made him their king. After all, they believed me to be a Dragon Lord and saw that I protected him."*

We entered the center of the oasis, conveyed by the many colors of pools that surrounded it. Each pool had a bridge that spanned across it, and in the center of each bridge was a bright sand-stone statue of Wanjala, built solely from the sands of that pool's color.

So, there *were* dragon statues. Just not of actual Dragon Lords.

*"We were going to make an escape after we replenished our supplies. Then, as we were sneaking out a few nights later, we saw the people about to sacrifice a woman to the black pool."*

I looked around until I saw the black pool settled in with the others. Nothing indicated it was special except it had no bridge or statue, and there were many more guards surrounding it than the other pools.

*"My human rushed to stop it and I helped him. The people were astonished that I stepped in to stop their barbaric ritual. My human felt we couldn't leave yet, lest they try again once we were gone, and he eventually fell in love with the woman we rescued."*

I took note of the other pools around us. Their colors were overwhelmingly beautiful. A green that brought to mind every color of home in the spring. Somehow a mix of all the brightest and darkest leaves, waving in the wind, catching sunlight. A red that reflected both the gleam of the brightest tomatoes in Mama Iris's garden, and the deepest notes of a crimson wine, swirling together in perfect harmony. A purple that could only be described as belonging in the finest palaces and adorning the most regal of royals among men, though I had never been in the presence of such nobility. A yellow that filled me with warmth and joy, like feeling the first ray of sunshine on my skin after a long, cold winter. An orange that screamed flavor that would wrap its recipient in citrusy warmth akin to the porridge I had been graced with that morning.

And yet, the way I viewed them still seemed unworthy of their beauty.

The black pool was different.

Staring at it filled me with unease. A mysterious, painful regret sprang up deep in my inner core. The discomfort seeped into my bones and screamed at me to run. Much like the feeling I got in the tomb.

*"Be careful,"* Uri said, and I looked at him. He was staring at my feet. I looked down and saw I was standing on a wooden door spanning the ground. I stepped off it and Uri said, *"Wanjala says to be careful, because that wooden panel keeps the venomous creatures of the rainbow sands trapped.*

The pit? In the middle of the colorful pools?

Then he continued as though no warning had been made. *"Despite the language barrier, she became his queen and bore him five children. He learned their language well enough, and as the children grew, knowing both languages they were able to help with communication in a way we hadn't experienced before."*

Much to my dismay, we moved away from the pools, into the forest of tall, unusual trees. There was a mass assortment of leaves around us, and I could smell a mixture of refreshing water in the air, laced with citrus that made my mouth desire a taste.

*"The rituals stopped. The aggression toward one another stopped. The people began to live in harmony and peace and work the land to make it better."*

I realized there were people up in the trees, tossing harvest down to those holding woven baskets. Someone approached me with half of an orange that had been ground to a pulpy liquid. I gratefully accepted it and sipped the amazing juice as we continued walking.

*"My human's queen knew what I was. My human loved her dearly and could hide nothing from her and she cared not. We had saved her life."*

Movement from above caught my attention and I saw monkeys swinging through the trees, causing the branches to bounce and dance above. Another person approached me and eagerly offered me a handful of dates, which I accepted and snacked on, along with my juice.

*"She feared that if the people found out about me not being a real Dragon Lord, they would return to their old ways. So, she begged us to keep up the charade and help the people of Aljonnah live in peace."*

Around me the people were working steadily, giving off an air of joyfulness and contentment. There was much smiling and conversation as they worked the land, even as we moved from the trees into fields akin in appearance to Papa Theo's garden, though empty of crops.

People were tending it, scraping at the earth and laughing with one another.

They didn't look rebellious and unhappy as Anahita and Joah had led us to believe.

*"My human eagerly agreed, so when the time came for me to attach to another, I did as he wished. Only one of his children had the glow of one who could take on a tippoo. And so, when the time came and my human breathed his last breath, I severed our bond, at his request, and bonded to his youngest. A new king."*

I looked off and saw someone approaching us with an odd-looking beast. It stood well above his head, and had a thick, furry body set upon long, knobby legs. It had large hooves that lazily padded into the ground as it allowed itself to be led over. It was a dusty brown color, with extra dark tufts of fur that curled upon its head and around its long, curved neck that jutted from the bottom of its chest and reached high above its back. A back that was misshapen with two large humps, that also housed dark tufts of fur atop each one.

From beside its wide, shapely snout, two massive tusks jutted forth. The animal was quite frightening as it approached, but the friendly demeanor of the man leading it so easily forced me to find my courage and stay put, rather than run for my life.

He stopped nearby and held out his hand for mine. I looked up at Wanjala, who nodded gently. I set my empty orange bowl down and laid my hand in his. He lightly gripped my wrist and pulled me toward the beast. He laid my palm on the nose of the creature and moved it up and down in a petting motion.

"Geelibamba," he said with a smile.

I nodded and responded, "geel .. ee .. bom ... buh ..."

He excitedly nodded and smiled, then bowed himself away, taking the creature with him.

Wanjala continued when we began walking again.

*"It was then I understood the people. The queen died shortly after her husband, and when the generation of the new king had passed away, the secret of what I was passed with them."*

I absently wiped my hand on my tunic, surprised by how velvety the creature felt when it looked so coarse.

*"That was many, many generations ago. And through the generations, I have learned that the people rely heavily on the colored pools to lead them and their decisions in life. They believe them to contain wisdom in and of themselves. Like sentient beings. So, I have allowed them to continue to indulge in*

*their customs, not wishing to tear down the traditions they hold dear. The only thing I stopped were the sacrifices."*

I let his last words settle on me. I didn't know what to think. He didn't seem to be the vicious, evil tyrant that Anahita and Joah described. If anything, he seemed just and virtuous.

*"So, you see, my purposes are noble. I love these people."*

"And you want me to keep your secret," I said softly.

*"I beseech you to act with discretion,"* he agreed. *"It would destroy everything they have become. And in exchange, I will help you with whatever task has brought you to us."*

I decided I needed to be bold with him. I needed to test his allegiance and see if he was really noble, or full of trickery.

"There is a real Dragon Lord here," I said. "In the black pool."

Wanjala froze in his tracks for a moment, and I looked up and saw his eyes wide.

*"The black pool offers no mercy to those who enter it. They never return."*

"That is where she is," I pressed, letting the tingle of my blade spread through my fingers. This was his chance. If he wanted to fight, I *would* win.

He turned only his head and gazed into my eyes, a softness in his. *"Then I will do whatever you ask of me. I will help you free her, for the greater good."*

I worked to pull the tingle back in and marveled at his resolve. Maybe he wasn't the monster I believed him to be.

"All I need is access to the pool," I said. "Once she is free, we will be on our way."

Wanjala looked down at Uri, a massive beast towering over a tiny kitten, and Uri said, *"I'm not THAT small."* Then Uri looked at me and said with a humph, *"He says your tippoo is young and small."*

Then Uri's eyes went wide, and he looked back up at Wanjala. With an excitement in his voice he stood and faced me, *"He says he can teach me! He says he can show me how to leap any time I want and teach me the secrets of being a tippoo! Things that took him hundreds of years to learn on his own."*

My breath caught in my chest and I looked at Wanjala, wide-eyed. Could it be true? Was he really an ally? If so, I needed to know what he knew.

"What of the rebellion?" I asked boldly. Although I couldn't discount Anahita and Joah's feelings about Wanjala since he *was* lying to them, I needed to know why he decided not to mention it when telling me his story.

Wanjala turned and faced me, an unreadable expression on his scaly face. Then Uri said, *"He wants to know how you know about that?"*

I didn't know what to say. I didn't know if I should tell the truth about what happened in the desert or lie and say it's because nothing can be kept from the Dragon Born. Before I could weigh both options, I blurted out, "There is a band of people out in the desert. They said you are cruel and tyrannical. They said you control the people and don't let them flourish."

Wanjala cocked his head and looked away.

Uri said, *"He says the oasis isn't big enough to support everyone if they were allowed to 'flourish'. He knows Anahita and Joah, and he knows they are upset about what happened to Zaire. It was a tragic misunderstanding. He didn't throw Zaire in the black pool, as they accuse. Zaire was bent on destroying the house of the Dragon and dove into the pool, knowing his sacrifice would be just what was needed to fan the embers of his movement into flames of rebellion. He was a traitor, and enemy to the crown."*

"How is that fair?" I asked, bewildered. He *wasn't* a real Dragon Lord. What right did he have to keep hold of a people who wished to be free?

He froze for a moment, and then Uri said, *"He says you're right. It has all gone too far. However, if he were to admit his deception now, he fears what it would do to the people."*

This was perfect. "You don't have too," I said with a relieved smile. "The people believe you to be a Dragon Lord. When I free the Blue Dragon Lord, she will leave. You can do the same. It will seem natural and not give you away."

After another silence, Uri translated, *"Perhaps this is what is best for Aljonnah. But where will I go? I have not had another home in a millennium."*

I looked down at Uri, and he was looking up me, completely at ease.

*"He should come with us,"* the kitten suggested.

When Brantley left it *would* be nice to have someone to help in tough situations. Who better to accompany the Dragon Lord, than a dragon? Tippoo or not.

I nodded and he turned toward Wanjala.

After a moment, Wanjala bowed his head and Uri said, *"He is grateful we have come and is thankful we are placing our trust in him."*

I was happier than I expected. I wasn't sure what the ominous tone to my dreams surrounding him were, but as long as he stopped pretending to be a Dragon Lord, I saw no fault in him beyond what he had already done.

*"He would like to begin training with me immediately,"* Uri said excitedly. *"He says you should go back to the huts and await my return."*

"What about the black pool?" I asked anxiously, though most of my angst was at the thought of leaving Uri.

*"He says the laws of the land are absolute, and even the Dragon Born needs to follow them to gain access to the black pool."*

"What 'laws'?" I asked.

*"He says he will explain everything to me during my training. For now, you should go back to the huts and await further instruction."*

I didn't like the way things had taken a sudden turn. Who was he to tell the Dragon Born what to do when he was only a tippoo? Still . . . it would really help if Uri knew how to control his abilities. Besides, I needed to tell Darsey and Brantley everything I had learned and see what they thought.

I hesitantly nodded. "Are you sure, Uri?" I asked.

He barely heard me as he was back walking beside Wanjala, a happy bounce to his gait.

A servant came up and bowed, then motioned for me to follow him. I turned and saw Darsey and Brantley some ways behind me. I joined them and we followed the servant back to the huts in silence.

"You told him *everything*?" Brantley asked, furious.

I crossed my arms defensively and said, "He told *me* everything. I wanted to see how he reacted to the news about the Dragon Lord in the black pool and the rebels."

"Great," Brantley said, his tone indicating it was the opposite of great. "Now he knows exactly where to keep us from. *And* if he didn't know about the rebellion before, he certainly does now."

"Unless he's telling the truth," Darsey argued. "If he really does want to leave Aljonnah and come with us, he could be very useful."

"So, we're just going to hide the fact that he isn't really the Dragon Lord from the people?" Brantley asked.

"Since when did you start caring about anyone other than yourself?" Darsey inquired as he crossed his arms.

"Yeah," I agreed, getting frustrated that he was unhappy with what I had done. "Isn't this exactly how you would *want* to handle it? Discreetly. In and out. Leave them be? Everyone will be happy this way."

Brantley laughed without humor and said, "I didn't realize we were doing things *my* way now. You should have told me." He drew his sword and moved toward the flap.

I leaped forward and grabbed his arm. "Don't you dare go out there and undo what I've done!"

"I don't think I *could* undo what you've done. You've given us up! If we can't trust him, he knows our secrets now."

"He doesn't know where the source of Adalee's power comes from," Darsey pointed out. He faced me. "I think you did a great job. You may have earned us the most powerful ally we could have."

Brantley scoffed and sheathed his sword. "And you think Uri won't tell him everything else? He has already proven that the dragon can take information from his memory without his permission."

"If he's telling the truth, which Adalee thinks he is, then we don't need to worry about anything he discovers. He wants to help us."

"I don't think he does," Brantley said firmly. "And neither should you," he said, pointing his finger at me. "You're too naïve to be the Dragon Born," he growled.

"And you're too cynical," I barked back, causing Darsey to jump and look at me in wonder. "And you're right, I *don't* want to do this *your* way. I want to do it *my* way. And I'm trying to figure out what that is. So, just give me a chance to make this happen. If it doesn't work out, and he does end up being traitorous," I pointed to my blade, "then I'll handle it. He has no idea what I'm capable of. Can't you be content with that?"

Darsey was beaming beside me and Brantley had an impassive expression on his face. He nodded stiffly and said, "If anything goes wrong, I'm taking over."

I clenched my fists as he exited through the back.

*One step closer* Madame whispered so near I thought she was beside me.

My hair stood on end and I shook my head.

*One more mistake, and he will tell Darsey. Just wait and see.*

"That was amazing," Darsey said upon exhale. "I am completely behind you. I trust you."

I forced a smile, then sat on the bed, pondering the validity of Madame's concerns and waiting anxiously for Uri's return.

It was hours before Uri's sweet voice sounded in my head. Darsey slept soundly on the bed behind me, exhausted from the day.

*"Adalee, are you here? I'm back!"*

I jumped up, the movement causing Darsey to stir. I ran to the flap and pulled it aside. Uri approached with three servants in tow, each carrying red bundles in their arms.

He trotted in and the servants stopped at the threshold and bowed their heads, holding the bundles toward me.

I made sure the tingle was fully contained before I let them stack the bundles in my arms, one on top of the other. They stepped back and waited.

I looked down at Uri and he said, *"We need to change and go with them."*

Brantley came walking in the back. The scraping of the door made Darsey sit up quickly, and look around drowsily.

"What's happening?" Brantley asked seriously.

The flap closed once I had the bundles and I faced him. He took them from me and set them down.

Darsey stood up and stretched. "What did I miss?" he asked with a yawn.

"Uri says we need to dress in these and go with the servants outside."

Brantley arched his brow and asked, "Why?"

I looked at Uri and he said excitedly, *"It's a surprise!"*

"He says it's a surprise."

Brantley crossed his arms and demanded, "Make him tell us what we are walking into. We don't know for sure if we are in the presence of enemies or allies."

Uri hung his head and I could see his feelings were hurt. I was angry that he was still undermining me and I turned to him. "We're doing this *my* way, remember?"

*Getting closer* Madame cackled.

"*Not* if your way is going to get us killed," he argued back.

"Uri wouldn't let us walk into a trap," Darsey interjected.

"If he *knew*," Brantley said as though we were fools. He scoffed and looked at Uri. "You can't trust the dragon, no matter how much you like him. If you do, then you align yourself with our enemy."

"Don't talk to him like that," I growled, stepping between them. "Don't talk to him at all. You talk to *me*."

"Fine," he said, stepping close to my face. I could feel the tingle of the blade spread futilely at his obstinance. "We need to know everything that was said so we can decide what to believe. If he can't tell us that, or *won't* tell us that, he isn't helping anyone."

*"They're making you members of the tribe!"* Uri cried out.

I turned to him and he looked sad and defeated.

*"Wanjala said that the black pool is off limits to everyone, and if an exception were to be made, it would only be made for a member of the tribe. Otherwise everything they have built would crumble and he would be risking them returning to their old ways once he left."*

I cocked my head in pity for poor Uri, who only wanted us to be surprised with what he saw as wonderful news.

I turned back to Brantley and relayed the message, then informed him that he had hurt Uri's feelings.

"I don't care about his *feelings*," Brantley said with disdain. "I care about our survival."

*"I won't hide anything again, I promise,"* Uri said.

"He said he won't keep anything from us again," I told him. "He deserves an apology."

Brantley laughed and said, "He won't get one."

Fifteen | Who Would You Die For?

The bundles were red robes that draped from my shoulders to the floor and down the length of my arms to my fingertips. I looked like a child wearing my mother's gown, as did Darsey and Brantley when they returned.

Though I felt ridiculous, Uri said the servants were waiting to take us to the ceremony, so we stepped out of the hut together. I was surprised that the robes were weighted perfectly so they gathered behind us as we walked, leaving our steps unhindered.

The sun quickly set, and it was only by the glow of the torches held by two of the tribesmen that we were able to see the path before us. The other two held staffs with red flags that trembled gently with each step. The sound of drums beating in the distance echoed around us and made the path feel more ominous than the first night we traversed it.

"Keep your guard up," Brantley whispered as we descended. "It could be a trap."

"I'm ready," I assured him, feeling the buzz of the blade at my side, though I felt there was little need for it.

"I hope there's food," Darsey added.

Brantley turned to him and said, "You won't be laughing when you're full of arrows."

"That depends on how they taste," he snipped back.

Brantley didn't respond as we entered the trees and headed to the center of the oasis where the pools resided.

As we approached, we were met with what appeared to be the entirety of Aljonnah. The people were all dressed in red robes and adorned with pounds of gold jewelry. We walked amongst the crowd who greeted us with silent smiles. They were amassed throughout the center of the pools in a way that made the wooden cover to the pit impossible to see. I wanted to be sure I steered clear of it.

I glanced over them for gold bracelets on the correct wrist, and was disappointed to see everyone wore so much, there wasn't a single person without the bracelet on their wrist, plus ten more.

Did Anahita really lie about it?

"Be ready for anything," Brantley reminded us, his tension now spreading to me.

The people made a path and as we walked past their smiling faces. My angst began to ebb, and melted away completely when we came upon a massive, low table covered in an extravagant feast of colors, smells, and flavors I couldn't wait to indulge in.

"Yes," Darsey whispered excitedly.

There were three red cushions on one side of the low table, and a single, more lavish one on the other side. Before each cushion was an empty golden chalice.

*"Adalee, you are supposed to sit on the middle cushion, and Darsey and Brantley are supposed to sit on each side of you."*

I relayed the information to them, and we sat. The people crowded in and sat on the ground as near us as they could get. The only sound was of their movements and the constant drumming spilling forth with low, baleful booms.

I looked at Brantley who was staying still and stoic, though I could see his eyes darting everywhere, taking it all in. I glanced at Darsey who was taking in the assortment of meats, fruits, nuts, and bowls of spices before us.

*"Can I sit on your shoulder?"* Uri asked sweetly.

I made sure the blade was contained, then nodded and said, "Of course. And if not for the power, you needn't ask."

He clawed his way up the thick robes to my shoulder and cheerfully said, *"I know."*

After a moment, the thunder of the drums was echoed by a different, softer boom. The boom I had come to recognize as Wanjala moving.

Everyone prostrated themselves on the ground as he approached, the old king on his back. They were both adorned in red robes like everyone else in Aljonnah, and I was amazed that Wanjala himself had some made to his specifications. Like he was truly one of them.

Instead of gold jewelry, both Wanjala and the king had gold crowns fitted atop their heads, the king's more intricate and ornate than the dragon's. Another testament to his humility, no doubt.

Two attendants jumped up and fluidly helped the king dismount and seat himself on the cushion opposite us. It was the first time I had really peered into his aged, milky grey eyes.

The drumming stopped as soon as he sat, and the attendants returned to their faces.

With a shaky hand, the king picked up a rod of wood intertwined with gold and tapped his empty chalice, which let out a ring.

Immediately, our chalices were taken, and we watched as they were filled with water drawn from the red pool. When they were returned to us, my heart raced, curious and anxious about what might come next.

*"He has begun the ritual,"* Uri said. *"It is a silent ritual, but Wanjala wants to set you at ease. When you drink from the red pool, you will see what you would die for."*

His description did not set me at ease. What did that mean? How would I see what I would die for? Was it drugged, like the wine on Surin's ship?

I looked around and saw everyone had a golden chalice in hand and were lined up all around the red pool, only retreating once they filled it to the brim.

Their faces were spread wide with smiles, and some of them smelled the inside of the chalice, closing their eyes as though the smell brought them joy.

I subtly leaned forward and sniffed the red water. It smelled of nothing.

"Do we drink it?" Darsey whispered, leaning toward me.

His voice, though spoken softly, seemed to ring out like clashing swords in the silence.

I jumped and looked up at Wanjala. He was staring at me, then closed his eyes and tilted his head forward.

*"He says you can translate for your,"* Uri giggled, *"servants."*

I moved past the assumption that amused Uri, and softly repeated his earlier explanation.

Brantley huffed, and I feared he wouldn't drink, which made me even more nervous. I hoped he had enough sense to not offend them by refusing.

Darsey's eyes went wide and he looked upon the chalice with a smile on his face. His smiled spread to me, and I decided if I wanted to successfully keep the blade's power in check, I needed to stick with Darsey. I needed to let his good humor lighten me up and let Brantley brood on his own.

Once everyone filled their chalice, they stood around us, expanding all the way to the other pools. Wanjala was right. There were so many people in Aljonnah, it was a wonder the oasis could support them all.

The king held his chalice up with a shaky hand, and movement of everyone around us doing the same caught my eye.

*"Do what they do,"* Uri reminded me.

I grabbed my chalice and held it up, Darsey eagerly following. I heard Brantley breathe deeply, then saw his cup raise from the corner of my eye.

The king brought the cup to his lips and drank. Everyone did the same.

I pulled the chalice down and looked into it, my heart racing. I looked over and saw Darsey drinking deeply.

I swallowed past the nervous lump in my throat, closed my eyes, placed my trembling lips on the chalice, and turned it up, feeling the cool, sweet liquid flow over my tongue, fill my mouth, and cause my senses to erupt in warmth and light that spread through me like how I might feel if one I loved more than any other were to tend to me in my hour of need.

I set the chalice down and opened my eyes. I was no longer seated at the table but was instead standing by the willow back in the village. Darsey and Uri were resting together in one of the large knees of the tree's roots. They both seemed at peace and happy. Carefree, even, and I remembered what Uri had said.

I would see what I would die for. It was them. I would die for them.

The vision faded, and I reached up and scratched Uri's head. He eagerly pressed into my hand.

The people around us erupted in cheers and began to embrace one another. The king lifted his hand and once the noise had ebbed, Wanjala roared loudly. A sound that would have caused me to shrink down and hide beneath the table were I not in such high spirits.

*"The feast has begun,"* Uri said. *"The ritual is over."*

Our plates were filled with wonderful looking foods and people began to move about, talking and laughing, while they grabbed things to eat.

I felt a hand on my face, and Darsey turned me toward him and smiled as he stared into my eyes.

"Guess who I saw," he said softly, full of glee.

I smiled and he placed his hand on the back of my head and pulled my face to his, touching our noses and foreheads.

"I saw you too," I whispered, then lightly kissed his nose, feeling more playful than I had in a long time. "And Uri," I added when the kitten began purring and rubbing against my cheek.

He smiled and shrugged, "You *and* my parents."

"You two make me sick," Brantley snapped.

I turned and saw him sitting like a pouting child, his arms crossed. His chalice was empty, yet his dark demeanor told me he had disposed of it somehow.

"Maybe you should just go back to the huts then," Darsey suggested, though his voice held no venom.

Brantley held up his singed wrist and said, "I wish I could."

The motion didn't seem to hold any weight in Darsey's eyes, much to my relief, and he said, "Then go look around. No one is forcing you to stay here." Then he looked at me and asked, "Right?"

I nodded. "Uri said the feast has begun. The ritual is over. I think we can do as we please."

"See?" Darsey said. "It's a party. Go enjoy it!"

Brantley shook his head and said, "And leave you two alone? You would die without me."

"Speaking of dying, what did you see?" Darsey asked.

"We should wake the star-runners," he said.

"Yes," Darsey agreed excitedly. "They would love to see them!" He opened his canteen and dipped his finger in.

"Not here, you fool," Brantley scolded. "Let's find a more open space."

Darsey laughed and said, "I guess I'll just follow you two."

I stood and followed Brantley.

*"I'll tell Wanjala what we're doing,"* Uri said, and I was grateful he was watching out for us and could communicate.

We moved through the crowd, and people were pressing into us and smiling, grabbing our hands and speaking excitedly in their language.

I was thankful the red water had put me in such high spirits that the tingle of the blade felt distant, and I didn't fear when people touched my skin.

Brantley ignored them and pulled away from their touch. Darsey was gladly returning their phrases and laughing when they laughed. I smiled, though I felt awkward, and wished I could fit in like he always did.

We slowly worked our way out of the crowd, beyond the edge of the pools, and stopped when there were fewer people around with just enough torchlight to see by.

The revelry was still all encompassing and music began to ring out, the sound cheerful and exciting.

Darsey was the first to awake his star-runner, and when the stardust began pooling up around Cosmo, some tribespeople rushed up, looking both terrified and thrilled. They kept their distance, trusting curiosity spread across their faces.

When Cosmo stood and shook the dust off, the people gasped and began jumping up and down.

Darsey, being the show-off he was, ran to Cosmo and jumped up, hugging his neck.

Cosmo, obviously feeding off his energy, trotted around with Darsey still dangling off the ground.

"Not too far!" I sang after him, laughing lightly.

My head was swimming in care-free waters and I couldn't remember the last time I had enjoyed such relaxation. Watching Darsey play around with Cosmo and interact with the people set me fully at ease.

I awoke Starla next while Brantley sneered at Darsey's playful display. The people reacted similarly to her awakening, and I let them gather in and pet her. Brantley sauntered off a way before I saw the starlight from Astraeus awakening in the distance.

His disposition was making it apparent he didn't drink the red water, and I momentarily hoped he would stop making it so obvious, when Darsey rode up beside me and clumsily slid from Cosmo's back.

"Did you see that? Did you see what I did?"

I laughed at his childish charm and shook my head.

"Okay," he said breathlessly, holding up a finger. "I'll do again. Watch this time." Then he scrambled back up on Cosmo and the crowd around us quickly gave them room as he darted off, bouncing helplessly atop the star-runners back.

A woman stepped in front of me, her face almost touching mine. In a shock I stepped back, only to bump into another woman. I tried to apologize as they spoke softly to me in their language, stroking my skin with their fingertips. I could see the wonder in their eyes and let them explore, as I was sure they had never seen someone as light as I was.

Another woman approached and delicately lowered my hood, letting my hair spill forth. Uri leaped from my shoulder to Starla's back and climbed up to her head. They both watched as the women ran their hands through my hair, working out tangles and feeling the texture with their fingers.

They were gentle in their curiosity and I enjoyed the soft tugs and pulls in my hair. It reminded me of Mama Iris when she used to pull through tangles and show me affection.

Another woman approached and unhinged one of her golden necklaces. She presented it to me, and one of the women held my hair back while the necklace was latched around my neck. They laid it gently across the robes on my chest and let my hair fall. Then another woman removed one of her bracelets and slipped it onto my wrist. By the time they were done adorning me with their gold, I was laden with two necklaces, a bracelet on each arm, an anklet on each ankle, and four rings on my fingers.

The heavy jewelry made me feel welcome. So welcome, in fact, I wondered if the band of rebels in the desert, were the *only* ones unhappy with Wanjala. These people were embracing us, just as Wanjala had.

Darsey rode back up, stopping outside of the crowd around me and leaned up over, trying to see me. "Did you see that time?" he asked, though I hardly heard him.

The first three women who had come to me took me by the arms and began leading me back to the feast. I happily went with them, listening to their sweet words, though I didn't understand them. They pointed to various things along the way and spoke slowly to me, much like the way the man with the beast had earlier that day. When I pointed and repeated the words, they would either correct me gently on my pronunciation, or cheer and clap.

Before long I had lost sight of both Darsey and Brantley, though I was filled with carefree indifference. Uri and Starla stayed close, and I trusted if anything were amiss, they would let me know.

Once we made it back to the table, which was not nearly as crowded as the beginning of the feast, they had taught me at least a hundred words, most of which I was sure I would never remember. I was happy for the interaction with them. For once I was beginning to feel like how Darsey must feel.

He never struggled to talk to people. He never struggled to fit in. Friends came to him, rather than him seeking them out. He was the one everyone always wanted to be around. And yet, these women were making me feel like one of them. They were making me feel honored, simply by being me. The ritual of drinking the water had made me one of them, and for the first time in my life, I felt truly welcomed among people.

I looked over at Wanjala, and realized it was because of him I felt that way. He had saved us from the pyres. He had agreed to help us. He was going to step down and allow the people of Aljonnah the freedom some of them so desired. He had set the ritual in motion to make us one with them. It was because of him that I felt so welcomed, and I began to realize that his presence was a blessing rather than a curse.

I looked at Uri and smiled at his sweet innocence. What if *that* was the true nature of a tippoo? Innocent, helpful, and loyal? Although I didn't think it right for Wanjala to pretend to be one of the Dragon Lords, he was truly doing it for the right reasons.

So, what of my dreams?

The music changed and I was quickly pulled from my thoughts as the women ushered me from the table and began to teach me the steps to one of their dances. It was a light-footed dance that I could only see the details of when they lifted their robes and let me see their legs, which were adorned with golden jewelry halfway up to their knees.

I spent much of the evening learning their dances and trying to retain words they taught me until the sun crept over the rainbow dunes and cast a purple hue across the sky. Only then did the music stop, followed by a loud cheer that echoed across the oasis.

Starla burst into dust and with exhausted laughter I moved through the crowd and retrieved her orb. Uri climbed to my shoulder as I secured her orb around my wrist and told me that the celebration was over, and we could return to our huts and sleep.

With cheerful hugs and kisses, the people of Aljonnah began to dissipate, confirming Uri's words.

I found Darsey quickly, stumbling about, having indulged in too much wine. He was laughing with a few men who had partaken in the drink as well, and I noticed he didn't have Cosmo on his wrist.

"Help me find Cosmo," I whispered to Uri.

Then Brantley appeared with an orb in his hand and took Darsey's wristlet, wrapping Cosmo up and securing him to his own wrist, all while mumbling unhappily. I approached him and he glared at me through deep set, tired eyes.

"Uri says we can go back to our huts and sleep now," I relayed.

"Finally," he sulked.

"What?" Darsey asked, stumbling up and falling upon me.

I braced myself and wrapped my arms around his waist. "Whoa, you're heavy," I grunted.

"I don't want to be *done*," he sputtered with a laugh, sending rancid, drunken breath into my face.

"Come on lad," Brantley said, as he heaved him from me and pulled Darsey's arm around his shoulder. "To bed with you."

"The party is over," I told him as we began walking back to the huts without an escort.

The walk was silent, and I realized how exhausted I actually was.

When we returned, we took Darsey into his own hut and Brantley slung him carelessly across his bed.

"Be gentle," I scolded, as I went to him and untied his sandals.

"Only a fool would get drunk while we are on enemy terrain."

I looked at him and shook my head. "I don't think they're our enemies," I said. "They made us a part of their tribe tonight. We're one of them now." Then I remembered that Brantley hadn't partaken in the ritual and I added, "Well, Darsey and I are one of them. *You* scorned their ritual and remain an outsider."

He left the hut and I followed him, frustrated that he didn't follow my lead. "Do I need to remind you that we need the trust of the people to gain access to the black pool?"

"Need I remind *you* that it is not the *people* standing in our way?"

"Wanjala seems to be trying to help us," I countered.

He clenched his jaw and began breathing heavily. "If you think," he said through tight lips, "that I would follow your lead blindly, you're mistaken. I will always do what I think is best, and trusting that beast is not going to happen."

It didn't matter, really. He didn't need to trust Wanjala because as soon as the Blue Dragon Lord severed our bind, he would be gone. Still, at the moment, I needed his cooperation, lest he take the path Madame constantly threatened he would, and tell Darsey the truth about why he was there.

I sighed and said, "Then at least give the people a chance. They are welcoming and kind."

He stifled a laugh and said, "The same people who tried to kill us for merely showing up in their land?"

"And Wanjala saved us," I pointed out.

He came close and grabbed my arm, hissing for me to lower my voice. Then he looked around and whispered, "Don't say his name. We don't want any extra attention."

I ripped my arm away and said, "They might have tried to kill us, but *now* they love us. That should mean something."

"I don't want their love," he growled. "I don't want to be a part of their tribe. The only reason I'm playing along is to get close enough to free the *real* Dragon Lord."

The way he said he didn't want to be a part of their tribe struck me as odd. Instead of sounding like he never wanted to be a part of their tribe, it sounded more like he had been rejected from being one of them.

"What happened to you tonight?" I asked, taking a leap of faith, not knowing if it would yield anything.

He huffed and crossed his arms. "Nothing."

"You didn't drink the water," I pointed out.

He didn't respond and I realized I might have been wrong.

"What did you see?" I asked softly, genuinely curious.

"Nothing," he growled, as he turned and stormed toward his hut.

I was taken aback, and Uri asked, *"He wouldn't die for anyone?"*

"There is *nothing* you would die for?" I asked after him.

He paused at his flap, then said over his shoulder, "And don't you forget it," before disappearing inside.

I stood there for a moment, and the sun made itself more apparent in the sky. Exhaustion caught up to me quickly as the excitement of the night wore off. Quietly, I turned and entered my hut, grateful for the bed that I lazily fell upon.

Uri rolled off my shoulder and stayed where he landed, stretching out and closing his eyes with a yawn.

Before I let myself drift to sleep, I remembered the blade pressed against my hip.

I unhappily forced myself to sit up and dig around under the robes until I found it and unlatched it. I let it clatter on the floor beside the bed, and welcomed the softness of the pillow, letting the comfort of the robes wrap me up and cradle me while I slept.

The wind howled aggressively outside my hut and jerked me awake. I stood from my comfortable bed and groggily made my way to the front flap on tired legs. I brushed it aside and looked out.

The oasis was gone.

Only golden sand as far as the eye could see lay before me. Had the whole thing been a dream?

Frightened, I released the cloth only to find that my hand held nothing. I spun around and realized I was standing in the desert, no hut to be found. No oasis. No friends. No Uri.

Then the howling grew louder and I looked to the distance and saw a great, grey sandstorm moving toward me. It was as tall as the sky, wide as the desert, and dense as stone. It descended upon me quickly, and I stepped back defensively. However, just before it slammed into me, an equally large mass of orange sand appeared, shielding me from the grey sand that was forced to part around it.

Then the sand disappeared. I was on my back and opened my eyes to peer at the ceiling of my hut. It was a dream.

Laughter played in my ears from outside. The light spraying in from the cracks around the cloth door was bright with afternoon sun.

I laid my hand down to rest upon Uri, and realized he was gone.

"Uri?"

He didn't respond.

I jumped up and went to the flap. I peeked out and saw Uri playing with two young children.

Shielding my eyes, I stepped out and the boys ran up to me, smiling wide.

"Can we take him with us to watch the monkeys?" one of the boys asked, pointing toward the oasis.

*"Please can I go?"* Uri pleaded. *"It will be so much fun!"*

His eagerness was overwhelming and I wanted nothing more than to make him happy. After all, what harm could two small children bring to him?

I smiled and nodded. "Of course, you can. Have fun!"

They cheered and Uri hopped up on the other boy's shoulder as they bounded off down the path. Once they were out of sight I stepped back into my hut.

I was surprised to see Darsey sitting in the middle of the floor, writing in a scroll. Before I could speak to him there was a knock at the back door. Darsey didn't seem to hear it, and I was sure it was just Brantley coming to scold me for letting Uri out of my sight.

Then another, louder knock sounded. The urgency behind the knock made my heart race and pound. The room began to get darker, and I tried to make out Darsey's features in the waning light.

The knocking continued, getting louder and more brash, and soon mixed with the ringing in my ears.

I turned to run from the tomb door, but fell, unable to move. I looked back and saw it swing open, a cold rush of air blasting into the hut. The air swirled around me and then began to mercilessly pull.

I slid across the floor, turning everything I grabbed hold of into ash. I couldn't stop the pull! As it drew me closer to the tomb, the ringing became more aggressive.

Suddenly, Darsey was before me, still writing in the scroll, though he stayed oblivious to my desperate pleas.

I closed my eyes and waited for the cold to take me and lock me in the tomb with the other bones. This was it. I couldn't fight it.

Then the air released me. The ground stopped sliding beneath me. The coldness began to fade. The ringing drifted away. Warmth swam throughout my body. Then heat. Oppressive heat.

I opened my eyes when I was sure there was nothing more to fear and found myself lying in the same position I had fallen asleep in early that morning.

A dream upon a dream. Or rather, one dream and one nightmare.

I reached up to pet Uri's soft fur, only to feel nothing more than blankets and a pillow.

I pushed myself up and looked around. He wasn't in the bed.

"Uri?" I asked, sitting up and rubbing my eyes. I had dreamed of his disappearance before, and he had always sworn to me he would never leave my side while I slept. Yet, he didn't respond.

I jumped up and shouted, "Uri?"

Again, nothing.

I ran from the hut, looking for any sign of him, and was met with the aggressive noon sun blasting into my eyes.

"Uri?" I called.

Silence.

I ran to Darsey's tent and tore his flap open. "Uri?" I called in, but other than Darsey's exhausted inquiries, no one answered.

Ignoring him, I ran to Brantley's tent and ripped open the flap, "Uri?" I shouted.

Brantley sat up, his sword in hand and looked around, wide awake.

"What happened?" he asked, his voice on edge.

"I can't find Uri!" I shouted, frightened tears springing into my eyes.

Darsey stumbled in behind me as Brantley stood and left the hut. "What's wrong?" he asked.

I wrapped my arms around his neck and sobbed, "Uri is gone. I don't know where he is."

*A fool you were to let your guard down. Now the rebels have a bargaining chip to control you,* Madame goaded.

I didn't try to push her suggestion away. Instead I cried out, "They took him. The rebels took him to control me!"

Darsey wrapped his arms around my waist and pulled me in. "That isn't what happened," he said gently. "The rebels aren't here. The people are kind."

"Unless we're wrong about them," I sobbed.

"Did you check the tomb?" he asked.

I leaned away from him, surprised that I hadn't thought of that. Then I rushed to Brantley's back door and flung it open, no longer fearing the dark or cold.

"Uri!" I screamed into it, answered only by the echoes of my own voice.

Brantley reappeared and quickly lit a torch he had waiting by the door. "I'll see if he is in the tomb," he said as he moved into the cavern, and disappeared into the tunnel.

A moment later he returned and shook his head.

I sat down, shock flowing through me.

"Where do you think he is?" Darsey asked.

*Being prepared for a stew,* Madame laughed.

Brantley snuffed out the torch and said, "It doesn't matter. We have to find him."

I looked up at Brantley, feeling for the first time he cared about how I felt and was worried about someone other than himself.

"You'll help us find him?" I asked, surprised and grateful.

"He's our only means of communication with these people," he clarified. "We need him."

Darsey held his hand towards me, and I took it. He pulled me up and said, "We *will* find him."

"Yes, we will," Brantley agreed, and we all left the hut.

SIXTEEN | Hidden Values

We ran down the path toward the oasis and were quickly met by four guards, laden with whips.

Brantley jumped to the front and held his sword out. "Come on, lads. Try your luck," he goaded.

The guards threw their hands up and fell to their knees, speaking quickly in their language. Whether they armed themselves with their whips or not, I was ready to fight.

"What have you done with Uri?" I shouted, stepping forward.

Darsey quickly rushed in between us and threw his hands up, pleading for calm.

Brantley backed off only slightly, and I leaned in, waiting for whatever trick he might have up his sleeve.

Darsey knelt down and drew a picture of Uri in the sand, pointing to it once he was done. "Uri," he said clearly. Then he pointed to me and tapped my shoulder. "Uri," he said again.

The men looked at one another and nodded. "Ahh, Oori."

Darsey nodded and smiled. "Yes, Oori." Then he threw his hands up and made a spectacle, looking around. "Oori?" he called as he pretended to search.

They seemed to understand and after a moment of whispers, one of the guards disappeared quickly down the path.

Darsey faced Brantley and said, "Put your sword away. I think they're getting him."

I sighed in relief.

*That easy?* Madame asked. *Then you proved you are nothing more than an illogical, emotional child.*

This time I did focus on pushing her away.

Brantley huffed and sheathed his sword. "He shouldn't have run off in the first place," he sneered. Then he looked at me and said, "Get control of your pet."

I ignored him and watched the path, waiting for the guard to return. He could say what he wanted, all I cared about was getting Uri back.

The other guards stood quietly, looking at each other and down at the sand.

Brantley began pacing back and forth behind us, his impatience making me uneasy. I was sweating profusely under the robes from the night before and looking forward to changing into something less oppressive.

As we stood there, quietly waiting for the guard's return, the melodies of the oasis reached my consciousness. The thrum of the wind whistling through the trees, the cawing and singing of birds lounging on branches, the hoots and hollers of monkeys as they went about their day, and of course the daily movement of the people, talking and laughing as they lived on in revelry.

I thought of the great celebration the night before, and how kind the women had been to me. How wonderfully they had treated me. How they made me feel like one of them. And now, how readily the guard ran to retrieve Uri once they understood my plight.

These people were kind. They hadn't done anything wrong, and I felt a bit of guilt for thinking they had. For thinking the women from last night would do anything to hurt me or someone I loved. We were one of them now.

Though I didn't know what made Uri run off, I was now convinced he had left of his own volition. And when they brought him back, I would find out why.

Finally, I saw the guard returning with something in his arms. As he approached, I realized he was carrying a large bundle, and not my tiny Uri.

Darsey and Brantley must have noticed too because we all looked at each other in confusion.

The guard reached us and held out an armful of clean clothes.

I stared at the clothes for a moment, then looked at the guard. Where was Uri?

"I don't want clothes!" I screamed; all calm fleeing as new tears formed in my eyes. "I want Uri! What did you do with him?"

My voice reached a new pitch with my cries and I felt Brantley grab onto my elbows just before I could knock all the clothes to the ground.

Darsey immediately began trying to calm me down, but I wanted nothing to do with reason.

Brantley yanked me back against him and whispered in my ear, "We are still in our ceremonial robes. It is probably against their laws to go out in them."

Darsey said, "Yes, I bet that's it!" Then he turned and I couldn't make out what he was doing through the tears that clouded my vision.

Brantley shook me and whispered, "Get a hold of yourself. You're not acting like the Dragon Born and they can see that."

Darsey turned back around and said, "I think if we change clothes, they will take us to him."

I was having a hard time regaining my composure and Brantley began dragging me back to the hut. "Get the clothes and come on," he ordered Darsey.

With a rough shove, he threw me into his hut and blocked my way out.

"What if they ate him?" I cried. "What if he tried to get to the black pool and fell in?" I added. "What if the rebels threw him in the pit?" I wailed.

Brantley roughly shook me, shouting, "Get a hold of yourself!"

Darsey shoved him aside and laid his hands on my arms gently. "Adalee," he said softly.

I looked down and closed my eyes, feeling the hot tears squeeze out and roll down my face in streams.

"Adalee, he is fine," Darsey continued. "I promise. The rebels are not here. These people are good. He is important to them too. He is the only way they can speak with us. I'm sure he's just exploring."

"What if he's not?" I squeaked out, not wanting to imagine what it would be like to live without Uri.

"Then he needs you to pull yourself together so we can go help him," Brantley snapped, yanking up the clothes that Darsey dropped on the ground when he rushed to me.

Darsey pulled my attention back and said, "He's right. If Uri does need our help, we need to go."

I nodded and wiped my tears away, trying to stop new ones from forming. They were right even though I felt I would not be able to stop crying until he was in my arms again.

Brantley handed out the bundles and we turned our backs to one another, quickly changing out of the robes, into the desert clothes. Only this time, there was no headpiece.

Once I regained control of my tears and steadied my breathing, we exited the hut and met the guards partway down the path. They were now wearing turbans and masks and offered each of us the same.

"What is this for?" I asked softly.

"Just wear it," Brantley said.

When our heads and faces were covered, save our eyes, we followed the men down the path, but quickly stepped from it once we were at the bottom.

Instead of leading us through the oasis on the well laid trails, we traveled through the brush, staying out of sight, and being directed to keep quiet.

Nothing about this seemed okay. Why did we have to sneak? Had something terrible happened? What were we not understanding?

After much hidden travelling, we came upon the pools from a new direction.

The men stopped in the trees and pointed. I followed the direction of their fingers and saw Wanjala and Uri lounging by one of the pools, completely alone and relaxed.

I ripped my mask down and shouted, "Uri!"

He jerked in my direction and stood. Wanjala's eyes fell on the guards and they prostrated themselves before him.

*"What are you doing out?"* Uri asked, sounding worried.

"Why did you leave?" I asked, not caring about the audience we had.

Almost as though he didn't hear me, Uri said, *"You need to go back to the huts."*

My jaw dropped at his dismissal and I said, "Not without *you*."

He then looked up at Wanjala and after a moment, he darted over and climbed up to my shoulder.

Without another word we turned; the guards stood and led us back the way we had come. When we reached the huts, Darsey, Brantley and I all went to my hut and I finally broke the silence.

"Why did you leave while I was sleeping?" I asked, frustrated.

He hopped from my shoulder, his eyes wide, and said, *"You said I could go. You told me to have fun!"*

The dream of Uri and the children wanting to watch monkeys played in my mind and I shook my head, calming down with understanding.

"I was dreaming," I explained. "I was talking in my sleep."

"What does the dragon want with him?" Brantley interrupted.

*"He was teaching me about what tippoos can do, remember?"*

I nodded and sighed, feeling foolish. "That's right," I mumbled, rubbing my face.

"What?" Darsey asked.

I faced them and said, "Wanjala is teaching Uri how to control the things he can do as a tippoo. I forgot he said he would."

"You *forgot*?" Brantley asked, astonished. "Uri being able to control when he leaps would be one of the most useful weapons you could ask for, and you *forgot?"*

I looked at Darsey for backup, and though he looked like he was agreeing with Brantley, she shrugged and said, "I think it will be amazing when Uri knows how to do it on command."

"Let me guess," Brantley continued. "You have too much going on to remember something like that? Just like you *forgot* your blade when we ran off to find him this morning?"

My eyes widened and I grabbed my side, realizing it wasn't there.

Brantley laughed in frustration and pointed to the side of my bed. "Honestly, lass, if you *had* had your blade, you would have burned the lot of Aljonnah down in your frenzy."

I leaped to the blade and picked it up, feeling the rush of tingle spread quickly through my body. I still wasn't calm. I wasn't in control. I closed my eyes and took some deep breaths, surprised at how forceful the tingle was when I had hardly felt it at all the night before. Was my mood really that much different after drinking from the red pool?

*"You shouldn't have come for me,"* Uri admonished, catching me off guard. He had never scolded me before and I looked at him, astonished still.

"Why?" was all I could think to ask.

*"Until you are members of the tribe, you have to stay hidden unless summoned by Wanjala."*

I stared at him, trying to comprehend his words. "What do you mean? We became members of the tribe last night."

Brantley looked back and forth between us and asked, "What's he saying?"

I held my hand up for quiet and Uri said, *"You only did the first part of the ritual. You have to drink from all five pools, all on different nights. It's a long ritual."*

"We have to stay hidden for five days?!" I shouted, feeling the power surge through me with extra fervor.

Brantley scoffed and said, "Five days of keeping us hidden away is five days for him to figure out how to keep us from the black pool."

"So, he *doesn't* want to help us free the Dragon Lord?" Darsey asked.

"Of course not!" Brantley huffed, putting his hands on his head and pacing.

Uri adamantly argued, saying, *"No, it isn't like that. It's a tradition, and the ritual has begun. The only way to stop it is . . ."*

"Is what?" I asked when he didn't go on.

*"Execution,"* he said unwillingly.

I stared quietly, trying to comprehend what he was saying.

"Tell us," Darsey pleaded, and I realized they still didn't have the full picture.

I cleared my throat and said, "The ritual lasts five days. Last night was the first. We will drink from a pool every night until it is complete, right?" I clarified with Uri.

He nodded.

I nodded back and continued, "And we have to stay hidden until the ritual is complete."

"And if we don't?" Brantley challenged.

I looked at him and furrowed my brow. "The rules say we stay hidden. They also say the only way out of the ritual once it has begun is death."

"Death?" Darsey asked, sounding unsure as the word rolled from his tongue.

"We already haven't stayed hidden," Brantley pointed out.

I looked at Uri.

*"Wanjala isn't evil,"* he defended. *"He said I should come back and explain everything to you before returning for my lessons. You will be spared."*

"Wait, return for lessons?" I asked, shaking my head. After discovering everything about the rituals, I felt uneasy letting him out when I was not allowed to follow. "I would feel better if you stayed right here, by my side."

"Is he going to execute us?" Darsey asked, nervousness growing in his voice.

I looked at him, shocked by the fear in his eyes. "No," I said. "He let Uri come back to explain it to us before he 'returns to his lesson'. We're *spared* for now," I mocked angrily.

Brantley stepped up and said, "We need to let Uri go back."

I eyed him and said, "Absolutely not. He's my tippoo, and I want him here where I can protect him. As a tippoo, Wanjala will understand."

"This isn't just about him learning how to *be* a tippoo. He can gather information for us. He might be able to learn something useful to help us when the time comes to free the Dragon Lord."

"Wanjala *does* like him," Darsey agreed.

I looked back and forth between them. "No," I shouted. "He's a baby."

*"I want to help!"* Uri added eagerly.

I shook my head and said, "That wouldn't be fair to you. You *like* him. Brantley wants you to betray his trust and lie."

*"I do like him. But I love you. Let me help."*

I stared down at him and could see the determination in his eyes. He was sounding less like a little child and more like a determined teen, though his voice sounded as young and sweet as always.

*He's foolish and will mess everything up,* Madame intruded.

It was all I needed. I remembered how she kept me hidden away my whole life, never trusting me or allowing me to learn things for myself.

I couldn't do that to him.

I nodded.

"Great," Brantley said as he leaned down close to Uri. "First of all, find out everything you can about the black pool."

"But don't bring it up yourself," I added, not wanting him to seem suspicious. "If Wanjala talks about it, then you can ask."

"Listen to everything he says," Brantley continued. "We need to see if he is lying about anything."

"I *want* to trust him," I added.

Brantley shook his head and said, "How can we when his very role here proves him a liar to the people? There is nothing keeping him from lying to us as well."

Uri nodded and said, *"Okay. I got it."*

"Be careful," I cautioned. "If something feels off, then don't be afraid to run. Get back to me as fast as you can. I will protect you."

He trotted to the flap and as he darted out excitedly, he said, *"I will. Remember to stay hidden, and I'll see you at the ceremony."*

"Wait, the ceremony?" I asked, moving to the flap, receiving no answer as Uri was already out of reach. I turned around and said, "He said he'll see us at the ceremony."

Darsey approached and said, "He'll be okay. Give him time to do his part."

Brantley nodded and agreed, "Aye, let him be." Then he mumbled, "He better not mess this up."

I ignored him and looked down. Trapped for four days while Uri spied on Wanjala sent my mind reeling. I didn't feel like Wanjala was our enemy. He seemed to genuinely want to accompany me on my quest. He seemed to feel it best to leave Aljonnah so they never learned of his betrayal and turn back to their barbaric ways. He seemed excited to help Uri learn to be the best tippoo he could be. He didn't feel like a threat, despite Brantley's untrusting nature determining otherwise.

The blade blazed wildly at my side and I decided the best use of my time would be to get it under control before the ritual that night. It didn't seem to want to obey.

We descended the path as soon as the sun disappeared over the horizon, and the distant drumming began. Our robes were many shades of yellow and fit just as the red ones had the night before.

At Brantley and Darsey's insistence, I put on the jewelry that had been gifted to me during the red pool celebration, though I wasn't feeling very interested in adorning myself with gold.

We followed four tribesmen. Two carried torches, and two carried intricately woven, yellow flags. It had taken much of the evening for me to harness the tingle of the blade. Never before had it struck out with such fervor, save when I was inside the pimeys.

Today it had felt different. Almost desperate. Like it *needed* to be let loose.

I had nowhere to safely unleash its power, and Brantley insisted I keep it on me at all times. So, I did what I could to pull the blaze back in, and it seemed to be reluctantly obeying.

I didn't know what to expect when we drank from another pool. More than ever I knew I had to keep my wits about me to maintain control and not hurt anyone. Or, as Brantley put it, burn the lot of Aljonnah down.

We wove through the oasis and came upon the pools by way of the main path. It was exactly as it was the night before, only this time the smiling faces were wearing yellow robes, rather than red.

We were led to three plush yellow pillows seated near the center of the pools and though I could smell food, I saw none.

Uri sat by the pillows, adorned in a tiny yellow robe. He looked to be happy, well-groomed, and smiling.

*"Sit like you did last night,"* he instructed me.

I sat in the middle and Brantley and Darsey sat on either side. The drumming stopped and was replaced by the pounding of Wanjala's steps as he approached the pools.

I noticed the wooden cover of the pit was within eyesight, and I realized I forgot to tell anyone about it. I whispered to Brantley and Darsey, quickly pointing it out, and Darsey looked on it with awe, while Brantley stiffened and said to us both, "Keep your wits about you tonight."

Uri moved and sat in front of us, between mine and Darsey's golden chalices that rested on golden stands jutting from the sand. Wanjala appeared with the king, both wearing yellow robes and their crowns.

Wanjala looked in my eyes, and I looked away, not able to bring myself to face him after our incident earlier that day.

Surely the people had told him how I had acted. I just hoped he didn't see me as weak.

*"Your cups will be filled with water from the yellow pool, and when you drink it, you will see what you want more than anything in the world."*

I softly whispered Uri's words to Brantley and Darsey, and they both nodded as our cups were taken and filled, along with everyone else's in the tribe.

Once they were returned to us, the king held his up and spoke softly, though his voice carried power and authority. The people held their chalices up and responded, then everyone turned their cups up and drained them.

When the liquid touched my tongue, its sweetness was overwhelming. Suddenly, I was surrounded by vast meadows. I was not hindered by the clothing I wore, and instead donned a lightweight dress that allowed complete movement. I weightlessly ran across the tall grass.

My desire for more was overwhelming despite it only being a vision. I pushed my legs and moved just as fast as Starla. I came to the edge of a cliff and leaped off carelessly, slowly drifting down to the sea below.

Once I landed on the water, I felt it tighten beneath my feet, not allowing me to sink into the depths. I bent down and jumped, feeling myself leap high into the sky and soar far over the waves, coming down slowly and jumping again as soon as I landed.

Then I thought, why land? How far could I jump?

I jumped again, and this time I willed myself forward, and laughed joyfully when I stopped descending just above the waves, and flew along, nothing holding me back or slowing me down.

Faster and faster. I closed my eyes, feeling the wind on my face. No one could catch me. No one could control me. Nothing could hinder me.

I opened my eyes and saw the king's milky gaze staring deep into mine. Instinctively, I leaned back, and Uri said, *"He wants to know what you saw."*

I explained my vision to him, and after a moment, he nodded. Then he turned to Darsey and waited.

I whispered, "He wants to know what you saw."

Darsey had a wide, carefree smile on his face. "I was back home, and everyone was happy to see me. There was a grand party put on for my return, and even Balbas wanted to hear the tale of our adventures. Everyone was gathered, and my parents were so proud of me as I shared all that we had been through."

I realized that the thing Darsey wanted more than anything was to be home, and it stung deeply. He had always talked of staying by my side, and now I feared it was more than he bargained for.

I looked at his face and realized he didn't see how his words sounded. He didn't even acknowledge that I wasn't there with him in his vision. He cared more about Balbas seeing him as a story-teller, than making it home with me.

*"It's Brantley's turn,"* Uri said, pulling me from my thoughts.

I absently glanced at Brantley and said, "Your turn."

Brantley cleared his throat and said softly, "I was standing upon the throne of my land, and by my order, the nobles brought forth the enemies of my people. They begged for mercy and received none. When their blood stained the stone floors, the nobles who did not actively stand against them were brought forth and met the same fate."

His words shocked me to my core, and I felt my mouth fall agape. He was dark. He was merciless. He was dangerous. Worst of all, the thing he wanted more than anything in the world was power.

Just like Madame.

The king spoke again, and three tribespeople stepped forward, one of them coming to each of us. I looked up and saw an unfamiliar, kind face.

She smiled and lightly touched the furrow in my brow, attempting to gently smooth it out. I then realized that the blade was completely under control and I felt not even a hint of a tingle. I smiled and stood as she tugged lightly at my hand.

*"Adalee, you will feast with the others who value freedom more than anything."*

Freedom. Is that what I was envisioning?

*"Darsey will feast with those who value acceptance."*

I looked at Darsey and told him, feeling a bit better that his vision was about being accepted when we returned home, rather than wishing to be home already.

*"And Brantley will feast with those who value justice."*

Justice? I looked at Brantley and quickly relayed it to him.

Darsey happily stood and embraced the man who came for him with a hug. Brantley stood and nodded stoically at the one who came for him.

*"I will stay with Wanjala and meet you when you head back to the huts."*

Uri was no longer asking permission. He was letting me know what he would do, and while I wanted to argue with him and tell him he needed to stay with me now, I still didn't want to limit him.

I had just envisioned myself desiring freedom more than anything, and I was contemplating taking some of Uri's freedom to satisfy my own comfort. It was wrong, so I forced a smile, nodded at him, and went with my new friend.

She held my hand the whole way as we moved away from Darsey and Brantley.

The people dispersed throughout the oasis, and the crowd I came to was made up of a couple dozen. There was a banquet table filled with delicious looking and smelling foods, though no one was indulging as they talked amongst themselves.

The girl pulled me along and called out to the group. They turned and greeted me with excited smiles, greetings in their language, and lots of explorative caressing.

Just like the women from the night before, many people gathered around me and touched my hair and skin. A child approached and tugged at my robes. I kneeled down and he grabbed one of my curls and lightly pulled it, his eyes widening when it sprung back into place once he let go.

There was great laughter amongst the people, and everyone headed to the table. I was offered a yellow cushion, only slightly less ornate than the one I had sat on for the ritual, and a plate of food was brought to me.

Everyone talked to each other, and many people talked to me, not seeming to care I couldn't understand them. Just like the night before, I felt included and welcome, despite the language barrier. They took to teaching me words and some of the women placed even more jewelry upon my skin. I looked for familiar faces and found none. I wondered for a moment what my friends from the night before saw when they drank.

I also pondered what Darsey and Brantley's experiences were like. I was a little worried that Brantley would start a fight and cause upheaval, yet I had no choice but to trust him. I wasn't worried at all about Darsey. If he really was around others who wanted to be accepted, I was sure he was having an amazing time.

After eating an assortment of the flavorful foods I had come to expect in the oasis, a small group began playing music and I recognized the song as the one the women had taught me the steps to the night before.

Many people started happily dancing, and I turned around on my cushion to watch. Those who weren't dancing were clapping along to the song, and I began clapping as well. The happy laughter was contagious, and the more I sat aside and watched the people, the more comfortable I became.

I found myself bouncing from side to side with the music, and one of the women hopped over to me, holding out her hand. I looked at her hand, then up at her smile. She wasn't forcing me. She wasn't trying to coerce me. She was simply offering me the option. Letting me know I was free to join them.

In that moment, I *was* free.

Free from the burdens of my quest. Free from the Brantley's criticism. Free from being overshadowed by Darsey's amicability. Free from worrying about Uri. Just free.

I happily took her hand and jumped up, joining in. There was an eruption of cheers and I danced alongside the people of Aljonnah, remembering each step with a proud heart. I linked arms with those beside me and the dance changed directions with the music. Though the song was just as upbeat, it was one of my lesser known tunes from the night before. I tried to keep up with the moves but found my steps foundering and having to follow their lead, always a half step behind. It didn't matter. I was having too much fun to want to quit.

We danced until the moon was shining above the oasis, then the music stopped. The people clapped and embraced one another, including me. Then they began to disperse, and I realized the festivities were over.

Uri found me as I was saying goodbye to one of the women and asked, *"Did you have fun?"*

I was smiling and laughing, though the energy I exerted on the little sleep I had was catching up to me. "I did," I assured him. "Where are Darsey and Brantley?"

*"I'll show you,"* he said as he began to trot away.

I rushed up to him and playfully scooped him up, lightly tossing him in the air as he shouted, *"Whoa!"*

I caught him and held him close, not caring that his extended claws were digging into my hands. "Sorry," I said with a laugh.

He laughed too and began to purr, pulling his claws back in.

I met up with the others and we headed back to the huts, sharing our experiences.

Darsey was now adorned with gold like me, though not as much, and he shared the rules of a game they played. He smiled and said they were wonderful people and how he almost wished we never had to leave.

Brantley seemed to have had a much different experience, dining quietly amongst a very apathetic bunch. According to him, they didn't seem to have the same patience for the language barrier as Darsey and I experienced. To my surprise, he said he quite enjoyed it, and was glad he didn't have to waste his time playing games or dancing.

I was curious as to when he became such a stoic man, when he was so carefree when I met him. Was helping with the quest that much of a burden? Would Darsey become the same way the longer he carried on with me?

We reached the huts and Brantley suggested we wake the star-runners before we went to sleep. I had forgotten about Starla, and immediately felt ashamed and embarrassed. I couldn't forget her! The stars would take her back if I didn't wake her every night.

We woke them, then went straight to bed, letting them mingle amongst themselves, talking about whatever star-runners talk about.

Seventeen | Selfish Motivations

Once again, I stood in the desert with no memory of how I got there.

The same dark storm loomed on the horizon. A grey mass of sand drew close, thrusting a violent wind upon me.

I covered my face and stepped back, quickly finding relief inside the swirling orange sand that once again came to my rescue.

It billowed around me, and I could see the grey sand surround it, not coming any closer than the orange sand allowed.

*Come out,* an unfamiliar voice sounded in my head.

Was . . . someone calling me?

With squinted eyes, I peered past the orange sand into the grey, trying to focus on who was out there.

Slowly, a large form took shape in the distance, shrouded by the grey. It was dark and tall. It slowly moved forward, and elongated itself toward me.

Though I couldn't make out any features, I could tell it was some kind of beast. The orange sand pulled in close to me, giving the beast more opportunity to near.

Then its face became clear for only a moment. A strong, gaunt, and familiar face.

Wanjala.

"Listen."

I sat up quickly, the sound of Wanjala's voice still echoing in my ears.

The grey sand. It was Wanjala?

I looked down at Uri who was sleeping soundly near my pillow. I sighed in relief; thankful he hadn't disappeared again. Did that make him the orange sand, keeping Wanjala away? Was that one of the things he was being taught?

I rubbed sleep from my eyes, causing my bracelets to slide down my wrists and clang together. I yawned and began removing all the jewelry, realizing I had been so exhausted I slept in them.

I gently placed them by my bedside where the dagger laid, and I vaguely recalled putting it there before I fell asleep.

As quietly as I could, I carried the golden adornments to the other side of the room and put them on the little shelves carved out of the wall. I felt the gifts deserved more respect than being piled up on the floor.

Darsey and Brantley entered at the same time, Darsey yawning and stretching above his head; Brantley extending Starla's orb to me.

I wrapped her gently in the wristlet and smiled at Darsey as he finished his stretch and sat down on the floor, looking exhausted.

"Is Uri here?" Brantley asked.

I nodded and yawned in response to Darsey's yawning.

"What has he said? How did it go?" he asked.

I shrugged and rubbed my eyes again. "He's still sleeping," I whispered.

"Wake him up, then," Brantley ordered. "We need to know what he found out."

"No," I said indignantly, crossing the room to stand between him and the bed. "If he's sleeping then he needs it. I'm not going to wake him."

Brantley shook his head and said, "If you were home, that would be well and good. Out here we are fighting for our lives. Sometimes we don't have the luxury of a restful night."

I looked over at Uri and contemplated Brantley's words. Then I turned back and shook my head. "I won't wake him. *I* have something you might be interested in hearing." Now that the sandstorm dream had taken on a new life, I felt it was important to tell them about it and see if anyone had an interpretation I was missing.

Brantley and Darsey both leaned in, quietly waiting.

I quickly told them about the dreams and when I was done, they silently stared at me.

Finally, Darsey said, "You think Wanjala spoke to you? Is that possible?"

Brantley added, "And you think the orange sand was Uri, keeping Wanjala away?"

"Well," I said thoughtfully, "it seems that way. The first time I dreamed it, the grey storm couldn't get near me. The second time, though it was closer, it still couldn't touch me. Last night it was the closest it has ever been. I saw and heard Wanjala."

They both looked at Uri and Darsey said, "Maybe we should ask him about it."

"Wake him up," Brantley said definitively.

There was a shuffling outside and Brantley darted to the doorway, placed his hand on the hilt of his sword, and ripped the curtain aside.

Four tribesmen stumbled back, offering frightened, undiscernible words.

Darsey jumped up and said, "Breakfast!" He rushed over and took the bowls they were holding. Brantley relaxed and sat down as Darsey handed out the meals.

I took my bowl and another servant approached with a small, plush looking pillow.

"Look," Darsey said excitedly. "Another pillow."

The servant recoiled as he neared him and shook his head. He nodded into the hut and said, "Oori."

"Oh," Darsey said as though he understood. "They brought Uri a pillow. That's nice." He nodded and said, "Yes, Oori." He reached for the pillow, but the servant pulled it away.

Darsey cocked his head and clarified by pointing at Uri, "Oori?"

The servant nodded and patted the top of the pillow, then pointed down the path. "Oori. Wanjala."

I didn't need Darsey to tell me what he thought the servant meant. I understood perfectly well, and to my surprise it infuriated me that Wanjala thought he could call for Uri any time he wanted, and Uri would come. Uri was *my* tippoo. And right then, he needed his sleep.

I stomped over and grabbed the curtain that Darsey was pushing back with his shoulder.

"No," I said slowly and firmly, ripping the curtain closed and spinning around. "He's sleeping," I reiterated to Darsey and Brantley when they stared at me silently.

Brantley shrugged and said, "I agree. He doesn't go anywhere until we question him."

Darsey looked back at the curtain nervously and said, "Do you think Wanjala will be angry?"

I looked at him and felt a fire in my eyes. "I don't care if he is. Uri is *mine*, not his. If he wants to join us, he better learn that."

Darsey glanced at Brantley and I saw them exchange a look.

"What?" I asked, demanding to know what they were thinking.

They both shook their heads and Darsey mumbled, "Nothing."

"Honestly, I find it refreshing that you're finally taking charge of something," Brantley said as he took a spoonful of food.

I calmed down after I ate, and we spent the day going over what we had experienced the night before.

Though we had already shared our experiences on the way back to the huts, Brantley wanted a breakdown of every look, word, and movement. It was exhausting trying to recount everything to him.

I didn't tell them what I had first thought their visions meant. I didn't want Darsey to feel guilty if he really was missing home, and I didn't want to start an argument with Brantley or give him any ideas about obtaining power. We just needed to navigate through our time in Aljonnah so we could free the Blue

Dragon Lord, have her remove the bind, and let Brantley be on his way.

Every moment with him was like living under a dark cloud, hoping the rain will hold off until it moves on. I needed him to move on. I needed him to not tell Darsey the truth and ruin everything. I felt I was always one decision away from losing his cooperation and I didn't want to live with that fear much longer.

Many tribespeople came to the hut throughout the day, requesting Uri go with them. I turned every one of them away, growing more irritated each time.

"Wanjala must really want to speak to him," Darsey commented after the last servant left as the hours marched into the afternoon.

"That tells *me* that Uri must know something the dragon doesn't want *us* to know. You really should wake him," Brantley suggested again.

To my surprise, throughout the day his orders had waned to suggestions, and though I wanted to believe it was because he respected me as the leader, I felt he was only doing it to use against me later.

As the day edged close to evening, Uri finally stirred.

"He's waking up!" Darsey exclaimed.

I rushed over and knelt beside the blade, leaning over the bed.

"Hey, you," I said softly.

With his eyes still closed he yawned and reached his paws out, extending his claws in a deep stretch. Then he stood and extended the stretch through his back and yawned again, before sitting and opening his eyes in little, sleep laden squints.

"Finally," Brantley said upon an exasperated exhale.

"You slept all day," I told him gently. "Brantley has a lot of questions."

His eyes opened wide and with sudden energy he said, *"Oh yeah! I found out stuff!"*

"He says he learned some things," I relayed.

Brantley and Darsey both rushed over and squatted down.

"What does he know," Brantley asked hungrily.

*"The rainbow sand didn't just come from the pools. It spread out over the desert, like magic! And though the people only drink from the pools during ceremonies and rituals, nothing stops the animals. The monkeys love the yellow pool, and they like to eat the food that grows near it."*

"What's he saying?" Brantley asked.

I shook my head. "Nothing useful."

Brantley scoffed. *"I'll* decide what's useful. Tell me everything."

I quickly relayed what Uri had said and Brantley shook his head. "Tell him to tell us something useful," he hissed.

Darsey stifled a laugh and Uri continued. *"Okay, I found out that tippoos can live forever by attaching to people. And if they don't attach to someone, they die. All people can be attached to, just not by all tippoos."*

He puffed his chest out proudly and looked at me with gleaming eyes. *"Wanjala didn't even know that. When we were together and talking about people we could attach to, not all the people were the same! He can attach to people I can't, and I can attach to people he can't. Some people we can both attach to. Like you. Neat, huh?"*

"Well?" Brantley asked.

I shook my head and said, "You wouldn't care."

Darsey said, "I'd like to know."

*"Anyway, that is how Wanjala is over a thousand years old,"* Uri continued.

I nodded and told them what Uri said and Darsey seemed amazed, while Brantley furrowed his brow. "I thought Wanjala was going to teach Uri how to *do* tippoo things. And how reliable is he if he didn't even know that about attaching?"

*"I'm the first tippoo he's ever met."* Uri said matter-of-factly. *"And we start training next time,"* he added proudly.

I shared what he said, and Brantley sighed. "Tell us what you know about Wanjala. Did you discover *anything* new?"

*"He told me how the kings are chosen,"* Uri offered.

I told them what he said, and we all looked at one another.

*"He always tried to attach to a descendant of the man who he came here with. Except a few centuries ago, when more than one sibling had the glow, they began to fight and kill each other for the right to rule. He didn't think the first king and queen would like that, so he changed the rules so that anyone in Aljonnah with the glow could become a candidate to rule."*

I shared his words and Darsey excitedly asked, "Glow? Is that how tippoos know who they can attach to? The person glows?"

Before he could answer, Brantley asked, "What does it mean to be a candidate? How does he choose?"

*"Yes, people who we can attach to glow."*

I waited for him to go on, but I realized he wanted me to tell Darsey before he would continue.

I told Darsey and he asked, "Do I have the glow?"

"Answer *me* first," Brantley butted in.

Uri faced Brantley and I translated alongside him as he said, *"He gathers together everyone who has the glow. Anyone who wishes to step down from candidacy does so right then. The remaining candidates compete in various tests to demonstrate survival. He wants the strongest person to rule with him."*

"What kind of tests?" Brantley asked.

Darsey stepped in, "My turn. Do *I* have the glow?"

*"No,"* Uri said simply. *"Adalee is the only person among us who glows for me and Wanjala."*

I told Darsey what he said, then started translating again as he spoke to Brantley. *"He chooses the ones who can find water and food the easiest. Those who can hunt and harvest without tiring. The three best ones are given these huts to stay in the night before he selects the new leader."*

"Then why are *we* in the huts?" Darsey asked nervously. "We're not candidates, are we?"

*"No. Staying in the huts is the greatest privilege Aljonnah has to offer, and he felt that since there were three of you, and three huts, it was meant to be for us."*

I told them what he had said and Darsey asked, "What about your dream? Does *he* know what it means?"

"Oh, yeah," I said, turning back to Uri. "Have you been protecting me in my dreams?" I asked plainly. "As orange sand?"

Uri cocked his head and said, *"I don't dream. How would I be orange sand?"*

His words confused me and I wondered what else it could mean.

I had just finished translating when there was a familiar rustling outside and Darsey went to the curtain, pulling it aside. A servant offered him a pile of purple robes and bowed as he turned around to wait.

Darsey came over and said, "I guess it's time to get ready for the feast."

Brantley stood and began going through the robes to find his. "Is all you ever think about food?" he asked absently as he pulled the longest robe out and turned around to change.

Darsey handed me my robe and we all turned our backs to each other as we quickly stripped from our yellow robes and donned the purple ones. When I opened my robe, a tiny one for Uri fell out and I couldn't help smiling at how cute it was.

I clasped it around him and patted his head, then went to the shelves and began putting the gold jewelry back on. Darsey noticed what I was doing and left by way of the cavern, returning shortly thereafter with his gold. Brantley had none.

I offered him some of my bracelets and he smirked and shook his head. "I'm not much of the jewelry type, lass."

"If they haven't gifted him with any, we better keep it that way," Darsey pointed out.

"He's got a fair point," Brantley agreed.

I returned the bracelets to my wrists and went to retrieve my dagger. When my hand touched it, the tingle shot through my arm, causing me to recoil.

"What's wrong?" Darsey asked, coming over.

I was holding my arm, though I was completely unharmed. "I don't know," I admitted.

"What happened?" Brantley asked.

"I'm sure it's nothing," I said as I reached down for the dagger again, preparing for the blast.

I touched my fingers to it and felt the blade surge through me, only this time, instead of pulling away, I let it wrap its fiery grip around me. It took all I had not to tremble as I lifted the blade and attached it to my side. The tingle it sent through the center of my body was overpowering and I immediately scolded myself for not spending the day working to regain control of the blade like I had the day before.

The drumming that signaled the beginning of the ritual began to sound in the distance.

"Are you two ready?" Brantley asked.

Darsey smiled and said, "I'm always ready. I want some more of those olives."

I nodded quietly and then looked at Uri. "Don't ride on my shoulder," I warned, feeling the tremble of the blade seep out all over my body. "Walk with us."

He hopped down from the bed and kept his distance, seeming to understand my concern on a level the other two didn't.

*"Is it really strong?"* he asked.

I nodded silently.

*"Don't worry,"* he said lightly. *"I know you'll get really good at it."*

I hoped he was right.

Brantley opened the curtain and Uri trotted out, followed by me, then Darsey.

The sun was so low only an orange hue mixed with deep blue tones stretched across the sky, painting the oasis in a warm glow. There were two servants holding torches, and two more holding purple flags with similar intricacies as the previous nights.

The one who had brought our clothes and was meant to lead us to the pools, audibly gasped and fell to his face before us. He was shaking his head back and forth on the ground and mumbling something in great distress.

"What's wrong with him?" Brantley asked as he stepped out behind us.

The servant sat up on his knees, tears streaking his face, and continued his rantings as he pointed to his ears, wrists, neck, and face. I realized after a moment he wasn't wearing any jewelry. Darsey must have noticed as soon as I did, because he said, "He doesn't have any gold!"

"Should we give him some?" I asked as I took off one of my bracelets and offered it to him.

He dropped to his face again and continued to mumble, shaking his head. Then he sat back up and moved to push my hand back toward me. I quickly recoiled and hid my hand inside my cloak. He then pointed to the other servants waiting to escort us down. None of them had jewelry on, though they donned the same cloaks we did, as they had every night before.

I looked down at Uri and asked, "What is he trying to say?"

Uri looked as perplexed as me and said, *"I don't know. We didn't talk about tonight's ritual. I don't know what this pool does."*

"I think he wants us to remove our jewelry," Darsey concluded, as he began taking his gold off.

The servant smiled through his tears and nodded, leaning over and grabbing Darsey's hands to kiss them.

I feared he would do the same to me once I began removing my jewelry, and I didn't want to risk turning him to ash as the blade was still out of control, so I turned and went back to the hut.

"Open the curtain for me," I ordered Brantley, and to my surprise, he obeyed, stepping in behind me and letting it close.

"What's going on?" he whispered.

"I'm removing my jewelry," I said.

"No, I mean what is going on with the blade?" he pushed. "I saw you recoil from it; I saw you keep that servant from touching you, and I heard what you said to Uri."

I sighed as I carefully placed the gold back on the shelves. "It's really strong tonight," I admitted. "It was strong yesterday, but not like this, and I spent the whole day getting it back under control."

"So, what are you going to do?" he asked.

"Keep my hands inside my cloak. Not let anyone touch me. And spend the walk down focusing on pulling the power back in."

He nodded and said, "Good answer. Let me take Starla from you for the night."

I nodded and held out my wrist, allowing him to unhook the bracelet and attach it to his own.

Then he held the curtain open and we headed back out. Darsey was returning from his hut, sans gold, and Uri was waiting beside the servant for us. He jumped up and bowed a few more times before turning to lead us down to the pools.

I hardly noticed when Brantley positioned himself between me and Darsey, since I was so focused on reigning in the power of the dagger. I kept my hands inside my cloak and my head down, not even having to be mindful of low-lying branches that might brush against my face, as Brantley moved them aside as we walked.

Darsey caught on to what was happening and helped move anything aside that I might brush against and set to ash, all while keeping a safe distance. I appreciated them and didn't know what I would have done without their presence.

We reached the pools much sooner than I had hoped, and I had no greater hold on the dagger than when we began the walk. Once again, the people were gathered, only with somber faces. They moved aside as we were led through them to the feasting table, and Darsey and Brantley positioned themselves on each side of me as we sat on purple pillows. I made sure my robes were between me and the cushion, and I stared at the golden chalice before me, wondering how I would pick it up without control of the dagger.

Then the drumming stopped and was replaced by Wanjala's pounding feet as he made his way to the feast.

Brantley leaned over and whispered, "If you need to, you can slide me the dagger."

I shook my head and said through determined lips, "I can do this."

He nodded and sat back up.

I only needed the power to pull away from my hands and lips. At least, to begin the feast. The last two nights, the water had put me in such a mood that the dagger proved to be no issue at all. I hoped that once I drank from the purple pool, it would happen again. All I needed until then was one hand and my lips.

So, as Wanjala's steps came closer, I focused. I pulled as hard as I could, though it felt like trying to remove dried sap from between the fibers of a cloak. I closed my eyes and sweat beaded on my forehead as I pulled against the tingle, working to assert my dominance over the flames. They wanted to burn. They wanted to vanquish. They wanted to break free and ravage the land.

I couldn't let the dagger have its way. Dragon's fire was all consuming, and for the first time I began to understand what Gavyn meant when he told me that such magic was not meant for me.

I was determined to prove him wrong. I was the Dragon Born. I could do this.

Wanjala's steps ceased and a moment later, Uri began to speak.

*"This is a solemn ritual. The purple pool will reveal to you what motivates you in life. Some will see happy things; some will see less happy things. You will keep what you see to yourself, and we will feast in silence, as everyone mulls over the meaning of their vision. Then you will return to your huts in silence and retire for the evening. You may now explain this to your servants and then not speak again for the rest of the night."*

I realized then that the words were being spoken only to us. I opened my eyes and saw the king sitting quietly, staring above our heads at nothing, waiting for Wanjala to finish explaining it.

I quickly repeated what Uri had said then returned to asserting control over the dagger. I would have lost everything I had worked on with the interruption, except I hadn't made any progress so there was nothing to lose. The servants came and took our chalices, moving toward the purple water.

Time was almost up, and I didn't want to have to hand the dagger to Brantley. I took a deep breath and continued willing it to calm. The servants filled our cups and began to walk back.

The tingle gave one more burst of resistance, then edged away from my fingertips just enough to refuel my resolve. The people of Aljonnah were lining up to fill their chalices, and I continued to work on pulling the power back in. Slowly, it ebbed down my fingers, like honey dripping from a comb on a cool day. I carefully urged it to go faster, mindful that the smallest deviation from my concentration would send me back to the beginning. Once the tingling was held at my wrists, I worked on pulling it from my lips.

Almost all the people had their chalices ready, and soon all of Aljonnah would drink. I needed to be ready to take part in the ritual. I continued pulling the urge of the dagger back, until my lips were finally free of the tingle.

The king lifted his cup, and we all followed suit. Brantley eyed me and looked back at the king when he saw I wasn't going to turn the cup to ash.

The king drank, and we each did the same, along with the rest of Aljonnah. Immediately, I was standing in a place void of all. Only white.

Not bright white. More like what I imagined it would be like in a cloud. A thick, dry mist that hid everything from my sight.

Then, the air began to thin, and I saw something in the distance. I squinted, and realized it was Darsey walking toward me. He had a smile on his face and something in his arms.

As he neared, he held up a beautiful child whose skin color was close to his, with pink undertones like mine. Her hair was reddish brown, and piled in tight, soft ringlets all over her head. Her eyes were bright, and light brown, glimmering as mine do in the sun, though they didn't hold the power of the Essence. Her toothless, big-lipped smile was beautiful, and her rosy cheeks were sprinkled with freckles.

I looked up at Darsey, and realized he was older. His face was no longer boyish and cute. Instead, he looked fierce and handsome.

He was smiling and said, "Isn't our daughter beautiful?" His deep voice resonated within me.

"Our daughter?" I asked.

Then more mist dissipated, and we were standing in the house we had built in our imaginings right after we left home. Darsey laid the child in a small, wooden crib, and a large tail came into view from above. I looked and saw Uri lounging on a branch just above the crib, in his largest form. Relaxed and peaceful.

My eyes were drawn to the tree he was in, and Darsey said, "The tree in the middle of the house was a great idea. Uri sure does love it."

Then Uri jumped down and changed to his smallest form just before landing in the crib and cuddling up beside the baby.

There was a sound behind me, and I turned to see Mama Iris and Papa Theo standing there, smiling.

"I brought you some stew," Mama Iris said, and Darsey rushed to take the bowl from her.

"You two have made a beautiful home," Papa Theo said, as he walked over and wrapped me in his warm, protective arms.

I stepped away and looked at everyone, then couldn't help the smile and tears that sprang into my eyes. This was exactly what I wanted.

The vision disappeared as suddenly as it appeared, and I was staring at the milky-eyed king. I looked over just as Darsey came to his senses. He looked taken aback and smiled. He looked at me, a gleam in his eye. Had he seen the same thing I had?

I glanced at Brantley, and he looked stoic as always. Unreadable.

There was a collective sigh throughout the tribe, as the multitudes came out of their visions.

The king placed his chalice down and began eating, signaling the beginning of the feast.

As expected, everyone ate in silence. Before I reached for anything, I checked the status of the dagger, and the tingling had completely ebbed. The dagger felt like a normal weapon. Whatever the pools did to me, they seemed to make me powerful enough to control the dagger without issue.

I ate in silence alongside the people of Aljonnah and thought of the vision. It was a future with Darsey and his family. A future where we had a child, and the house we imagined, and his parents right there. It was a happy life.

That was what motivated me. The hope that one day we would have that.

*Selfish.*

Madame's intrusive voice caught me off guard. She wasn't wrong.

As the Dragon Born, my motivation should be nothing more than freeing the Dragon Lords. More than anything I should want to help save Pylertchia from the descendant of the Great Deceiver.

It was the destiny Madame wanted for herself. She had always said I wouldn't be able to fulfill the will of the Dragon Lords. For the first time, I wondered if she really *was* the villain? Had I done Pylertchia an injustice by taking away her chance to obtain the Dragon Essence? Had I doomed everyone?

*We shall see*, she cackled.

I glanced at Darsey. I wanted to be with him, and I wanted all that I had seen. Was that something I was allowed to want; to indulge in?

Would I be able to complete my task if the only thing driving me forward was a happy future for myself? The more I contemplated the vision, the more I felt I shouldn't share it with him.

It wasn't fair. I didn't ask to be the Dragon Born, yet it was given me, and if not for my task at hand, we *could* have that life.

If I told Darsey about what I saw, would he want us to abandon the quest and return home? If he did, would I be able to deny him?

Despite my desires, deep down I knew it wasn't what I was *meant* for. I killed Madame for the right to carry this burden. I was destined to do great things, and only after those things were completed would I have the freedom to have that life.

And yet, if he suggested we abandon Pylertchia for ourselves, a strong part of me would want to agree. I was tired of traversing the world. I was tired of the anguish and danger that awaited around every corner. I was tired of living in peril. All I wanted was the peaceful future in my vision.

The feast ended early in the evening since there were no festivities beyond filling our bellies.

When we were headed back to the huts in silence, as instructed. Wanjala approached from behind, his heavy footsteps shaking the ground as he came.

We all turned, and Uri trotted toward him happily. The only voice was the translation that Uri offered.

*"He wants to know if I can continue my lessons in the morning."*

I wanted to say 'no'. I wanted Uri to stay with me, even though I knew it wouldn't be the best thing for our mission. We needed him to find out more information, and he still hadn't learned anything very useful about being a tippoo. I also knew he greatly enjoyed Wanjala's company and I didn't want to deny him, so long as he promised to be careful.

I nodded solemnly, and Wanjala answered me with a silent nod. Once he turned and began back down the path toward the pools, we continued to the huts.

The attendants left as soon as we were in sight of the huts and we each went to our own, as we had grown accustomed to doing each night.

Moments after I entered, Brantley and Darsey knocked at the back door. I unlatched it and they swung it open.

"Why do you keep it locked when you know we are coming?" Brantley asked as he entered.

I envisioned my frightening dreams about the tomb, but only shrugged and said, "We don't know how far back it goes. What if someone else, or some*thing* else is lurking within?"

Darsey froze and looked at me, eyes wide. "You think there could be?"

With a dismissive wave, Brantley said, "You can't let fear win over logic."

"Maybe she *is* being logical, though," Darsey suggested.

"It doesn't matter. Sorry I asked," Brantley said. "What I really want to know, is what did Wanjala want?"

"He wants Uri to join him for lessons tomorrow morning," I answered.

"You said he could, right?" Brantley asked, eyeing me like he expected me to have ruined his plan.

"Yes," I said indignantly. "I understand how important it is."

"Good," he said simply.

His ownership of the decision frustrated me. I didn't need his approval, though with it I knew my secret was still safe.

"I want to know what everyone saw in their vision," Darsey interjected as soon as the subject was closed.

Brantley shook his head and laughed softly. "I saw myself killing my enemy." A smile played on his lips while torchlight danced across his dark eyes. "There was much suffering. He begged for mercy. He begged for forgiveness. He received neither."

I furrowed my brow and Darsey pointed out, "I know they said you value justice more than anything, but that sounds like revenge."

"It is most definitely revenge," Brantley easily agreed.

"That's not very noble," Darsey accused softly.

Brantley looked at him, his eyes burning, and said, "And who ever said I was noble?"

"Okay," I said to break up the intense stare between them. Brantley looked back down, while Darsey looked at me.

"What did *you* see?" he asked. "And please tell me it wasn't the blood of your enemies raining down on your head."

I pictured myself dancing in a rain of blood and laughed so suddenly I snorted, which made Darsey double over laughing.

Even Brantley pulled from his brooding and smirked, letting out a chuckle.

I shook my head and tried to stop laughing at the ridiculous scene he had painted. I could get no words out to set him at ease.

When we finally stopped laughing, I asked him through tears, "What did you see?"

With humor still on his voice, he said, "I saw you, happy. We were back at home in the village. The people were treating you as one of them. Everyone saw you the way I always have. You were the shaman and you loved it. The village honored you as you should be honored."

I contemplated his words, then said softly, "That all sounds wonderful, except one thing."

"What's that?" he asked curiously.

"I'm *not* a shaman. And nothing I do will ever make me one. You saw what happened with Veda in the clearing. How the dialons swarmed to protect her. They will never do that for me because I do not bear the mark."

"A healer then," Darsey rushed past my concerns. "It doesn't matter. I just . . . want to see you happy."

"I see now why my lack of nobility offends you" Brantley pointed out. "One as noble as yourself can only look for nobility in others, I take it."

I was surprised that his words held no hint of irony, and Darsey puffed up with pride and his smile beamed.

"Don't be too honored by my words, lad," Brantley warned. "Nobility is foolish, and it will do nothing aside from get you, or the ones you love, killed."

Darsey seemed taken aback by Brantley's words. After a moment he shook them off and smiled at me. "What about you?"

I didn't yet know if I wanted to share my vision with him, so instead I said, "I think we need to wake the star-runners and get Uri ready for his lessons tomorrow."

"There's plenty of time for that," Brantley said as he faced me. "I, too, am curious as to what motivates the Dragon Born."

I looked back and forth between their eyes; Darsey's eager and Brantley's expectant.

I then decided it would be more foolish to hide something else from Darsey. His whole motivation in life was to see me happy. I owed him enough to tell him what my motivation was. I just needed to make it clear that it couldn't happen until *after* the quest was complete.

I took a deep breath and quickly shared my vision and what I thought it meant.

Brantley rolled his eyes and turned away while Darsey never looked happier.

"You saw us with children?" he asked with a smile.

"*A* child," I specified, blushing. "Only one."

"We want the same things," he said gleefully, as though it was a brand-new discovery on his part.

"We mustn't rush it," I added. "We have so much to do before we can have that life."

He nodded, but I didn't feel like he was really listening.

"Darsey," I said, trying to pull his attention back. "I mean it."

"The tree was *in* the house, right? How would we do that? Should we build around an already established tree, or grow one and prune it ourselves as it ages through the years?"

"Darsey," I said again.

"Give it up, lass," Brantley said. "He's not going to hear another word at this point."

"That's not true," Darsey argued back then focused on me again. "I'm sorry, what else were you saying?"

"That life can't exist until Pylertchia is safe. We can't even think about it until the Dragon Lords are freed and the descendant of the Great Deceiver is destroyed."

"Of course!" he hastily agreed with a nod.

Though we moved on from the subject after that, preparing Uri for his lessons, waking the star-runners, and heading to bed, I knew where Darsey's mind was, and I wondered if telling him was a good idea or not.

EIGHTEEN | A Terrible Idea

The grey sand swirled around, just like the night before. I was
protected by the orange sand that Uri claimed wasn't him. What
was it, then?

The silhouette of Wanjala approached, just outside my
orange shield, and his face came into view.

"Listen," he said, his mouth moving with the words. His
voice was difficult to hear above the sandy tumult, and I leaned
forward, trying to draw closer.

"Wanjala?" I asked.

His mouth moved and the orange sand spun faster,
howling loudly, drowning out any words I might hear.

"What do you want?" I screamed. The orange sand
hastened out before me and the grey sand was pushed back.

"Wanjala," I said loudly, waking myself.

I sat up and looked around the hut tiredly. The robes from the night before were still wrapped around me, and I fell back into my bad, breathing in a deep, comfort-filled breath.

Was Wanjala really trying to speak directly to me?

I turned my head to find Uri and instead found the empty space where he had been. A quick search of the hut told me he left to pursue his lessons with Wanjala. Finding him gone made me sick to my stomach and I hoped when he returned, his time with the older tippoo would prove fruitful in some way.

I peeked out my front curtain and saw that the sun had barely broken over the edge of the sky. Starla was already asleep, and I quickly retrieved her orb, along with Cosmo's and Astraeus's.

I gently placed Cosmo and Astraeus on my pillow and attached Starla to my wrist.

It felt odd being alone in the hut. I was used to always having someone around. A servant brought my breakfast and placed it outside the door, almost completely disappearing down the pathway before I realized they had come.

I brought the bowl of warm porridge in and sat in the middle of the floor. I considered going to Darsey's hut but as we agreed, I would need to go through the cavern so as not to be seen by anyone, and I wasn't keen on that idea.

Though I hadn't had any nightmares since the first night of the ritual, I still felt uneasy about the cavern and tomb.

My indecision didn't last long, as I heard knocks on my cavern door after just two bites of my breakfast.

I jumped up and unlatched it. Brantley swung it open and ducked inside. Darsey followed him, arms full of fresh clothing and a smile spread across his face.

"We're sneaking out today," he said proudly before I even had the door closed.

I turned to him, not sure I heard correctly.

"We're what?" I asked.

"I told you she wouldn't go for it," Brantley said nonchalantly as he began wandering about the hut.

Darsey pushed the clothing into my arms and excitedly said, "I got them to bring us some clean clothes. As long as we keep to the shadows of the trees, no one should see us."

I didn't know what to say. I wanted to smack him in the forehead for not thinking clearly.

"That's . . . a terrible idea," I finally said.

"Which one is mine?" Brantley asked and I glanced over, seeing he found Cosmo and Astraeus on my pillow.

"The left one," I said quickly before turning back to Darsey. "Why?" was all I could think to ask. "Why would we risk going out today when the penalty is *death*?"

He rolled his eyes and laughed lightly. "They aren't going to *kill* the Dragon Born," he said as though the thought were ludicrous.

Though I knew he was probably right, I couldn't fathom breaking the rules for anything other than necessity. "They *could* decide not to continue the ritual," I pointed out.

He shrugged and I added, "They could banish us from Aljonnah."

"Like the rebels who found us," Brantley reminded him as he attached Astraeus to his wrist.

"Exactly," I agreed.

Darsey shrugged again and said, "Once Wanjala leaves with us, they'll be welcomed back. He isn't a real Dragon Lord; we don't need to worry."

"We don't know if they'll be accepted back," I said. "The people still don't know the truth."

"And it's going to stay that way," Brantley said behind me. I turned and saw him eyeing me, one hand still cupping Astraeus's orb. He let the orb swing on his wrist and approached me slowly. "We agreed it isn't our business to tell them."

"I know," I said, frustrated that he mistook my words. "I didn't say we were going to tell them. It's just that . . . the rebels have every right to be angry, don't they? There must be something we can do to make it so the people will welcome them back."

"Why help a people who tried to kill us?" he asked.

"They saved us from the desert first," I pointed out. "Then they allowed us into Aljonnah."

"Knowing the people would try to kill us! Don't you see? It was just another way to try to get rid of us. Those bracelets they gave us did nothing!"

"Shouldn't you trust Wanjala, then?" I asked, trying to turn the argument back on him.

He looked confused and asked, "What does that have to do with anything?"

"You don't trust him. You think he is hiding something. You think *everyone* is hiding something—"

"Because everyone is!" he cut me off. He looked at Darsey, then back to me and said, "*Everyone.*"

I knew he was talking about our lie to Darsey and I looked away.

Darsey took the bundle from my arms and said, "You two do as you like. I can't stand being in these huts for the entire day again. I'm going to explore." He separated the clothing until he found what was meant for him and dropped the rest on my bed. "I'm going to eat and then change. If you decide to join me, you better make it quick." He turned toward the door, then paused. He turned back, grabbed Cosmo, secured him to his wrist, gave it a small tug and nod, then threw his clothing over his shoulder and strutted out the back.

After he was gone, I looked back at Brantley and said, "Maybe everyone does have a secret. That doesn't make them untrustworthy."

"How sure are you about that?" he challenged.

I sighed heavily and shook my head.

"Shouldn't you be worrying about Darsey instead of me?" Brantley asked. "He could ruin everything because he feels pent up."

I scoffed at the idea, having been a prisoner my whole life, and said, "I understand how he feels, but at least there is an end in sight to our imprisonment."

"Apparently that end is today," Brantley chuckled.

"It's a bad idea."

"Aye, it is," he agreed readily. "I spent most of the morning trying to make him see the error of his ways. The lad isn't budging. I imagine he spent most of the night planning it out."

I huffed and rubbed my face. "What if Uri comes back while we're gone?"

He looked at me, eyes wide and bright. "While *we're* gone?" he asked, humor in his voice.

"Yes," I said obstinately. "If I go, you have to go."

"That's where you're wrong, or have you forgotten? If you try to go, and I don't, *you'll* be drawn back to me. Then the lad will know the truth."

I looked about wildly, suddenly fearful that Darsey was within earshot. Was this the moment? How often did he think about exposing us?

"Don't worry," Brantley continued. "I have no problem with going."

"That wasn't what it sounded like to me." Then I sighed and asked, "Then what *is* the issue?"

"Quite a few things. For one, you find this to be a folly idea, yet you will go along with it to . . . *protect?*. . . Darsey? Another problem is that you are right about Uri. What if he *does* come back and you are not here to receive him? Will he run back to Wanjala? Will he give us up?" He held up his hand when I opened my mouth to protest. "Let me finish, lass. I don't believe he would. He is young, and often foolish. Still, he loves you fiercely and would do nothing to harm you. Now, can the same be said for Darsey? You told him you don't agree with his plan, yet he intends to follow through with it either way. It appears to me, he is choosing to indulge in his own desires, rather than focus on your *needs*."

"That is not—"

"Aye, it is," he said aggressively, though without ire. "You *need* to gain access to the black pool. You *need* to be a tribal member to do so, and he is casting both of those needs aside to relieve his *boredom*."

I hated that Brantley wasn't wrong. Regardless, I shook my head and said, "One thing I can assure you, is that he is not *intending* to cast my needs aside."

"I don't doubt it," he said with a smile.

Frustrated with the way the conversation was going, I sighed heavily.

"Either way," Brantley added, "who's to say they won't exile the lot of us for the folly of one?"

I tried to think of what to say to Darsey to stop him while Brantley continued. "Or, who's to say they *won't* execute him if he is found? After all, *he* isn't the Dragon Born."

I clenched my fists and said, "Fine, we need to stop him."

There was a quiet knock at the back door, and both Brantley and I turned. The door was unlatched, and it swung out. Darsey stood there in the new clothes, looking less determined than he had when he left.

"What did you decide?" he asked hopefully.

"You are putting your wants ahead of my needs," I snapped, not meaning for Brantley's accusations to come out of my mouth.

The satisfied smirk on Brantley's face made me want to smack him too.

Darsey's jaw dropped and he slowly shook his head. "I said all that stuff," he admitted, "but did you really think I would go without you?"

I let myself relax a little, and he stepped in, pulling the door closed behind him. "I came back over," he said, "to see if I could convince you to change your mind. If not, that's fine. I'll stay and sit and wait. I was just hoping we might be able to see something a little different today than the inside of these huts."

"It's just two more days," I assured him as I laid my hand on his shoulder.

"If the old tippoo is speaking the truth," Brantley interceded.

"We have no reason to doubt him," I defended.

"Isn't it reason enough that he keeps his plans to himself and only shares them with us when we *need* to know?" Brantley asked. "After all, he knows exactly what will happen after the ritual is done. Do we?"

Darsey and I looked at each other and Darsey turned to Brantley and asked, "I thought you said sneaking out was a foolish idea?"

"Aye, if you're only doing it to indulge your curiosity. However, if you are doing it to gain information, then it might be necessary."

"Wanjala said we would gain access to the black pool once we were members of Aljonnah," I reminded them.

Brantley held his hand up and said, "No. He said we could not have access to the black pool unless we were members of the tribe. He never specified if we would be granted access once we became members."

Darsey looked frustrated and he threw his hands out. "Then what would be the point of all this?"

Brantley shrugged and said, "A distraction? A way to buy time?"

"Time for what?" I challenged.

"We don't know! That's exactly the problem, isn't it?" Brantley asked as he looked over at the curtain.

"So, you *do* want to sneak out?" I clarified.

He smiled deviously and nodded. "We have the clothes. Might as well."

Darsey was bouncing up and down with excitement.

"And if we get caught?" I asked.

Brantley looked around and found my blade on the other side of my bed. He held it up and offered it to me. "If we get caught, then we take our access to the black pool by force."

"We won't have to!" Darsey interrupted. "We won't get caught. No one will see us."

"How can you be sure?" I asked him.

Darsey looked at the blade, then at me. After a moment of thought, he said, "Because I know you would never hurt them. And if we get caught, that might be what has to happen. So, we *won't* get caught, because that isn't something either of us could stand doing."

Brantley laughed and tucked the blade under his arm, clapping his hands. "Quite moving little speech lad," he said humorously. "I would point out the senselessness of it, if I were not arguing alongside you for the same cause."

Darsey didn't pay him any mind and kept his eyes on me. "I won't put you in that position. We *won't* get caught."

The sincerity behind his words settled into me with great conviction. I didn't know how what he said could be infallibly true, yet I trusted him. I nodded and he smiled.

They left the hut while I changed from my robes to the regular clothes and came back moments later. We all looked the same, and Darsey helped tuck some stubborn hairs up in my turban.

"You should keep your eyes down," Darsey suggested. "Their sparkle could give us away."

I smiled at the way he complimented my eyes while Brantley guffawed and said, "Our light skin will give us away before her eyes do!"

Darsey ignored him and gave me a reassuring smile before covering his mouth and nose with cloth.

Brantley held my blade out for me again.

I reached out to take it and the moment my hand touched it I felt it resonate all over my body, causing me to rip my arm away and stumble back.

"Are you okay?" Darsey asked quickly.

Brantley growled and demanded, "Okay, tell us what is going on with this thing!"

"I don't know," I admitted once I caught my breath. "It has been getting harder and harder to handle."

"Why?" Brantley asked. "Are you tired? Scared? Hungry?"

"No, none of that! I . . . I don't think it's *me*."

His eyes narrowed and Darsey asked, "Is the blade getting stronger?"

"It doesn't feel stronger . . ."

"What then?" Brantley asked impatiently.

"It feels . . . angry." Then I looked at Darsey and added, "Pent up. Like it wants to have a chance to burn freely and is angry that it can't."

"Are you meaning to say that the power in the blade is . . . alive?" Brantley asked, sounding unsure for the first time.

"I know it sounds ridiculous," I admitted.

"Aye, it does," he agreed.

"That doesn't mean it can't be true," Darsey defended.

"You *would* be the only one of us to know," Brantley agreed.

"When did it start?" Darsey asked eagerly.

I tried to recall the first time I had trouble with the blade, and realized it was the day after the ritual began. I told them and Darsey asked, "Do you know why?"

"You didn't seem to have any problems last night during the feasting," Brantley pointed out before I could answer.

I nodded slowly and said, "When I drink from the pools, they make it easier to handle. They make it feel like a normal blade."

"The waters make you stronger," Darsey said in awe.

"That's what I think," I agreed.

"Or they make the blade weaker," Brantley suggested.

Darsey glared at him and asked, "Are you honestly saying the powers of Aljonnah surpass those of the Dragon Lords?"

"It was only an idea," he said coolly.

Though he took the suggestion back quickly, his words played over in my mind. What if, somehow, the pools did make the blade weaker?

"Can you handle it, or do I need to carry it?" Brantley asked.

"I will keep it hidden," I said. "Along with any skin. As you said, we don't need anyone noticing us."

He nodded and held it out.

I braced myself, prepared for the aggressive spread of power, and gripped the hilt tightly. It immediately resonated throughout my body, emanating from my very being. I felt moments away from losing myself to an explosive episode. I clenched my eyes shut and willed it to calm, and though I could not pull it away from the edge of my skin, I could sense it would go no further without my approval.

That would have to be good enough.

Keeping my concentration up, I moved to secure the blade to my hip. To my surprise, Brantley grabbed my wrist and slipped the blade from my grasp.

"What are you doing?" I asked.

"On second thought, I might hold onto this for you. Turning the oasis to ash would definitely draw some unwanted attention. I'll give it back if the need arises."

I looked at Darsey and he nodded. "It's not a bad idea."

"Okay," I acquiesced, somewhat relieved I wouldn't have to spend the whole time concentrating on harnessing the power.

Brantley smiled and disappeared into the cavern for a moment, returning with a massive bundle of color that Darsey helped grab when he saw it. It took both of them to carry the colored fabric, and I cocked my brow, wondering how long this had actually been planned.

I grabbed some cloth that was dragging the ground and realized it was the robes from the previous feasts.

We left my hut and followed Brantley's lead. We stayed low and crept along the side of my hut to the vacant edge of the cliff. There was a drop off that stared out above the trees.

Brantley gathered the pieces from each of us and began working through them, tugging at each knot along the way. Finally, he nodded and tied a large knot around one of the ends and wedged it between a sturdy rock that butted up near the mountain.

He tugged at it and then smiled at us. "Who wants to go first?" he whispered.

My eyes widened and Darsey said, "You do."

Brantley shrugged lightly, looked over the edge, then tossed the end down. He gripped the makeshift rope and hopped off the cliff backward.

The cloth flew up from the ground and held taut. Darsey and I rushed to the edge and looked over. Brantley walked backwards down the wall, using the robes to keep him from falling. As soon as he landed, Darsey touched my back and said, "You're next."

I didn't argue, though I wanted to abandon the plan right then. I wasn't sure I would be able to descend with the same ease as Brantley.

I took as deep a breath as I could muster through my stifling disguise and nodded. I laid on my stomach and inched my legs over the edge, holding tightly to the robes. As soon as my waist made it over, I slid down to the first knot quickly, barely able to hold on. My legs dangled in the air and I clenched my eyes shut, holding my head close to the robes, wishing I was back in the hut.

I wasn't, though. I was in this now.

I opened my eyes and looked up at Darsey's face as he leaned over and watched me. I looked down and saw Brantley waiting for me at the bottom.

I realized then, seeing their faces, how foolish it was of me to be frightened by such a simple feat. Determined, I clamped my feet over the robes and moved my hands below the knot, sliding down until I felt the next knot. I moved my feet and slid until my hands caught it. I continued down the robes like that until I reached the bottom and Brantley gripped my arm to help me stay steady as I backed away from the rope.

"Good job," he muttered, and we both watched as Darsey climbed down in similar fashion as Brantley had.

Once we were all down, Brantley motioned for us to follow him. Darsey went so willingly, it occurred to me that they had planned this together. I was annoyed that Brantley had claimed we needed to seek out the truth because of Wanjala's secrets, when *they* were hiding plans from *me* the whole time.

It was too late for me to voice my concerns or accuse them of treachery, as we were moving along the mountain in the shadows, staying low in the brush to avoid detection. We moved slowly, inching along as quietly as possible. Only a few times did we come close to being spotted, as Brantley did well to keep us hidden.

Eventually, I heard the sound of the monkeys who enjoyed the yellow pool, and realized we were drawing close. How he had managed to map out the oasis in the short moments we had moved through it amazed me. I had no idea where we were headed or where we *should* head to reach *anything*.

We came up behind the pools from a direction we had yet to enter by. Sadly, we could get no closer, as there were more guards than seemed necessary posted everywhere. With one look from Brantley, I could tell we needed to abandon the mission.

Slowly and quietly we made our way back.

Only, this time, there were children playing in the brush we had crawled through, and Brantley quickly redirected us a way we had yet to explore.

I started to panic. Would we get lost? What if there was no way to get back to where we had crawled down the robes? What if they *found* the robes and began searching for us? This was a terrible idea!

Brantley and Darsey moved with confidence, and I did what I could to draw courage from them. We crept along, somewhat aimlessly, and continually had to redirect due to villagers in the path.

However, we could catch glimpses of the mountain through the trees, and I knew Brantley was working on moving toward it as much as he could while keeping us hidden.

After much more time than I liked, we found ourselves butted up to the mountain again. Only, we were near the edge of the oasis and could look out onto the rainbow sands.

Brantley motioned for us to follow the back of the mountain to get to the trees, and we quickly came to an unfamiliar structure.

It was built out of the rainbow sands, like everything else, and though I believed it to be another palace at first, Brantley quickly pointed out the difference in shape and height. This was something new.

"Is this part of Aljonnah?" I whispered in wonder.

"Let's check it out," Darsey suggested so low I scarcely heard him.

Brantley nodded and we crept into an opening against the mountain that seemed more like a mistake than a pathway. It was narrow and required us to shimmy our way through on our stomachs. I didn't like the plan, but at that point there was little I could do, as Brantley was before me and Darsey behind.

We reached the end of the tunnel and Brantley softly whispered, "It's a dead end."

"What?" I asked, unsure I would be able to back out with how small the tunnel was.

"Wait," he added. "The sand is loose. I'm going to see if it leads to anything."

A moment later he moved forward without a word and I followed. I came out into a dark room and felt him grab me under my shoulders and stand me up on firm ground. I heard Darsey come out and we both grabbed him and pulled him from the tunnel, helping him stand.

"Where are we?" Darsey asked.

"Shh," Brantley said quickly. Then he placed his hand on my shoulder, and slid it down to my hand, pulling me along. I reached out blindly and grasped at the darkness until I grabbed Darsey's collar and pulled him along, sliding my hand into his once we were moving.

It wasn't long before Brantley stopped.

"What is it?" I asked softly.

"Bars," he said, barely above a whisper.

"Like a prison?" Darsey clarified.

"We're in a cell," Brantley said.

"What?" I asked, panic in my voice.

"Hey," Darsey said gently. "We're not trapped. We'll go back the way we came."

"Hold on," Brantley said. Then I heard the scraping of metal against hardened sand. "It's not locked."

"We should get out of here," I whispered. Instead of listening, he pulled me along.

We silently moved along the wall in complete darkness. No people. Nothing in the walkway. No deviation from the solid wall.

Finally, a small light appeared ahead. It blasted into the darkness like a powerful beam, illuminating the wall across from where it came.

"We'll check that out, then go back," Brantley whispered, and we moved toward it.

As we came closer, sounds began echoing around us. Grunts and roars of anger and pain. There was the snapping of whips and the clanging of swords. We all froze for a moment, then Brantley moved toward the light swifter than before. We reached it and peered out carefully from a hole in the wall that acted like a window.

What I saw made me drop both of their hands and brace myself against the wall. I couldn't tear my eyes away.

It was a stadium full of warriors. Scarred and bleeding. They fought against one another, equipped with whips, swords, and shields. I watched in horror as they snapped their whips, cutting into the skin of their brethren. Swung their swords, some of which landed against shields, some of which clashed against other swords, and others still that sliced through flesh. It was fierce and full of aggression and hatred. I saw no mercy. I saw no peace. I saw nothing that represented what Wanjala had told us the people had become since his arrival.

"The rebels," I whispered.

"There might be more than what we thought," Darsey said in awe.

"We should tell Wanjala," I said. "He needs to know that they are training to win their freedom. He needs to tell them he is leaving with me when we free the Blue Dragon Lord. This is not what he would want for these people."

Brantley pointed and said, "Are you sure?"

I followed his gaze and saw Wanjala sitting atop a great throne at the head of the stadium, watching peacefully.

I felt sick. What was he doing? Why wasn't he stopping them?

"We need to find Uri and warn him that Wanjala is a liar," Darsey whispered.

Was he, though? Certainly, there was an explanation beyond my understanding. Something reasonable. Wanjala wanted to help us. He wanted to accompany us. He loved these people and wanted what was best for them.

"I don't think we'll have to search far," Brantley said, pointing.

I followed his gaze and realized that Uri was sitting right beside Wanjala, watching the fighters just as peacefully.

I wanted to scream for him. I wanted to climb through the window and bring him back to me. I wanted us to run from this place and never return. Brantley and Darsey both grabbed one of my arms and forced me back down the corridor into the darkness.

I was in a daze as we reached the cell and found the tunnel back out. I hardly registered when we rushed around the side of the mountain, less careful than before, while still avoiding detection. Anger rose inside me as I held on to the end of the make-shift rope and they hoisted me up.

I barely noticed when Brantley unwedged the robes and he and Darsey carried them back into my hut. As soon as the curtain closed, I ripped my turban and mask off.

Before I could speak, Darsey tore his mask away and asked, "What *was* that?"

"An abomination!" I answered. "The opposite of what Wanjala told us he had brought to these people. That was not *peace*."

"I don't understand why you two are so appalled by what we saw," Brantley interjected flippantly as he removed his turban and mask.

I turned on him and said, "I don't see how you can be okay with what we saw!"

He shook his head and smiled. "It is natural for people to have warriors. I didn't know stumbling across where they are trained would affect you so."

Darsey shook his head as he removed his turban. "Wanjala said they were a peaceful people, and even if they weren't, why would they *need* warriors if they have a *dragon*?"

"Yes," I agreed. "The people believe he is a Dragon Lord. Why would they need to train warriors if they have a Dragon Lord living among them? It doesn't make sense."

Brantley's eyes were wide, and he looked back and forth between us like he couldn't believe what he was hearing. "Have you forgotten," he asked, "about the welcome we received when we first arrived?"

Darsey and I looked at one another and he continued.

"They attacked us," Brantley said seriously. "*Warriors* attacked us. Without thought. Without question. Without Wanjala, they were going to burn us to death. Have you really forgotten that?"

I huffed and said, "I didn't forget. We scared them!"

"It was more than that," Brantley insisted. "It was protocol. It was purposeful. What reason would a peaceful people have to stand sentry at their borders?"

I thought for a moment and Darsey said, "The rebels?"

Brantley nodded. "They were there to kill the rebels should they return. Not capture. Kill. And you two were foolish enough to not see it, and instead believed the tippoo's story about peace and good will."

Darsey crossed his arms and said, "So you didn't believe a word from the beginning?"

"Of course not! Only a fool would!"

I slowly sat down on the bed and stared at the wall while they continued their rantings. It was too much.

Wanjala was a liar and Uri was with him, though under what premise I didn't know. All I knew was I wanted to get him back, free the true Dragon Lord, and get out of Aljonnah.

Now, more than ever, I felt unsafe. More than unsafe. I felt trapped. Like a rabbit in a snare.

And yet, there was a tiny glimmer of hope shining on the outskirts of my mind. If Uri was with him, then he must know something that we didn't. I trusted Uri, and if Uri trusted Wanjala, I had to put my faith in that.

"Here," Brantley broke into my thoughts, holding out my blade. "You need to work on harnessing this before they come for us tonight."

I looked at the blade then up at him in a daze. "Tonight?" I asked.

"The ceremony," he clarified.

I looked back at the blade and asked, "We're still doing it?"

"Have you not been listening, lass?" Brantley asked.

Darsey broke in and informed me, "We are going to go along with Wanjala's plan. We have the upper hand because he doesn't know everything we know about him. He doesn't know where your power comes from, and he has no idea that we suspect him of being untrustworthy. We need to keep it that way and your blade can't leave your side. We have to be ready."

"What if I can't control it?" I asked, staring at the red gem bursting forth from the tip of the blackened hilt.

"I don't believe the Dragon Lord's would have entrusted it to you if you didn't have it in you," Brantley said softly.

I looked up at him, surprised at his kind words. Then I nodded and reached for it. The blast almost pushed me off the bed. I maintained my composure and willed the blade to calm itself. Once again, I felt it would go no further without permission.

I moved to the middle of the hut and sat down, laying the blade in my lap. I closed my eyes and imagined Serefina speaking to me in her soothing voice, this time for concentration rather than meditation.

I stayed that way until the sun began to set and a servant brought us our orange robes for the ceremony.

By then, I had a certain handle on the blade, though I felt it obeyed me only out of obligation mixed with the assertiveness of my desires.

I opened my eyes and reached out, confidently grabbing the orange robe from Brantley.

I stared at the robe with uncertainty and Darsey asked from across the room, "What's wrong?"

"Uri's still not back."

NINETEEN | Painful Memories

Clad in our orange robes, we walked down the path without Uri.
I hoped that Brantley and Darsey's assumption that he would join
the ceremony with Wanjala was correct.

When we arrived at the feasting table, the king was
already there, standing as tall as he could, eyes defiant and angry.

Did they know we snuck out?

I was even more worried than before, and I could feel the
blade responding to my emotions, fighting for the chance to burn
the oasis to the ground.

Brantley gripped my arm and whispered, "Calm down.
You're beginning to singe."

I looked around and realized the ground was starting to
smoke and blacken. I took a deep breath and willed the power

back in. It wasn't as hard as before, since I had focused so explicitly on controlling it all day.

The king raised his hand and I couldn't help the gasp that slipped from my lips as Anahita was brought forward, bound by rope, head hung in defeat.

Before I could say anything to her, the king began speaking for the lot of Aljonnah to hear.

When he was done, Anahita said, "Once you drink from the orange pool, you will relive the most influential moment of your life. You will then share your vision with the people and reflect inwardly on how you have been influenced by what you saw. Then the feast will begin."

Without another word, Anahita bowed toward the king and he nodded, raising his hand again. Servants came and took our chalices to fill.

This was all wrong. Where was Uri was and why Anahita was before us as a prisoner? She refused to meet my gaze no matter how hard I tried to make eye contact with her. She looked broken and I felt responsible.

She wanted me dead because she was afraid I would ally myself with Wanjala and be Aljonnah's downfall.

And now she was their prisoner.

Where were the rest? Did they escape? Was she the only one they found?

Our drinks were placed before us and we waited while the rest of Aljonnah filled their chalices. I noticed Anahita was without one and still wore her desert clothes as opposed to orange robes like the rest of us. I silently begged her to look at me. I wanted to know what had happened. What had Wanjala said to her? I wanted her to know we were not in league with the imposter Dragon Lord.

More importantly, I wanted to know if she had seen Uri and knew if he was okay.

Then the king lifted his cup and drank.

It was time. Unlike the other nights, I wanted to get the ritual over with so I could get my questions answered and find Uri. I took a deep breath and gripped the chalice through the fabric of my sleeve, hastily throwing the liquid to the back of my throat.

Immediately, I was small again, sitting before Madame. She was showing me how to mix a certain elixir and I couldn't mix with the right speed. She shouted at me to try harder or she would bring Livia back.

I begged her to give me another chance. "Please, Mother!"

She froze as she reached for a willow vine to punish me for being unable to mix the elixir correctly.

"Mother," I said again in my innocent, scared voice. "Please let me try again. I know I will get it."

She turned her back to me, her hand tightening around the vine, and said, "It's Madame."

I furrowed my brow and asked, "What, Mother?"

She released a pent-up breath and said. "Don't call me that. Never again."

"W-why?" I asked, as frightened tears spilled down my cheeks.

She faced me with a fiery hate in her eyes and said, "Because I can't be your mother anymore."

"But . . . you *are* my mother," I said, confused.

She brought the willow vine down across my face. I fell back with a scream and grabbed my cheek and chest, which were already whelping up.

"I said I'm not your mother," she spat venomously. "You will call me Madame."

I was still screaming and crying and asked, "Why, Mother? Why are you doing this?"

Then the vine whipped across my arm and down my side, causing me to cry out again and grab the whelps that formed.

"I am Madame and you are my apprentice! You are nothing more to me than that."

"M—" I caught myself. "Madame," I said the unfamiliar word weakly.

She let the vine rest by her side and said, "Yes, child. Say it again."

"Madame," I said through tears.

She nodded, then turned me around and ripped my dress down my back. "Now, brace yourself for your punishment. Elixirs need to be perfect and this will help to remind you there is no room for error." Then she brought the vine down upon my bare back.

I opened my eyes and sucked in a pained breath as I arched away from the whip, tears spilling from the brims of my eyes. Only there was no whip, and Madame was gone.

I was facing the king.

He spoke and Anahita said, "Share what you saw, Dragon Born."

I quickly wiped away my tears and forced my voice to come out steady. "I saw—" I began before having to take a moment to regain my composure. "The moment my mother left, and I became a shaman's apprentice," I said with a cool, steady voice.

Anahita spoke to the king, then he nodded at Darsey.

"I relived the day my father started teaching me how to write." His voice was light, and his eyes were beaming.

Anahita spoke to the king, then he nodded at Brantley.

Brantley cleared his throat and said, "I was with my mother as we laid my father to rest."

Anahita shared with the king, then the king spoke out to the people and everyone began approaching the table and grabbing food before walking off to eat.

"The feasting has begun," Anahita said.

Darsey reached for a piece of fruit, whereas I had no appetite. As if separating me from my tippoo without any explanation wasn't enough, they made me relive one of the worst moments of my life.

Enough was enough.

I slammed my hand on the table and asked, "Where is Uri?"

Anahita's head shot up and she stared at me, eyes wide and mouth agape.

The king focused in on her and spoke.

She looked at him, then back at me, and then at him again before speaking.

He sat back and began laughing, waving me off like a greedy child.

I crossed my arms and Anahita said, "There are no second chances at the pools. One may drink only once during the ritual."

I furrowed my brow and opened my mouth to argue, pausing when Brantley rested his hand on my arm.

"Calm down and eat," he said in a low, fierce voice. "We'll find him."

Darsey leaned over, taking care not to touch me, and whispered, "Wanjala likes him. I'm sure he's okay."

I sucked in a deep breath and begrudgingly took a handful of olives, eating them slowly and thoughtfully. My mind was wholly focused on Uri, and I couldn't enjoy the feast like they wanted me to. Wherever he was, whatever he was up against, he needed me. I could feel it.

The feast ended early and the king had Anahita led away before anyone else left. When we were dismissed, we followed the servants back up the path in silence. They left us once we awakened the star-runners and entered our huts.

The moment they were out of sight, I ran to the back door and unlatched it, shoving it in. I was furious and ready to find Uri. I didn't have time to fear the dark as the cold air rushed in upon me. I ducked in and ran to Darsey's hut next door just as he was coming out with a lit torch.

"What do you want to do?" he asked as he closed the door behind him.

"We need to find Uri," I said, breathlessly. Then I thought of Anahita's imprisonment and added, "And we need to get to Anahita." She shouldn't be punished for not trusting in Wanjala. He was, after all, being deceitful.

"You won't be able to reach her," a voice echoed from deep within the cavern, near the tomb.

Darsey shoved me behind him and held his torch out to the dark. "Who's there?" he demanded.

A sword unsheathed behind us as Brantley stepped up. "Show yourself," he added.

A disheveled and dirty looking man stepped into the light and I recognized him immediately.

"Joah," I exclaimed.

Brantley jumped in front of us and angled his sword out. "What is your business here?" he growled.

"To beseech your mercy," he said weakly.

"What mercy do you deserve after you sent us into Aljonnah, *knowing* the people would try to kill us?" Brantley asked.

"Did the bracelets really mean nothing?" Darsey implored.

Joah shook his head and said, "We were just trying to weaken Wanjala."

"At the cost of our lives?" Brantley roared.

"I would do anything for my people!" Joah roared back. "They are unhappy and trapped. The Dragon Lord is using Aljonnah for his evil practices. We shouldn't have to be subject to a ruler we didn't choose!"

"The people seem happy," I pointed out. "The only ones who have a problem with Wanjala are your band of rebels in the desert."

He shook his head and said, "We have more allies inside the oasis that are staying hidden. Even now, our 'rebels' are settled on the outskirts of the oasis, unharmed by the guard, as they are with us."

"Then for what reason do you beg for our mercy?" Brantley asked suspiciously.

Joah shook his head and had tears in his eyes. "For Anahita. She wasn't supposed to be captured, and I would do anything to get her back safely. I already lost my son; I can't lose my wife too."

Brantley spoke before I could reassure him we would get Anahita back. "What trade would you offer for her life?"

Joah sighed deeply and said, "If he releases Anahita back to me, we will leave. We will go back to the mountains and never return to Aljonnah. We will no longer be a threat to him, or you."

"Tell him," Darsey whispered.

Brantley let out a long breath and said, "Might as well." Though he didn't lower his blade.

"Tell me what?" he asked, then his face took on fear. "Is Anahita okay?"

"Yes," I said quickly. "We just saw her at the feast. She was unharmed."

He sighed in relief and I looked at Darsey and Brantley to be sure we were all in agreement, then back at him. "Wanjala isn't a Dragon Lord," I revealed.

Joah's looked confused as his emotional breaths slowly steadied.

"What?" he asked, barely above a whisper.

I took a deep breath and explained, "He's a tippoo, like Uri."

"What?" he asked again. "What is . . . a tippoo?"

I explained what little we knew about tippoos, and how Uri and I were attached.

When I was done, Joah sat back on his knees and mumbled, "So you don't speak to the animals."

"He's been lying to the tribe for over a thousand years," Darsey added, bringing the attention back to Wanjala.

"And he knows we know the truth," Brantley said.

I nodded. "He claims his reasons were noble. And he plans on leaving with us when we go—"

"He killed my son," Joah growled.

I froze and felt Darsey lay his hand on my shoulder, urging me to go inside the hut. I ignored him and waited for Joah to continue.

He looked down and clenched his fists. "Wanjala will die."

Brantley stepped up and eagerly said, "How many men can you muster to fight?"

Joah's voice went from a distraught husband and father, to a cold soldier as he said, "I don't know. How many will we need?"

As much as I had seen, I had to believe that Wanjala was still good. Uri wouldn't be giving him so much of his time if he weren't. And he planned on leaving with us once the Blue Dragon Lord was free. Surely, it needn't come to fight. We were almost there!

"As many as possible. Wanjala has lied to all of Aljonnah for far too long."

Joah nodded and Brantley slowly lowered his blade and continued, "He has killed your people."

Joah agreed.

"He has forced you to worship him."

Joah snarled.

"He has made you believe that an attack against him is an attack against the Dragon Lords themselves."

"He is an abomination!" Joah roared.

"The people need to know the truth, and they need to turn on him together."

"They will," Joah agreed fiercely.

"We need his weakness." Brantley looked at me and added, "Something Uri was supposed to help us discover."

"Uri could be in trouble," I snapped back, surprised that although I was trying to believe in Wanjala, I was still worried about Uri. Then I continued, "We need to find him before we plan an uprising."

"How sure are we that an uprising is what we need?" Darsey asked, and I was grateful I wasn't the only one thinking reasonably.

Joah turned to him and asked angrily, "You would have him get away with his crimes?"

Darsey shook his head and said, "No. The people of Aljonnah need to know that he has been lying to them, but maybe there doesn't need to be bloodshed to do it."

"Darsey's right," I agreed. "If enough people know the truth, Wanjala will be forced to admit his wrongdoings. Then he will leave with us. We're only a few days away from gaining access to the black pool and freeing the Blue Dragon Lord."

Joah looked at me, his eyes narrowing. "Tell me, child . . . do you *trust* the deceptive beast?"

Darsey jumped in and said, "Wanjala is the liar, not Adalee. She *is* the Dragon Born. Don't disrespect her."

We all looked at Darsey and I marveled at the stony set of his eyes as he stood up for me.

"My apologies," Joah offered, then continued, "Do you trust him?"

I sighed and shrugged my shoulders. "I don't know. He *has* been kind and trusting to us. He has kept us fed and sheltered. He is making us members of the tribe so we can access the black pool. He says he is going to help us free the Dragon Lord."

"He told you that only members of the tribe can access the black pool?" Joah asked.

I hesitantly nodded.

"*He* is the one who made it off-limits. *Not* the people. You don't drink from it during the ritual and I don't believe he plans on granting you access."

"Then what has been the point of all this?" Darsey asked, distraught.

"I told you," Brantley shouted. "To buy time."

Joah nodded and said, "It may end up being the cause of his downfall."

"How?" Brantley asked.

"The people of Aljonnah will not trust or defend one not of their tribe. If we fight against Wanjala on *her* word," he pointed to me, "then she needs to be a tribe member. Or else, her word means nothing."

"Even though she's the Dragon Born?" Darsey asked.

Brantley answered, "The people have been scorned by one they believe to be a Dragon Lord. In Aljonnah, being the Dragon Born doesn't help."

Joah nodded again.

"So, we finish the ritual? Become members of Aljonnah?" Darsey asked.

"If the Dragon Born becomes a member and *then* tells the people the truth about Wanjala, they will listen," Joah confirmed.

Darsey shook his head and said, "If the people hate Wanjala so much, why wouldn't they be willing to listen right now?"

"They might think it is a ploy to reveal those who stand against him," Joah explained.

"And kill all the rebels," Brantley finished.

*"Adalee."*

"Uri," I gasped, as I rushed back through the door to my hut. "Uri," I said again as he walked tiredly past the curtain.

I scooped him up, relief taking the place of angst. "What happened? Where were you?"

Darsey and Brantley came in behind me.

Uri yawned and stretched in my arms. *"How was the orange water? Wanjala said Anahita came back and could translate, so we kept training."*

"I was so worried," I scolded, pulling him to my face.

*"Why?"* he asked, confused. *"I was only with Wanjala."*

"I know, and I saw where you were," I whispered.

Uri's ears perked up and he looked at me, cocking his head. *"When?"*

"When all the people were fighting. And you and Wanjala were watching."

*"Oh! You mean this?"*

Then the world around me faded and I saw only the arena before me. It was filled with roaring warriors, throwing themselves at one another, weapons screaming out as they clashed upon one another. Some were glowing yellow.

I was astounded by the vibrant glow, then my vision twisted until I was facing Wanjala, his face more animated than I had ever noticed before. His grey skin glowed yellow just as the people in the arena, and his eyes were energized and focused.

"The king is very old," Wanjala was saying in an ancient, deep voice. "His time is almost complete."

"Will you miss him?" Uri asked.

"I miss them all," the dragon said with a nod. "I have been his tippoo for almost seventy years, and he has been a good and faithful king to the people of Aljonnah."

"So, he knows you're a tippoo, right?"

"The people do not understand tippoos," he explained. "They believe what I tell them, and that is that I am their Dragon Lord."

The vision spun back to the arena, and Uri asked, "And why do they fight? What are they training for?"

"They are preparing for the games. The weakest third of them will be buried in the tombs. The strongest three will be housed in the huts until the final test. The victor will be crowned the new king and the attachment ceremony will take place."

"How do you switch from one person to another?" Uri asked curiously.

"I will simply sever the bond and attach to the new king."

Then it disappeared as quickly as it came, and I was staring at confused looks from Darsey and Brantley.

"What was that?" I asked breathlessly.

*"Is that not the place you saw?"* Uri asked innocently.

"No, it was," I said. "Just . . . how did you make me *see* it again?"

*"Oh! That is how normal tippoos talk to their people. Wanjala showed me. They can't talk with words like we do, but they can push pictures into their mind. I can show you what I see and what I think."*

"What is he saying?" Brantley asked.

I ignored him and asked, "Why were some people glowing? What tomb? Do people die in that arena?"

*"They were all glowing for Wanjala. The ones I could see glowing are the ones I can pair with. That's what you look like, too."*

"What is he saying?" Brantley asked again, frustrated.

I shook my head and quickly explained what I saw to them.

Joah stepped inside and said, "These huts are reserved for the three strongest eligible warriors in the tribe. The tomb behind them is where a third of those who wish to be crowned end up."

Brantley turned to him and asked, "So the challenges result in death?" Before Joah could answer he looked at me and said, "That is quite different than what Wanjala made us believe."

Joah said, "Not directly. As we said before, they lose the right to bear children. Their line ends with them. The bottom third of competitors are sacrificed and put into the desert until their bones are picked clean. Then they are brought back and laid to rest in the tomb."

I felt nauseous. "The tomb behind these huts?" I asked weakly.

He nodded and Darsey asked, "Why is the tomb so near where the strongest warriors are housed?"

"To remind them what has been lost already. To encourage them to do their best in the battle. And to motivate them to protect the people of Aljonnah, should they be chosen."

We all stared at Joah and Uri said, *"That doesn't sound right. I don't think Wanjala would do that."*

I didn't share his concerns with them, as I didn't want anyone turning against Uri for his trust in the tippoo.

"He is evil," Brantley concluded.

Joah nodded. "Believing he was the Dragon Lord made it seem righteous. Now that I know he is nothing more than a tippoo . . ." he trailed off and I saw his jaw set firmly.

"We need to plan," Brantley said.

Joah nodded and they went back into the tomb.

Uri stretched and yawned in my arms, before turning around a few times and curling up.

I turned to Darsey and whispered, "This doesn't feel right. Uri doesn't think what Joah is saying is true."

Darsey nodded and said, "I don't think we should be aiding in the rebellion when Wanjala plans on going with us in a couple of days. He's *leaving*. Why rush to fight?"

"Exactly," I agreed. "Uri?" I asked.

*"Hm?"* he responded right before gently slipping to sleep.

"He's asleep," I said. "The poor little guy is exhausted, but he *trusts* Wanjala. We don't even know Joah and Anahita that well."

Darsey nodded. "And why is Brantley suddenly so excited about allying himself with him when he despised him so?"

"I don't know." I gently shook Uri. He stirred only a moment, then went back to sleep. "I can't wake him," I said helplessly.

"Should we warn Wanjala?" Darsey asked hesitantly.

I shook my head quickly. "I don't know what that would do. Even though I want to trust Wanjala, it could put innocent people in danger."

"If Joah is lying, we might lose our chance to have a *dragon* join our quest. Imagine how helpful that would be," Darsey pointed out.

I sat down, still cradling Uri, and focused on what to do. Brantley and Joah's voices disappeared when they closed the door behind them, and I wondered what their plan entailed. We needed to know.

I looked up at Darsey and said, "You should go with them and help them plan."

He scrunched his brow, then nodded with understanding. "So, if we do need to warn him, we'll know what's happening."

"Yes," I confirmed.

"What are you going to do?" he asked.

I looked down at Uri and said, "I'm going to sleep. I think something has been happening in my dreams, and I'm going to try and see if I can speak to Wanjala through them."

Darsey cocked his head and asked, "Is that possible?"

I shrugged and said, "I'm going to find out."

The orange sand swirled around me, and just outside of it was the grey sand, with Wanjala's silhouette on the edge.

If it was him, I needed to know. If he had really spoken to me, I needed him to do it again.

I neared the edge of the orange sand though it stayed aggressive, not allowing Wanjala to come any closer. As it whipped by, threatening to shred anything that tried to cross, I slowly moved my hands forward.

It was a dream, after all. I shouldn't be harmed.

I pushed my arm into the sand, and it immediately calmed and fell to the ground. The grey sand did the same after a moment, and I was left facing Wanjala.

"Finally," he said.

"Wanjala?" I asked, not moving.

He nodded and said, "I have been trying to reach you since you first arrived." His voice was deep and ancient. Every word was laced with guttural growls, though I felt it was merely from his age, and not his temperament.

"In my dreams?" I asked.

"Tippoos can only communicate with those who they are attached to," he explained. "So, I have been trying to come to you in your dreams. Only now do I realize it is possible. Your Uri finally trusts me enough to let down his guard."

I looked at the orange sand that rested around my feet. "Uri has been keeping you away?" I asked.

"Not to his knowledge," he said. "He should have no memory of it. I believe it is his consciousness protecting the one he is attached to."

"And he was strong enough to hold *you* off?" I asked, bewildered.

The dragon smiled and said, "Apparently, all tippoo auras are equally powerful. I could not have come to you, had he not allowed it."

"Why?" I asked. "Why have you come to me?"

"I greatly wish to attach to you when I accompany you on the quest."

I thought about what it would be like to have *two* tippoos attached to me, and wondered if it would make Uri jealous. I also wondered if I would be filled with the same protectiveness and love for Wanjala that I felt for Uri.

"That would be great," I said. "So long as Uri is okay with it."

Wanjala nodded and said, "I understand. You have great devotion to him. Just know, that should I attach to you, you would feel equally devoted to me. It is the blessing of the tippoo."

I nodded absently and asked, "Why ask me now? Why didn't you ask me when we first arrived? We could have already saved the Blue Dragon Lord and been on our way."

"We must respect the laws of Aljonnah," he explained.

Confused, I mentioned, "I heard that it is only *you* that has made the black pool forbidden. Not the people."

His eyes narrowed and he asked, "Who has been in your ear?"

I shook my head and said, "It's not important. What *is* important, is knowing that you're being honest with me. I can't have you as my tippoo if I can't trust you."

"Very well," he said. "I will show you everything."

He stared into my eyes and a moment later, the world around me faded and I saw him as a tiny lizard, a skink, on the shoulder of a man wandering the desert. He came upon Aljonnah, and the next thousand years played out before me as quickly as a blink, just as Wanjala had claimed they happened. I saw the people's barbaric ways. Their sacrificial rituals. Wanjala offering the bottom third of candidates up as sacrifices to appease the peoples' savage roots. Zaire diving into the black pool himself.

Then the vision skipped forward. I was riding upon his back and he brought all our enemies to their knees as we passed.

We stood in the desert with all the Dragon Lords facing us. They offered their gratitude for his part in freeing them and made him one of them! Then they made me his rider, and we ruled over Pylertchia alongside the Dragon Lords for the rest of time.

Then the vision faded, and I was once again facing him. "Wow," I said.

"I have so much I can offer you," he told me.

"You wish to become a Dragon Lord," I said in awe.

He nodded and said, "I wish to be with someone forever, instead of needing to sever bonds every one hundred years. It is painful to say goodbye to them."

I thought about having to say goodbye to Uri, and it pained my heart greatly. "I understand."

"Now," he said, "I wish for you to trust me as greatly as Uri does."

"I wish for that too," I said, honestly.

"And I don't want you to be frightened or misunderstand when it happens," he explained further.

"Okay," I said softly.

"You are right that becoming a member of the tribe does not gain you access to the black pool."

I nodded, though I was surprised at his admission.

He continued, "And so, instead of completing the ritual tomorrow night, I will instead hold the Choosing."

"The Choosing?" I asked.

"I will sever the bond with the king and attach to you before all of Aljonnah."

I sucked in a deep breath at the revelation and asked, "Then we will free the Blue Dragon Lord?"

"Yes," he confirmed. "When you awake, Uri will be gone. Fear not, for he will be with me. His presence is vital for the Choosing to take place. You need not fear."

"He is young," I defended gently.

"He is. Do you understand what severing a bond means?"

I shrugged at him moving on and said, "You disconnect. When Uri and I connected it came from looking into his eyes. I guess one of us would decide to no longer be connected and look into each other's eyes."

He shook his head and said, "The connection is final. You don't disconnect from a tippoo. They become a part of you. Your fates are intertwined unless one of you sever the bond."

I tried to understand what he was saying, then I asked, "How do you sever the bond?"

"One of you has to kill the other."

Suddenly, a burst of blue light exploded in the distance, and we both looked. The sand rolled up in a wave and billowed forth, towards us.

"What's happening?" I asked, shielding my eyes.

"I don't know!" Wanjala called out in a fierce voice.

I looked back toward him as the sand rolled in and pushed him away, wrapping itself completely around me, and stealing my sight.

I crouched down and covered my head.

Then it ceased.

Slowly, I opened my eyes and saw I was standing by the black pool. Had the Blue Dragon Lord come to remind me she needed rescuing. I knew she did.

I hadn't forgotten her!

Maybe she wanted to show me what was beyond the black waters. I readied myself to dive in.

"Wait," a voice sounded beside me, and I turned. Gavyn stood there in his warrior form.

"Where have *you* been?" I asked angrily. Not that I wanted him around, I was just irritated that he chose this moment to reveal himself.

"Watching," was all he said.

"I don't have time for you," I bit. "The Blue Dragon Lord needs me."

He offered me his hand and said, "You don't have to free her. I can take your dreams away. I can stop the Dragons from Calling you."

His words felt like poison and I said, "You mean you can stop me from *hearing* them. You can't stop the Calling."

"You don't have to submit to this path," he said gently. "There are others."

"I want nothing you have to offer," I said flatly.

"Remember what I said before."

I tried to recall all that he had said to me, though it felt like I last faced him a lifetime ago.

"If you—" he began, but I dove into the black pool, not caring for anymore of his deceit.

Twenty | A Trustworthy Dragon

I awoke in a sweat to Darsey nudging me.

"Where is Uri?" he asked.

I sat up quickly and looked around.

Remembering Wanjala's words, I rubbed my face and softly said, "It's okay. He's with Wanjala."

"Things are getting bad," he whispered. "There are more people in Brantley's hut. Joah brought the rebels in and they are dispersing throughout Aljonnah, preparing for the uprising. I think they are going to do it tonight, at the Choosing."

I eyed him in surprise and asked, "How do *you* know about the Choosing?"

"It was announced early this morning. The entire oasis is abuzz with it. They are rushing the uprising to stop it."

I jumped up and shouted, "Well, they shouldn't!" I snatched up the blade and the power knocked me off my feet.

Brantley came in and said, "Now *that* is the kind of power we need." Then he picked up the blade and added, "Just not yet."

Darsey helped me up and I asked, "The uprising is *tonight*?"

Joah stepped in and said, "We can't let him choose another king."

"You don't understand," I argued. "I spoke to him. I saw him in my dreams."

They all stopped and stared at me.

"You really did?" Darsey asked eagerly. "What did he say?"

I told them what happened, leaving out the part about Gavyn and once I was done, Joah scoffed.

"You think that *means* something?" he asked.

"She doesn't dream as others do," Darsey defended.

Brantley shook his head and said, "She just wants to stop the uprising so she can have a dragon on the quest with her."

I crossed my arms, taken aback by his disregard for my words when he knew what I was capable of in my dreams. "How can you say that?" I asked in disbelief.

"Okay," Joah said, nodding. "Let's pretend for a moment that you are telling the truth. There is one detail of the conversation that *proves* he isn't your ally."

"What's that?" I challenged.

"He is stopping the ritual," he said. "He is having you go directly to the Choosing, knowing that if you were to reveal him, it wouldn't be enough to make the people stand against him. They would have no reason to trust you."

"Where's Uri?" Brantley asked, looking around.

I waved him away and said, "With Wanjala, preparing for the Choosing."

His eyes went wide, and he growled, "So you *do* trust him. Completely. You're not even one of us anymore!"

"*You're* not one of us anymore!" Darsey shouted at him. "You are allying yourself with the rebels, and not heeding the Dragon Born's wishes."

"Because we have a better chance at freeing the true Dragon Lord if we trust the people, not the tippoo! *She* has forgotten that! She has become so obsessed with making her own journey easier, that she is distracted and not trying to move us forward." He paused and then added with great emphasis, "I will not be slave to her longer than I have to be!"

"Okay!" I shouted, stepping in the middle before Darsey could respond. "Okay," I said more calmly. "Can we finish the ritual? Can we become full members of Aljonnah?"

"Yes," Joah answered. "You don't need Wanjala for it. All you need is to drink from the five pools."

"Why?" Brantley asked, facing me.

"Let's finish it. Let's become members and not tell Wanjala until we get to the Choosing."

"Go to it willingly?" Brantley asked.

"Yes. And I will be the one to determine if a fight is necessary or not."

"I assure you," Joah said, "it is."

"Still," I said putting my hand out, "let me decide. I promise, I will do what is best for Aljonnah. I do not want bloodshed, and I want your people to be free."

Joah looked at Brantley and he nodded. "She is right about that," he admitted. "She hates bloodshed."

"So, we put our fate into the hands of—"

"The Dragon Born," Darsey interrupted, standing beside me. "And I assure you, your fate is in good hands."

"Come, then," Joah said, motioning for us to follow him. "We will tell the people the new plan."

I looked at Darsey and he grasped my hand protectively. We followed Joah to the cavern, Brantley behind us, acting more like a guard than a friend, and into the tomb.

There were many torches lit, and I was shocked to see at least thirty people standing around. Their talking ceased when I entered and Joah held his hands out to them.

He spoke in their language and I stood between Brantley and Darsey. There was a little bit of grumbling, though they all seemed to agree with the new plan.

Joah turned around and said to me, "They are worried about trusting you, so I hope you know what you're doing."

"I do," I said confidently.

A tall, thin boy about Darsey's age stepped up and spoke to Joah. Joah turned toward us and said, "This is Faraje. He wants to make sure Zaire will be getting the justice he deserves."

I knew the truth. I knew Zaire had jumped into the pool on his own. Wanjala had shown me, but I couldn't bring myself to reveal it to them. It would break any trust I had of theirs, so instead, I nodded and said, "There will be justice."

Joah translated and Faraji smiled at me, and slightly dipped his head.

He then turned and told the people what Joah had said to him. They all cheered and he moved to them as they gathered and placed their hands on his shoulders, embracing him with kisses.

"It has been decided that Faraje will be the next king," Joah explained as we watched the exchange. "The people love him, and they loved his parents. He will fiercely defend Aljonnah with his life, and everyone sees it."

It was important that Wanjala remained alive, no matter how much I disliked lying to the next king of Aljonnah. He would be a greater ally to me than the people, and he had already proven himself.

Joah directed us back to the huts and we went, though I wondered at what point in the night did Joah gain so much control over our actions. Brantley seemed to be in sync with him and all I saw when I looked at them were two soldiers, ready to do whatever it took to gain what they wanted.

Brantley had proven to me time and again that he could kill without a thought. Joah seemed to be cut from the same cloth, and I feared for the people of Aljonnah if that was what their leadership would look like. No wonder Wanjala said they were a barbaric people.

The day drew on, and people came and went from the huts in stealth. Wanjala's attention was divided with preparations for the Choosing, and it appeared to give the people more freedom to move about.

I stayed in my hut with Darsey, working on harnessing the blade. Its power was unimaginable and after many hours of trying to contain it, and only succeeding in singeing the ground around me, we decided it would be best for Darsey to hold onto it until after the final ritual.

We both assumed the water would make me strong enough to control it, and I couldn't risk an accident before then. The people seemed to barely trust me despite the kindness we had experienced during the rituals.

It made me wonder if they had faked it the whole time, and I became even more concerned for Wanjala's safety. All he wanted was to be able to live on without having to sever anymore bonds. He didn't like saying goodbye to his people, and I didn't blame him. It would be painful.

Faraji secured green robes for us as night began to fall.

We changed quickly and Brantley went over our part of the plan once more. We were to drink from the green pool, get to the arena, and then I would decide if Wanjala was our enemy or not once he saw our green robes.

Joah determined he would be livid that we became members without his blessing, though I was quite sure he wouldn't mind, as all he wanted was to bond to me and leave.

Joah opened the curtain of my hut and asked, "Are you ready?"

"Yes," Brantley answered, and he motioned for us to follow.

We rushed down the path toward the pools, though all I could think about was getting to the Choosing and finding a way to convince the people to spare Wanjala. Too many of them knew the truth now, and they were holding off because of me.

We reached the pools and rushed to the green waters.

"We don't have chalices," Joah explained. "Drink from it as you would a river."

The three of us dropped to our knees and I leaned over, pulling the water up into my mouth through my lips. It was cold and sweet.

Immediately, I was upon a Dragon Lord, high in the sky, looking down at Pylertchia. I had done it. This was the eighth Dragon Lord, and I had just freed him. My quest was complete. I was filled with satisfaction, relief, and exhilaration.

Then the oasis returned to my vision. I looked at Brantley who had a smile on his lips. He almost seemed happy, albeit confused. Then I looked at Darsey, who had a stone cast face and tears streaming down his cheeks.

"What does this pool show you?" he asked, looking up at Joah.

"It shows you a vision from your future."

"Really?" Brantley asked as he stood. "A sure vision? Or just what *could* be?"

"A sure vision," Joah answered. "What the pool shows you cannot be changed."

Darsey jumped up and wiped his eyes. "Let's go," he said. "We have to get to the Choosing." His voice was flat and sounded irritated.

"Follow the servants." Joah instructed. "Faraji and I have another task at hand."

We turned and I saw three servants waiting with torches.

"Are you okay?" I asked Darsey after we started moving and Joah and Faraji disappeared in a different direction.

He only nodded and paused to set my blade down. "Here, you'll need this."

I grabbed it, readying myself for the kickback.

Nothing.

I looked at Darsey and said, "It's powerless."

Brantley rushed up beside us and said, "I doubt that. You just need to be strong enough to tap into it."

I nodded and strapped it to my side.

We followed the servants through the oasis until we heard the roaring cheers from the arena. Though our guides didn't falter in their steps, my heart grew more anxious with each one.

The arena came into sight and we approached a great open doorway, spilling out with firelight.

"Are you ready?" Brantley asked me.

I nodded as we entered the open door. Immediately, I was led away from Darsey and Brantley, despite our objections.

Darsey started swinging at the men but Brantley grabbed him and held him back. I tried to turn and see what was happening. Brantley was whispering in Darsey's ear, then he calmed down.

I was led through a small, dark doorway and down a corridor. I could still hear the cheering echoing across the sandy bricks and the servants led me to some stairs. We climbed up and eventually came out at the top, where Wanjala was seated, along with the old king, and Anahita bound beside them.

"Wanjala," I said breathlessly as I stepped out into the firelight, eyeing Anahita.

She silently looked at my green robes.

He looked down at me and stared.

"Uri?" I asked, looking around for him.

The king spoke, and Anahita translated, "He is readying himself for his part of the Choosing. I see you have completed the ritual to become a member of Aljonnah."

I nodded and said, "I did. All three of us did."

Anahita translated my words to the king and I was surprised Wanjala didn't understand me as he had in my dream the night before.

The king responded after a moment and Anahita said, "That is not what we discussed. What reason have you to become a tribal member, unless you have found deceit in my words?"

"No," I said gently. "It isn't like that. We just wanted to be sure—"

Wanjala let out a roar that made me jump back.

The king stood and held his hands out, quieting the crowd. He spoke, his words echoing across the stadium.

"Let the Choosing begin," Anahita whispered.

The grating of a gate opened down in the arena, and I leaned over the low wall and watched as someone carried Uri out, a collar tightly wound around his neck.

"Uri," I whispered in a panic.

The man ripped the collar off and tossed Uri down. Uri leaped into his largest tiger form before he hit the ground, and three warriors came forward, weapons raised.

He was going to be slain in the ring.

I desperately willed the blade to spread its power through me, though it remained stagnant.

"Uri, run!" I screamed.

He dove out of the way as one of the warriors thrust their spear through the air.

"Get out of there!" I ordered as I frantically began searching for a way down.

"The bond must be severed," Anahita said, and I spun around and faced Wanjala.

"*Your* bond!" I cried. "Not mine!"

After the translation was through, Anahita said, "There can only be one."

"One what?" I asked, hearing Uri roar angrily. I wanted to turn and see what was happening, but Wanjala had me trapped in his gaze.

"One king?" I asked. "One Dragon Lord? One what?"

Uri roared in pain and I spun back, seeing blood spill from his side as a spear stuck from it.

Then I understood.

One tippoo. Each person could only have one tippoo.

"No!" I leaped over the edge and landed roughly on the compacted sand.

I scrambled up as one of the warriors approached Uri, lifting a sword high above his head to finish him off.

"Stop!" I screamed.

Before I could reach them, Wanjala tore past me and picked the warrior up in his teeth, biting him in half and letting the pieces fall to the ground, blood spilling from his mouth.

He spit it out and I met his eyes as I reached Uri, leaning down over him.

"Uri?" His eyes were barely open, and his breathing was labored.

Darsey made it to my side and asked, "What do you want me to do?"

I examined his wound in a panic and cried out, "I don't know! I don't know how to heal him! Stop the bleeding?"

Darsey pulled his ceremonial robe off and handed it to me. Carefully, I wrapped it around the spear that still jutted from his side.

"Uri, can you hear me?" I asked in a broken voice.

*"It hurts,"* he said weakly.

Hearing his voice filled me with hope. "It's okay. I'm going to fix this," I tried to say calmly.

*"Sever the bond,"* he said.

His words dashed my hope away. "No," I said. "Don't give up. I'll save you; I promise."

Then he pushed an image into my mind of him dying, and me dying beside him, despite having no wounds. I sucked in a deep breath when my surroundings came back and I asked, "Uri? Is that what will happen?"

*"Yes,"* his sweet voice said. *"Do it so you can live."*

I shook my head. "No. I won't."

I felt a swoon come over me and I wavered on my knees, leaning over him. My face was against his fur and he was beginning to grow cold.

"Adalee!" Darsey cried, wrapping his arms around my shoulders. "Are you okay?"

"No," I whimpered.

I wasn't ready to give in. I couldn't let Wanjala get away with what he was doing.

Then Faraji's voice cried out over the arena from where the king and Anahita stood.

Joah reached our side while Faraji addressed the people, and Wanjala stood unmoving, in a catatonic state of shock.

"The people know now," he said quickly. "They know what he is. They know you are members of the tribe. They know what he's doing to you and Uri."

"They know too late," I wailed as I buried my face in Uri's fur.

"What do you want me to do?" he asked.

Everyone was asking what I wanted them to do. All I wanted was to die in peace next to my Uri. If one of us died, so did the other.

I weakly looked up at Wanjala's face as he stared out over the crowd, fear in his eyes. Then I looked at the old king, seated on his throne, watching it all play out.

They wouldn't get away with this.

In a rage-filled voice I cried, "Kill the king!"

Joah immediately stood and loosed an arrow that struck the king in the chest.

Wanjala, breaking from his shock, roared loudly and rushed back to the king, knocking everyone aside who stood in his way. He took the king up in his mouth and killed him just as he had the warrior.

The people of Aljonnah, filled with a rage that rivaled my own, screamed and rushed toward him. As soon as the king's body was halved, Wanjala disappeared.

Joah ran toward the tumult and I turned my attention back to Uri. Darsey shook me gently and asked, "Is he going to be okay?"

It was getting harder to breathe as Uri barely held on to life. I shook my head. I couldn't imagine going on without Uri.

Gavyn appeared, a sudden calm in the storm raging throughout the arena. All the screams, pounding of feet, and roars of rage and uncertainty slowed to a crawl around us.

I looked up at him, his otherworldly presence sending both fear and calm through me, an unwelcome duo.

"Please," I pleaded, not knowing what I expected him to do. "Please, save him."

"Sever the bond," he said coolly, his voice echoing around me.

I shook my head and wrapped my arms around Uri, both our bodies shivering. "I can't. I won't live without him. Please. Please don't let him die. Don't let us die."

"What power do you think I have?" he asked.

"I've seen it," I said desperately. "Please, you have power. I'll do anything. Please. I'll do whatever you want! If you can, save us."

The warrior leaned down and gripped the spear. He whispered to me, "There is hope for you yet." Then he ripped it from Uri's side, dropped it, and turned back into the Falcone and flew away.

Immediately my strength came back, and I sat up, looking over Uri. The wound was nowhere to be found, and Uri's breathing steadied, though his eyes didn't open.

"What was that?" Darsey asked breathlessly.

"Gavyn healed him," I said, stunned. Then I looked at Darsey and said, "I think I messed up. I made a deal with him—"

"Who cares?" Darsey said excitedly. "He's okay!" He wrapped me in his arms and held me tightly. "What did you mean by 'save us'?" he asked.

I took a deep breath and said, "Our fates are intertwined unless one of us kills the other."

He sat back and stared at me. "You said," he said slowly, "that you wouldn't live without him." Then realization and anger rushed over his face and he asked, "Were you going to let yourself die?"

I nodded, not caring about how ridiculous it sounded to anyone else. No one could understand the bond we had.

He scolded me with great frustration, though I hardly heard his words as I searched the dark sky for Gavyn. What would he expect of me in return?

Then a sharp tug pulled at my wrist and I looked down. The black char that tethered me to Brantley was stinging. I spun around then pushed away from Darsey and asked, "Where is Brantley?"

"The black pool," he said solemnly.

I jumped up. "Where? Which way?"

Anahita rushed up and grabbed my arms. "He got away. You must help us find Wanjala. I saw it with my own eyes. He turned into a skink when he killed the king."

I faced her. "Take me to the black pool. Now."

She stared at me for a moment, then nodded and I was grateful she didn't question me, and instead began to lead me from the tumult.

Darsey ran up beside me and said, "I'll do whatever I can to help."

I slid to a stop and grabbed him. "Stay with Uri. Let no harm come to him. *That* is what I need you to do. I'm the only one who can traverse the black pool."

He unhappily nodded and rushed back to Uri, though no one was paying him any mind, as everyone was searching for Wanjala. It appeared Joah and Faraji's plan had worked, though the inner workings of it still remained a mystery to me.

Anahita and I ran through the oasis, the light of a single torch as our guide. The sting of the bind lessened, and I spotted Brantley leaning against a tree, facing us.

"Finally," he called as we neared. "Let's go!" Then he turned and darted off.

"Stop!" I cried as I chased him, leaving Anahita behind. It was foolish to rush in without the power of the blade no matter how badly I wanted to free the Blue Dragon Lord. I had no idea what awaited us in the black waters; if they would burn like the fire stones, or how deep they ran.

His brazen, know-it-all attitude sent me reeling and I wanted so badly to put him in his place.

Uri almost died. I almost died. Wanjala got away. And all he could do was focus on himself.

I was the one who had freed a Dragon Lord before, not him. He was rushing into a dangerous situation, forcing my hand, and he had no idea what he was doing! It was infuriating!

He reached the black pool before I did, and it was only by the torch in his hand I could see his face. He looked at me and smiled. Then dropped the torch and jumped into the pool.

I raced over and slid to a stop by the bank. "Brantley!" I screamed out, searching over the waters. There wasn't so much as a ripple indicating he had submerged, and if I hadn't seen it with my own eyes, I might not believe it just happened.

Anahita rushed up behind me and asked, "Where did he go?"

"Into the water," I said.

"No one emerges from the black pool," she warned.

"I know," I said softly.

Then I took a deep breath and jumped off the bank.

**Twenty-One** | Into the Black Pool

Darkness.

Pressure. No sight. No sound. No breath.

No fire.

I thrashed about but couldn't swim. The water wasn't like water. It was like . . . sap. Thick, overwhelming, and everywhere.

Air. I needed air. There was too much pressure pushing in on me. Squeezing the life from my body.

Held in place, I had no idea which was up or down.

I had to hurry. Without air I would die!

Unable to wait any longer, I opened my mouth and sucked in deep, my lungs filling with what felt like river stones piling upon one another. They weighed me down and forced their way in, despite me trying to push them back out. Panicked, I grabbed at my mouth, unable to close it.

The tingle of the blade flamed to life at my side and spread through my limbs, exploding around me. It raced through the water akin to lightning in a fierce storm. It burst forth, pushing the black water back, leaving me suspended. It continued to spread, illuminating the darkness. Nothing was left hidden.

And to my surprise, the excruciating pain in my lungs subsided for only a moment, while I took in the vision of dozens of blue orbs floating amidst the darkness, mostly filled with piles of bones.

Then the light faded, the pain forced its way back in, and I fell. I landed on something smooth and slick, and retched up the stones settled in my lungs, though all that came forth was a torrential fall of black water.

When I could breathe again, I looked up and saw that I was in a blue, illuminated orb. It was like the others, only not as vibrant. Outside was the black water, looming lazily, existing for the sole purpose of stopping anyone from breaking through.

The blade was still tingling at my side, having been only momentarily appeased with its explosive fit. It wanted more.

Then the orb began to fill with vibrant blue water, though I couldn't pinpoint where it was coming in. I jumped up as it raised steadily up my calves. It was cold against my skin, and I instantly feared finding myself trapped beneath it, unable to breathe again. Unable to escape.

"No!" I cried out, and the blade reacted with another powerful blast, shattering my orb like a bubble, sending it to the far edges of the pool. Then it fired out again, illuminating all the other orbs around me.

A new one quickly formed, and I landed on the smooth bottom.

Again, it began to fill with blue water. The power of the blade was no longer responding, as though it had satisfied its rage and was ready to rest.

I didn't need it to rest now!

The water spread up my calves, past my knees.

"Come on!" I cried out, trying to force the blade to react.

The water continued to rise past my waist, and I turned and shoved my hands against the orb. It sizzled and my hands reached through, though it closed up around my wrists, and the black water fed into my fire, causing it to spread and illuminate everything again.

Then I saw it. A bubble with Brantley floating inside, unconscious. Full of water.

He was dead. Or dying.

"No, no, no," I mumbled as I swiped my hands across the bubble, only to have it close up as soon as they passed through. "Let me out!" I screamed as the water reached my neck.

I stumbled back from the wall and stood on the tips of my toes, trying to breathe in as much air as I could before it filled.

I lifted my chin above the water and sucked in one last breath as it covered me completely, leaving no space for refuge.

I swam to the edge and tried to shove my hands through again. They didn't break the barrier and the blade felt even more powerless by my side.

Futilely, I shoved against the wall, with nothing to brace myself. My lungs began to burn and I knew that without air, I would soon be like Brantley.

All my efforts were proving in vain, and I couldn't hold out any longer.

I opened my mouth and sucked in a deep breath, feeling the cool water rush in upon my tongue and fill my lungs.

I cringed and braced for the burn, yet somehow this water satiated my desire for air. I breathed it out and opened my eyes, sucking in another breath. I marveled at the fact that though I could feel it filling my lungs, it didn't hurt as I knew it should.

Not only that; it felt good. My panic ebbed and my heart slowed.

I closed my eyes and pulled in deep, relaxing breaths, relishing the peace each one brought. Everything else faded away and I let the comfort wrap around me. No longer was the water cold. Each breath brought it closer to my temperature until I couldn't tell the difference between myself and it.

I relaxed into the warmth.

Screams.

Fire.

Madame.

Uri and Darsey swirled around me, smiling down. Then quickly vanished as I freely flew across the sea. Suddenly I saw Darsey holding our daughter and a doting Uri looking over them. They disintegrated as Madame's willow vine slashed across my back, only once, as I was lifted into the air on the crest of the Great Dragon Lord.

Darsey came back to my vision, begging me to take his hand. When I reached for it, Madame struck him with a stick. He turned away sadly, and as I ran after him, I fell down a sandy dune. I sat up quickly, only to discover I was standing in the middle of a steep pillar that dragons were circling. Not Dragon Lords. Just regular dragons. Angry dragons. Evil dragons.

I felt the blade blaze at my side, and I released it upon them. I wouldn't let them take my life.

My eyes shot open, though the water still tried to lull me to sleep. I couldn't let it stop me!

I pulled out the knife, sucked in a deep breath, and stabbed into the side of the orb. It burst like it had before and the black water rushed in on me, trying to squeeze the blue water from my lungs.

The power of the blade resonated throughout my body and branched out, illuminating everything.

I searched quickly for Brantley's orb as a new one was already formed around me. Before the light of the fire faded, I spotted him. He wasn't far.

I breathed the blue water out painlessly and sucked in air before the orb had filled. Then I stabbed it with the blade. It burst around me, and the darkness lit up with the fire of the blade spreading throughout it. With the blade firmly in my grip, I swam toward Brantley.

Each time an orb formed around me, I slashed through it with the blade and kept moving. I couldn't let it stop me from saving him, stupid as he was.

I finally reached his orb and stabbed through it, grabbing his robe with my free hand before I lost him in the dark. Another orb formed around us both and we landed softly on the bottom. I tucked the knife under my arm and grabbed his shoulders, shaking him violently.

He didn't stir.

The orb began to fill, and I screamed for him to wake up, my cries landing on deaf ears. The water was getting too high. I leaned down, holding him close, and used the blade to pop the orb.

We floated for a moment, then another orb formed.

Frustrated, and with a sense of great satisfaction, I slapped him across the face.

It did nothing, so I did it again. Then again, each slap feeling better than the last. He opened his eyes just before I landed a fourth.

Grabbing his face, he rolled to the side and breathed out blue water as I had, then mumbled, "Why, Nadine?"

I rolled my eyes and said, "Not Nadine!" Then grabbed his robes and said, "Hold your breath."

Then I popped the bubble and clung to him, though he was thrashing about, which made it difficult to keep my grip.

A new orb formed, and we landed on the bottom of it. I let out my air and Brantley began coughing up black water.

"Why didn't you warn me?" he asked angrily when he could speak again.

"Don't breathe the water," I said sarcastically.

He stood up and faced me. "I got you down here," he said triumphantly.

"And I had to save your life," I bit back.

He rubbed his bright red cheek and said, "Yes, I can still feel it."

The water was up to my knees and I said, "Let's get you out of here so I can free the Dragon Lord."

He nodded and held on to my robes.

"I'm going to burst the orb, then we need to swim up," I explained.

"How will we know?" he asked. "It's too disorienting."

I looked down at the blade and said, "Open your eyes and follow the light."

He nodded and I burst the orb.

We swam up as best we could discern, and I slashed every orb that formed around us after we replenished our breath. But no matter how long or far we swam, we never broke the surface.

Finally, Brantley grabbed my arm just as I was about to slash through another orb and he said, "We're not going to make it out."

"We have to almost be there," I reasoned.

He shook his head and said, "Anyone who enters, doesn't come out, remember? It's not going to *let* us out."

The blue water was rising past my ankles.

"What should we do then?" I asked, frustrated.

"Swim down," he said. "Find the Dragon Lord."

I nodded absently, then mumbled, "The pool looked a lot smaller from the outside."

"We can do this," he said.

We sucked in deep breaths and I burst the orb. Then we swam down, using the light from the blade as our compass.

It was easier to swim down, though the farther we got, the more often orbs formed around us. We took advantage of each one, taking in fresh breaths before continuing. As we delved deeper, the orbs were almost on top of each other, stunting our progress.

We stopped taking breaths with every orb and only used every other one. Then they started coming so frequently I was slashing through multiple ones at a time. We only needed air every ten orbs or so, and when we did stop to breathe, they filled much faster than the ones closer to the surface.

"We have to almost be there!" Brantley shouted, breathlessly.

I nodded and sliced through the orb, and we continued down, me slicing through the onslaught of orbs that were now flying at us from every angle, not even forming around us anymore, as it seemed we were getting too close to where they were coming from.

Then the black disappeared, and we were laying on blue sand, breathing in clean, fresh air.

I looked up and could still see the black looming above us. We were beneath it now. In a huge air bubble?

My limbs felt weak from all the swimming. I sat up and Brantley said, "Adalee."

Hearing him say my name infuriated me. Uri almost died because he ran off.

"Adalee, look," he said.

I shook my head. "Give me a minute to rest."

"Now's not the time to rest, look!" he shouted.

I jumped up and screamed, "What is your problem?"

He couldn't respond before I continued, "Because you left, Uri almost *died.* And I *still* saved you, even though you didn't deserve it! I just got us through all those orbs, pulling you along with me!" I was carrying on quickly, not taking a breath between words. "I'm exhausted and all I want is a moment, just a moment, to catch my breath! Is that too much to ask for?"

He smirked, grabbed my chin, and forced me to face what he was trying to show me.

My jaw dropped and eyes widened as I stared out over a vast city. There were glorious temples and domes spread throughout, made from blue sand; illuminated with light akin to the other pools.

The sandy walls of the pool had multiple doorways in them all around the city, with steps etched into the sides, making each doorway easily accessible. It was beautiful and preserved with no crumbled buildings or decaying walls.

"It's a whole kingdom," Brantley whispered.

I nodded and asked, "How is it down here?"

"Let's find out," he said with a mischievous note to his voice.

I looked at him and saw he was staring behind us rather than out at the incredible city. I turned and saw a small, round hole in the wall.

He moved toward it and looked inside. "Interesting," he said, then he quickly sat down and disappeared into the dark.

"Brantley!" I shouted, rushing to the hole. I peered in and saw that it dropped down.

"Come on!" he shouted, and I looked over the edge of the pillar. He was standing on the ground, looking up at me with a smile on his face.

"You're a fool!" I shouted down as I moved toward the hole and slipped in as he had done. Immediately, I was sliding down a smooth, glass like surface that twisted and turned, landing at the bottom of the pillar.

I stood up from the edge of the slide, and looked around for Brantley, who had once again disappeared.

"Brantley?" I asked.

"Over here," he whispered.

I followed his voice to the front of the pillar, and we stared down a path that led into the heart of the city.

"Want to explore?" he asked.

"The Dragon Lord is here," I reminded him. "We need to find her."

He nodded and said. "So . . . explore?"

I nodded and couldn't help the excitement I felt at discovering such a forgotten place. "Yes," I agreed. "Explore."

We walked down the wide, sandy path that eventually turned into something resembling cobblestone, made from the blue sand.

The city was fully intact and seemed to be waiting for life to return.

"Who do you think lived here?" I asked as I looked into the window of an abandoned shop.

"Whoever it was," Brantley said as he examined an open doorway, "they left quickly."

"It seems almost . . ." I said softly, not knowing how to finish the statement.

"Frozen in time?" he asked.

I nodded and we looked at each other, a gentle dread pushing against the outskirts of my mind.

We continued, walking slowly and meticulously throughout the streets, both of us on edge as though at any moment someone would appear and call us down for being foreigners in their beautiful blue world.

"Look at these designs," Brantley whispered, making me jump.

Though his voice was soft, it seemed out of place in the complete silence of the world. He didn't notice and I shook it off, taking note of what he was showing me.

Etched in the stones we were walking on were designs and carvings so tiny and intricate, it almost seemed impossible for a human to have made them.

"What made those?" I asked, kneeling down. "They're beautiful."

"Yes," he agreed. "Too small for human hands, and too intricate for nature."

"Fairies?" I asked.

He shrugged. "Perhaps. Or something of the like. Water nymphs, most likely."

His confidence irritated and intrigued me. "If you believe in water nymphs why did you doubt the existence of fairies when Plume and her sisters came to our camp?"

"I never doubted the existence of fairies," he specified. "I merely doubted that Plume was one."

I eyed him and reminded, "You called Darsey childish for believing in them."

"And I am not saying I believe in water nymphs," he defended. "It was merely speculation."

"You seemed pretty sure it was water nymphs," I pressed.

"Is the Dragon Lord here, or not?" he asked abruptly.

I let it go, having got under his skin, and said, "I can meditate and find out."

He nodded and stepped away a little, still marveling at the structures and designs etched in them.

I took a deep breath and sat down in the middle of the path. I closed my eyes and focused on relaxing. It was easy to block out any distractions, as there was nothing save the sound of my own breathing in my ears.

Everything else disappeared quickly, and I heard a gentle voice call out to me.

"Help."

I opened my eyes and stood. It was her. The Blue Dragon Lord.

"Help," she called again, her voice echoing around me from every direction. I spun, unable to find where it came from.

"This way, Dragon Born," I heard her again, and this time I saw blue streams of sound emanate from the largest temple in the center of the kingdom.

"I see you," I answered.

I opened my eyes from my meditation and stood.

"What did you see?' Brantley asked, approaching me quickly.

"She called to me," I said. "I looked for her and saw her in that temple." I pointed where the blue sound had come from.

"Great. Let's go free a Dragon Lord," he said, and we raced through the city toward her.

The temple towered high above the rest, and as we neared it, it seemed to grow even taller.

"Is this the place?" he asked, slightly out of breath.

"Yes," I said, equally winded.

He pushed the tall, heavy doors open and we entered the looming, vast corridor.

Immediately, Brantley froze, and I stepped past him, taking in the most welcome sight.

There she was, the Blue Dragon Lord, frozen as stone. She was enormous like the Red Dragon Lord, though her body was more serpentine, and she resembled a dragon that was more closely related to an eel or fish.

Her body was coiled up, and long ribbon-like tendrils streamed in the air away from her, as stiff and solid as the rest of her. Her face was stretched out toward the sky, like she was trying to escape before she became stone.

I walked around her and stared up at her massive jaw. Wider and flatter than the Red Dragon Lord; equally dangerous. She had flat, ribbon-like tendrils coming from her jaw line as well, and I followed them with my eyes down her thick, scaly, muscled neck.

I was surprised to see she had gills on the side of her neck. They were spread open, like how a fish's gills look when they are gasping for breath.

Did she need water to breathe?

I stepped back and looked her over, finding no wings large enough to support flight, though smaller wing-like fins spread from her body, poised and ready for action.

"That's her?" Brantley asked, breathlessly.

I had never heard him so awestruck and I nodded without facing him. "It is," I answered confidently.

"Wow," he whispered. Then he cleared his throat and said, "Do what you do, and let's get out of here."

I turned to him and asked, "Do what I do?"

"Yes," he said. Then he motioned toward the Dragon Lord and said, "Do whatever Dragon Born magic you do, and free her so we can get out of here."

His switch from awestruck to nonchalant irritated me and I snapped, "I don't know what to do! I don't just wave my hands and she is suddenly free!"

"Okay," he said defensively. "Pardon me for thinking you knew what you were doing."

I spun on him and said, "I've only done this once before! Before this, I was just a girl in a village, trying to live as normal a life as I could. There is no magical knowledge that comes from the Essence. There is no magical scroll that appears to me and explains in detail what I need to do."

"Fine!" he shouted over me. "Then just do what you did last time!"

I quieted and sucked in a deep breath, turning away from him. "Just be quiet and let me think," I muttered.

He didn't respond and I tried to remember everything from the first Dragon Lord. I thought about the freezing cold hole in his back and decided to look for the same thing on the Blue Dragon Lord.

I gently stepped on her coiled body and climbed all over it, looking for anything like what I had found on the Red Dragon Lord. Unlike him, she was solid, without blemish. I climbed back down and walked around her, looking for any clues as to how to free her.

"Did the first Dragon Lord take this long?" Brantley asked.

I ignored him and kept searching, yielding nothing.

"Let me help," he pleaded impatiently. "What did you do last time?"

I shrugged and said, "I found a hole in his neck. It was freezing inside. I had crossed through fire to get to him, and I put some of that fire into the hole in his neck. That's it."

"Okay," he said as though we had it figured out. "So, we find the same thing on her—"

"No," I cut him off. "I already looked. There isn't one."

He rolled his eyes and said, "Maybe you missed it. Look again while I try to start a fire." I watched him for a moment then turned back to her. I returned to her face and looked up, trying to see if there was something I missed. My eyes fell on her outstretched gills, and then it occurred to me.

I had used fire to free the Red Dragon Lord, and fire is what I passed through to reach him. What if fire was not the key for the Blue Dragon Lord? Gills would make it difficult to breathe fire, as she would need to be underwater to breathe at all.

"What if it isn't fire," I said over my shoulder.

He stopped what he was doing and asked, "What then?"

"Water?" I suggested. "The black water?"

"Okay," he said, entertaining the thought. "Where would we pour it?"

My eyes darted back to her gills. "It's interesting," I thought aloud.

"What is?" he asked, walking up to me.

"She looks like she was struggling to breathe before she was turned to stone."

"And?"

"If we get her air, maybe she will turn back?"

"And by air, you mean—"

"Black water."

We rushed from the temple and looked around. I pointed where we had descended from, but Brantley shook his head and said, "We'll never make it back up the slide."

I turned and continued to search when Brantley laid his hand on my shoulder. He pointed up and I followed his gaze to see the black water hovering right above the highest point of the temple.

"Up there?" I asked.

He grabbed my wrist and we ran back inside. He pulled me along, past the Dragon Lord, to the other end of the corridor, showing me a wide staircase that disappeared around the corner. Embarrassed I hadn't noticed it on my own, we raced across the threshold and began climbing steps.

The stairs opened up to another floor, which was open in the middle. We stumbled off the stairs, my legs burning. I looked over the edge of the center opening and stared down at the Blue Dragon Lord's beautiful face. Then I looked up and saw there were many more floors, all with holes in the center that she would be able to escape through.

I peered up as far as my eyes could see and realized the top of the temple was open. From the outside it looked like a massive steeple. From the inside I could see it was completely open to the water.

"This isn't the highest point," I said breathlessly.

"Then let's find some more stairs," he said and we both took off across the floor, peering into doorways until I found a new set of stairs, less grand than the others, still moving in the direction we needed.

"Here!" I shouted and he joined me as we raced up the steps to another floor.

Without saying anything, we both searched doorways until Brantley called out, "Come on!"

I ran to him and we raced up the stairs he found until we came to the next floor. Again, and again we found staircases that only led up one floor and had to search for more.

"This place is a maze!" Brantley shouted in frustration.

"At least we're going in the right direction," I tried to encourage him. He only grunted and we kept moving.

Finally, we came to a floor with no more stairs. I was exhausted, sore, and trying desperately to catch my breath.

The ceiling towered above us, and the hole in the steeple was larger than I thought.

I had no way to get up to it. I could see the black water swirling above, but it might as well had been a mountain away.

Brantley leaned out a window and looked up. "There!" he shouted. "If you climb up the side, you can probably reach the black water."

My heart sank. Climb? Outside? How high were we?

I met him at the window and looked out, feeling sick at the thought of falling from such a height. He grabbed my wrist when I tried to back away. "Don't tell me you're afraid," he mocked.

I ripped my wrist from his grasp and said, "No more afraid than *you*."

He lifted his brows and chuckled. "*I'm* not the Child of Essence. *You* are."

I hated that he was right, and this was *my* responsibility. I stepped back to the window and looked up, avoiding the height, towards the black water.

"It looks steep," I said, staring out over the edge of the steeple that jutted up with very small steps ingrained in it.

"You'll have to be careful then."

I came back in and faced him. "I need something to gather the black water in."

He thought for a moment, then emptied his water canteen and handed it to me. I emptied mine and my eyes settled on the canteen of stardust by my side.

I gently untied it and handed it to him.

"What's that for?" he asked without taking it.

"Just in case I fall," I said hesitantly. "Make sure Starla gets to see the world before she goes back."

He took the canteen and said, "I'll hold it for you, but be warned, if you fall, she is going back to the stars because I'm not handling *two* star-runners."

I clenched my jaw and said, "And *you* be warned that if I fall, you'll die down here. Alone."

He shrugged and said, "Then I guess it's in both our interests that you don't fall."

I cut my eyes at him and faced the opening. I took a deep breath and calmed my nerves before stepping out on the bottom of the sill. I steadied myself by holding on to the top of the window and I felt Brantley grab my waist.

"Alright, lass, easy does it," he encouraged me. "I'll give you a lift."

I nodded and stepped into his hand. I gripped the top of the window tightly as he lifted me up. I leaned forward, laying against the roof, and was happy to feel it had some tread to it. Exactly as compacted sand would. It was rough and when I lifted my other foot and put it against the grate, I didn't slide back or feel like I would slip.

I pushed myself up and left Brantley's hands, then laid upon the roof of the temple. With my cheek pressed against it, I peered up and saw the black water was very close.

With great care, I moved up another step, keeping my whole body pressed tightly against the sand. One careful step after another, and I saw the darkness right above me. I didn't even know if it was possible to collect the black water, and I hoped I wasn't on the tower for nothing.

Once I was within arm's reach of the suspended black pool, I opened Brantley's canteen and thrust it up, shoving the opening into the black water.

I felt the canteen fill and I pulled it down when it was swollen with water. Then I did the same with my canteen and I very slowly and carefully attached them to my sides.

Now all I had to do was make my way back down.

I loosed one of my feet.

It didn't budge.

I gently pushed off the roof and tried to step down.

The foot I was bracing myself with slipped.

I screamed and slammed myself back into the roof. My feet couldn't firmly plant as I slid down the side, my face being scraped up by the rough sandy top.

"Brantley!" I screamed out as I felt my legs fall freely.

Then they stopped and I bent backwards at the knees and slammed against the side of the temple. I stared in horror at the ground far below, suspended in place.

"I got you, lass," Brantley grunted, and I felt him lift and pull me into the window, his arms wrapped around my knees.

I landed roughly on the floor, grateful to be alive.

"Did you get it?" he asked immediately.

Breathing heavily, I stared up at the intricately designed ceiling, somehow finding it in myself to nod. I patted my sides where the canteens of black water were settled.

He laughed and said, "Great!"

I sat up and said, "Let's go free the Blue Dragon Lord."

He helped me up and we walked toward the stairs.

"If your theory works," he added.

I stopped and stared at him. Then said, "If it doesn't, *you* can climb the next temple."

Then I went ahead of him and began the long descent back down.

## TWENTY-TWO | The Blue Dragon Lord

I stood before her, staring up. Another climb, though this time the fall wouldn't be deadly.

"Want me to help?" Brantley asked. "She has two sides of gills and we have two canteens."

The fact that he thought I needed his help at that point was irritating. I rescued him from the orbs. I got us through the black water. I climbed up the side of the temple. And now he suddenly thought his presence was useful in some way?

"Nope," I said with finality. "Your time with me is just about done." Then I stared him in the eyes and said, "I need nothing more from you."

He held up his hands in retreat and said, "Very well, lass. I meant nothing of it."

I looked back at the Dragon Lord without a word and began my climb to her gills. Her serpentine body coiled around itself gave me many places to step. I avoided the tendrils, as I feared they might break off, seeming so delicate and dainty.

Once I reached where her neck jutted up, I laid against it as I had the roof, and climbed until I was even with the gills. Her neck, which was wider than I expected, made it so I couldn't reach both sides at the same time. I was forced to carry my weight upon the fins and tendrils that were sprouted out. To my surprise and relief, they were firm and strong, with no hint of weakness or ruin.

I shimmied to one side of her neck and settled myself in the groove between a tendril and fin, then I pulled out one of the canteens, opened it, and poured it over each gill.

Immediately, the water was sucked up, though there was still no movement in the stone.

"I think it's going to work!" I called out, wanting to share my excitement with anyone who would listen, even if it was Brantley.

"Great! Do the other side now!" he said.

His order quashed my excitement, and I wanted to shout back that he wasn't in charge and I knew what I was doing.

Instead, I threw the empty canteen at his head, but he caught it with a smile and attached it to his side.

I then worked my way around to the other side and found a place to wedge myself. I opened my canteen and leaned over, poured its contents into her gills and watched it soak up immediately.

Then they began to flap. Brantley ran over to the side I was on and said, "Something's happening!"

"She's waking," I said to myself as the spaces between the scales where I was nestled began glowing a vibrant blue. The tendril I was standing upon turned flaccid and I slipped down.

Brantley broke my fall, though the impact knocked him to the ground.

I shoved against him harder than necessary as I stood and stepped back, staring up at the Blue Dragon Lord. Her body was beginning to uncoil and the space between her scales glowed so brightly I had to shield my eyes.

When the blue light subsided, I looked back and saw her standing there, as long and flowing as in my vision. Her color a beautiful blue, her tendrils like ribbons floating in the air around her. Her fins opened and closed along her back and face. She spun and ran from the temple on short legs I hadn't noticed before, knocking the great doors off their hinges as she burst through them. Her movement was sleek and fluid.

"Where is she going?" Brantley asked breathlessly.

Then I realized she had left without us. "Catch her!" I screamed and we darted from the corridor.

Having not gone far, she stood at the base of the temple, looking up. She was going to climb!

"Hold on to her!" I ordered Brantley, and for once he obeyed me without a snide remark.

I jumped up and grabbed a tendril that was near her shoulder. Then with the movement of her jump, it slipped from my hands and I crashed down on the blue sand, Brantley beside me.

We looked at each other in horror and he asked, terror in his voice, "What now?"

I jumped up and watched as she climbed up the side of the temple. She reached the top quickly and stuck her head into the black water.

There she stayed.

"The black water is hers," I said, remembering how the Red Dragon Lord had sucked all the fire back into his body. "She's breathing it back in!"

"So, what do we do?" he asked, articulating each word. "Will she come back for us?"

"I don't know," I said honestly, facing him.

"How do you not know?" he screamed, grabbing his head.

"She's frantic to get out!" I shouted back. "She might not even be thinking of us!"

He looked up and pointed. "There! Her tail! See that?"

I followed his gaze and saw the end of her tail swishing in front of the window I had climbed from.

Without a word, we raced back into the temple and began climbing the steps, making our way to the top of the tower as quickly as possible. It took everything I had to reach the top and my legs were burning by the time we found the window.

Despite the pain, I ran over, Brantley beside me, and we grabbed on. The end of her tail spread out into two, firm fins, and we each stepped on one, holding tight to both her and each other.

"Don't fall this time," I shouted at him as I looked up and saw the black was almost gone and all that was left was crystal blue water of many different hues.

"I was going to say the same to you!" he shouted back.

The last of the black streamed into her gills and water began to swirl around her, like it had in my meditations.

"Here we go," I said, making sure my grip was tight.

Then she launched up into the blue water, and if not for my foothold, I would have easily lost my grip. She swam through the blue water like it was nothing, though the pressure rushing past me made it difficult to hold on, and impossible to open my eyes.

Finally, the water stopped rushing, and I felt air surround me. I opened my eyes and saw her stepping onto the bank, where much of Aljonnah stood and stared in awe.

Once her tail was over land, I let go and crashed clumsily to the ground, Brantley beside me. The Blue Dragon Lord let out some chirps, like a happy bird, and I sat up wearily to see that water was still flowing around her, only it was very dark blue, like the deepest recesses of the sea.

Then the people of Aljonnah began to gasp and rush forward.

I turned and saw others emerging from the waters, most of them very old. Piles of bones were washing up on shore, and I realized that all the orbs beneath the water were cages, trapping them.

"Zaire!" I heard Anahita cry and watched as she and Joah rushed forward and wrapped their arms around a handsome boy, close to mine and Darsey's age. His skin was only slightly lighter than Anahita's and when he opened his eyes, they were brilliantly blue beyond any eyes I could ever imagine. His surprisingly dry hair was light brown and coiled softly atop his head.

Then Faraji stepped forward, his brow laden with a golden crown, and the king's scepter in his hand. Zaire left his parents and rushed to his friend, embracing him in a hug that left them both laughing.

The Blue Dragon Lord chirped again, and Zaire looked at her. I watched as their eyes met and he stepped away from Faraji. A smile spread across his face and he went to her. She lowered her head and he climbed up her leg to her shoulder and straddled the base of her neck. She stood up tall, and Zaire's voice, intertwined with the brightness that I imagined was hers, spoke out.

"People of Aljonnah," she began.

Brantley leaned in and said, "They won't be able to understand her; she's speaking our language."

I looked at the people and saw their awestruck faces listening intently.

"I don't think language is a barrier for her," I whispered back.

"You were once a thriving and happy people, derived of six clans. The Blue Clan, the Red Clan, the Yellow Clan, the Orange Clan, the Green Clan, and the Purple Clan. Named for the waters that the rainbow sands come from. You were not land dwellers; rather dwellers of the pools, living in your kingdoms beneath the waters."

The people looked at each other in confusion and I was beginning to realize that *all* the pools had kingdoms like we had seen, not just one.

"You were peaceful, and happy. Then the Deceiver came and trapped me beneath the blue pool; took my power and used it to keep you out and displaced every member of the Blue Clan.

"You were not discouraged, for you are a hearty people. The other clans took those in who no longer had a home, and there was peace and happiness once again, despite the loss of one of the pools.

"Now you may return to your homes. Drink from the blue pool and it will show you where you belong. Appoint your clan leaders, and remember that if one clan outshines another, all will suffer."

Zaire slid from the Blue Dragon Lord's back and began speaking to the people in his language.

I touched Joah's shoulder and he turned to me, his eyes glistening and a smile on his face. He nodded, understanding my silent request, and began translating Zaire's words to me.

"Wanjala came and destroyed the life we lived. He pretended to be the Dragon Lord and decreed that the pools were no longer a place to inhabit. Those who refused to believe him were slaughtered. Those who followed him were given leniency, though many of them were given over to the venom of the stillemas."

I looked at him and asked, "The what?"

"A snake whose venom steals your voice," he explained. "The stories of our history could not be passed down until Wanjala's truth was all we knew. He bred us to be obedient to him."

Everyone looked at Zaire, listening intently. Then he began speaking again, smiled at Faraji, and mounted the Blue Dragon Lord.

Joah was smiling and said, "He said the blue waters showed him he was the rightful ruler of the Blue Clan and he trusts Faraji to lead it until his return."

Anahita looked frantic and rushed up to the Blue Dragon Lord and Zaire. She asked him something in her language and he responded, "Do not worry, Mother. I will return once my quest is complete."

"Wait!" Brantley said, surprising me as he stepped forward. "Can you remove the bind?" he asked desperately.

The Dragon Lord looked at him and they said, "I cannot. What is done with Dragon Fire cannot be undone."

It felt like the wind was knocked out of me and I stared off, shocked and shaken.

"We will always be bound, then?" he asked, unbelieving.

"Take heart, warrior," she said. "Embrace the nobility of your chains and commit yourself to the Dragon Born's service. Her task is of great importance and must not be hindered."

He fell to his knees, looking as distraught as I, and said softly, "I understand."

The people slowly began to fall to their knees as Brantley had done and bowed down to the Dragon Lord and Zaire.

"I will now join my brother and make preparations for the rest of our brethren," she said, then faced me. "Dragon Born, it is with great responsibility you have wielded Dragon's Fire, for it is not one easily controlled."

I immediately thought of all the times I had let it get out of control and felt admonished for my inabilities, despite her praise.

"It will only become more difficult from here," she warned. "Take this and use it well."

Zaire unhooked a whip that was attached to his side and the Blue Dragon Lord turned her head and opened her mouth. He tossed it in, and she swallowed it. Her eyes glowed blue, then calmed and she opened her mouth, laying the weapon on the ground before me.

The whip now had a deep blue stone imbedded on the end of the handle. I picked it up and bowed my head.

Then she turned and water swirled around her from nothing. She leaped into the air, swimming away in a river that made its home the sky.

I looked back down at the whip and ran my finger over the beautiful, smooth stone that reminded me of stones that rested in rivers. Inside it swirled with blue water that deepened the longer I stared. Endless and massive, despite its constraints.

Once she was out of sight, the people stood and began embracing their long-lost loved ones.

"It appears our situation is permanent," Brantley said stoically.

"It does," I agreed unhappily, as I found a place on my belt to attach the whip. I looked at him and said, "I am going to tell Darsey the truth. I can't live with the lie, nor you using it to control me as you have been."

"I don't recall trying to use it to control you, lass," he defended. "However, I thought our time together would be short, or I would have tried harder to make a better impression."

I began walking away and said, "I think the impression you made is accurate."

He followed me and asked, "Where are you going?"

"I want to find Darsey and Uri. I need to check on Uri and Darsey needs to know everything that's happened."

"You're going to tell him *now*?" he asked.

I thought about it for a moment, then nodded. If I waited any longer, I might lose my resolve, and I needed to tell him while I felt courageous.

As we made our way back to the arena, he asked, "Aren't you going to practice with the whip?"

"It doesn't feel as aggressive as the fire. I'll practice later."

We continued walking and he said, "You did great down there, by the way. Freeing the Dragon Lord. That was impressive."

"Don't try and get on my good side now," I warned him, irritated. "You've shown me who you are, and nothing is going to change that."

"Very well," he conceded. "Although a 'thank you' would be nice."

I looked at him and asked, "Thank you for what?"

"For me saving your life," he said matter-of-factly. "When you fell off the roof and I caught you. You're welcome."

I stopped and said, "I saved your life way more than *that!* I saved you from the black water, and the orbs, and—"

"It doesn't matter," he cut me off. "The point is, you're welcome."

Then he continued walking ahead of me and I clenched my fists and caught up to him, grabbing his shoulder and spinning him toward me. "No, *you're* welcome," I snapped.

He smiled and looked down. "Are you sure?" he asked.

I followed his gaze and saw deep blue water swirling around my feet, not touching me or the ground. I looked back up at him and his smile deepened.

"This is going to be fun," he said with a smirk.

I sighed and kept moving. The arena came into sight and I stopped.

He looked at me and asked, "Second guessing your decision?"

"No," I said vehemently. "Just . . . don't hurt him if he attacks you," I said.

Brantley chuckled and bobbed his head. "Aye," he agreed. "The last thing I want is to mar our union any more than I already have."

I nodded and continued on to the arena.

I was surprised at how many people were still there, searching for Wanjala.

"Adalee!" I heard Darsey yell. I turned as he rushed up to me and wrapped his arms around my waist.

*"Adalee,"* Uri's sweet voice entered my mind.

"Uri?" I asked.

Darsey stepped back, a relieved smile on his face, and said, "He's okay." Then he stepped aside, and I saw Uri sitting on the ground behind him in his smallest form.

"Uri," I cried out in relief as I rushed to him and scooped him up. "I'm never letting you out of my sight again. From now on, you stay with me. Always." I held him up and looked in his face. "Always. Do you understand?"

He wriggled from my hands and clawed his way to my neck, pushing his head into it and purring. *"I promise,"* he said.

"Adalee, I need to talk to you," Darsey said.

I faced him, still clutching Uri. "And I need to talk to you."

"Please," he said, holding up his hand. "I know what you have to say is probably very important, but please let me go first before you say anything else—"

"I lied about Brantley," I cut him off.

He froze, horror on his face. "You can't *love* him," he said cautiously.

"No," I said quickly. "I don't. I really don't. I don't even like him."

He let out a relieved sigh and Brantley muttered, "You're not exactly my favorite either."

"The truth is, he wasn't chosen by the Dragon Lords to accompany me. He knew Madame and was the reason she had everything she needed to transfer the Essence. She made a deal with him and whoever else he was working with. When we escaped, he thought *I* was Madame, and tried to force me to go with him by means of a magical bind." I held out my wrist and he looked down at the singe without moving. "The only thing is, my Dragon's Fire got out of control, and I singed both of our binds, locking us together . . . forever."

Darsey looked down, furrowing his brow. "What does that mean?" he asked.

"It means we can't be very far from one another, or we will be drawn back against our will, and we can't hurt one another." I stepped up to him and said, "Darsey, I'm so sorry I lied."

He looked at me with tears in his eyes and a sad smile on his face and said, "I forgive you."

"You do?" I asked in bewilderment while Brantley asked the same thing in disbelief.

He shot an unhappy glance at Brantley then looked back at me. "Of course, I do," he said, taking my hands and kissing them. Then his voice turned serious and he said, "Adalee, what happened in this arena was way too close. You can't do that again."

"What do you mean?" I asked.

"You were going to *die*," he reminded me. "You were going to die, rather than sever the bond with Uri. If you are *ever* faced with that again, you *must* sever the bond." He was staring at me with his deep, pleading eyes. "Please." Tears spilled from his eyes and he said, "I know you don't want to live without him, but I can't stand the thought of living without *you*. You must *always* stay safe. *I* will always make sure you're safe," he vowed.

I pulled him into an embrace and held him tightly, both of us sobbing as the reality of everything that had happened crashed down upon us, and at the relief of being forgiven so easily.

Rain began to fall on us and Darsey laughed. "This is the first rain since we entered Aljonnah," he mused with his face against my neck.

He was right. I looked up and realized the water was *only* on Darsey and I, swirling around us and pattering against our skin. "It's the power of the Blue Dragon Lord," I marveled quietly.

Darsey stepped back and wiped his eyes, looking around. "Wow," he said breathlessly. He looked at me and I moved my robe aside so he could see the whip and the blue gem. "I take it that means she is free?"

I smiled and nodded.

"I'm sorry I missed it," he said longingly.

I touched his face and said, "You won't miss the next one, I promise."

"The night wears on," Brantley interrupted. "There will be plenty of time for this later. For now, we should search for Wanjala with the people. So long as he is running free, Uri and Adalee are both in danger."

We nodded and I said, "Where do you think we should start looking?"

"Darsey and I will look. You need to practice your new power."

I knew he was right. I was more use to them in control of my new power than out of control.

The search continued throughout the night.

It wasn't as difficult to control the whip as it was to control the dagger. I harnessed the power easily in the same way I harnessed the fire.

Though I was too distracted by the frantic search to truly discover what the weapon could do. Like Brantley said, we weren't safe so long as Wanjala was free.

We awoke our star runners before dawn and after a long night, Faraji found us, along with Joah and Anahita.

They both embraced me and Brantley, thanking us for bringing their son back to them.

"He'll get to see his aunt again," I said with a smile.

Anahita, tears in her eyes, nodded and said, "I am grateful for that."

Faraji led us to the temple that Wanjala had built for himself and the king, and offered us a room, as opposed to the huts we had been staying in.

We gladly accepted and he had people bring us clean clothes and assured us we could sleep, and they would bring us our star-runner orbs once the sun came up.

The room we stayed in was large and had enough beds for almost twice as many of us. Each bed was sectioned off by a beautiful tapestry that depicted a different pool. I chose the red, Darsey chose the purple, and Brantley chose the green.

Uri laid close to me, and I had the whip and dagger settled within reach, though the fire of the blade had yet to come back since we were in the blue kingdom.

"We need to take shifts," Brantley said as Darsey and I settled into our beds.

Darsey nodded and looked at me. "He's right. Until Wanjala is found, we need to watch over you and Uri."

I sat back up and said, "I can take the first shift. I would like the quiet to work with my new power."

Brantley thought for a moment, then nodded. "Wake us if you see Wanjala, or if anything happens or seems out of place."

Darsey came over to me as I grabbed the whip and stood. "Are you sure you want the first shift?" he asked. "I don't mind taking it for you."

I smiled and stroked his cheek with my fingertips. "I'm okay. I wouldn't be able to sleep right now anyway."

He nodded and we touched our foreheads and noses, closing our eyes, before he went back to his bed and was soon snoring away.

Uri sat up on the bed and watched me call up water droplets over and over again. I could make them float around me and with a thrusting movement I could weakly scatter them.

It was odd. The Dragon Fire was a force to be reckoned with. Difficult to control. Raging against my authority. Whereas the Dragon Water was . . . tired. Lazy, almost.

I knew that couldn't be true, and I felt guilty for even having such a disparaging thought against the power.

For many hours into the early morning I practiced while the boys slept. Uri also fell asleep quickly and I never let him leave my line of vision.

I spent much time trying to recreate the swirl of water Brantley had pointed out on our way to the arena. When I conjured the droplets, I willed them down, around my feet. I moved my hands in a way to make them swirl, yet every time they got behind or beside me, they would fly off and disappear.

Some servants knocked on the door and when I opened it, I saw our star-runner orbs sitting on some pillows just outside. Darsey came up behind me, rubbing his eyes.

"You're up," I whispered, surprised.

He nodded and helped me pick up the orbs.

"You get some sleep," he said gently, helping me attach Starla to my wrist and attaching Cosmo to his own. "I'll keep watch."

"Thank you," I said sweetly, and gladly went to my bed, unhappy with the little progress I had made with the Dragon Water.

However, I fell asleep as soon as my head hit the pillow.

Silence. Too much silence.

I needed sound. Voices. Someone to talk to. Someone to listen.

Here, there was only silence.

I opened my eyes and all I saw were unnatural stony walls. A prison built around me. A man-made prison.

They couldn't keep me here. All I needed was one. One sound. Give me back my voice.

"Adalee, wake up," someone whispered in my ear.

I opened my eyes and saw Brantley leaned over me.

"What?" I asked drowsily, stretching my arms above my head and yawning.

He covered my mouth and motioned for me to follow him.

I sat up as he looked over at Darsey. I picked Uri up and Brantley grabbed my weapons. I quietly snuck past the sleeping Darsey and we stepped outside of the room.

"What's wrong?" I asked. "Did they find Wanjala?"

He leaned down close to me and whispered, "He's hiding something."

His ominous words sent a chill down my spine and asked, "Who? The new king?"

He shook his head and said, "Darsey."

I dismissed him immediately and waved him away. "You should go back to sleep because you're not making sense."

He grabbed my hand and held it down, pulling me back to him so he could whisper. "I mean it," he said. "He forgave you way too easily for the lie. He didn't even *try* to come after me."

"So?" I asked. "He's more mature than you give him credit for, and he loves me. I'm not going to question his forgiveness."

Brantley huffed and looked irritated. "Just be smart about this. Why would he forgive you so easily, unless he had something that needed forgiven?"

I rolled my eyes and turned my head away.

"Just think about it," he urged.

Joah approached us in the hall with a bundle of clothing. "Good afternoon, saviors of Aljonnah," he greeted us.

We faced him and he held out the clothing. "King Faraji has requested your presence at the pools. The people are preparing to drink from the blue pool and discover their clan. He wishes for you to prepare them by sharing what you saw beneath the waters."

Brantley took the clothes and nodded with a smile. "We'll be ready in a moment."

Joah nodded and turned around to wait for us.

Brantley moved past me without another word, and we went back into the large room.

I woke Darsey and told him what Joah had said and he leaped out of bed, awake and energized.

I handed Uri off to him so I could take my weapons from Brantley. We quickly dressed behind our curtains and I was able to attach both the whip and dagger without the kick back I had been experiencing.

We stepped back out and I smiled at the normal tingle that spread through my being and nodded. "I think releasing the flames in the black pool satiated it. It doesn't feel any more uncontrollable than normal."

Brantley lifted one brow and said, "That's a relief," in a sarcastic tone.

Darsey smiled and said, "So, can I hold your hand?"

I looked down at it and then back at him. "Maybe later? I don't want to risk it until I'm sure."

He nodded and we left the room, following Joah toward the pools.

It was strange walking through the oasis during the day as we had been confined to our huts for much of our time in Aljonnah. I gladly took in the beauty of it as we made our way to the glowing waters.

"Is there ever a time that these pools *don't* look magnificent?" Darsey asked softly.

The people were crowded around, and there was much jubilation and cheer. Everyone wore white and Joah commented that it was to represent a fresh start for Aljonnah.

Faraji came up and embraced us, though I shied away from his touch, fearing to hurt him. He didn't notice and I was pulled into his arms. Happily, I had the dagger under control, and he wasn't turned to ash.

He looked at Joah and spoke to him. Joah looked at us and said, "Describe what you saw beneath the waters."

I began explaining the kingdom we saw, describing the temples, homes, and shops. I told them it was so intricately designed and well preserved that it seemed ready to be lived in again.

Joah translated to Faraji, and Faraji shared the news with everyone.

A loud cheer erupted from the crowd and Anahita appeared, looking dazzling in her white robes and turban. She kissed each of us on the forehead and asked us to stay and watch.

We gladly agreed and found a place to sit so we could see people drink from the blue pool. The first person who did it was Faraji. He stood up and his eyes glazed over for a moment. Then they came back, and he smiled, yelling out the name I recognized to mean 'purple'.

Then he ran to the purple pool and dove in, disappearing beneath the water without leaving so much as a ripple.

The tribe quieted and stared.

"What are they waiting for?" Darsey whispered.

Anahita leaned down and softly explained, "Faraji is checking it first to make sure no one in Aljonnah will be in danger by diving into the pools. When . . . and if, he emerges, everyone else will drink."

We waited for almost an hour in complete silence with the rest of Aljonnah.

Then, a rumbling of bubbles erupted in the center of the purple pool, and out from it floated a large orb that had Faraji standing in the center, donning purple robes. The orb easily destroyed the bridge with Wanjala's statue on it, then moved across the top of the pool and popped like a bubble when it rolled onto land, revealing him to be happy and dry.

He threw his arms up and shouted, which caused Aljonnah to join in with roars of gladness.

Then they gathered around the blue pool to drink, had their visions, and ran to their colored kingdoms.

Joah leaned down and excitedly told us, "He says there is a temple just like you described, with a pillar of water in the center. You get back to the surface by stepping inside it."

Darsey leaned in close to me and said, "This is a better ending for them than I would have expected. I'm so proud of you for really freeing these people."

I smiled and nudged him sheepishly.

"Wanjala is still on the loose," Brantley reminded us.

I left his statement to hang in the air and continued watching the revelry before us with Darsey.

When it was over, Faraji, Joah, and Anahita came to us and asked if we wanted to drink from the blue pool.

Brantley stood and smiled, saying he had a taste of it already and saw where he belonged.

I looked at him, surprised because I had been in the same water and had no such vision. Nor did I want to, much to my surprise.

Darsey reached down and grabbed my hand. He smiled up at them and said, "I know where I belong."

We were met with smiles and asked what we would like as a reward from the people of Aljonnah.

Brantley stepped forward and said, "When the time comes for us to be on our way, please provide us with the supplies we need to get well out of the desert."

They agreed and we began walking back to the palace, as we were all still exhausted from the long night before.

"It sure is quiet," Darsey mentioned. "I didn't realize how many voices you hear during the day when everyone is in the oasis. Now it seems like we are alone out here."

The way he said the word 'voices' made my dream come rushing back. I stopped and froze, staring at nothing as I recalled the dream I had just before Brantley woke me.

"What's wrong?" Darsey asked, pulling me from my thoughts.

I looked at him and furrowed my brow. "I think the next Dragon Lord is Calling me."

"Already?" Brantley asked. "Last time it took weeks for you to be Called again."

I shrugged and said, "Maybe we aren't moving fast enough."

He shook his head and said, "The star-runners aren't at their fastest. The moon is still on its way to becoming *full*, when they'll be no more useful than a regular horse. We have more than a fortnight before the star-runners will regain their full speed."

I looked at him and threw my hands up. "Oh, I'm sorry. Let me go meditate and tell the Dragon Lord that we can't come because our horses aren't fast enough."

He huffed and Darsey snickered.

"I don't see the humor," Brantley said.

Darsey shook his head and said, "Adalee needs to free the Dragon Lords. Maybe you want it to be easy, but I would walk across the world to help her with this task."

"Your devotion obviously reaches deeper levels than mine," he said flatly.

## Twenty-Three | Seeking Wanjala

We returned to the palace and I was surprised to see people moving about like the lot of Aljonnah had not just dove into the pools.

They offered us bowls of warm food and we returned to our room to eat and drink.

"Where did they come from?" Darsey asked, mid bite.

"Perhaps they didn't all dive in," Brantley suggested.

"Or they may not have stayed in," I said. "You saw how easily Faraji came out. I bet for a while they will come and go while they at least pack up their things to move to their new homes."

"I wish I had seen what was beneath the waters," Darsey said dreamily. "It sounded amazing."

"Maybe you can before we go," I suggested with a smile.

"Really?" he asked, his eyes bright. "Oh, I would love to be able to tell my parents about it. What a story!"

"After we eat, you should meditate," Brantley urged.

I nodded and said, "I will."

"What was the dream like?" Darsey asked.

I thought about it for a moment, then said, "It was quiet. I was yearning for sound. For voices. I was . . . worried about not having anyone to talk to or to listen."

Darsey nodded and said, "Sounds lonely."

Brantley cocked his head and asked, "Are you sure it was a Dragon Lord Calling?"

"I know it sounds different than the last two," I admitted, "but it *felt* the same."

We ate in silence for a bit, then Brantley said, "So what did everyone see when they drank from the green pool?"

I smiled as I recalled and said, "I saw myself atop the final Dragon Lord, successful in our quest."

Brantley raised his eyebrows and said, "That's a good sign. Was I there?"

I shrugged and said, "It was very brief. I don't think I got the whole picture. You might have been."

"And me?" Darsey asked.

I smiled at him and playfully said, "Might have been."

"What about you?" Brantley asked Darsey.

Darsey looked down, no smile on his face, and shook his head. "I didn't see anything. I don't think it worked for me."

I furrowed my brow and said, "What do you mean? You just saw . . . nothing?"

He shrugged and said, "I didn't take a very big drink. Probably not even enough for a vision."

"Or it means you're going to die," Brantley said nonchalantly as he took a sip from his cup.

"We all die," Darsey bit back bitterly, a heaviness weighing behind his eyes that wasn't there moments before.

"And we have no idea how far in the future the pool showed us," I pointed out, though I was worried about Darsey's lack of vision.

"Well," Brantley said brightly, "if no one is going to ask me, I'll share my vision anyway."

I reached over and caressed Darsey's arm, and he offered a small smile.

"I was with Nadine, and we were happy to see each other," he said with a smile.

I hardly heard him as I was trying to read Darsey's expression.

"And," Brantley continued, "while I was in the orb of blue water when the pool was still black, I saw myself with her, and we were sitting together on the grass. She was leaning on my shoulder."

Darsey reached up and gently touched my face with the back of his hand, and I feared he felt seeing nothing in his vision meant that he *would* die.

Was I going to lose him again?

"I feel like the Dragon Lord in your dream. No one to talk to and no one to listen," Brantley commented.

Darsey turned to him and offered a smile. "That sounds great. So, you and . . . Nadine? Who is that? Someone from your village?"

I turned and said, "Wait? Nadine? Like . . . from the ship, Nadine?"

Brantley bobbed his head and said, "I'm as surprised as you are! I knew she was beautiful, and we got along well. And she's a fantastic fighter, and very witty. I guess a part of me kept thinking about her, even though I didn't realize it."

"I'm trying to remember," Darsey said, looking at me.

"She's the one who killed Surin," I reminded him.

"Oh! With the short hair?"

I nodded and he smiled at Brantley, a genuine smile. "Finally, the pools revealed something not dark and twisted for you," he said through his grin.

"I have to be honest; I would have *never* gone back without that vision. Now, I can't wait!"

The bind that we now knew was permanent caused me to speak up, despite not wanting to crush his enthusiasm. "We still have six Dragon Lords to rescue."

"I know," he said dismissively. "I'm talking about *after*. When we go back."

"*If* we go back," I said darkly.

He looked at me, his face turning serious. "What do you mean 'if'?"

"You're not the only one who has someone to get back to," I told him. "Darsey wants to see his parents. We have a home. An entire village."

"And I am helping you on your quest," he said as though it validated his desires over my own.

"Due to your own selfishness," I reminded him. "Just because you have to help me on this quest, does *not* mean I owe you anything."

"Or," Darsey interjected, "afterward, when we're all alive and Pylertchia is safe, we can find Nadine and the girls and *bring* them to the village."

We both looked at him and he added, "It was safe there."

"We do need a shaman," I said thoughtfully.

"Thank you," Brantley said abruptly, as though Darsey were agreeing with him. Then he looked at me and said, "I'm quite sure you just want to see me suffer."

I shrugged without denying it.

We finished our meal in silence, and I prepared to meditate while they watched over me, in case Wanjala appeared.

I sat down in the middle of the room and laid my hands palm up on my legs. I closed my eyes and took a deep breath.

I pushed everything aside and waited. Nothing changed. I couldn't feel the Dragon Lord's presence. Perhaps it *wasn't* a Calling dream?

I opened my eyes and was taken aback to see I wasn't sitting in the room and was instead standing outside upon a large grassy hill that descended and spread out as far as the eye could see. The sky was deeply overcast with rays of sunshine breaking through, scattering over the land, revealing bright green patches.

"Hello?" I asked, and suddenly I was flying through the air, though no Dragon Lord appeared.

I saw over the land and fixated on a distant castle, widely built with multiple courtyards, gardens, farmland, and livestock. Scattered around the castle were humble homes that stretched beyond the rolling knolls.

"Hello?" I asked again.

Then the room returned around me and I opened my eyes to see Darsey, Uri, and Brantley staring at me.

"What did you see?" Darsey asked.

I scrunched my brow and said, "It was strange. The Dragon Lord did not appear and lead me anywhere. Yet, I was in a new place."

"What kind of place?" Brantley asked, though he seemed to have little interest.

"Very green. Large hills that reached the horizon. They were covered in thick, lush grass. Greener than any I have ever seen."

Brantley seemed to become interested as I described it and he asked, "What else?"

"The sky was covered in white and grey clouds, and rays of sunshine were scattered over the land."

He closed his eyes as if he were imagining it.

"Then I began to . . . fly, I think. And I came to a castle." As I described the castle, Brantley grabbed our breakfast bowls and combined the little pieces that were left into one bowl. Then he started moving them around.

Before I was finished, he held the bowl out and said, "Did it look like this?"

I looked at the design he had made in the porridge and was surprised to see how similar the shape was to what I imagined the castle would look like from the ground.

"Maybe?" I asked.

He huffed and said, "Maybe? Didn't you *just* see it?"

"From the sky!" I defended.

"Do you know the place she is speaking of?" Darsey asked abruptly.

"Aye," he confirmed. "*If* what she saw is true, it's the home of my enemy."

I stared at him, bewildered.

Darsey chuckled and shook his head. "You mean, the same enemy you kept having visions of destroying?"

"Aye, lad. The very same."

"How far are we from there?" I asked.

He thought about it and said, "Quite far. At least two months on the star-runners."

"Two months?" Darsey asked, astonished.

I was more interested in the fact that he was so far from home when I met him. "How long were you searching for Madame?" I asked.

He looked at me and said, "I was on the road for over a year. And that was *with* Astraeus."

"And . . . you were going to take her back to your homeland," I confirmed.

He nodded and said, "She agreed to help us destroy our enemy."

"What am I missing?" Darsey asked, looking between us.

I looked at Darsey and said, "Brantley has his own concerns to attend to if we go there."

"I'm not the one forcing you to, lass. The Dragon Lord is."

Suddenly, there was great commotion in the outer hall. We all looked at one another, then jumped up and ran out. The people were scattering, screaming, and taking up weapons.

"What's happening?" Darsey asked.

"We need to find Anahita and Joah!" I shouted, and we ran from the temple, toward the pools.

"Which pool did they dive in?" Brantley asked as we neared them.

"Blue, I think," I answered.

"Their son said he was the leader of the Blue Clan," Darsey confirmed.

We came to the pools and raced to the blue one, stopping short when we saw Joah and Anahita standing near it, Joah barking orders, and Anahita trying to calm people down.

"What's happened?" I asked frantically.

"Wanjala took Faraji!" she cried out.

"Took him? How?" Darsey asked. "I thought he turned back into a tiny lizard when he killed the king."

"He was a full-sized dragon," Joah confirmed. "He emerged from the purple pool with Faraji in his grasp. He carried him off, that way," he pointed.

The ground began to rumble, and people stood ready for battle, though they trembled with each resounding step.

Darsey faced me and said, "He must have attached to someone new."

"How do you know?" I asked.

"Because when he killed the king, he shrank. I don't think he can leap without a host."

"What fool would willingly attach to him?" Brantley growled.

*"Faraji,"* Uri said.

I looked at him on Darsey's shoulder and asked, "Are you sure?"

"Sure about what?" Darsey asked loudly, trying to be heard over the growing tumult of the frightened people.

*"Wanjala is close and his mind is frantic! He attached to Faraji and hid him away."*

"He attached to Faraji and is hiding him so we can't kill him," I told them.

"No," Anahita said in horror. "Faraji would never align himself with Wanjala."

"You're right," Darsey said quickly. "We believe you."

"Find him," I said, looking at them. "Find Faraji. If *he* kills Wanjala, then he can sever the bond without dying. He needs to do it before Wanjala decides to sever it himself."

"He doesn't stand a chance!" Anahita cried, just as Wanjala burst through the trees and snapped his large jaws at the people, causing them to scatter.

We quickly ran to the underbrush as Wanjala dove into the blue pool.

Brantley turned to them and said, "The Dragon Born will weaken Wanjala. Now go! Find Faraji! Bring him here!"

Anahita and Joah both ran off and I looked at Brantley. "How am I going to do that?" I asked.

"We just needed them out of the way. You need to kill Wanjala or this won't end. He's too powerful."

Darsey looked at him, horror struck. "You just said we would help save Faraji. What you suggest would *kill* him."

"Then he shouldn't have allowed Wanjala to attach to him!"

"Maybe he didn't allow it," I suggested quickly. "Maybe Wanjala forced the attachment. Right, Uri? Can that happen?"

Uri hung his head and said, *"Wanjala taught me that we can only attach to those willing to attach."*

"What did he say?" Brantley asked.

"It doesn't matter," I snapped back.

Orbs began raising to the surface of the blue pool and people began to rush up on land and hide behind their armed brethren.

Brantley faced me and said, "You know we have to do this."

"Fine!" I screamed. "We'll subdue him, but only to make it easier for Faraji to finish him!" I faced Darsey and said, "Stay here with Uri."

"Not a chance," he said forcefully.

I didn't have time to argue, and we all ran toward the blue pool, ready to dive in.

Then a massive orb lifted to the surface containing Wanjala. He was grinning evilly when he saw us.

Uri cowered and said, *"He destroyed the city. He said he will destroy them all so the people have to stay on the surface with him and submit to his rule."*

I let the tingle of the blade reach my fingertips and said, "I'll take out his legs so he can't move."

Then I ran toward him, my hand outstretched for the claws nearest me.

He leaped from the orb and swept his large talons over the sand, flinging it upon me, knocking me to the ground, fully buried.

The blade reacted and the sand took on the consistency of ash, and to my surprise it lifted away from me in a wild vortex. I jumped up and saw it swirling around me, much like the water had done the night before, and when I had eyes on Wanjala preparing to dive into the orange pool, I ran for him and the vortex fell to the ground behind me.

"Wanjala!" I screamed, feeling bold and empowered.

Yet when he faced me, I was filled with terror and felt like a tiny child. He did not charge as I expected. Instead, he grinned, then dove in.

I screamed as I ran after him, but Brantley tackled me before I got to the pool. "Stop! Stop!" he yelled over my screams.

"Why?" I asked angrily.

He straddled me and held my arms down, yelling, "We don't know what the water will do to the blade!"

"You had no problem a moment ago!" I shouted.

"And it was a foolish idea!"

"He's destroying the city!" I reminded him.

"They will rebuild," Brantley growled.

"Okay!" Darsey yelled, standing over us. We both looked at him and he continued. "Let's have a plan for when he comes back up."

Orbs began forming at the top of the water, filled with terrified people.

Brantley let me up and stood. "We need to get these people out of the way," he said, looking around.

"Before they get hurt," I added.

"Faraji," Darsey said as though he had an idea. "They can help find him!"

"Except we don't have a translator!" Brantley reminded him as Darsey ran off and began trying to communicate with the people.

Within moments, the people were all saying Faraji's name and rushing off.

Darsey returned to us, a satisfied smile on his face.

"You're telling me you could communicate with them the whole time?"

He shrugged and said, "I'm good with people."

"And they understand they're bringing him here, right?" I asked.

He shrugged again and said, "Maybe?"

"Good enough," Brantley growled, as a large orb that held Wanjala emerged.

I let the fire reach my fingertips again and this time I chased him to the next pool. He dove in before I could reach him.

I let out a frustrated scream as he disappeared beneath the waters of the red pool.

Darsey rushed over and said, "I'll tell the people to search for Faraji as they emerge."

Brantley ran up and asked, "Can you harness your power enough to climb that tree?"

I looked at where he was pointing as people began to emerge from the red pool. Darsey stopped them and tried his best to explain what we needed, and I saw the tree Brantley spoke of, dangling over the water.

"I can jump on his back from there!" I said.

"Exactly."

I did my best to pull in the power and when I was sure it would be contained enough for the climb I worked my way up the tree with Brantley giving me a lift and my adrenaline carrying me the rest of the way.

I held on, leaning over the pool, ready for him to emerge. As soon as I saw his orb rise up, I leaped down, letting the fire spread through me, arms wide, ready to burst his orb and immobilize him.

I hit the orb and slid off, landing in the red water. Immediately it sucked me down with a powerful current that spat me out on a cliff similar to the one in the blue pool, only here everything was red.

I jumped up and looked around. The city was vast, empty, and in ruins.

In the center was a swirling red vortex that looked to be moving upward, yet never left the ground. Just like Faraji described.

I turned to use the slide and saw that it had been filled with sand.

Frustrated, I carefully climbed down the side of the pillar and fell once I was halfway down. I jumped up, unharmed, and raced to the center of the city toward the vortex.

By the time I reached it I was breathless, and I carelessly thrust myself into it. An orb formed around me and flew through the vortex to the top of the water. Once I was above the red pool, I saw Uri in his largest form standing between Wanjala and the green pool, a snarl upon his face.

The orb released me onto the sand, and I rushed to them. To my surprise, Wanjala was not attacking. Instead, it looked like they were talking. Uri looked angrier than I had ever seen him.

Darsey and Brantley met me as I closed in on them, not wasting any time. I leaped forward, my hand extended, and grabbed onto Wanjala's back leg.

Wanjala turned and looked at me, his face full of dark humor and he kicked me away with his still intact leg.

I flew back and landed roughly on Darsey.

"Are you okay?" he asked.

I was too focused on watching Uri leap up and latch onto Wanjala's exposed neck to answer. Wanjala swung around and Uri, still attached, flung about with the motion.

"Uri!" I screamed, jumping up and running to them again.

Brantley grabbed me and said, "You have no power! The pool did something to the blade!"

"Let me go!" I cried, trying to reach them.

Darsey ran past me with a spear in hand and stabbed Wanjala in the back of his leg. He reared back and roared in pain, and when he came back down, Uri slipped from his neck, landing on his feet.

Wanjala swiped at Darsey who was already out of arm's reach. Then he turned back to Uri and knocked him into a tree. Uri's back hit the tree and he shrank to his smallest size upon landing.

He moved toward Uri and I heard a voice cry out, "Wanjala!"

I turned and saw Anahita standing beside Faraji, who looked stoic and resigned.

Wanjala froze, his eyes wide.

Darsey rushed to them and drew a knife, grabbed Faraji by the hair and angled his head back roughly, pressing the knife to his throat. "Tell him to let Uri go or he dies right now!" Darsey screamed.

Wanjala quickly swung his tail around and knocked the cover off the pit that rested in the center of the pools. He ripped the unconscious Uri up from the ground and dangled him over it by his little orange tail.

"Uri!" I screamed and Darsey let Faraji go.

"No!" he yelled, laying the knife down at his feet. "Please don't hurt Uri," he pleaded as though he were begging for my life.

I ran at them but Wanjala easily grabbed me with his free talon and held me up to his face. He smiled cruelly, then held me over the pit, and dropped Uri.

"No!" I screamed as Uri fell through the air toward the hole of snakes, scorpions, and spiders.

Just as Uri passed the threshold of the opening, Darsey overtook my vision as he grabbed Uri, spun in the air, and threw him back out of the pit, onto the ground.

My eyes widened as I watched in horror as Darsey landed on the bottom of the pit and was covered and overcome by all the venomous creatures that inhabited it.

Then Wanjala roared and I was thrown back. I landed roughly on the sand, face to face with Faraji. Blood was spilling to the ground and I sat up in horror as I saw a blade jutting from his neck, his own hand wrapped around the hilt. His eyes were stony, and dead.

I jumped up and ran to the pit, past where Wanjala was shrinking to his small size and dying. I landed beside it and looked down.

"Anahita!" I screamed.

Brantley rushed over and grabbed me by the arms. "Don't be a fool," he whispered. "You can't go after him."

"He's still alive!" I cried.

People emerged from the trees, and some came over and began kicking sand into the pit, sending the venomous creatures back into their holes. Then two of them fearlessly jumped in and retrieved Darsey, handing his almost lifeless body to those ready to receive it.

He was covered in bites and stings, though his chest was still rising and falling as he gasped for air. "Darsey?"

He didn't respond or open his eyes.

He was sweating and losing his color.

The people behind us began to mourn loudly for the loss of Faraji, and I looked at Brantley and said, "We have to do something."

"I don't know what to do," he said helplessly.

"We can't let him die!" I screamed.

Anahita came over, tears streaking her face, and said, "The blue water."

I looked up at her and asked, "What?"

"I don't know what it means, but the blue water can be used."

"How do you know that?" Brantley asked suspiciously.

"She's a curator," I said, realizing what it meant. "She knows what things do; she just doesn't know *how* to do it."

She nodded and spoke to the men who had helped get Darsey from the pit. They lifted him up and carried him to the blue pool.

I stayed right by his side and heard Uri say, *"Adalee?"*

Feeling embarrassed and mortified that Uri's wellbeing hadn't entered my mind, I turned and rushed to him, picking him up from the sand.

"You're okay," I said to him. "Darsey saved you."

We rushed over as they laid him down by the blue pool.

"Now what?" I asked, looking at Anahita.

She shook her head and I shoved Uri into Brantley's arms and knelt by Darsey's side, scooping some of the blue water up with my hands.

"Open his mouth," I ordered.

Anahita squeezed his mouth open, and I dribbled the water past his lips. He instinctively swallowed, though his color didn't improve, and he was still unresponsive in every other way.

"The wounds," I said to myself as I ripped a tattered piece of my clothing and soaked it in the blue water. Then I squeezed it out across his body, covering every bite and sting I could find.

Still, nothing improved.

"What do I do?" I cried frantically.

"He has to breathe it," Brantley said as though he just realized.

"Get him into the pool," I said without question. "Lay his head under the water and don't let it pull him down."

Anahita translated and they did so. I watched with anxiety coursing through every part of me. Slowly, the wounds healed on his body and the color of his arms and legs returned to normal.

"Okay," I said, and they pulled him back up.

I leaned over him and said, "Darsey?"

Silence.

It didn't make sense. His color was back. His wounds were healed. Why was he not waking?

I looked at Anahita and asked, "What is happening?"

Anahita said, "The people who emerged from the pool after having been lost said they were put into a sleep in the orbs. That the blue water sustained them, though they could not wake."

"So, he won't wake up?" I asked, tearfully.

"We need pearls," Brantley suddenly said.

I turned to him, still cradling Darsey. "What?" I asked weakly.

He dropped Uri and jumped up, beginning to pace. "We need pearls." He looked at Anahita and added, "As many as you can spare. Do you have any from tribespeople? What do you do with their pearls?"

"What are you talking about?" I screamed, seeing the confused and appalled look on Anahita's face.

He knelt back down and said, "I know someone who might be able to wake him. If anyone can, she can."

"She uses the pearls of the fallen?" Anahita asked hesitantly.

"As payment," he said as though the words disgusted him. Then he looked at me and said, "She's a witch in my homeland. She can do things no one else can. She bears both marks."

"Like Veda?" I asked hopefully when I realized what marks he was speaking of.

"Aye. She told me how to find the star-runners. She gave me charms and scrolls. She sent me to find your Madame."

I tried to comprehend what he was saying when he continued. "She's powerful. She's ancient. She's discerning."

That was enough for me. "Anahita, please," I beseeched, staring up at her with tearful eyes. "Do you have *any* pearls we can trade? Please."

Joah approached and held out a pearl to Brantley. "Faraji offers his pearl," he said gruffly.

Anahita hissed and stepped between them. "You offer the pearl of our son to a witch?"

"He is already *gone*," Joah said fiercely. "Many of our people are *gone*. They have no need for their pearls any longer, and Faraji died protecting this tribe." Then he pointed at Darsey and said, "*He* is one of us. Faraji would be ashamed if we did not do all we could to save him."

I pleadingly stared up at Anahita's pain-stricken face and let out a great sigh when she hung her head and stepped aside, allowing Brantley to take the pearl.

Joah softly told him, "We will give you all you need."

"We should leave as soon as possible," I said, looking back down at Darsey's still face.

"There's something else you should know," Brantley hesitated to say.

Our eyes met and he held my gaze.

"She demanded I bring her the Dragon Born."

A tense silence fell between us.

I looked down at Darsey and stroked his face. "Gather what we need and wake the star-runners." I wasn't going to let Darsey's vision of nothing come to pass. This would not be his fate.

"Are you sure?" Brantley questioned.

I stared up at him and said, "I need Darsey to be okay, and your witch needs me. What else is there to be sure about?"

He nodded and rushed off with Joah.

Uri came up and sniffed Darsey's hair.

*"Is he going to wake up?"* he asked.

"I swear by it," I vowed.

# Acknowledgements

No one has supported me throughout this process more than my loving husband, Matthew. He has believed in me from the beginning and his confidence has never wavered. To him, I want to offer the most sincere, loving, and appreciative thank you.

To my darling children, who have grown so much this year, thank you for sharing in my ideas with an excitement that matches my own. It wouldn't be the same without the two of you in my corner.

Thank you to my wonderful editor, Chelsie. You have a way of presenting edits less like problems to be overcome, and more like opportunities to enhance the experience. I couldn't ask for a better editor.

I am grateful for all my family and friends who have supported me in this endeavor by not only reading the book but suggesting it to others. Thank you for showing me how much you love me.

Last, but not least, I want to offer a huge thanks to the fans of the series. Many of you have reached out to me personally to express your love of the story. Each and every interaction inspired me to keep going and never quit. I have a story to tell.

-Rachel N Kaufman

Made in the USA
Monee, IL
28 January 2022

90111881R00254